SEASON OF CHANGE

SEASON OF CHANGE

Connie Monk

St. Martin's Press
New York

Library of Congress Cataloging in Publication Data

Monk, Connie.
  Season of change.

I. Title.
PR6063.0486S4   1984   823'.914   84-11764
ISBN 0-312-70819-X

First published in Great Britain by Judy Piatkus (Publishers) Limited of London .

First U.S. Edition

10 9 8 7 6 5 4 3 2 1

Chapter One

Instinctively Frances pressed her small body into the feathers of her mattress, lying rigid, hardly daring to breathe.

'Stop it, please, please stop it,' silently she pleaded, 'please be friends with each other.' Her heart was beating so hard she could feel it right up to her throat, or so she imagined, and inside her a thousand needles seemed to be pricking. She didn't want to hear what they said, yet she strained her ears to listen.

'. . . and that I'll never give you, I swear I won't,' Myrtle Ratcliffe's voice carried, but Clement's reply was lost.

Her mother was always so gentle; now she sounded like a stranger. Frances didn't know what it was about, she couldn't even hear all they said, but she recognised the spite.

'Please don't say anymore, please be quiet – don't you remember what day it is?' This wasn't even an ordinary night. When they woke up in the morning it would be her birthday, 1st September 1890 and she'd be five years old. Didn't they even remember? For months the date had had a ring round it in her mother's engagement book, but now they seemed to have other things on their minds. She dreaded the sight of them but if they were to see her they'd remember about her birthday and stop fighting; anyway she needed to go to the lavatory.

She hurried out of bed and opened her door wide; if she wanted to attract their attention there was no point in creeping. Along the landing she padded, then forgot the object of her trip at the sight of them in the hall at the foot of the stairs.

'I've stood it for years. I don't know another woman who's had to put up with what I have.'

'And whose fault has it been?'

'You don't love me, don't pretend. It's never mattered to you. What have we ever shared? All you want is some common whore. Well, I wish you joy of her.'

'You . . ., you take that back!'

'Whore? And what else is she to take a married man to her bed? I'm your wife, I bore your child and nearly died of it. What do you expect of me? Why cannot you be content? I run your home, I care for my appearance, why –'

'You really don't know. God help you, you don't even start to know. Myrtle, this isn't a proper life, not for either of us, this is no marriage. She's prepared that you cite her; but please for the child's sake if not for mine give me my freedom to marry her.'

'Child!' she spat at him and upstairs Frances bit hard on the fist she'd pushed in her mouth trying to hold the sobs back. 'Her child! What of mine, born in wedlock? Is she to have no father? Is she to grow up making do with whatever home I alone can make for her?'

'What sort of home has she now? If you think this is what a home should be then pray God gives you wisdom.'

'Don't you bring God into this. What do you know of God or faith or love either! All you ever used me for was hateful, dirty – you had no love, no sympathy. Now because I don't let you do the things you want you stand there accusing me. If I came to you, prepared to suffer –'

'No. You could come to me begging. I wouldn't touch you. How I ever did God alone knows. You've got ice in your veins, ice in your heart, for all your pretty ways.' His voice was low but each word so clear that it carried to the child who stood barefoot on the dark landing. Then without a backward glance he turned away, picked up his hat and cane from the hallstand and went out, shutting the front door quietly but firmly behind him.

There was no sound save for the hissing of the gaslight in the hall. Then a frightened sob from Frances attracted Myrtle.

'Frances! Whatever are you doing out of your bed at this time of night? You should have been asleep hours ago.' How calm she suddenly felt, almost relieved.

'. . . aren't well . . .' Her face crumpled. Once she started to speak Frances couldn't fight her tears. '. . . got awful pins pricking in my tummy – and it's my birthday nearly . . .'

'So it is. Poor baby.'

Clement had gone, gone for good. There was no doubt about that. Yet it wasn't that that kept Myrtle awake so long during the night, but Frances who, like so many only children, kept her emotions repressed and secret. 'Pins pricking her tummy' gave them both something they could accept; here they were on familiar ground, Frances turning to her mother for care and Myrtle warm in her response.

Ice in her heart did he think? When finally, the night

3

half gone, she looked at the sleeping child, there was no ice but a burning rage. How dare he with his animal lusts do this to their innocent baby. She remembered his cutting contempt that she'd not understood and she honestly believed the faults were all his.

Frances, it seemed, had more perception. If things had been a clear black or white she wouldn't have been so torn by what they did.

When Myrtle told her: 'Papa has had to go away on business,' she knew it wasn't the truth but she pretended to believe it, it helped to push the memory of last night away. An ordinary day might have been more difficult but this was no ordinary day, it was her birthday. What could be more natural than that Myrtle should lavish all her affection on her? Cast off by Clement she needed to focus on someone else and today, still uncertain and frightened by the night, Frances needed all her love.

In the afternoon Frances's cousins were coming, Gina and Dickie. For weeks she'd thought about this milestone, to be five and ready for school had been the height of her ambition; she would have caught up with Gina and Dickie. In fact Gina was six all but two weeks and Dickie eleven months younger. As far as Frances was concerned their visit was the important part of the celebrations; the others were company for her mother but it was Gina and Dickie she looked forward to, them and the new dress Myrtle has made for her. The satin felt smooth on her shoulders as she slipped her arms into it. Excitement took over. Such a beautiful frock, fine white net over a pale-pink satin underskirt, a pink sash tied behind in a large bow. Her long straight tawny-brown hair was to be held back with a ribbon of

4

the same shade and the colour of her stockings and satin pumps was so near that if she half shut her eyes as she looked she really could imagine they were the same.

She went to the window and peered down the road. No sign of them coming yet. She supposed Grandma and Grandpa would arrive with Aunt Ella and Jessica – a cab would drive them from the railway station – but Aunt Cynny would bring Gina and Dickie on the 'bus. If she were honest she had to admit she wished Aunt Ella and Jessica weren't coming – well, Jessica didn't really count one way or another, but Aunt Ella was Myrtle's elder sister, hers and Aunt Cynny's too, and somehow when she was there Myrtle always sat straighter in her chair and Cynny never laughed quite so loudly. As for Jessica, at fourteen she fitted in nowhere; her young cousins' games were beneath her and the adults still looked on her as a child.

'Let me look at the birthday girl. Stand still while I do up your buttons.'

Because she was only five and being full of her own importance she assumed that because she had recovered so her mother had too. She may not have consciously considered it but the house was a happier place when her father was out.

'It's going to be so gorgeous. Does you tummy feel all bubbly and excited, Mama? Not because of the party, it's just the day – it's –'

'Magic?'

The little girl nodded. 'You know Mama, five is what I've always wanted to be.'

Myrtle's eyes were suddenly full of tears and before she could stop it one ran down her cheek. Frances expected it was because she had that bubbly feeling too, that must have done it, and it was by no means the

5

first time she'd seen her mother cry. So she gave her a
quick hug to show that she understood how difficult it
was to contain one's emotions on such a day, then
turned back to her reflection.

Indeed the walnut-framed pier-glass showed a pretty
pair, the child in her party dress, her huge gingery-
brown eyes shining, promising that one day she'd be as
lovely as her mother, although never as dainty. And
Myrtle? Even today, despite her pale face and the
shadows that told of a sleepless night, she was a
beautiful woman and one of those never disfigured by
their tears. Her eyes could brim with them (and very
often did), she'd blink and they'd roll down her cheeks,
but never would her eyelids be stiff and swollen or her
nose turn pink. 'For Christ's sake don't turn the taps on
again!' How often she'd heard him say it. Time had
been when the sight of her moved to sadness had been
enough to mould him any way she wanted. She sat back
on her heels and fastened the last button. Ah yes, time
had been . . . but how long ago? In those day's he'd not
accused her of turning on the taps. When had things
started to go wrong then? The first years had been so
different, and then Frances had been born. After that,
small wonder if she had changed – but surely it was he
who'd altered? Was it her fault if she found more
pleasure in the advertisements in *The Times* than in
news so often of places she'd not even heard of? She'd
looked after her appearance, was as pretty now as in
the beginning. Was it her fault if he never looked at
her? Was it her fault that after an evening of silence (if
indeed he was home at all) he'd expect to make love to
her in the darkness of the bedroom, wordlessly, using
her as if she were just a woman, any woman, and she
couldn't respond?

She wished the day could be over. Today she'd have

to tell them; she couldn't put it off any longer. 'Is Clement not coming home in time for tea?' She could imagine the surprise on her mother's face, the criticism on Ella's. Cynny would be full of compassion when she heard, kindness and sympathy that would be hardest of all to bear.

'Hark, Mama, there's the omnibus, the horses are stopping.' Frances ran to the window. 'They've come, Gina and Dickie, they've come.' She banged on the window and waved. 'Look, she's got a new frock too and Dickie's wearing his Sunday suit.'

Frances had no eyes for her aunt: well built and homely, Cynny was taken for granted. She didn't even notice that for this gathering of the family she too had donned her best, even to the straw hat that until today had only come out of its box on Sunday mornings for the family visit to St Stephen's. A light Italian straw, its large bunch of cherries never failing to set them on their way to church in high spirits, Richard telling the children to watch out that the birds 'don't see your mother coming.'

Dickie was in his best suit, the long trousers of charcoal grey and short black jacket, the high Eton collar round his small neck, and perched on top of his thick blond curls a grey flat cap. He was a small child for his years, inches shorter than Frances. Gina was small too and with a natural daintiness that made the family say: 'But for her blue eyes she's so like Myrtle'. As they saw Frances and her mother at the window three beaming faces turned upwards.

'Come along then, down we go,' Myrtle held out her hand.

Every night for weeks as Frances had curled up for sleep she'd imagined this day, she'd even crept out of bed to peep under the sheet that wrapped her dress so carefully. Now her throat felt tight and her tummy was pinching, the joy was almost too much to bear. Wordlessly she followed her mother downstairs, but as soon as she was with her cousins, excitedly opening the box they'd brought her, she forgot everything but the wonder of being five.

That birthday was to be the dividing line. Always if she looked back to her early days it would be 'we'd did that before my birthday' or 'that was just after my birthday'.

While the grown-ups talked in the drawing-room and in the kitchen the cake stood ready to be carried in at tea-time with its candles lit, the three children played croquet, usually missing the hoops with the heavy balls and concentrating harder on their finery than on the game.

'Let's play two-ball. Have you any bouncy balls, Fran?'

'Yes, there's one in the shed drawer. I'll have to ask Mama about another one, though I'm sure there is one. You put the mallets away while I go and get it.'

She ran through the kitchen, stopping for a quick look at the cake, it looked splendid, she'd blow the candles out in one huge puff. Up the basement stairs and across the hall she went. What made her stop and listen instead of running in to ask about the other ball? Memories of last night? Something in the grown-ups' voices?

The news had to be told but Myrtle hadn't rushed into it. The usual chatter of a family coming together was pleasant, she dreaded the moment that must come.

'Richard is going to close the shop up so that he can come over for a while. Not in time for tea, but we'll ride home together,' Cynny had said.

'I can't think why he doesn't keep his own trap. So inconvenient having to use those beastly 'buses and trams, and not right for the children. Full of germs those places are, and vermin too I wouldn't wonder.' Ella had a way of putting her sisters on the defensive, something in the tilt of her head as she sat erect, and her habit of pulling the skirt of her dress close to her as if to be sure she'd not be touched by the outside world.

'We really don't have need of a trap; why Ella we're both home all day. And there's nothing amiss with the trams. To be honest I enjoy them, there's usually someone to speak to. Anyway a horse costs a deal of money to keep even if we had the need – which we don't.' Then she'd turned back to Myrtle: 'He'll be here about 6 o'clock but we won't stay for supper. He just likes to see everyone. A shame Thomas couldn't come,' she'd added to Ella (she wouldn't want her to think she'd been unfriendly saying what she had about the trap), 'he's the only one missing. What time are you expecting Clement home, Myrtle?'

It was while Cynny had been speaking that Frances had come across the hall.

'Clement won't be coming home.'

How quiet the room suddenly was. Her grandparents had been talking to each other but as her mother made her announcement their words died a natural death.

Myrtle stood and faced them all. 'Clement won't be coming. He's deserted me.'

They'd all known their parts so well, the loving parents, the eldest sister whose task it was to show the ways of wisdom, the next one who never failed to see a joke or roll up her sleeves even if only metaphoricially and give practical help. Now seeing them all speechless she felt she'd cheated them, played a card no one had known was in the pack. To help them back on the road

9

(and in any case it all had to be told) she went on: 'You're all taken by surprise I can see. Well, of course you are. I am myself, although dear knows why, for he's had little enough interest in me. It wasn't until last night that I found there's been someone else.'

The room was full of silence. Cynny was the first to recover. 'Do you still love him, Myrtle?' That must be the only way to find a solution. Without love what hope could there be?

'He doesn't see me,' her eyes swam but it only made her prettier, 'we never go anywhere. If he goes out it's alone (or so I've thought) to some concert, or a Liberal meeting. He used to take me; not that I cared for that sort of thing, but it was nice to get dressed and perhaps have supper afterwards.' He used to tell her how lovely she looked, not a woman to compare; he used to pin flowers to her coat, hold her arm as though she'd been made of Dresden china, bring her home and make love to her so that she felt cherished. . . . But that was in the beginning, long ago now.

The family had found a second wind. Now they were all talking.

'When did you suspect things weren't right?'

'Young swine. Ought to have a stick to his back,' Frances heard Grandma say, and peeping through the keyhole she saw she looked quite capable of the task.

'He'll keep the house going of course; you're his wife, he's responsible for you,' from Ella.

And in the background as if he was talking to himself: 'Dear, dear, oh dear me, what a business, dear, dear me,' from her grandfather.

Frances crept back across the hall. Home, parents, these were the things one took for granted, things that were always there. She didn't want to watch, nor yet to hear what they said, didn't so much as look at the cake as she went back to the garden.

10

'Mama doesn't know. There's a rope in the shed, let's play skipping.' She didn't mention what she'd heard; she wanted to forget it, pretend it hadn't happened.

Indoors the practical Cynny asked: 'What have you told Fran?'

'Just that he's had to go away on business for a few days. After her birthday . . .,' her tears spilled, 'not now though . . . poor little girl. . . .'

'A good hiding. I'd do it . . .'

'Now then Janie my dear, don't get too excited. You know it upsets you, gives you indigestion.' Myrtle's father laid a hand on his wife's knee.

'Beggar the indigestion. I'd like to give him indigestion. Now then, Myrtle child, don't you cry. We'll find where the rascal's run off to, we'll see he comes back.'

'No, Mama. . . .'

'I dare say if you did but know it he's had a woman or two before this.' Ella put herself in charge; 'A pity you came to hear of it. Always struck me he had an eye, if you understand me. You might have been better to let him think you forgave him; he'd soon have come eating out of your hand.'

'You don't understand. It's not like that. He wants me to go to a solicitor – but I won't. I told him I won't divorce him.'

'Indeed not.' Her father sat forward on the sofa, his knuckles showing white as he gripped the stick planted firmly between his knees. 'I should think not indeed. You took him for your husband, dear me, dear me, more's the pity.'

'Wipe your eyes, Myrtle. It's so difficult to decide what's to be done when you stand there like that.' Ella had seen her do this as long as she could remember.

11

When things went wrong, she would cry, silently, making no attempt to mop the tears that now rolled down her face and on to the bodice of her pretty lilac gown.

Cynny the practical spoke: 'It seems to me that if Frances has been told her father is away for a few days, now is the time for an unexpected outing. Take her away, have a change of scene – pack a grip and come home with Richard and me. What better day for a surprise than a birthday? Give yourself a chance to think away from the house. And Frances would love it, she could share Gina's bed. What do you say?'

'But would Richard want us?' How pathetic she looked, a harder-hearted man than Richard would have rushed to help her.

'Richard will insist, you'll see. He'll be here later and he'll tell you himself.'

'Now then, my girl, just blow your nose and wipe your face. No man's worth it, least of all one who doesn't know how to keep faith.' Jane Pilbeam sniffed her disdain for the son-in-law she'd never been comfortable with. Jane came from country shock, not landowners but country folk. Her own father had worked his way up to being head gardener at Chilbury Manor and when she'd married Ernest Pilbeam it was but to move some seven miles to Ipsley House where, at thirty-nine, and twenty years her senior, he already held the same position. That had been not far short of forty years ago and there they'd stayed until only last year, living in the same cottage and watching one generation at the big house follow another. A less kindly family might have asked them to move on long ago, for it was a good many years since he'd done more than keep an eye on the younger men who did the work in the large gardens. But he'd been part of the establishment and right up to the time he and Jane finally let Ella sweep them off to live under her roof, his eagle eye had made sure the gardens were a pleasure to the family he'd served so long, and the vegetables a credit to their table. Of their nine children only the three girls lived near enough to visit each other, in fact of their nine, only six lived at all.

The domineering Ella was the third eldest of the remaining family, married to Thomas Stowe. A kindly enough man and apparently successful with his one-man printing business. He must do quite well for their home never went short and Ella always appeared well set up. Only one child there and not because Ella was weakly, more likely she kept the poor little man at arm's length, Jane suspected. Jane had always been something of a spitfire herself but even she was wary of Ella.

Next was Cynthia, or Cynny as they all thought of her, uncomplicated and content with her Richard. And so she should be. A good man was Richard, his blue eyes ready to smile and his voice never raised in anger, at least not to Jane's knowledge. The sports shop he kept in Highworth would never make him a fortune but more people seemed to have the shillings to buy fishing rods and cricket bats these days, and then there were the repairs. In his room behind the shop Richard would patiently mend a keep net or re-string a tennis racquet. There was the bait to catch too, the 'tiddlers' that he and the children took from the stream at the bottom of their long garden and brought back to the tank in the shop to be lifted out in a little net as the customers wanted. A steady trade was Richard's; his family would never have riches but he and Cynny had found the secret of a good life; one look at her told Jane that.

The last of Ernest and Jane's family was Myrtle, the baby and everyone's pet. Not one of them had been as pretty, dainty and gently spoken. No wonder Clement Ratcliffe had been bowled over by her. For eight years they'd been married, the eighteen-year-old girl had matured into a beautiful woman. What a fool the man must be! Picked up some loose woman, Jane supposed, while he ought to be filling his nursery at home. That's what they needed, both of them, more children to hold them together.

Dear me, she did wish the girl wouldn't cry like that. Most upsetting it was to see her with her lip trembling and the tears rolling unchecked down her face to plop on that pretty dress, making wet blobs. 'That's the thing to do,' she said briskly, 'go back with Cynny for a little break. I dare say he'll get home and find you gone, then he'll come running.'

Go to Highworth. Yes, they'd do that. Mama was wrong, he'd not come home and she wasn't sure she'd even want that life again, not as it had been. Away from here she'd be able to think. It wasn't that she wanted what she'd lost, it was a relief in a way to feel she belonged to herself. For a long time they'd shared the house as strangers. She supposed men were different but even if they'd been remote from each other downstairs he'd still expected to make love to her. Sometimes she couldn't find an excuse; there were limits to how often she could say 'I'm not well', and apart from that he asked nothing of her. In the beginning it had excited her to have the power to move him to passion. Strange how for so long none of it had mattered, it had become something to endure and when it was over she knew it was exhaustion not contentment that carried him to sleep. How was he with this other woman? And how much did she honestly care?

She dabbed her cheeks with her lace-edged

14

handkerchief. 'We'll do that Cynny, we'll come for a few days.' She even smiled through her tears. 'I think I shall enjoy it, really life's been very tedious lately. You seem to have such fun at the shop.'

'No time for idle hands, that's the secret, child.' Jane said it kindly enough, somehow even giving the impression that the comforts Clement had bestowed on his wife had taken away her chance of the fun she deserved.

So half an hour later, the candles blown out in one huge puff, the children heard the plan. Hadn't Frances known that this birthday was something special? But even she hadn't imagined anything like this. Mama was smiling again, seeming pleased that they were going. The prospect was enough to put last night's scene and all that had followed into the shadows; a holiday at the shop, sharing Gina's room, that was something she could understand. A future without both parents was beyond her comprehension, they were permanent and reliable, as certain as tomorrow's dawn.

The party over, Jessica was sent to the cab rank to order a hansom to take them to the station, and while the others were still at the front gate waving the departing visitors on their way Frances ran upstairs to get ready. She pulled off the exquisite frock that for weeks had been a symbol of this day. In her eagerness for the next step it had lost its wonder. Clothes to play in were what she'd want at Highworth. She'd help Uncle Richard catch his bait, she'd climb right out over the stream on the branch of the willow, shed –

'Now we're ready,' Myrtle fastened the strap of the wicker box that carried their luggage; 'Run and tell Uncle Richard I've packed our things, the grip's ready for him.'

If anyone thought it more than they'd need for a few days no one said so.

15

Already Myrtle was recovering, things would work out, of course they would. It was too soon after last night's scene to know exactly what she hoped. She couldn't imagine having no husband. Why, he'd seen to everything, even the grocery bills he'd paid. It wasn't fair of him; tears welled up when she thought of the injustice.

'I'm picking blackberries tomorrow if the weather holds.' Cynny pretended she hadn't noticed. 'We'll make bramble jelly.'

It sounded like the old days, there in the cottage at Ipsley where she'd been free and secure, no worries, no responsibilities. 'Lovely. Oh Cynny, all I ask is to live in peace and happiness. Is that so much?'

If it seemed a tall order to Cynny she didn't say so.

Richard shouldered the wicker box and, the three children with him, set off to the corner where the horsebus was due at any minute. If Myrtle hadn't gone back to check that everything was left tidy she would have missed the lad who came up the path as she was locking the front door behind her.

'Mrs Ratcliffe, ma'am?'

'Yes, I'm Mrs Ratcliffe.'

'I have to give you this letter. It's from Cowdery & Elphinstone, ma'am.'

The name was vaguely familiar. She'd seen the brass plate outside the tall ivy-clad house at the far end of Broad Street. Why should solicitors write to her?

Cynny glanced over her shoulder as she read.'Think about it later.' She squeezed her sister's arm. 'Time enough then. Look, Richard's signalling, the 'bus must be in sight.'

'It's only a small room, I hope you'll manage.' Cynny

16

had always been proud of having a spare bedroom, the cushion on the little armchair and the frill along the mantlepiece stitched of the same material. Now here she was apologising for it, mentally wondering whether she might take the rug from her side of the bed and put it over that worn patch of linoleum. At her own home in Belmont Road Myrtle's room was very different.

'Of course I'll manage. It's lovely to come. Oh Cynny, I never thought this time yesterday . . . you can't imagine . . . supposing Richard did it to you, left you to fend on your own?'

'You're not on your own; why you've got all of us. He'll realise when he sees what he's lost. There's Frances too; it's not as though he doesn't love her.'

'He can't do or he'd not have done this to her. He doesn't care about either of us.' With her wicker basket on the bed she looked forlorn. All Cynthia's instinct was to protect her, her beautifully cared for hands clasped ('so people really do wring their hands', the thought struck the elder sister). 'I don't understand it, truly I don't. There have been women before, I'm sure there have. All that sort of thing, he knows I don't like it, I don't like talking about it even, but you know what I mean. But Cynny, I'm always even tempered, you know that's true. The home is comfortable. I've tried to keep myself the same, to be smart and fashionable, not grow old just because I've had a child. Why couldn't he have been like your Richard? I doubt if he ever notices that you change. You're part of his home, the same as the children are. He'd never look at other women. It's not fair, Cynny, it's unjust of him.'

Unfair, unjust – but what of the lack in her life without him? Cynny suspected that Clement as a person had ceased to matter long before this; Clement as a provider and a barrier between his pretty wife and

17

the responsibilities she'd never had to face was the man who'd deserted her.

'Give it a little time, try not to worry. You know we will love having you and Frances here. Just put it aside for a few days and give yourself time.'

Myrtle didn't answer, but her mouth drew into an unfamiliar tight line as she turned to unfasten the strap of her grip.

Was it true, did Richard not notice the changes? And if he didn't, was it because he no longer really looked? Cynny let her gaze wander to the mirror on the deal wardrobe door (so used to it had she been that now she seemed to see it for the first time, see it through Myrtle's eyes – poor-quality wood and the thin backing to the glass of the mirror so worn that it was covered with brown speckles). Yes, she'd changed, her hips had broadened and her hands told a story of house-cleaning and gardening. Her hair was as thick but not as glossy, brushed less, if she were honest; her complexion had lost the rosy glow of youth. Her bust looked matronly these days; fourteen years ago when she'd been a bride she'd been plump, 'cuddlesome' he'd called it. Did he see? Did he notice? And if he didn't was that because they'd grown so close she was like a part of him, or, as Myrtle implied, because it wasn't important any more?

'I'll leave you to unpack your things and go and see about a bite of supper for the children. Just look at them out there, Myrtle, how they're enjoying being together.' Then she knocked sharply on the window pane, pushing the bottom sash up as she shouted: 'Dickie! Come away from that water. What did I say to you? No getting that Sunday suit dirty.' Her tone brooked no argument; kindly she may be but the children knew better than to cross her.

'Sorry, Ma. I was only looking.'

18

'Then look somewhere else, my lad, I know you when you get to the edge of that stream. Time to wash your hands for supper in five minutes; I'm just off down to make your bread and milk.'

Myrtle was still unpacking when Gina appeared in her doorway bearing an offering of Michaelmas daisies from the garden.

Later in Gina's bed Frances lay awake a long time. Whispering their plans for the next day she'd had no room for worries, but the moment came when, despite her urgent whisper, 'Gina, wake up. Don't let's got to sleep yet, Gina', her cousin's only answer was a deep sigh.

She hadn't felt comfortable with the grown-ups today even though it had been her birthday. Grandpa had looked at her and shaken his head as if he was sad she'd grown to be five. Grandma had tapped her foot in a fidgety sort of way, and why had he put his hand on her arm like that and said: 'Now, Janie my dear, you'll do no good like that, just try and have faith m'dear?' And Grandma's reply hadn't sounded a bit like herself: 'Poor child, poor baby,' then with something of her familiar spirit, 'Faith! Faith you say! It's that bounder should have faith. If I could lay my hands on –'

'Hush now,' said her grandfather with a nod in her direction as Frances had hovered near them. The atmosphere had been uncomfortable, not a bit like a birthday.

Still awake, she heard the grown-ups come up the linoleum-covered stairs to bed. At the top they stopped, still speaking but she couldn't hear what they were saying. The voices went on and curiosity got the better of her. Very gently, careful now not to wake Gina, she eased herself out of bed and went to the door. Kneeling down with her eye to the keyhole she looked straight along the passage to where they stood. Mama was crying again and Aunt Cynny had an arm around her while Uncle Richard stood to one side. He looked so worried Frances wished she could have told him her mother often cried; then he took a large folded handkerchief from his pocket and shook it open.

'Come now, tomorrow's another day, Myrtle;' he wiped her face. 'Come, let's see a smile. With the morning things won't look so bleak, and you know my dear you're not to be frightened by things you're not used to. We've eked our shillings out for years enough, we're dab hands at it, we'll see you manage.' His was the only voice that carried well enough to reach Frances.

Instead of cheering her mother it seemed to make her worse, and her quiet crying turned to uncontrolled sobs as she clung to him. This was different, Myrtle's quiet tears Frances could accept, but this was different. In her stomach there was a horrid fluttering feeling and as she watched the scene along the passage deep inside her invisible hands were tying her in knots.

She gripped her teeth firmly together, only milk teeth but she'd already learnt that was the way to hide her hurts. She squared her jaw and tried to will her heart to stop its banging; she could almost hear it. She wouldn't cry, she wouldn't. There was nothing to cry about, hadn't Uncle Richard said so? Eke out their shillings, what did it all mean? And her mother really crying like that, she was frightened by what she'd never seen before, what she didn't understand. The grown-ups turned away and went into the room Myrtle was using, shutting the door, shutting her out.

Under her bare feet the linoleum was cold, the room was dark and unfamiliar. She groped her way back to bed.

20

'Gina,' she whispered, hoping even for a grunt. But no, Gina was beyond recall. There was comfort in her nearness all the same and Frances snuggled closer; she needed to cling to something and Gina was part of the past and the future too.

Chapter Two

Nothing looks as bleak by daylight and the next morning at breakfast Myrtle announced her intention of taking the omnibus to Tarnmouth.

'I'll go in by myself. Franny will be better left with the children.' Frances listened to her mother's plans. Yes, in the morning sunshine the insecurity of the night had gone. Wearing a calico playdress with a white pinafore over it she was ready for anything, even glad to hear that her mother's eye wouldn't follow her activities.

'You're going back to collect up things from the house?' Richard held his cup towards Cynny for a re-fill but he looked at Myrtle in concern. 'Wait until tea-time. I'll shut the door early and give you a hand; you don't want to go back there on your own.'

'No, not the house. I don't intend to so much as step inside there again. No, I'm going to see this Mr Cowdery who wrote to me.'

'You've decided to give him his freedom?'

'Hush!' Cynny frowned at him, 'Remember little pitchers. . . .'

'No.' By daylight Myrtle was full of determination. 'I've thought things through and I'm going to find a

22

small house to rent, perhaps here in Highworth. Could you stand to have us on your doorstep?' She turned to Richard and surely she must know no man could resist those large gingery eyes when they pleaded like that? 'I'll do my best not to be a burden, I'll get used to being on my own and I'll learn to manage.'

'My dear, a burden you'll never be. We want you nearby, where we can help. We want to be involved. Eh, Cynny?'

'As if she needs telling!' Then to Frances: 'So you stay here with us, duckie, while your Mama goes to do a few things in town. And mind, all of you, no dabbling in that stream. Summer's all but over I fear; quite a nip in the air when I fetched the wood in this morning.'

'Ah, no paddling,' Richard agreed, 'but you can take your nets down (I'll find one for you Franny) and a jar apiece and see what you can get me. A farthing for six tiddlers, that's what they get Franny and I'll pay you the same.'

She puffed out her chest in pride. A job of work to do, proper work that mattered for the shop, not like being given a duster and told to dust the dining-table that gleamed already. It was more than just the coming of daylight that banished last night's fear, it had something to do with all sitting together round the kitchen table for breakfast, the lid of the big black kettle bobbing up and down on the range (even the fire burnt with a newness, the flames more orange, not the dull red glow of the later hours of the day), the steaming saucepan of porridge, the bowl of boiled eggs, the crusty loaf and dish of butter, the home-made marmalade that Aunt Cynny had ladled out of a brown earthenware jar on to a pot on the table. Yet was it really anything to do with what they ate? It was something she couldn't define, something she couldn't see or hear, a sort of safe feeling.

'Eat up Franny, sitting there dreaming . . .,' Myrtle prompted.

She dug her spoon into the yolk of her egg.

The letter from Cowdery & Elphinstone had left Myrtle in no doubt; Clement had no intention of coming back. His arrangements for her were clearly set out. The tenancy of the house in Belmont Road was to be made over to her and she was to have an allowance sufficient to run it. What the amount would mean she had no idea for up until now she'd had no dealings with money. He'd paid the grocer, he'd paid the coalman, the painter, the dressmaker, even the two daily women who cooked and cleaned. Myrtle hadn't given a thought to these things, she'd not lived extravagently but neither had she practised economy. To Richard and Cynny the figure sounded more than adequate but Myrtle was honest enough to know that she enjoyed pretty clothes, hats seemed to beckon to her from Madame Zeigler's window and her cooking wasn't of the stew-and-dumpling variety that sustained Cynny's household.

So, leaving Frances behind, she took the omnibus to Tarnmouth and made her way through the bustling mid-morning of Broad Street to the offices of Cowdery & Elphinstone. Yesterday the elderly solicitor had talked to Clement and imagined a very different woman from the lovely girl who was ushered into his book-lined sanctum.

'Mrs Ratcliffe, you've no doubt come in answer to my letter.' He bowed his head courteously over the gloved hand she rested in his. She was given a seat, the chair moved from its position facing him squarely across the desktop so that she sat at a slight angle. Then he pushed his own chair farther back and relaxed into it. Somehow he hoped it set their interview off on an

24

easier vein, he'd appear less formidable to this gentle-looking little lady. As he let his gaze linger on her he thought Clement Ratcliffe must be a complete fool.

Myrtle was never less than beautiful and to be honest she'd taken extra pains today. She knew the soft pink of her velvet suit flattered her, she knew the nipped-in waist showed a figure that would have done credit to a girl ten years her junior and that the trimming on her pink hat was the exact shade of her tawny eyes. This Mr Cowdery would be sure to see things from Clement's point of view, probably imagined she was some sort of harridan a man would be glad to shed.

His manner was inscrutable. Was it her imagination that his expression softened?

'I've read your letter, Mr Cowdery, many times. So my husband has deserted me, left me and little Frances.'' She turned those remarkable eyes towards him and he saw how they suddenly brimmed with tears. He might have been excused if he'd been annoyed; the middle of a busy morning was no time for dealing with weeping women who arrived unannounced. Had she been different he might well have felt that way about it.

'There now, dear lady, you know I'm here to give you what assistance I'm able.' He cleared his throat. 'I understand from Mr Ratcliffe that you have no wish to terminate the marriage.'

'Mr Cowdery, until forty-eight hours ago I imagined all was well. How can I think of myself as a divorcee; suddenly, from being a respected married woman to be made an outcast? I'm not prepared; and there's Frances. . . .'

'Indeed, indeed, yes. You want me to intermediate for you, is that it? It's not ethical, dear lady, but it grieves me to see a partnership flounder.' Stupid man

25

Ratcliffe must be, the longer he talked with her (and looked at her) the more he thought it.

'No, I'm not asking that. He tells me he's given his affection elsewhere' (perhaps Clement hadn't disclosed his affair with the other woman but Myrtle couldn't bring herself to mention the coming child, she was frightened of where such an indelicate subject might lead) 'and I couldn't try to hold him against his will.'

'But I understood you to say you'll not free him to re-marry?'

'No, indeed! Dear knows I cannot do that. We made vows. If holy vows mean nothing to him they do to me. I can take no other husband and he can take no other wife. This new affair of the heart will be the easier for him to put down when he tires. He may well come to thank me one of these days.'

Poor woman! So that was it. 'One of these days', she said, hoping no doubt he'd see the folly of his ways and come back to her.

'Why I've come to you is that I cannot face living in Belmont Road as things are. It's too full of memories – neighbours would point a finger at me. I'd be a figure of gossip. But, Mr Cowdery, I've no experience, so I've come to beg you to help me. I intend to look for a house to rent in Highworth, something smaller, then I'll decide just what furniture I need to keep. Will you help me? My husband will have to know I'm leaving Belmont Road, I really don't wish to have any contact with him. . . .'

'Dear me, I dislike having to press you, but are you sure. Gossip is short lived, the house you have is familiar; surely it's better not to rush away and be on your own in a strange place?'

'Highworth is only a few miles up the road and I have a dear sister there. She and her family have welcomed us.'

If it crossed his mind to wonder why, with a family

behind her, she should ask him to help her he didn't say so. Poor child, for she looked hardly more, not a line on her lovely face and eyes trusting and innocent. He'd not want her to think he was less than willing to do as she asked.

'And Mr Cowdery may I leave you to arrange with my husband that he tells the daily women he no longer requires them? He engaged them, he's always paid their wages. It would upset me too much to be the one to put them out of work, for I know they both depend on the shillings they earn; I just couldn't do it to them. It's been such a shock to me, I can't tell you. . . .' Her mouth quivered and the unshed tears trembled on her long lashes.

'Of course, of course. Indeed you did right to come to me, it's not for you to be faced with such unpleasant tasks.'

So, a clean break made with the past, Myrtle returned to Highworth. Her family were firmly behind her, the responsibilities that had frightened her seemed to be satisfactorily taken care of and her view of the future was surprisingly pleasant.

For Frances every day was fun. For instance at Belmont Road she'd never been bathed in a zinc tub in front of the kitchen fire, bathed then wrapped in a towel warmed on the tall brass-rimmed fireguard, for in Belmont Road the small bedroom had been made into a special room with a bath and a gas geyser. Perhaps because she was the visitor she was the one now to have the water first. Gina would climb in when she was lifted out and last would be Dickie, a pan of cooling water skimmed off and another of hot added. Twice a week they followed this ritual and afterwards, on Saturdays,

27

in nightclothes and slippers they'd line up ready for the next stage.

'Open wide. . . .' Cynny never asked if the medicine was needed, but again turned first to Frances, 'Syrup of figs'. Deftly she scooped a spoonful into each mouth, the same spoon just as it had been the same bath water. Perhaps it wouldn't have been approved by the hygienists but it certainly was by Frances who until now had been one on her own.

There was something else apart from the fun of sharing that she learnt from these fire-side ablutions. Her face was a study on the first Saturday evening as Dickie stripped off his clothes. Whatever could be wrong with him? She heard her aunt's: 'Come on lad, in you get, I don't know where you get the dirt from.' She opened her mouth to speak, thought better of it, realising that what she saw wasn't interesting anyone else, and closed it again. Could all boys be like that? Sitting on the wooden chair she drew her knees up and wrapped her nightgown over her feet. Gracious, but she was glad she was a girl! So much tidier!

By the time the tub was filled the following Tuesday she was prepared for what she would see and after another week or two she ceased to bother to look.

In those first weeks life was much too full to worry about her father, or her mother either for that matter. She went to Miss Searl's school with Gina and Dickie, if it could be graced with the name school. Miss Searl took in about twenty children of ages five to about nine. In her two ground-floor rooms they sat in two classes, one for the younger ones and the other, taught by a Miss Turnbull, for the older. In Miss Searl's class they learnt the three Rs, each child having her full attention for a few minutes of each day, then all joining together to listen to tales of Greek mythology

or readings from the Bible. Both classes combined to march round the garden at drill time, but apart from that they saw little of each other. Frances was happy there and she learnt her lessons well.

'I've got an idea!' How often they'd hear her say it. 'Up on those fat branches, let's make a tree house,' or 'Let's ask Uncle Richard if he wants any tiddlers', or 'Can you do a backward somersault? Peter Chamber can, he showed me. Come on, let's practise; I'm going to.' Dickie followed her lead, even egged her on, to a higher branch or to advance from a headstand against the side of the shed to a perambulation on her hands.

'You want to see Fran do. . . .' this or that, he'd boast at school. No doubt, she was the very best sort of cousin to have.

Gina was nearly a year older; she felt she should have set the pace yet often she'd watch the other two in bewilderment. All very well for Dickie to do these things, young harum-scarum she'd heard her mother laugh many a time, but when he was there Frances never seemed to want to play girls' games. Mothers and fathers was her favourite; she would be mother, happy with the wooden perambulator and crib Richard had made her, Dickie father, off to work or sometimes hunting or fishing for their food. Frances was unpredicatable but whatever her role the game seemed to revolve around it. 'Send your child to school, I'm teacher' or 'Dickie, you work on a farm, I'm the farmer' (sometimes it was 'the farmer's wife', male or female, it was all one to Frances). Then there was, 'Let's have your baby christened. I'll be the parson.' She soon got tired of that one, though. It seemed she wasn't cut out for the cloth. The pull of the tree was too strong and she was soon climbing its familiar branches.

'Come down, Fran, don't spoil the game,' Gina pleaded.

'But I have to go to the steeple; something's gone wrong with one of the bells.' There was no getting the better of Frances.

'I'll help you,' Dickie called up to her. 'I'm coming up. I'm a bellman, 'tend that's my job.'

Gina turned back to her pram, she knew it was no use expecting the game to go on. It wasn't fair, Fran never settled down to play properly.

But at night when they were shut away by themselves in the bedroom they now shared, Frances belonged just to her. Sharing had been no new thing to her, yet even in the happy family life she'd always known the closeness between them was something she'd never felt before. In the dark bedroom on the cold nights of that winter they'd cuddle together, pull the covers over their heads to make a tent and shut out the world. Then Frances was just hers. Spoken aloud what they said to each other held little importance but whispered for their ears alone there was a magic in the intimacy. Frances felt it too, it was something that would stay with her always.

Myrtle didn't take long to find a house, Mallard Cottage in Duck Island Lane just off the High Street. It was set back only six feet from the cobbled pavement, the small front garden crying out to be planted with colour. As soon as she'd settled in she'd find a man to dig it. The house was small and pretty, she'd make it just what she wanted; she was like a child with a new toy as she chose material to stitch the curtains and mantle runners. If anyone should hint at her solitary state those all too ready tears would threaten, for she honestly believed she'd been badly used. But if a good fairy could have waved a wand and put Clement into this new home she was making she'd not have wanted it. As there was no such fairy the question didn't arise,

and it's doubtful if she realised how much better suited she was to her new life than her old.

'Myrtle's gone to Tarnmouth to buy curtaining for Franny's room.' Cynny came into Richard's workroom where he was mending a doll one November afternoon. 'Whose is that? Whatever are you doing with a doll?'

'Molly Higgins brought it in to see if I could do anything with it. It belongs to that poor little mite with the clump boot; you know, Cynny, we've seen her go by sometimes.'

'The cripple child? But you don't mend dolls, Richard.'

'Seems I do.' He held it up, surveying his handiwork. 'It happened yesterday tea-time. Gwenny (that's the child) was coming up the road carrying it and a couple of young buggers jumped out on her right outside Molly's window. Called her that too, like we did: "cripple" they said and snatched it, dodging round her so that she couldn't reach it. You can just picture Molly: out she went ready to give them the hiding of their lives and before you could say knife this is what they did, each pulled an arm and a leg and the whole thing fell to bits. Then they dropped it and were away before Molly could get them.'

'Oh Richard, poor little soul.'

'Ah. Good job it was Molly who saw it. My guess is that she gave her a shoulder for her tears. She said she took her home and promised she'd have Esmeralda (this is Esmeralda) as good as new by this evening. So you see I mend dolls now it seems even if I didn't before.'

The room was very still, only the clock on the mantlepiece broke the silence. He carried the doll to the window and looked at it closely as he gently pulled each of its limbs to make sure the elastic was just as tight as it should be, then he tilted it forward and backward checking that the round eyes opened and shut.

A moment of awareness held Cynny. She seemed suspended in time – a morning of cooking and cleaning behind her, followed by an hour in the garden pulling up decaying plants; in a minute she'd be attacking a pile of ironing (already two flat irons were on the range upstairs in the kitchen). But this moment was apart from all that. She hardly realised she had moved, as she held a hand towards him, dear, dear Richard.

'What's up? You all right?'

She nodded. 'Richard, we're so lucky, we've got so much.'

He glanced round the barely furnished workroom, his eyebrows raised in laughing enquiry. 'Luxury indeed,' he laughed. But perhaps he understood her message, for he carefully put Esmeralda on the table and tilted Cynny's chin up with a hand that was gentle. 'Ah, so we have, Cynny. No one ever had more.'

For tears to spring to Myrtle's eyes was common-place, but it was a rare thing for Cynny's vision to mist. A light kiss on the nose might not be every woman's idea of romance but to her it spoke volumes. She laid a work-roughened hand on his shoulder – and the clanging shop-bell put an end to their interlude.

Contentment stayed with her as she smoothed her way through the pile of ironing. With two extra in the house she had plenty to do and Myrtle hadn't been used to looking after her own things.

The hissing of the gaslight, the occasional crackle of the fire in the range, the iron as she thumped it down on each fresh article she took from the folded pile in the wicker laundry basket, the kettle lid that bobbed up and down until she pulled it to the back of the range, all

these were a background to the life she found
thoroughly satisfying. The children would be home
from school any minute and Myrtle from town. It was
getting dark early today and the fog coming down fast,
yet that only made the kitchen more comfortable, a
haven of warmth waiting to welcome them home.
Three of them soon arrived, bounding through the
shop and up the stairs, rosy cheeked and hungry for
their tea.

'You've timed that well,' she turned her smiling face
to them, pink and warm from her hot and steamy job.
'Just that second finished the last thing.' She carried
both her irons and stood them in the fender of the tall
brass-rimmed fireguard. 'Mind you don't let anything
touch those, they'll be hot for a bit yet.'

'Can I do the pulley, Ma?' Dickie went to the far end
of the kitchen, the rope in his small hands ready for him
to pull.

'Just a jiff while I make sure it's all hanging to rights.
Yes, up it goes then.'

He pulled the thick cord with all his might and the
girls added their muscle to his. The sight of the parallel
wooden beams hoisted almost to the ceiling and hung
with airing clothes was so much a part of their daily life
that Gina and Dickie hardly noticed it. Frances did
though, for if clothes had been aired at 11 Belmont
Road (and she supposed they had) she'd seen nothing
of them. In fact Mrs Grant, the cleaning woman, had
taken the washing away each Monday and brought it
back each Friday, but Frances hadn't known that
either. Here things were different, washday something
that affected all their lives. Downstairs behind the
room where Richard did his repairs was the wash-house
and, come rain or shine, fog or snow, Cynny could be
found there on Monday mornings, the water bubbling

and steaming in the copper and her brush on the washboard defeating even the most obstinate marks. On a dry day the long garden would be festooned with the results of her efforts, on a wet one the upstairs kitchen filled with steam from the mangled garments draped on the pulley and round the top of the guard. Cold cut of yesterday's joint and bubble and squeak would be waiting for them at dinner time and by tea-time the character of the house would be changed again. Monday tea-time they all shared Cynny's sense of achievement, her task was over for another week.

Tuesdays saw stage two of the battle and final victory. No matter what befell the outside world. Tuesday tea was taken under the awning of neatly pressed linen. The family's shirts and undergarments, sheets and pillowcases, all to view displayed. Frances loved Tuesday tea-time; of all the week it was her favourite (her things and her mother's hanging with everyone else's); she didn't stop to consider why it was but she knew that Tuesdays she always felt warm and happy.

Today that glow was to be short lived.

'That's the 'bus, I think. The horses are stopping over the road. I dare say your Mama will be home on this one, Fran.' Cynny said as she spread the cloth over the kitchen table ready for their meal.

What happened next she wasn't sure. There was a shout, then a thud (or was it a thud and then a shout?), then the horses took fright, neighing and stamping out of control. The whole thing was muffled by the fog and when the four upstairs pulled back the curtains to look out the driver had managed to quieten the frightened animals. Already a group was gathering around the figure and Richard was running across the road.

*   *   *

34

Richard carried her up the straight, steep flight of stairs and laid her on the sofa in the parlour.

'I'm so sorry – my own fault – ouch, oh, it's my back. Be better if I can just lie still. Have your tea – I'll be all right –' she shivered.

'I'll put a match to the fire,' Cynny said, 'and get you a blanket.'

'Cynny I'm sorry – nuisance . . .'

'Silly! Nuisance indeed! Musn't let you get cold though, it's a shock to tumble like that.'

'My mind wasn't on what I was doing. I'd just heard – he's gone away, sold out of the business and found work in Brighton. Ouch – can't talk, oh . . . oh. . . .' But she did, talked through the tears that rolled unchecked down her face. She tasted the salt of them and it only made her more miserable, more aware of her unhappy state. 'Met Mrs Higman, she never did like me, crowed when she told me. Ouch, if I try to move – right on my back his hoof seemed to come. . . .' Fortunately she exaggerated in retrospect.

The warm closed-in feeling of Tuesday tea-time had gone. Frances stood helplessly just inside the parlour doorway. 'Gone'. That must mean her father.

'I'm off to fetch Dr Saunders. Let him have a look at you,' Richard said. 'We'll hold tea back, Cynny. Won't hurt the kids to wait. I'll lock the shop on my way out, you stay here with Myrtle. Just put a match to the coals.'

'Richard, could you just push me to the kitchen,' the sad eyes pleaded. 'I don't want to be on my own and I really don't believe I can manage a chair. Please, I don't want to be shut away.'

Somehow they wriggled their sofa out of the parlour where none of them would dream of sitting on it except on special days and when they were in their best

35

clothes, and into the kitchen. The large table had to be moved back to give it space so that she could be near the fire.

Myrtle smiled, somehow conveying how brave she was being and how much she needed the love of her family. And so she did; not for a moment was she less than honest. If, in seeing how they rallied round her, she thought 'how upset they are to see me like this' rather than 'how kind they are' perhaps she may be forgiven, for she was as she was and why should she look for faults in herself when they saw none and all loved her so dearly? All? This wasn't the time to think of Clement. She didn't want to remember what Mrs Higman had told her. Her back hurt and she let her mind dwell on that; in truth it hurt sufficiently to put even Clement's treatment of her into the background.

Dr Saunders banished all of them except Cynny from the kitchen. Richard and the children waited downstairs while her back was examined. Backs were something of a mystery to him. She could move her legs, nothing seemed to be broken.

'Rest is the answer. You stay here on the sofa for a week or two. You'll help her to bed, won't you, Mrs Sellwood, and see she doesn't try and bend for anything? And even when the pain seems to have gone you'll have to be careful – no bedmaking or ironing for some time, nothing that puts any strain on it. The trouble with backs – I'll just listen to your breathing – ah, yes; as I say, the trouble with backs is that you never known when the trouble will recur. A burden you may have to live with, I fear. I've seen it so often, a person thinks "Ah, I'm better" and takes a liberty, reaches for something, bends to put coals on the fire, that's all it might take. You'll need to bear it in mind, cosset yourself a little, even when the pain has gone.'

As he talked he'd been putting his stethoscope in his bag; he knew where he stood with that. Give him a good case of bronchitis, a throat that was red and raw, even a crop of spots, but spare him from backs. 'I'll look in again in a few days, but as I say it may well leave a weakness you'll have to cosset.' It seemed psychology was another of Dr Saunder's weak suits!

The family came back upstairs after they heard Cynny see him off through the side door and they listened respectfully to the advice he'd left.

'Easy for him to tell me to be careful, a woman on my own. . . .'

'You'll never be that my dear,' Richard's hand rested on her shoulder.

'Indeed you won't,' Cynny agreed. 'Now then a good strong cup of tea and I'll put your food on a tray. Can you bear it on your knee?'

'I'll manage,' she nodded bravely.

Frances came to stand close by her not knowing what to say or how to help. All her earlier happiness had evaporated. She wanted to be useful, she wanted to be included, to be told about her father. 'He wants to live with someone else instead of us,' her mother had told her weeks ago – and now he'd gone right away, to some place called Brighton. That he'd left home on her birthday of all days had worried her, she couldn't understand it. She wished Myrtle would tell her some more, she was frightened that the tale would be told when she wasn't there, something just for the grown-ups. It wasn't fair, he was her Papa, he belonged to her, not to them. But she was happier at the shop than she'd ever been at home and in truth she didn't miss him as much as she imagined.

The tears had dried on Myrtle's cheeks and now, looking pale and weak, she was lying back with her eyes closed. She didn't so much as notice the child standing close.

'Tea-time,' Cynny said. 'Sit up, Franny, there's a good girl.'

She did as she was told and took a slice of bread and butter when the plate was passed. The rule was one slice with noting on it before they started on anything else: jam on the bread, sometimes a piece of pie, or fruit cake. Today Frances's plain slice was like sawdust, and her tummy was screwed in knots, half nerves and half unhappiness. She forced the food down, dreading that anyone might suspect how she felt.

She was right about one thing: it wasn't until the children had gone to bed that Myrtle told the others what she had learnt about Richard and his new love.

Cynny was busy darning the heel of Gina's stocking, the thread weaving backwards and forwards as she gripped her wooden mushroom. Equally industrious was Richard. He'd let the fire in his workroom die down early and closed the shop, the fishing rod he was re-ferruling could be done upstairs in the kitchen. Myrtle was lying quietly, her head on the pillow Cynny had brought out from her bed; they both believed she was asleep.

'We'll make sure that they stay until after Christmas now. No rushing off before she's ready,' Cynny whispered.

'Ah. One way and another she's taken a knock today.'

'It was hearing about it' – so she hadn't been asleep – 'that's what upset me. I wanted just to hurry back here. I shouldn't have tried to cross the street in front of the horses. I should have waited and gone behind the omnibus. Then the boy on the bicycle skidded on something and swerved, that's what frightened the nags as I stepped off the pavement.'

'I didn't see any boy. Did he fall, was he hurt?' Richard had hurried to the doorway as soon as he heard the commotion.

'He didn't come right off, just saved himself. Frightened he'd be in trouble for creating a stir, I expect, he rushed straight off when he saw me go down; didn't even wait to see how badly I was hurt.'

'Never mind, I expect he panicked. You'll soon feel better. We thought you'd dozed. Is there anything you'd like? A nice warm milk posset? There's a drop of brandy in the sideboard.'

'I'm sorry, Cynny, being such a nuisance.' The drink might put some heart back in her. 'It's always been the same with him, never cared about his home, always filling his mind with some lecture or other. I never could understand the things that interested him. I didn't know until Mrs Higman told me (I didn't say so to her of course), this woman of his is just the same. Since her husband died she'd been a teacher. She even speaks at some of the Liberal meetings; you remember he was always so keen to go to them, perhaps for the talk, perhaps for her. And I never knew. Not a girl, she's all of his age and no beauty it seems. A widow with a son of about fifteen. "The boy needs a father about the place," how Mrs Higman leered when she said it. He thinks more of them than of you and your girl, that's what she meant.' She sat upright, cried out as the pain stabbed her and fell back again. They forgave her the unusual venom in her tone as she rasped: 'What a happy family they must make.'

'Here dear, get this down you and you'll feel brighter. Don't look back, Myrtle; the future's going to be good.'

'Oh, Cynny, I just hope so, but how can I tell? I didn't know he was tired of me, I always tried. . . .

39

Perhaps I'll make the same mess of the future. Oh . . . oh, my back . . .,' she bit her lip. 'Truly I don't know what's happened, my life seems to have fallen to pieces. . . .' She took a spoon to her posset and they watched her, both full of pity, both determined nothing else should hurt the gentle little creature.

So Frances learnt no more about her father and when she mentioned him to Cynny she was only told: 'Best not to worry your head, duckie, and don't ask your poor Mama, it might upset her. We wouldn't want that, would we?' She knew better than to make an issue of it.

But her fantasies were her own. The father she created in her mind bore little resemblance to the reality. He listened to her when she told him about her lessons at Miss Searl's school, about how pretty Mama looked in the hat she'd just bought from Madame Zeigler's (and in her mind he smiled approvingly at Myrtle and she at him), about being able to jump higher than anyone else in her class; she made him her confidant in a way he never would have been had they stayed together in Belmont Road. Now that he was gone it was easy to forget how the house had seemed to relax when he went out of it and stand to attention when he came home.

Myrtle took Dr Saunders's advice and let Cynny wait on her. All idea of moving into Mallard Cottage before Christmas put to one side. Then in the New Year came a cold spell that dragged on into February.

'Bide your time, the cottage has been empty all winter, you don't want to move in at this time of year,' Cynny persuaded.

'You're right. The least chill seems to plague my poor back. We'll move for Easter. Can you bear us until then?'

'Bear you indeed! What nonsense the girl talks!'

So it was that they were still there when the school holidays started, the day that Richard held out a hand to yet another lame dog.

'I don't want anything the boy can't handle. Something with shorter joints would be easier for him. Only seven yet. Would want the two joints; wouldn't like to think it only a toy, d'yer see?' Roderick Smart laid the fishing rod he'd been examining back on the counter. 'Two joints it had better be – shorter lengths, what?'

Highworth was a small town (hardly a town at all, the future was to see it no more than a suburb of Tarnmouth, but that day was still a long way ahead). The tradespeople all knew one another and even though the gap was wide between Richard, the keeper of a small sports shop, and Roderick Smart, importer and merchant of timber, they weren't strangers.

'Try and get him out of the house now that school's finishing, d'yer see? It's my wife – not at all well – not the place for a child. Thought, let him have a packet of sandwiches – amuse himself by the river.' Roderick had a way of throwing out his sentences, tossing information at one. 'Day or two – must keep her quiet, d'yer see? No place for the boy. . . .'

Richard did see. Indeed he saw more than Roderick realised.

'The youngsters are of an age, likely they know each other from school. Look here, Mr Smart, send the lad to my Cynny, she likes nothing better than children around the place. Dickie's got space in his bed for another.' If Richard hadn't read beneath the bluster of his customer's words he mightn't have suggested it. 'No place for the boy'. Well, that was true enough.

'Would Mrs Sellwood let him board for a few days, d'yer suppose? Just till this bout passes.'

'Indeed she wouldn't. She doesn't take boarders, but she welcomes visitors. Send the lad to us, we'll take his mind off his Ma. Not right for nippers to be involved with sickness.'

So almost within the hour Gregory Smart was sent from the large grey house on Matley Heights to share a bed in the attic of the shop in the High Street. Strangely enough that was a Tuesday afternoon, and looking across the table at the guest that tea-time Frances wondered whether he could feel the magic. Gina smiled encouragingly and in response his lips stretched into a smile that didn't reach his eyes, such startling light blue eyes. Frances chewed her first slice of plain bread and butter, it just wouldn't go down, her throat was dry and stiff. Gregory's eyes showed no traces of tears, they showed nothing, yet she knew exactly what he was suffering. Couldn't they see it didn't help to ply him with food? Aunt Cynny had even offered him jam on his first slice.

'Eat up, Franny. What's happened to your appetite today?'

'Nothing, Mama.'

'It's your favourite vanilla cake. I'm sure you'll manage your bread and butter for that.'

She took another bite of her bread and felt the blue eyes watching her across the table. His mother must be very ill for him to have to be sent away. How could they expect him to eat?

'More bread and jam, Gregory? Or are you ready for a piece of vanilla cake?'

'I'd like the cake, please,' he said and for the first time Frances saw his eyes show a hint of warmth as, for a second, he looked across at her. The vanilla cake, her favourite Myrtle had said.

'May I have a piece too, please, Aunt Cynny?' she

42

asked and taking it plunged her teeth into it with relish. Between the two children a silent message passed. 'This is good' it said. But even more important was that she suddenly knew he felt the magic of Tuesday tea-time.

Later, lying in the big bed they shared, the covers pulled over their heads to make a tent, Gina speculated about the guest. 'She must be terribly ill for him to be sent away. I expect she's going to die.'

''Course she isn't. It's only 'cos there's no one to cook his dinner and look after him. Of course she won't die.'

'You can't know that she won't. She may. If she does and there's no one to look after him do you suppose he'll come to live with us?'

'She won't, I tell you. . . .'

'I'm only supposing. He's awfully handsome isn't he, Fran? Why do you think we haven't noticed him more at school?'

''Cos he's old, I suppose. He's in Miss Turnbull's form. He wouldn't play with us.'

'He will now though. Have you ever seen anyone with eyes like that, Fran? Don't you think he's handsome? You must do.'

'Let's play a game, Gina. Let's pretend something.' She tried to change the subject, she didn't want to talk about him.

'All right. I'll be Gregory's Ma, you could be his Pa – or the doctor. I bet you this week's bait money she dies and he stays with us for ever.'

'Please no, let's not be them. It's as if we wished it would happen. I'll bet she won't, and I've still got a farthing from last week, I bet that too.' She threw in all the weight she could to tip the balance in the poor woman's favour.

It semed she did the trick. The very next day Gregory went home.

'What a fuss to make, sending him off like that. When he went to find out how she was, there she was up and dressed, told him to come and get his grip and go back home.' Myrtle supposed (and do we detect a shade of jealousy?) that Roderick Smart put his wife's well-being far ahead of all else, but even so to banish a child for anything so trivial seemed unnecessary.

A glance passed between Cynny and Richard.

'She gets those turns from time to time,' was all Cynny said.

That was just before Easter and on the Monday the shop, of course, was closed and everyone helped Myrtle and Frances finally move to Mallard Cottage.

If they'd gone there straight from Belmont Road Frances would never have known what she'd been missing, but after nearly seven months in Cynny's household, her heart sank as she and her mother made their tour of inspection. The unpacking was completed, the others had all gone back to the High Street.

'Our very own little home, Franny, just for you and me! Isn't it the prettiest house you ever saw? Have you even seen drapes so dainty?' Really she was talking to herself, as excited as a child with a new toy. 'I stitched every one and what fun it was too, looking forward to having this dear pretty little house. Your Uncle Richard is going to bring his fork and scythe and set about the garden.' She stopped and hugged Frances. 'I can hardly believe it all,have you even known a day so exciting?'

Frances held her face into the expression she knew Myrtle wanted. It was lovely to see Mama so happy; if she'd ever shown her disappointment or displeasure by anger it wouldn't have been so important to try and please her. But she didn't. When things went against Myrtle she would be so sad that it hurt Frances to look at her. So now her own sense of loss in leaving the High Stree must be kept hidden.

'Anyway,' she sought to cheer herself, 'I'll be with the others at school and lots of times as well. I'm big enough to go to Aunt Cynny's by myself – and I will, I'll go ever so often.'

And so she did.

Then, quite once in a week if not more, Myrtle would say: 'Aunt Cynny's giving you your dinner today' – or 'your tea' – 'I shall take the omnibus to Tarnmouth and have my bath.' Since her accident she had formed the habit of visiting the Turkish Baths on the seafront; she enjoyed the outing and whether or not it benefited her health it certainly put her in a cheerful frame of mind. What better than a trip to town? and, the bath over, it would be a waste of an outing to hurry straight home.

When Miss Searl's school opened again there was no sign of Gregory. It was some weeks before Richard heard that he'd been sent away to school.

'At his age?' Cynny was appalled. 'Poor little love.'

'Better for him than living in that atmosphere.'

Gina repeated the conversation she'd overheard to Frances, and was disappointed by her cousin's apparent lack of concern.

'I expect his Papa knows what's best, Gina. Let's tie a rope and play jumping.' Anything to turn the subject away. She didn't want to imagine the hurt in Gregory's blue eyes, she shied away from picturing him in some harsh boarding school where the big boys might bully him and all the time at the back of his mind must be fears about his Mama.

'I do think you're mean about him, Fran. Don't you care if he's miserable?'

45

'Stupid, 'Course he's not miserable. He'll be having lots of fun. You jump first then I'll tie it up a bit more. Come on Dickie, we're seeing who can get the highest.'

It was a carefree period in the children's lives and memories of Gregory faded. Except that they slept under different roofs they were seldom apart. Frances might be the youngest but she remained the tallest; in fact the gap widened. Sometimes Myrtle would watch them together and feel ashamed of her disloyalty to her own daughter. Truly though, it did seem unjust when she herself had always taken such pride in her appearance. If a stranger were to see the two girls and be asked to guess which was hers and which Cynny's surely anyone might be forgiven for thinking little Gina belonged to her. About Gina there was a natural daintiness. Even after a morning at play she was never untidy, her dark curly hair would still be held in place by its ribbon and her buttoned boots never caked with mud. Not so Frances! When she played she gave no thought to anything as unimportant as her appearance. How could one be expected to worry about a hair ribbon when one was intent on reaching the topmost branch of the oak tree, and how could one fish for tadpoles and not get muddy boots? The girls had a different approach, each was a complement to the other. And somewhere in between was Dickie, usually with them at that stage. finding much more fun in their games than he would have had without Frances.

'Do just look at those children, Richard,' Cynny laughed, watching them from his workroom window, 'walking on their hands, would you believe, or trying to?'

Dickie managed six steps, Gina's feet hardly left the ground and then it was Frances's turn. While Gina rubbed her hands together cleaning off the dirt from the grass, then smoothed her skirt (not conscious of what she did; she simply wasn't comfortable unless she was neat) Frances leapt into a handstand, poised to hold herself steady before she moved forward.

'What a display of bloomers! Good thing her mother can't see her,' Richard laughed.

Her long straight hair fell forward like a curtain, her skirt was up-ended and covered her shoulders as, on her hands, she plodded across the grass. One, two, three, four, five, she rocked, stopped, steadied herself, then off again, six, seven, eight, nine, ten – then down she went amidst cries of mirth. Yes, it was a good thing Myrtle couldn't witness the exhibition; the child was turning into a hoodlum, all arms and legs.

Because it was a carefree time for them the seasons passed happily for the children. They progressed from Miss Searl's class to Miss Turnbull's, then finally to different schools, Dickie to 'the grammar', as the boys' school in Tarnmouth was known and the girls, still in Highworth, to Warwick House. If they thought of Gregory at all they must have assumed he came home for the school holidays, but more likely they were too busy with their own affairs to think at all of a boy they'd known so little.

Frances was nearly ten when she saw him again, more than four years later since the day he'd been welcomed into Cynny's home. That was almost half her life and she'd not thought about him for ages. When she heard the sound from the shelter of the willow tree by the river she peeped between the hanging branches in curiosity.

Four years had changed them both but the gap was bridged in a second.

47

Chapter Three

Boarding school at seven years old is sure to do one of two things. Perhaps it will crush a boy, make him timid and cowed, or perhaps it will make a man of him ahead of his time.

Gregory prided himself he was a man. Occasionally he came home for his holidays, but more often he went to his grandfather's house in Hastings. That's where he'd expected to go for the summer break this year as his father's last brief note had told him, 'Your mother's health keeps her to her room – you will fare better at Hastings'.

The portmanteaux were being carried out to the waiting carriages, everyone was ready to leave, when Dr Baker, the headmaster, summoned him.

'A telegram has been delivered. You may read it.' He passed the buff envelope.

'Thank you, sir.' It read: 'Unable to receive grandson Gregory Smart. Please arrange conveyance to Highworth. Horatio Smart.'

'Alter the labels on your boxes, boy, and report back to me. I shall have you escorted to the railway station for the five minutes past one train. You will alight at Tarnmouth. You understand me?'

'Yessir. Is my grandfather ill sir?'

'Stupid boy. You have read the telegram, you know as much of the reason as I do. Perhaps more. Are you sure you conducted yourself well during your Easter vacation?'

'Yes, sir, I did. Grandpa enjoys the holidays.'

'Then no doubt he has a good reason.' And with a sudden softening of his normal austere manner. 'There are weeks of holiday before you, I dare say some of them will be spent in Hastings later, eh?'

'I hope so, sir.'

'You're confident of your journey?'

'Yessir.'

'Good man.'

So the good man was put on the train and duly alighted at Tarnmouth; then, leaving his boxes at the station, he took the omnibus to Highworth.

There was no welcome waiting for him at Matley Heights. He was the only traveller to get off there (indeed the Heights was the upper-class area of town; there wasn't a house there without its own carriage), a solitary figure in his grey tweed suit with its Norfolk jacket, his stiff collar uncomfortably tight on the hot afternoon and his round black cap perched on the back of his head. At twelve he was a tall, well-built boy, no one would have wondered at his making the journey alone. Even so he felt less manly than he looked as he marched, just a small wicker case strapped and holding his overnight needs in his hand, up the lane towards home.

The door was opened by Betsy, the housekeeper who'd been there as long as he could remember. Often enough she'd been on the verge of going but never quite carried out her threat.

'Why, young Master Greg! Whatever are you doing here?'

'It's holiday, Betsy. Grandpa sent a wire, said I had to come home.'

'Oh dear, oh lawks! There's a thing! Come away in then, bless the boy, whatever are we going to do with you here? The old man never said – the elderly gent. I mean, old Mr Smart – never a word to us. Been taken ill has he?'

'I thought you'd know. How is Mother?'

'Kept to her room,' she sniffed. 'Best keep yourself out of her road till your Pa tells you. Fancy you coming.' This time he could tell that under her surprise she was glad to see him. 'Quite the young man you're growing. That collar's too tight. Don't know how to look after your things at that place. Shrink your clothes in the wash likely.'

'I expect I've grown, Betsy. Don't you think I've grown?'

'Ah, that you have. You grow up and we oldies grow down. Enough to grind anyone down in this place. Why I stay I'll never know. Your Pa don't see what's round him; never in the house if he can be out of it, and who can blame him? As for your Ma – oh well, we are as the good Lord made us, but seems He made a fine mess of some of us.'

He ought to want to go upstairs and see his mother; any other boy would be rushing up. He told himself he should and he was ashamed that when Betsy had told him to 'keep out of her road' his feeling had been relief. Now when she led the way down the basement stairs he was glad to follow.

'Best come down to m' kitchen. 'Tis the only bit of comfort in this barn of a house. Home they call it! Some home!'

'Nice down here though, Betsy. I say, I'm jolly hungry. Is there a slab of cake or anything?'

'Bless the boy. I'll get you a bite of something. A nice boiled egg, how would that be?'

'Sounds good. Is there any cake, Betsy?'

'No, I don't make cakes these days. What's the use? I tell you, your Pa's never in and your Ma wouldn't eat a piece of cake if I took it to her. I'll set to and stir one up this evening. Bless the boy, he shall have a cake for tomorrow.'

He had an urge to hug the portly figure, but he'd long since learnt to overcome any show of affection. So he contented himself with finding an egg cup and spoon, then spreading two enormous slices of bread thickly with butter.

The meal was just over when Roderick's carriage was heard and Gregory went up the back stairs to meet him in the hall.

'Ah, so you've arrived.'

'Yessir. An hour or so ago.'

'Your grandfather – reached me by telephone – been trying all day. Came straight home. Housemaid – down with scarlet fever.'

'Is it Daisy?'

'What? Oh – I didn't ask any names. Don't know what you'll find to do with yourself. Best not disturb your mother.'

'Shouldn't I go up and see her, sir? Betsy said not. I've not even told her I'm here.'

'I'll see how she is first. You've got books and such in the nursery, I dare say. You must try and amuse yourself as best you can. Have you friends about?'

Gregory was a man, well almost. He held his mouth rigid so it wouldn't betray him and nodded rather than trust his voice. The end of term built up to a fever of excitement, all the chaps would be arriving home, this very minute their families would be welcoming them . . . he clenched his teeth together. Then after a few seconds he managed: 'I'm sorry about the scarlet fever.'

'What? Ah, nuisance just at holiday. You must do some fishing or something. Time will soon pass.'

Later in the evening Gregory was told he could go up and see his mother. The blinds were pulled against the evening sun and going in from the bright corridor he screwed up his eyes to focus on her. The room smelt sour and as he adjusted to the dimness he could see how tousled her hair was. He bent to kiss her and hated himself for instinctively pulling away from her foul breath.

'Is there anything you'd like, Mama? Anything I can do for you?'

'Greg,' she whispered curiously; 'you look like Greg.'

'That's right, Mama.' Perhaps her sight was failing. 'Greg, home for the holiday.'

In the poor light he discerned something that passed as a smile.

'Greg,' she whispered, gripping his hands, 'if you could get me – but go quietly – get some –'

'I'll see to what she wants. Get in the sunshine. Breathe some fresh air.' Roderick's voice cut in from the doorway.

Gregory retreated. His mother seemed a stranger to him and he was disgusted with himself, disgusted but incapable of feeling any affection for what he'd seen. Pity perhaps, but something remote from himself. He did as Roderick said, went outside, grateful for the clear, clean air of the July evening.

As far back as he could remember his parents had had separate rooms; and during that night it was from hers that he heard movements. She was banging on her door; how strange. Creeping out, he tiptoed along the landing. The key was in the outside of her lock while in her room she frantically twisted the handle.

'I'll do it, Mama. Is it stuck?'

'Back to your bed.' Roderick came out of his room at the end of the corridor. 'No place for you to be.'

'But Father, she can't get out; something must have gone wrong with the lock.'

'Do as I say.'

Only when Gregory had closed his door behind him did Roderick unlock Judith's room and go inside. After that Gregory didn't want to hear anything. There were voices, skirmishing, something tipped over, china breaking. . . . He didn't understand, he was frightened to try to understand and he hated himself for wanting only to escape from it.

By daylight things appeared more normal. He breakfasted with his father and agreed that a day's fishing would be a good idea. Instinctively neither of them referred to the night's disturbance. An outing with a packet of sandwiches and a couple of slices of the cake Betsy had baked the previous evening and life wouldn't be so bad after all.

While Betsy packed his food he went to the old nursey to sort out his tackle.

'Greg,' hardly more than a whisper and so close behind that it startled him.

'Mama! Should you be out of bed?'

'Ssshhh,' she held a finger to her lips. 'I feel a lot better. See I've brushed my hair and made myself pretty for you. Haven't you a kiss for your Mama?' Because she spoke so quietly she leant towards him.

He shouldn't care that she smelt of sweat and her breath was sour; she was his mother. He consciously tried to recall memories that would warm him to her but in truth he had none. Always it had been Betsy who'd cared for him. He supposed that even then his mother's bouts of illness had put a blight on family life.

'I'm going fishing. You don't mind if I'm out all day do you?'

'I want you to have a happy holiday. But Greg, before you go, just one wee little thing for your poor Mama. It'll save Betsy's legs, she has so much to do. Downstairs in the sideboard – a bottle of brandy. I need it – I think I've got one of my turns coming. Just the bottle, I've got a glass.'

'Are you sure it's all right for you to have it?' Somewhere he was sure he'd heard that if the doctor had given one medicine one shouldn't take alcohol.

'What do you mean – allowed? 'snot your business what I do.'

In a sudden flash he half understood so much that had been a mystery.

'Supposing it's locked? I'm almost sure it's locked, Mama.'

She gripped his wrist. 'Then find the key,' she hissed, 'in his study – the desk, that's where it'll be.'

'Oughtn't I to ask Betsy? She'd know.'

'Didn't you hear me! You won't ask Betsy. You'll fetch it, you won't ask Betsy.' Then changing back to her former wheedling tone: 'Musn't worry poor Betsy, so much to do. . . .'

Oh heavens, she was dribbling. He backed away hating to see the saliva hanging on the corner of her mouth. Still she came nearer, pleading, cajoling as, trying a new tactic, she rubbed the heel of her thumb against her chest.

'It's just here, that's where I get the pain. Shouldn't have eaten that breakfast; should have known today was to be a bad day.' As if to prove her point she stared straight at him, opened her mouth and belched. 'Be better for a sip, just to settle my poor stomach. There's a good boy.' Unblinkingly she held his gaze, belched

54

again and moved so near that her face was only inches from his (and how was he to know how useful her skill in forcing up wind had proved). 'Please, please. You're kind, you understand, you want poor Mama well.' He cringed at the touch of her clammy hands.

'No, I can't let you. Mother, I can't. Don't you see it won't help you. Come back to bed –'

Her long nails cut into his wrists, she was panting and he turned his head away, revolted and frightened.

'Get it, get it you young whelp.' She was blubbering now. 'That damned Betsy won't watch you. They watch me, they think they stop me, but I fool them. Can't see everything. Oh dear, oh dear,' she flopped against the nursery table. '. . . chair,' then sat limply with her hands dangling between her knees. 'No strength . . . so ill. . . .'

'I'll get Betsy.'

'No, no. Just a sip, just to lay my breakfast. You'll help me . . .'

'Mama, I cannot, you know that.'

Then she turned on him like a trapped animal. If her strength had left her before, just now it came back with a vengeance. She sprang up, taking him by the shoulders and shaking him; her hand came across his face with a force that left the marks of her fingers, then with a final effort she threw him from her. It had been too much, though, and she clung to the mantlepiece for support.

From downstairs Betsy must have heard. 'Off you go.' From the doorway her voice took command. 'Just leave your mother to me, lad.'

He didn't wait to argue, didn't so much as wait for rod or sandwiches. Out of the house, along the lane, over the stile and through the meadow. He didn't stop until he reached the stream. The memory of what had happened loomed in his mind; the touch of her hand, the

55

sly smile that wasn't a smile. Yes, that was the worst. If she'd been ill, even in the putrid state he'd seen her last night, he could have understood, tried to help – or so he told himself. This was something different though; it frightened him, set her apart. He hardly noticed where he was going as he hurried, hands deep in his pockets, along the path at the water's edge. What did it matter where he went as long as he escaped? By the time he reached the shelter of the willow tree he was crying; he wasn't even sure why but shock and fright had caught up with him. He sobbed as he hadn't for years.

It was the strange gulping noise that made Frances stop and listen. She was collecting a bunch of tall white daisies from the meadow. Tomorrow was Myrtle's birthday and secretly, at the shop under Cynny's guidance, she'd stitched a pretty lilac apron trimmed with coffee-coloured lace. Her talents in that direction were limited, Gina would have made a much better job of it, but Frances hadn't noticed the titivating that Cynny had given to her handiwork each day after she'd gone home. So now it was pressed and wrapped in tissue and the bunch of daisies was to be put in water in Cynny's wash-house until last thing this evening.

Now she dumped the flowers unceremoniously in a heap and gently pulled the overhanging branches of the willow apart to poke her head through. The boy was taken by surprise. He snorted, wiped the back of his hand across his nose, then turned his face away.

'Greg'ry!' She'd not seen him for so long, but even swimming in tears, she recognised those piercing light-blue eyes. Whether or not he wanted her there she didn't consider. In a second she was sharing his shady retreat, kneeling by his side. 'Is your Mama ill? Is that what's the matter?'

He snorted. 'No – yes –' He gulped, sniffed, wiped his

nose again. '. . . got a hanky?'

'Here.' She dug in the pocket of her white pinafore. 'It isn't very big,' his wet face and running nose looked more than enough for the minute square, 'but you can have it.'

'Thanks.' He blew, wiped, rubbed his eyes hard with the little ball of screwed-up cotton. 'Thanks. You're from the shop aren't you, where I was sent that time? I remember you – we had vanilla cake.'

'Yes.' It didn't seem at all strange to her tht he should remember the incident of the cake. 'My name's Frances, but you can call me Fran if you like. I don't live at the shop, not any longer. Mama and I live in Duck Island Lane.'

'I've often thought about it there. Is it always like that? Do you know what I mean?'

She nodded. 'It's funny, but even if you do something bad and get a wigging you still feel warm deep down inside, as if you know they're grumbling 'cos they love you.'

'Why don't you still live there?'

'We only stayed with Aunt Cynny while Mama found us a house. We used to live in Tarnmouth when I was young, until Papa went away.'

'Did he die, your Papa?'

'Dear me, no.' Instinctively she knew that while she talked he had a chance to recover, so she plunged on. 'He went to live with another lady. Mama is so pretty and yet, do you know Greg'ry, I listened one day when she was talking to Aunt Cynny and she said the lady he'd gone to wasn't a bit pretty. She said "She's no beauty and not even young". You'd think he would have wanted to stay with Mama and me wouldn't you?'

'Expect you're better off without him. Sounds like a bounder to me.'

'Oh no, Papa's a fine man, I'm sure he is. One day when I'm a grown-up woman and Mama won't cry – she cries usually if I do things she doesn't like you see – I am going to find him and show him how I am.'

Poor little kid, Gregory thought. Likely as not the rotter won't even care to see 'how she is'.

She'd talked far more than she usually did, purposely telling him things to take his mind off himself while he found his composure.

'Why don't you sit down? Your knees will get sore.'

She sat close by his side. 'I often come under here. If you sit very still you can hear the stream.'

'I couldn't; I was making too much row. I say Fran, I don't usually blub like that. I mean, well, I'm pretty well grown up. You must think me an awful cissy.'

'I think no such thing. Greg'ry if you want to tell me why, you can, but I don't need to know. I was just scared that your Mama had – you know. . . .'

'Died? Oh no, she's not going to die. Fran, listen, yes I'll tell you. I want to tell you. They've always said she's ill, but I know now what's wrong with her. There's a name for it – dip . . . something or other. It seems that her mind's gone fuddled with drink and she's ill because of it. Suddenly I could see that that was what's up. She's sort of mad, she smells, she's wild –' and by this time so was he, the horror had come back and his voice was choked with sobs he tried to swallow. Frances didn't understand about this 'dip – something or other'. She'd heard about the men who got thrown our of the Barley Mow of a night. When she'd been staying at the shop she and Gina had watched them sometimes as they went singing on their lurching way up the High Street, but this other was beyond her imagination. How could she help him? Timidly she slipped her hand into his but she didn't speak. Soon he mopped up in the minute wet handkerchief and she hoped he felt better.

'I'm sure Aunt Cynny would let you stay again. They've got a proper spare room now that Mama isn't using it. Shall we go and ask her?'

'No. I just wish I could do that but I was only a kid when father sent me there before. I must tell him I know about what's wrong. I must let him see I'm not a kid any longer.'

She turned her gingery eyes upon him with new respect. He was a man indeed.

'Fran, do I look as though I've been blubbing? I've not cried for ages, years – feel beastly ashamed of myself – honestly I don't . . .'

'Chump. I know that.' She dug deep for the right words to help him. 'Even grown-ups cry when they have heavy burdens to bear.' There! That sounded grand to her ears, so with added confidence she went on: 'Mama does it all the time.' Not so clever. He took his hand away and stood up. My, but he was tall! Could he really be only a year or so older than Gina? To Frances the lad who'd only just had his twelfth birthday was in a class apart.

'Go and wash your face in the stream, Greg. You can dry it in my pinafore. You'll look as right a ninepence if you have a wash.'

'Right-o.'

The cold water helped, and then they spent an hour hunting for butterflies before they finished gathering the daisies. Together they went to take the flowers to Cynny and, being the wise woman she was, she gave no sign of noticing his swollen eyelids. Gina was finishing a basket she'd been making for Myrtle and Dickie was out fishing. A glass of home-made lemonade and a piece of seedcake helped restore Gregory's equilibrium.

'Dickie will be home at 1 for his dinner. Sure as eggs are eggs he'll be at the river again after, Gregory. Shall I

59

tell him you might join him? I'll say to stay near the bridge, then you'll know where to find him.'

'I've got my tackle ready.' Gregory even smiled as he said it, the memory of his mother's interruption while he was sorting it seemed now to have lost much of its horror.

He and Frances left together and by the time they came to the corner of Duck Island Lane where they were to part company it would have taken a keener eye than Cynny's to detect traces of tears.

'Will you come to our tree tomorrow, Fran? If we meet the others we could start from there.'

'Yes, I will. Come early. Soon as you've had your breakfast.'

He nodded. Obviously there was something else he wanted to say; still he hovered. 'About this morning. . . .'

'I've promised. I'll not tell.'

'No, I know that. That wasn't what I meant. It's . . . er . . . I say, Fran, I'm jolly glad you came to the tree and I told you all about it – I was, well, I was jolly down in the dumps you know before you came. . . .'

She didn't answer but he understood that was because she didn't know how to find the right words. After all in years at any rate she was no more than a kid. But in her gingery eyes he read her answer. No doubt she was jolly glad too.

Next day was Myrtle's birthday, something Frances hadn't taken into consideration as they made their plans, something in fact she'd entirely forgotten despite the hours of stitching that had gone into the apron. A trip to Tarnmouth was to be the order of the day, a visit to the milliner, then their dinner at the Hotel Metropole.

'But Mama, wouldn't you have more fun if Aunt Cynny went with you?'

'Silly child. How can she with dinner to cook and a family to care for? And anyway I love us to have a little outing together, Franny. It's good for you to come to the fashion houses and learn to appreciate pretty things – and what fun it'll be taking our dinner at the Metropole!'

Frances knew when she was beaten. It wasn't that she was frightened of standing up for herself, but she dreaded the sight of her mother's lips quivering before the tears came; she couldn't bear to hear: 'I suppose I shouldn't expect us to be together as much as I do, but Franny you're all I've got.' Anger she could withstand but not that and especially not on a birthday.

So it turned out very different from the morning she had expected. No calico playdress and white pinafore today, but her best navy blue and white sailor top, white skirt, white stockings and black patent leather shoes that she must be careful not to scuff. Her hair hung to her waist now, still the same tawny colour and today topped with a straw sailor hat. Myrtle looked at her with some satisfaction. It was regrettable that she was growing so fast but she had to admit there was something about the child that caught one's eye. If, as a rider, she added 'as long as she manages to keep herself tidy' experience was behind the thought.

They took the omnibus to Tarnmouth. Frances sat obediently by while Myrtle tried on hats in Madame Zeigler's salon, they ordered a special birthday dinner at the Metropole where a trio played and the damask serviettes were stiff and shiny with starch. She tried to be as excited about it all as her mother expected but her mind was under the leafy tent of the willow. How long would he have waited? Would he think she hadn't really cared about being his friend?

When the horses came to a halt and they alighted from the omnibus on their homeward journey they saw Cynny

61

watching for them from her window. Not only a birthday dinner but a special celebration tea too it seemed. How long had she stood over the steaming pan while she beat the eggs to produce Myrtle's favourite sponge cake of such enormous height? Gina presented her basket, Dickie a wooden winder for her knitting wool (made under Richard's guidance) and no one so much as mentioned Gregory. Perhaps he'd not been to the shop today.

During the night she heard the rain and the air was still damp the next morning when she picked her way along the rutted path by the stream.

No Gregory waiting for her. But attached to the tree by a thin nail was a letter. The ink on the envelope had run, the word 'FRAN' had turned into blue teardrops down the paper. The single sheet inside was dry though, and sitting where they'd shared their confidences she read: 'Dear Fran, I told father I knew what was up but he didn't seem to understand. He'd already sent a telegram to his brother and I have to go and stay with him on his farm near Oxford. I don't want to go. The train is at 10 o'clock so I shan't be here when you come to the tree. Tell Dickie I'm sorry I shall miss the fishing. I'm to stay on Uncle James's farm until I go back to school. I haven't been told yet about the Christmas holiday. Next time I come to Highworth I hope I see you. Your friend, Greg.'

She read it through twice then carefully folded it and tucked it under the knee elastic of her bloomers. Walking home she could feel it scratching against her leg, something private and personal, a letter that was hers alone.

The girls had no secrets from each other (well, almost none, for Frances hadn't mentioned her encounter with

Greg under the willow). At one time Dickie had been one with them but recently they'd found things that had to be talked of out of his hearing. Like the August day of that same summer when Frances waited until he was out of earshot then whispered to Gina: 'You remember what Millie Bryant told us – about having hairs – well, Gina, I've got some too. Only just starting, but suddenly they must have come, quite a lot. . . .'

'Really! Let me see. Come on, Fran, show me. Let's go up to my room.'

'We mustn't be long. Dickie'll be out with the jars in a second.' For the secret had been shared while he was in the shed fetching jam jars for a tadpoling expedition.

'I'll tell him to go on; we'll run and catch him up,' Gina was already half way down the path to the shed.

'What are you going to do?' he wanted to know; 'Why can't I come?'

'Nothing to do with boys, and anyway you're younger.' Not quite true as far as Frances was concerned but he supposed she really meant too little, and how could he argue with that? 'We sometimes have grown-up things to talk about you know.'

Frances hoped she hadn't exaggerated last night's discovery; there wasn't a great deal to show. When she saw Dickie looking after them from the open doorway of the shed she almost wished she'd kept her news for another time or that she could share it with him too. 'Take the jars and nets, Dickie, we'll catch up in a jiff,' she called.

It took a little longer than that though for the examination had to be thorough, a count made. Her hint of adolescence had to be admired, touched, the darker colour wondered at; Gina had to be inspected, albeit fruitlessly. By the time they pulled up their bloomers Frances felt the subject was exhausted. So proud she'd been to carry her news to Gina but by now she was eager to answer the call of the tadpoles.

Myrtle was as aware as Frances of her body's progress and viewed it with misgiving, as she said to Cynny.

'If only she'd take life more gently perhaps she wouldn't grow so. Always jumping about or climbing – and swimming in the river too, that's what gives her a bosom already I wouldn't wonder. It's not right at her age. Gina is a little girl still – and so pretty, Cynny. My, but she's going to be a beauty.'

'Nought wrong with your Franny's looks. She's to be well built like her father; favours his features too. But she's got your colouring.'

That was some solace but even so Frances knew her appearance was a disappointment, something she should feel guilty about.

'Do try to be more delicate, dear, don't rush so. Your feet are as large as mine already and it's not seemly in a child of your age to have a chest. Such a disadvantage for a woman to be gawky.'

Frances squeezed herself uncomfortably into her tightly buttoned bodice, hoping to flatten the offending bosom into submission.

Only weeks after her tenth birthday she menstruated, painlessly and copiously. She listened as her mother gave her 'a little private talk' (not that anyone would have been likely to overhear, since they lived alone). She was half proud of herself for what in some way seemed to make her a more important person than she had been a few hours earlier and half ashamed that her body had once again pushed ahead too fast and disappointed her mother.

'Now this is something girls must never talk about, Franny. Remember that, and especially not a word to the boys, not Dickie. Promise me you'll say nothing in

64

front of him or Uncle Richard. It's what we call
Women's Secret. Oh dear, poor little soul, fancy being
burdened so soon. I'd said too that I'd wash your hair
this evening; now it must wait for a few days until this is
over.'

Feelings of shame took pride of place.

Later, when she saw Gina the scales tipped the other
way. In view of what had happened Cynny had also had
a talk to prepare her daughter, the bare essentials
accompanied by the same warning of secrecy; Frances
filled in the details in dramatic whispers from the shelter
of the wash-house, keeping watch that they weren't
disturbed and, by now, very pleased with herself for her
superior knowledge and seeing the respect her cousin
had for her feat.

Guilt did return though as with regularity and no sign
of pain each twenty-eighth day the floodgates opened.
Gina was to wait nearly two years and then suffer in a
way that Myrtle seemed to accept as proper.

The girls advanced towards maturity as full of hope
and confidence as any other and as full of their own
affairs too. Thoughts of Gregory faded; they were too
busy looking to the future to bother with the past. If he'd
come home it might have been a different story but when
Christmas came he was sent to Hastings, then again at
Easter and in the summer back to the farm in
Oxfordshire, a pattern that held for the next year too.
That he didn't come to Highworth didn't worry Frances.
She was even glad for him for the memory of his
unhappiness still made her uncomfortable. He was
especially her friend just as she was his and she'd much
rather he was having a good holiday somewhere else
than being miserable in Highworth.

And we mustn't imagine he was pining to see his new
friend either, for he had plenty more to think about. As

for the school holidays, whichever place he visited either was better than Matley Heights. At Hastings he had his grandfather, he had the old rowing boat and fishing rods, he helped the locals unload their catch and watched while they sold the fish by the shore. Then there was the farm, the long summer days when he learnt to match his strength to the men's who worked in the fields. Like any other young person he felt himself to be part of the fast-changing scene, a brave new world; everywhere one was aware of progress; there'd never been a time like it. Every generation knows the same urge to spread its wings and fly. Gregory was no different. His world was all around, young, new and eager. But through it all was a lesson he learnt from the farm, one that was to stay with him as long as he lived; he was humbled by the smallness of man against nature's bounty.

Frances never talked about him but somewhere safely tucked to the back of her mind he was there. It's doubtful if Gina had given him a thought as time went by and it was only overhearing the end of a conversation between her parents that called him to mind.

'. . . suppose she must be the latest woman. That's twice I've seen him go with her in the punt in this last week,' Richard said.

'Poor man – and her too. His poor wife I mean.'

'Doubt he misses out on much from the look of it. They came from under the trees where he'd tied the boat and from the look of them he'd been putting his time to good use.'

'But Richard, what a life, what a marriage. And can you wonder she drinks?'

'Yes, I can. Got no sympathy at all, if you want the truth. What about that poor wretched boy of theirs. Pushed from pillar to post every school holiday because of what she is. Can't think how she lasts. You'd expect it would have finished her off long ago. Keeps to her room these days, Bert Read told me – you know Bert, the postman who pushes the truck – his wife cleans there, he says –'

'I don't want to hear it. Pity folk haven't got more to do than listen to gossip about other people's troubles.'

Looking at her he was struck by something unfamiliar, what it was he couldn't be sure. A drawn look; her face was still plump and yet there was something. Perhaps she was tired; that could account for her sharp tone.

Listening, Gina knew nothing of his thoughts. The conversation seemed to be over and she recognised who they'd been talking about. She passed it on to Frances the next day and was disappointed in its reception. Frances always seemed singularly unconcerned about poor Gregory.

Once in a while Horatio Smart considered it right to organise things so that Gregory went home first, even briefly, before coming to Hastings. No matter what sort of a state Judith was in he wanted Roderick to be aware that his son was developing into a fine young fellow – or so the old man fondly considered. It was probably the thought of being tied for the next few evenings that had encouraged Roderick to make the most of his freedom.

By now Betsy had been relieved of much of her care of Judith by the strong, but gentle, Mrs Goddard. No chance these days of smuggling a bottle upstairs, yet it seemed that Gregory's diagnosis had been wrong. His mother's condition needed even more watchfulness. He was at a loss to understand.

'Ought I to wait for Papa or shall I see her now?' he asked Betsy.

'Can't do her any harm – but won't do her any good either. Doubt she'll know who you are. Be prepared, Master Greg. Her body grows stronger as her mind grows weaker.'

'Betsy, what really ails her? D'you know? It's as if I'm an outsider – I want to care, honestly I do. Suppose its because I'm always away, and father never tells me.'

'Look boy, if you're outside it just be grateful and leave it at that. Her poor mind's got all the devils at it; she can't help what she is. Just be gentle with her. Time was when she was different. Her own father, he was just the same. Died when she was still a child, so I've heard, and in the asylum for the last years while he waited for his call.'

'Asylum! And Mama. . . .'

'In her blood, poor soul.'

'But Betsy I thought it was drink, I'm sure it was drink and father didn't argue when I told him I knew.'

'A drop used to help her, take the fear out of her. No more it don't though. She knew what was happening then, came and went, she seemed to. Proper gone these days. Your father won't have her taken off, says her home is here. Dare say he's right, but to my way of thinking it'd make little difference to the poor soul. Well, if you want to pay your respects you mustn't expect too much. Have I said too much, spoken out of turn? Mayhap I have, but you're not a child no more, time you knew the rights of things and I doubt your father will put you wise. But not to mention to him how I've spoken; not my place to be the one. But, well, they've made their beds; it's you we have to look to. Don't want you to worry your young head about what can't be oddsed.'

He was lost for an answer and she turned back to her bowl of vegetables. In her simple way of caring about him hadn't she realised the enormity of what she'd told him? His mother wasn't sane, and her father before her. . . .

Last time he'd been at the house he'd hated going to her room; now it drew him. He had to see. It was more than curiosity that sent him up the stairs. He felt weak with fear, not fear for her, nor even of her. What had Betsy done to him!

He knocked and at Mrs Goddard's hearty 'Come along in' entered a bedroom far different from the one he remembered. The window was open top and bottom, lavender water was the predominant smell if smell there was and his mother sat in an armchair, her nightgown clean and her hair brushed and plaited. The blank stare she turned on him told him a salutory kiss would be out of place – and even Mrs Goddard's ministrations couldn't banish the memory of her unwashed mouth.

'Mama, it's Greg.'

Her only recognition that someone new had come into her vision was to hold out a woollen ball she'd been swinging.

'Pretty. Tell her how pretty it is Master Greg,' the nurse prompted.

'It is, it's a lovely ball, Mama.'

From the frightened pathetic animal she'd been when last he'd seen her she seemed to have gained a new strength, or if not strength at least a couple of stone in weight. Even her face was fat and her chin hung into her neck. Food had become almost the only thing in life. Now she held the baby's ball that Mrs Goddard had just finished making to give to her great niece and swung it backwards and forwards laughing delightedly.

'Pretty,' she burbled.

Greg wasn't sure what was expected of him so he put out a hand to pat the coloured ball. In a second her

69

pleasure vanished and she clutched her treasure with both hands.

'Go 'way, go 'way.' She was panting and in a sudden fury she turned on the ball plucking the woollen strands from it. 'Hate you, hate you, go 'way . . .' she was sobbing tearlessly, 'send her 'way, her eyes burn me. . . .'

'Mama.' Despite the 'her' Greg could see it was him she cringed from.

'Dear, oh dear, now you've upset her. Been such a good girl this morning too. Now I'll have a job with her dinner.'

'What can I do, can I help?'

'Done enough damage, you have. Off you go downstairs. Come along now, my luvvy, she's all gone.'

Heaven above, now the stupid creature was encouraging her! He fled from the room, he'd seen more than enough. But this time neither daylight, sunshine nor even dinner shared with his father with no mention of his visit upstairs could dim the memory. It haunted him. So too at one time it must have haunted her in the secret corridors of her mind.

What instinct made her become so docile after he'd left her? How much was planned and how much chance? We shall never know for we have no way of understanding, and may be we never have.

She pushed her plate away, the food untouched, and her look would have melted a sterner heart than Mrs Goddard's as she said: 'Milk, lovely creamy milk . . .,' her tongue licking her dry lips.

'You'd drink it up for me, dearie? Then I'll get it.'

Was it cunning that made her close her eyes as if she wasn't so much as aware she was being left on her own? The tray of uneaten food in her hands, no one can blame the nurse for not locking the door; after all she was coming straight back.

Judith might have grown fat but she moved deftly and

70

quietly out to the corridor, along to Roderick's room, then back into Gregory's carrying something in her hand.

The lucifers had been easy enough to find, standing ready to hand in the base of the candle-holder by his beside, but it wasn't Roderick she had in mind, it was Gregory she had to destroy. She had only one thought, to destroy him, and that he wasn't in his room made no difference to her objective; it seemed to her that to get rid of his things would remove him, wipe him out. Her reasoning was out of step but her cunning was sharp enough to tell her she must move quietly and lock herself into his room before she started her task. She laughed as she threw the key out of his open window, now no one could stop her!

By the time the milk was poured and the nurse had had 'just a quick cup then, seeing as you've got it in the pot', she had a good start. Smoke was already curling its way under the locked door and Mrs Goddard sniffed anxiously as she hurried back to where she'd left her charge. Even when she realised what had happened she wasted precious time trying to coax Judith to unlock the door. It wasn't until the first piecing scream rent the air that she ran back down to meet Roderick and Gregory already at the foot of the stairs.

'The mistress – locked in Master Greg's room – set it alight she must've –'

Roderick and Gregory ran to the shed and together dragged out the ladder to put against the side of the house. 'Take your cycle, quick as you can, get the engine.' Already Roderick was climbing towards the open window through which smoke was pouring.

Judith had done her job thoroughly, she'd gone round the room delighting in the bright flames she brought from anything that came to hand – the corner of the

71

counterpane; the mantle drapes; a pile of papers; his case of butterflies had to have the glass broken first and even then wouldn't flame so she crushed the wings between her fingers, thrilled by the power she felt as they crumbled. He'd liked his butterflies – now they'd gone, now they'd gone.

It was then that the fire lapped at the hem of her nightgown, the material seeming to stretch out to meet it. That's when she screamed.

Roderick found her in a crumpled heap on the ground, the first furious flames had eaten her gown, tried to eat into her flesh, frizzled her hair, and left her unconscious, the last orange tongues lapping round her neck. In the smoke-filled room he tried to grab something to wrap her in. The rug, he'd roll her in that. Already he was half choked by smoke. He pulled at the bedside rug – then he knew it was hopeless as he felt the searing heat and the wicked tongues licked out at the cloth of his own clothes. Self-preservation came first He rolled on the ground trying to extinguish the flames, his yells could be heard from the garden below like cries of a soul in the torment of hell.

It had all happened in minutes, even as Roderick's shouts turned to an unearthly choking and then to silence the fire truck had only just started on its journey.

Cynny, the practical, thought first of Gregory when they heard where the fire was, and it takes little enough time for word to spread. As the fire truck headed towards the Heights the usual group of sightseers followed, some on bicycles, some running, all speculating – then as soon as the excitement faded, all keen to be the first back to town to spread the news.

They hadn't seen Greg since that morning some two years ago when he'd called with Frances, but if what the gossip-mongers were saying was true who would there be for him to turn to? He'd come to them once before, and so he could again. Richard locked the shop and pedalled off towards Matley Heights.

Half an hour later he returned. Gregory and Betsy had gone home with Mrs Goddard, and folk were saying that a telegram had been sent to Roderick's brother. It seemed Cynny's hospitality wasn't needed.

It was the talk of Highworth for the next few days.

'Fancy, trying to save that wife of his, and him with all his lady friends. . . .' some said, leaving the way open for any snippets of his affairs they might have missed.

'Poor man. To give up his life for her, a poor enough partner she was too. Still he didn't stop to count the cost. . . .,' others elevated him to the ranks of the saints.

The fire that had taken two lives hadn't destroyed the house; only the back upper floors stood as evidence of Judith's handiwork. A tarpaulin over that corner of the roof, blackened brickwork round the boarded-up window, nothing more; the materials that had burst into flame so readily had been easy to extinguish, even the solid wood furniture was wrecked by smoke and water, not by fire.

No one had any idea how often Frances had thought about Gregory. Even the self-created father who shared so many of her secrets hadn't been told of the morning in the shelter of the willow. After the fire she went each morning to their tree; he'd know that's where he'd find her. But he didn't come. Perhaps he'd forgotten she was his friend, perhaps it hadn't really been important to him.

Always careful to show no hint of interest, she kept her ears open. His uncle had come to Highworth, then she heard that his grandfather was there too. It was the day after the funeral that she learned they'd all gone away. The house was closed; she supposed he'd never come to Highworth any more.

And perhaps that would have been the end of it but for a chance visit of Myrtle's to the grocer's to buy a dozen candles.

'Bad business, but as I always say, who are we to argue with our Maker?' Mr Pengelley, the fat, rosy-faced grocer carefully wrapped the wedge of cheese he'd cut for his customer, and looked up to greet Myrtle. 'Morning Mrs Ratcliffe. Ah, we all have to go when He's ready for us. Bad for the lad, as you say, but he seemed always pushed out of the nest if you ask me. Now is there anything more I can get you? Just cut a nice side of bacon, smoked just to your liking it is. How about a few rashers or a bit for the boil?' He nodded his head towards the half pig hanging over the far end of the counter but didn't press the point. Experience had taught him that folk opened their purse strings wider if one gave them time, so he went on: 'No, it's Betsy Ackroyd has my sympathy, the housekeeper, you know. Been with them goodness knows how many years, moved with them when they came from somewhere Hastings way. No family to fall back on, that I do know for she used to have a chat sometimes when she brought her order. Glad of a chin wag she must've been too, stuck there with the missus like she was. A real home-maker, you could tell just to talk to her, not that she had much chance in that – ah, a nice piece of middle cut, I'll see to it right away. Soak it overnight, then you'll find it'll boil a real treat.'

When Myrtle walked home, bearing a larger cut of bacon than she'd intended, she considered the problem of Betsy. It seemed she was staying temporarily with Mrs Goddard, the nurse. A real home-maker, he had

74

said, someone who could always be in the house. And why not? She made ends meet with some to spare and how much more pleasant to have a housekeeper living in than a daily (or more precisely a 'daily' every other day) to do the cleaning and someone else to take on the washing?

But for Myrtle needing to replenish the bedside candles, she would never have called at Mr Pengelley's shop that morning and probably would never have heard the whereabouts of this treasure who needed a home. Whether or not then Frances would have seen Gregory again, who knows. It seems more likely that she would have forgotten all about him, for life was full of promise as she grew to adolescence.

Chapter Four

To learn a musical instrument was the accepted thing and Cynny's parlour, like so many, boasted a piano. So no choice was given to Gina and Dickie (although he wriggled out of it after the first few months) and for half an hour of every evening scales, exercises and then one piece – like cake after bread and butter – had to be battled with. From October until May the parlour was often cold enough for Cynny's nightly reminder of 'Run and do your practice, Gina,' to be followed by 'You'll need your coat in there tonight.' Myrtle's parlour was always warm but it was such a pretty room, to fit a piano into it would overcrowd it; yet Frances ought to have a chance to learn.

It was an outing with the school to St Stephen's Hall to hear a visiting quintet that provided the solution. While most of her twelve-year-old classmates fidgeted restlessly Frances sat spellbound. She'd learn to play the fiddle. She could hardly get home fast enough to tell her mother what she wanted. Unless one lived in a town with a concert hall the only music one heard was what the family could make and Frances had heard so little. Church on Sundays where Dickie still sang in the choir, his treble lasting, to his shame, while all his friends had croaked their way out. He trilled as easily as ever to top A, never opening his mouth to find his voice betraying him. So the afternoon when Frances listened to Schubert new horizons were opened for her. She hurried home prepared to use every power of persuasion only to find Myrtle as keen as she was herself with the idea. A fiddle! What better? In the summer all the practising could be done in the attic playroom and in the winter Betsy kept the kitchen nice and warm; she'd enjoy having Frances in there of an evening. Why, it needn't upset the house a bit. If the doors were kept closed she'd hardly hear.

That Highworth had no violin teacher wasn't seen as an obstacle; the reverse. Each Thursday afternoon instead of going to school Frances went by omnibus to Tarnmouth, her fiddle case under her arm, and willingly Myrtle took the opportunity to travel with her and visit the Turkish Bath. Folk were used to looking to Tarnmouth for anything more than their daily needs. A prosperous harbour town, two theatres, a grand Town Hall with an organ fine enough to bring people from miles around to hear the regular recitals, a college that in the not-too-distant future was to gain the status of a university, and on the Esplanade the Metropole Hotel where Frances had first gone none too willingly on that birthday of Myrtle's. Each meal-time in the dining-room of the Metropole a trio played, more than earning their meagre wage as they romped through Viennese waltzes, popular operetta and, every day, Saint-Saëns' *Swan*, where the cellist came into her own, never failing to float downstream with her eyes closed. Myrtle enjoyed taking her tea there. Even before the Thursday fiddle lessons she'd enjoyed it, and now it became her meeting place with Frances. So satisfactory having a daughter almost grown up.

Frances always looked forward to her lesson and this week as she put her violin back in its case she was surprised to see how fast the time had gone; she was nearly ten minutes late in finishing. She'd have to hurry; she hated keeping her mother waiting.

She didn't run. To run in the street was only one stage worse than eating in the street and so inbred were the standards expected that a quick walk was her natural reaction when she saw the hands of the church clock. Round the corner and she'd be in West Street. Perhaps a tram would be coming. Luck was against her; as she rounded the bend the conductor punched the bell and before she could get to it the tram had rattled away down its track, along West Street towards King Street and the Esplanade. Another wouldn't come for ten minutes; she'd be quicker to walk.

Her long legs stretched out as she strode down the busy street, her leather music bag in her right hand and her wooden fiddle case tucked under her left arm in what she hoped was a professional manner. Under her breath she hummed and half imagined the score of the sonata she'd been practising, stepping out in time to the silent rhythm. Often Myrtle looked at her anxiously; so tall for fourteen and still growing, heaven knows where it would end!

When she saw Frances come into the dining-room though, she forgot her misgivings. Instead she noticed with pride the confidence in the girl's movements, the lovely glossy hair that hung below her waist, and the eyes exactly the same tawny shade (if she admired them especially, knowing the colouring was the one thing she'd passed on to her daughter, who can blame her? She couldn't be expected to have reached her age without realising the value of eyes like that), the clear complexion and, today, cheeks pink from hurrying.

78

'Am I awfully late, Mother? I did hurry, but we went on beyond time and I missed the tram.'

'Never mind, you're here now. You should have told Dr Russell I was waiting; he would have stopped and let you get away.'

'The time just flew, I didn't realise. Oh hark, Mama,' she reverted to the old name as she whispered, leaning across the table, 'here comes the Swan fluttering its wings for a glide. I do believe she must have waited for me! Oh, do just turn and peep, she's composing her face ready. Isn't she a dream?'

'Hush, someone'll hear us,' Myrtle giggled. This was delicious, having a joke to themselves, something they shared with no one. 'I've asked for muffins and gooseberry jam.'

'Nice.'

So each Thursday they met like this and went home together. An extravagance, Jane Pilbeam had considered when Myrtle had told her about their outings. It was on a day Ella had brought her to visit Highworth, dinner at the shop, tea in Duck Island Lane.

'Good job you're able to afford it. Metropole indeed!'

'It's somewhere I can rest and be comfortable after my Turkish Bath. They say the Bath is beneficial and I must admit I feel all my tensions easing while I'm there. It seems I'm to be plagued all my days with this weakness in my poor back, Mama.'

That had tipped the scales. 'Well, child, if it does good you must persevere. You're but young yet, too young for aching bones.' She'd patted Myrtle's hand lovingly. 'I dare say you're right to have a quiet sit in the warm after the rigours of the Bath.'

'Mama's right. And so you should be able to afford it too. You may be sure Clement doesn't go short, or that chit of his either. No more than right that he sees to

79

it you can be comfortable.' Ella had given her approval and so that matter had rested.

'And I do so enjoy an outing with Franny. Remember I've no one else.' The last words had been Myrtle's and hearing them Jane put all thoughts of extravagance away. Poor girl, how brave she was in her lonely life.

In truth Myrtle was very content with her lot. Certainly she had little cause to envy her sisters their married status, neither of them could please themselves as she could. Ella may rule the roost but from her expression she got no pleasure from it and Jessica had been swift to fly the coop at the first offer of marriage. Richard was a kind man but even so Cynny was very altered and aged lately, always tired. So, Myrtle considered, life was a deal easier without a man. Small wonder her lovely face stayed free of lines and, with the same instinct for dress she'd always had, small wonder too that many a head would turn as she took the air on the Esplanade. The high ruffled necks flattered her and even now that bustles no longer disguised the shape under a lady's skirt she had nothing to fear. Slim, elegant, a picture to behold and a joy to listen to with her soft, gentle voice. No, she didn't envy her sisters, nor anyone else for that matter, yet she wouldn't have been displeased with the impression she created. 'Such a lovely lady, poor dear soul.' Bravely she carried her cross, or so she liked to think.

If she could have arranged it, Myrtle would have liked things to carry on as they were, no one altering or growing older. She listened to Gina's plans for leaving school; she knew Dickie would follow suit in only a few more months. If only Fran looked forward to their being together as much as she did herself she would have

80

welcomed the end of her school days too, but every sign was that the girl wouldn't be content to pass her days at home. Time enough to worry when they had to. Myrtle shelved the problem by sending her back for another year. After all she was eleven months younger than her cousin. By then she might see things differently. Frances knew too that the future held a battle for independence. 'Perhaps she'll see things differently in a year,' was the thought of both. The time would come when they'd have to face up to it, but for now they both accepted a reprieve.

It was a hot afternoon at the end of August when Myrtle called, as she often did, at the shop in the High Street. Richard wouldn't have been human if he hadn't found pleasure in the sight of her as the jangling shop bell heralded her arrival.

'You'll find Cynny about the place somewhere, I heard her out in the back a minute ago. Tell her a cup of tea would go down well, eh? I'll be up in ten minutes or so.'

'Right, I will, I'll chivvy her along,' she laughed, then going straight through his workroom and out to the garden, called: 'Cynny, where are you?'

'You must be early Myrtle, or is it me late? Just can't seem to get done. Let me empty this bucket and put my brush away. Not two minutes finished the kitchen floor. I'd no idea it was so late.'

'It's gone 3 o'clock. You're like the old cow's tail today. . . .'

Something about Cynny wasn't right, yet she wasn't sure what. This last year or so she'd steadily lost weight, but then she'd been on the plump side; it wasn't a bad thing to be slimmer. But today it struck Myrtle how gaunt and aged she looked. Her breasts hung low and sagging, so different from the firm cushion that had

81

always cradled the children when they came to her with their woes. Her hands, always strong and capable even though hard work had roughened them long since, now were bony, the skin looked loose, and her single gold ring slipped round and round, only held on at all by the joint of her finger.

'You look tired, Cynny. Perhaps it's this heat. Are you all right?'

'Of course I am.' But even the answer worried Myrtle; it wasn't like Cynny to snap.

'Richard says to tell you he'll try and get upstairs in a jiffy for a cup of tea. Come on, put the pail away. I'll see to the tea while you get a tidy frock on. You're certainly all behind today, still in your overall.'

Cynny bit her lip but didn't answer as she led the way up the outside flight of stairs of the kitchen. There was no spring in her step, she pulled wearily on the banisters as she climbed the steep, straight flight.

Even with her dress changed Myrtle wasn't happy about her. She wasn't old; glory be, she oughtn't to let herself go to seed like it.

The bell told them Richard had a customer.

'You pour, Myrtle, you made it. Bad luck for two to handle the pot. Richard will be up when he's free.

'Are you sure you're all right, Cynny? You look quite wan today.'

'I'm tired. Myrtle, I'm tired to death . . . you don't know. . . .' She bit her quivering lip.

Myrtle had never seen Cynny near to tears, the sight frightened her. 'What ever's wrong? Is it something between you and Richard?'

'Richard? Heavens, no. It's me, I suppose it must be to do with the age I am.' She pulled herself together. 'Some women have it far worse to put up with I expect. No use fussing.'

'Nonsense, you never fuss. Anyway you're hardly past forty, too young for the change.'

'Then what? You tell me what. My back's so weary I feel like an old woman, dates mean nothing, and such floodings. Now these last few days I daren't eat; never had the gripes like it.'

'Haven't you sent for Dr Saunders?'

'No need for that expense. It's only since the weekend I've been so upset. The other, that's a thing that takes us all differently, I dare say; some sail through it, some don't. Must have eaten something I shouldn't at the weekend; took me different from the others. Got run down I expect, the way I've been lately.'

'Richard should see you rest.'

'And so he does. Nought wrong with Richard – and I've not been much of a wife to him these past months.'

'Gracious me, as if that sort of thing matters.' Myrtle shied from anything bordering on the intimate side of marriage and to cover her embarrassment changed the subject. 'Where's Gina?'

'She's gone to Tarnmouth to see Madame Zeigler. I was to have gone with her. I really ought to have made myself go but I didn't feel safe to risk the ride. She said she didn't mind. She's so excited that I don't think she'd mind anything, bless her. Monday she starts. Like a pup with two tails she is.'

Madame Zeigler's was quite the smartest millinery house in town and Gina had done well to get herself accepted to learn the trade there. As long as she could remember the salon in King Street had fascinated her. Like Myrtle she could never pass without admiring the creations. She'd looked forward to being old enough to learn to make hats as lovely. Then, alone and without a word to anyone, except Frances, of what she was intending, she'd gone to ask if Madame Zeigler could

83

find her a place. She'd be prepared to do anything if she could just have the opportunity. Vera Zeigler had taken an instant liking to the pretty, dark little creature with her pleading blue eye.

'And Frances? What's she up to?'

'Can't you guess? Practising that fiddle. The hours she spends at it, never seems to tire. This morning she picked me a big basin of brambles; early this year, aren't they? Betsy is what she calls "jamming them". Really, Cynny, I am lucky to have Betsy; she's just like one of us. "Bring your fiddle down out of that hot attic," I heard her telling Franny; "give me a bit of music while I see to the jamming".'

'Cuts both ways, dear. I dare say she has a happier home now than ever she did at the Smarts' place. Things have a way of . . . oh . . .' Sudden pain made her catch her breath. She bent forward over the table, fists clenched.

'I'll call Richard –'

'No, no . . . easing . . . oh dear . . .' She was sitting up again now, the pain loosening its grip. 'I hear Richard; you do his tea.' She leant on the table as she stood up. 'Have to go along the passage, not be long. You see to things. . . .'

'Are you sure you'll be all right?' Myrtle whispered. She didn't need to be told that Cynny wouldn't want Richard worried.

''Course I will. Back in a jiff.' She hurried away.

'Where's Cynny?' Richard took the cup Myrtle passed to him.

'Won't be a minute she said. Richard, shouldn't she see a doctor? She doesn't look at all well.'

'Try telling her that. I've told her. Time and again I've told her but she won't listen. Says it nothing unusual. I don't know much about these things but she's talked to your mother.'

84

'I don't like it. She's got quite scraggy.'

'Not to be wondered at. She eats nothing. Hush, here she comes. . . .'

Cynny seemed to have recovered. 'Hello, love. Got rid of your customer then?'

'Umph,' he turned a worried frown on her, seeing her afresh in the light of what Myrtle had said. 'Come and drink your tea before it gets cool. This weather there's nothing better.'

Cynny took the cup and raised it to her lips, but her pretence fooled no one.

The following Monday morning just after 7.30 Gina was on her way to Tarnmouth, a packet of sandwiches and an apple in her bag and determination in her heart. By the time Dickie and Frances set out for school she'd be there, a working girl, part of Madame Zeigler's establishment. The smile that played at the corner of her mouth seemed to have a will of its own, hard as she tried to look as if the morning rush was routine to her as much as to her fellow travellers; her lips would insist on turning up as soon as she took her mind off them.

And at the end of the day she could hardly wait to get home, there was so much to tell. The omnibus seemed purposely slow, as if the horses knew and wanted to keep her waiting. When at last the driver drew in the reins opposite the shop she forgot the dignity required by her new status and jumped down before they'd come to a halt. Ma would sure to be watching, she'd want to hear every detail.

She looked straight up to the window, ready to wave, quite unable to control the smile a second longer. No Ma! She hurried across the street and into the shop but her father was busy serving and had another customer waiting. So she went through the door at the foot of the stairs and bounded up to the kitchen.

'Ma!' she shouted, finding the room empty. 'Ma, where are you? I'm home.'

'Oh there you are, dear. I only left the window just for a minute. I'd been watching for you.'

'Ma, I've had a splended day, everyone was ever so friendly. Eight girls in the workroom and upstairs Madame and another lady, very smart. And Ma, you've no idea how finicky some of the stitching is, I won't be shown how to do that sort of thing yet, not until I'm ready. The trimmings have to be perfect. Madame examines every last stitch and she showed me – Ma, are you listening?'

'Yes, dear, of course I am; go on telling me.'

'Sure you listened? I didn't think you were.'

'You were saying about the trimmings. . . .'

'Oh, that's just one small thing.' Gina's first excitement seemed dampened. 'Well anyway I enjoyed it. Tea's late, isn't it, or have you had yours?'

'No. I'll get it now.' The smile was forced as she took the cloth from the dresser drawer. She would like to have sat down in the nearest chair and wept, sat down out of sheer exhaustion and wept in misery for her aching back and the pain 'like rats growing at my gut', as she silently put it. Today everything was an effort, every step forced, and now in the last half hour she'd started to lose blood again; she wondered she'd any to lose.

'. . . would you think, Ma?'

What had Gina said? Oh heavens, the waves of pain never faltered. If only just for a minute she could stand straight and feel well. She leant against the table, trying to hold herself erect.

'Ma I knew you weren't listening. I thought you'd be so excited.'

'Of course I am. Oh Gina I'm sorry dear, it's just that I've got such a nasty tummy. . . .' There, now she'd said it, she let herself sag, her eyes closed.

86

'Oh Ma, I didn't know. What is it, what sort of tummy?

'Just gripes. It'll soon wear.'

'I'll get the tea; you come and sit down.'

Gina set the plates round the table, put a ham and egg pie that Cynny had made ready in the oven to warm through, then cut a pile of bread and butter. Every now and again she'd glance at Cynny, worried because it was so unlike her to be ill, even frightened by the grimaces on her face as the waves of pain bit into her. Yet irritated too. She supposed it was because it was so rare for her mother to be sick that she was making this fuss. Cynny held her bottom lip between her teeth, her body writhed as if she couldn't sit still in the chair.

'Tea's ready, Pa,' Gina shouted down the stairs. Perhaps if he or Dickie were there Ma would find a bit more self control. It seemed she was wrong though, as she came back to find the kitchen empty.

'Where's your mother?' he asked when he came up.

'She said she didn't feel very good; nothing to worry about she said.'

Wouldn't you think he'd stay and ask her her about her day, chasing off after Ma like that? She poured her own tea, very sorry for herself and the lack of enthusiasm she'd met.

When he came back he cut a slice of pie and took his bread and butter. 'She's lying down for a while. I thought she seemed quiet at dinner time. Says she doesn't want so much as a cup of tea.'

'I expect she's better without if her tummy's upset. Do you want to hear – about how I got on?'

'Ah, that I do. Right from the beginning.' He could see from the look of her that Cynny hadn't paid much attention. He'd get Dr Saunders to her tomorrow whether she wanted him to or not. She'd been out of

87

sorts for weeks and it wasn't as if she showed signs that it would put itself right. Perhaps the doctor could give her something. Nearly crying she'd been just now, not like his Cynny at all, never seen her so down.

Gina chattered, a background to his thoughts. 'Anyone you own age?' 'Where did you go at dinner time to eat your sandwiches?' 'How long does she give you to eat?' He really did quite well, almost healing the hurt of Cynny's lack of appreciation of the importance of the day.

Her account had just worked itself through to the 'bus ride home when they heard Dickie putting his bicycle in the shed, back from a game of cricket on an improvised pitch at Matley Meadow.

'We won, Pa, licked the lads from Wheelers Green with two wickets in hand. Behold the hero of the afternoon – got thirty-seven and caught two chaps out. Not bad, eh? Where's Ma?'

'She's lying down, she's a bit off colour,' Richard told him.

'Ma? I say, that's awful; I mean for her to say she feels bad, she must be really rotten.'

Richard looked affectionately at the boy; he understood his mother.

Gina knew she was pouting. She even hoped Dickie noticed and was ashamed of himself. She thought he was jolly mean; at least he might show an interest. Anyway it was so stupid to look so panicky; just gripes Ma had said. By this time tomorrow she'd sure to be as right as ninepence. It was no use her saying that though, they'd think she wasn't bothered. . . .

'If she's not better by the morning I'm getting the doctor. I should have sent for him before, but she keeps saying she feels a bit better. Hasn't been well for weeks, months. You're not kids anymore, it's time you noticed for yourselves, but I tell you I'm worried about her. Doesn't eat, doesn't sleep, thin as a rake.'

Dickie played with the pie on his plate; somehow his appetite had gone. He'd never heard his father speak like that, talking to them as if they were equals, or more likely just talking, as if they weren't there at all. He'd never seen him look like it before either. Did he mean she was ill, really ill? Been sick for ages the old man had said, so it couldn't be just something she'd eaten had not agreed with her. He pushed his plate away and gave up the pretence.

'When we've finished tea I want to go and tell Auntie and Fran about my day, they're sure to want to hear. I'll do the dishes first.'

'Leave them, sis, I'll do them,' Dickie wanted to make amends. 'I never even asked you. It was hearing about Ma, put everything out of my head. All right being a working gal is it?'

Gina forgave him and accepted the opening. He was only a year behind her, of course he was interested. Perhaps not in the intricate artistry of the milliner's workroom but certainly in the plunge that had taken her from being a schoolgirl to a working member of adult society. This time next year it would be him, his school desk forgotten and the battle to earn his own way started.

Lying by her side Richard took hold of Cynny's hand. It reminded him of another night, sixteen years ago, that had started like this – but that one had ended with Gina making her appearance into the world. How the memories flooded back there in the dark, both so helpless this time. Then when the pain had made her catch her breath, when she'd gripped his hand, they'd known and understood. Tonight he was frightened. Her nails dug in as she clung to him and her head turned first one way and then another as if she fought to escape the pain.

'The warm oil might be a help. Just try a spoonful like Myrtle said. She left a bottle on the dresser. Can't hurt, love, and it might get things moving.'

For this evening even Myrtle hadn't given her full attention to Madame Zeigler. As soon as she'd heard about Cynny she'd left the girls and come to the shop.

He got out of bed and struck a match to light the bedside candle.

While he was out of the room Cynny forced herself to sit up, glad he couldn't see the effort it took her. The sight of her hit him as he came back carrying the cup, a splash of warm water from the kettle left on the range and swimming on top of it a tablespoonful of olive oil, an uninviting mixture. It wasn't simply how ill she looked, it was more. In the flickering candlelight the hollows of her wasted neck and her sunken eyes were exaggerated, her hair that this evening she'd not bothered to unpin hung in untidy strands, her wrists looked no more than bones. He was frightened.

'Here, love,' he put his arm round her. 'A big gulp and it'll be down. Oil's nice and gentle.'

And so it may be, but it did nothing to help Cynny.

As soon as daylight came Richard dressed and cycled to Dr Saunder's house. By then Cynny knew this was no time to worry about expense.

Too early to expect Myrtle to be up, but on his way home Richard put a note through her letter box.

'Richard.' He looked up at the sound of the bedroom window being pushed up.

'What is it? Is it Cynny?' She'd heard the gate open and hurried from bed not even stopping to put a wrap round her when she saw who the caller was. Her curly hair hung around her shoulders, her white nightgown was trimmed with pink ribbons at the neck and cuffs, and even straight from sleep she had all the freshness of a child waking. By contrast he thought of Cynny as he'd left her, her gaunt body and dull, sunken eyes. Dear, dear Cynny.

'I've been to ask the doctor to come. Bad night – don't know what ails her – can't seem to help her –'

'I'll get dressed. You go back to her, Richard, I'll come right away. The doctor will like to have a woman there and Cynny'll rest easier if she knows I'm there.'

That was on Tuesday morning, the first day Cynny kept to her bed. How thankful she was to hear the doctor say: 'She must stay where she is for a while. We'll try her on this mixture – and don't force food on her if she doesn't want it. Give her warmth to her back. To sit on a commode of warm water can be beneficial, the steam may comfort her. I'm a great believer in warmth.' Then he left them saying he'd call again the next day.

Later she was thankful too when Myrtle told her Betsy had called to see if she could do anything and had taken yesterday's wash back with her to Mallard Cottage to see to the ironing. They none of them knew the nightmare of battling with the boiler, the buckets of water, each growing heavier, the steaming sheets that had to be lifted out and plunged into the bath of blue water, then wrung and folded for the mangle. Just to get it all pegged on the line, that had been as far as she could think as she'd fought for the strength to conquer her Monday chore. Now the burden was lifted. All she had to do was lie still. Someone else was fighting her battle.

Poor Cynny, each day she let herself be helped to sit on the commode of steaming water, all to no avail. She seemed to be slipping away from them, cocooned in her own wretchedness.

91

Frances didn't like going to the shop. Nothing was right without Cynny, the hub they all turned on. Uncle Richard was different; no ready smile when she went through the shop to the door at the foot of the stairs; his mind was somewhere else. As for Dickie, he hung around the place hating to see his mother as she was, yet not able to pull himself away. And Gina, well she was the most normal yet even she was changed and Frances suspected she was resentful that something was intruding on her new life.

Cynny had been in bed for nearly three weeks when Frances called one afternoon on her way to Tarnmouth for her lesson to see if they wanted her to do any shopping. Over these weeks Myrtle had spent each day with her sister; she'd not given a thought to her Turkish Bath or tea-time treats at the Metropole.

Standing alone in the kitchen Frances looked at the room she'd known as long as she could remember. The pulley was draped today with just some sort of a drawsheet. The brass rim of the fireguard hadn't had time to tarnish but it had lost its shine, and the tap over the sink too that had always sparkled from Cynny's ministrations ('I'll just rub up my tap and then I've done'; Frances could almost hear her saying it as each day the tap was given the gleam they'd all taken for granted). The tablecloth was folded on the dresser, but not neatly, the edges were uneven; she knew that when it went back on the table it wouldn't look fresh. The room was an empty shell.

'Please make her better,' she silently pleaded, and because there were no secrets between her and her Maker, 'it's just not right here without her. Let her feel better soon – please.'

She went along to the bedroom and tapped on the door, then waited until Myrtle's 'Come in' answered.

Even that put a barrier up, one could always have run straight to Aunt Cynny. Even so when she entered the room there was nothing in her attitude to show her thoughts, no hint that only seconds before she'd prayed so earnestly.

Somehow she seemed to bring a gust of fresh air in with her. 'Hello, Aunt Cynny,' she beamed.

'Off to town?' Cynny played the same game, yet they both knew what lay unspoken below the surface. 'Enjoy your lesson.'

Frances nodded. 'Thank you, I will.' Then almost roughly she dropped a kiss on her aunt's brow.

'Franny – we've been saying – my hair – such a job to keep tidy. Get's tangled –' Even a few words seemed too much for her.

'I suggested we cut it short for her,' Myrtle surprised Frances. In fact over these weeks she'd been constantly surprising her, her voice so calm and matter of fact. 'When you get back from your lesson, can you help Cynny sit nice and steady while I shape it up for her? It's no use waiting for Gina, by the time she gets home the evening's all but gone.'

'What a good idea, of course I'll help. Then, Aunt Cynny, when you feel better we'll put some curl in it for you.' But as she said it a cold hand of fear gripped her. In that moment she knew, and she was sure her mother did too. And Aunt Cynny? Was she bearing it alone because of the fear they all had of the truth? 'Please, please, I beg you, please help her. It's cruel and beastly. Not Aunt Cynny.'

Later on though, when she got back from her lesson and Myrtle took up the dressmaking scissors, there was no denying it was Frances' strong young arms that bore the strain. Alone Cynny could no longer sit straight. Perhaps a message can be transmitted by touch, perhaps

Cynny was comforted by the surge of tenderness that gripped the girl, for when the job was done and her cropped hair combed her gaze rested in her silent gratitude and some thing more besides.

'That looks much better and as Franny says as soon as you feel well enough we'll put a curl in,' Myrtle's voice was gentle. Frances looked at her with new respect, she who'd always been the one to be protected yet now, faced with something so dreadful, she was strong.

So her strength grew, her calm supported them all, especially Richard who went about his work like a lost soul. If only Cynny would turn to him, for help, for comfort, in anguish, anything; but as the disease consumed her body so her mind grew distant.

Over the weeks of that autumn the family came to face what must be faced. Jane Pilbeam insisted she wanted to be in Highworth and it was Myrtle who took the arrangements in hand, with Betsy firmly behind her. Gina and Dickie were sent to Mallard Cottage where Betsy took them under her wing, and Jane too, for an hour or so a day at the bedside was as much as they let her have. She didn't argue, she felt old and useless and by contrast the 'children' felt young and useless. Just Myrtle and Richard stayed at the shop, taking turns to watch over Cynny day and night. A cleaning woman was engaged to come in two mornings a week and one might have expected Richard to insist on paying her wage, but he hardly seemed to notice her; he left everything to Myrtle.

It was towards the end of November when she came down to where he was sitting idly in front of his work table, a landing net he was supposed to be repairing untouched in front of him.

'Richard, Richard my dear, I think you should come. There's something different, it's her breathing. . . .'

He was up the stairs two at a time, straight to the bedroom.

94

With every breath Cynny took he could hear the rattle, death rattle he'd heard folk call it.

'Cynny, Cynny sweetheart,' he was on his knees, her hands in his, but she didn't seem to know he was there. For days, weeks, it had been like that, as if she didn't see him. Now his hands gripped hers trying to drag her back from the No Man's Land where she hovered.

Suddenly she turned to him, recognition in her eyes and love too.

'Richard,' then that rattle, that dreadful rattle. Did she hear it too? ''chard – we – s'much . . .'

He nodded, tears blinding him. 'Yes, my angel, no one's had more, no one. Oh Cynny, Cynny . . .,' and silently his heart cried: 'No, don't let it happen, don't take her', but he knew it was too late now for hope or prayer.

A deep rattling breath and she'd slipped from him again, her stare was empty of recognition. That was on a Thursday, but even then her wasted body clung to life. It was in the early watches of Saturday night when silence told them the end had come. Myrtle closed her eyelids and gently kissed her; now that the vigil was over Richard sat in the chair by the bedside, numbed, empty. Then the finality seemed to hit him, his shoulders shook as he sobbed helplessly in despair and exhaustion.

It was Myrtle, pale, tired but composed who carried the tidings to Mallard Cottage the next morning.

So often in November the air is heavy and damp with fog. Not so on the afternoon they gathered around the open grave to bid their last farewell to her. The sky was a hazy, light blue and full of promise.

Ernest Pilbeam hadn't come. Arthritis and old age had made him obedient to Ella's decision that he should

95

stay at home. Richard was the only man amongst them and all around him his women wept, even Ella dabbed a large white handkerchief across her eyes. Of them all only Frances was dry eyed, listening with all her mind to the vicar's words. If during the last weeks of Cynny's life it had been Richard and Myrtle who had been by her side, this surely was Frances's moment.

'. . . and is cut down, like a flower; he fleeth as it were a shadow, and never continueth in one stay.' '. . . suffer us not, at our last hour, for any pains of death, to fall from thee.' Oh but she hadn't, Aunt Cynny could never fall from Him. The coffin was being lowered, she didn't want to look. Next to her she heard a snort from Dickie and took his hand in hers. Her eyes were tight shut, but she heard the rattle as the earth was scattered on the elm coffin. The voice went on: '. . . earth to earth, dust to dust, in sure and certain hope of the Resurrection to eternal life. . . .'

It was at that second that Frances opened her eyes and looked towards the hazy clouds, and in the same second of her looking the sun broke through. It happened so fleetingly, she felt herself lifted out of the graveside misery. It was a moment of awareness such as she'd never known before, something so wonderful she wanted to share it. Gina, her face crumpled as she wept, if only she could tell Gina. The haze covered the sun again, the vicar raised his hand in the final blessing. It was over, yet they still stood, hating the moment when they'd leave Cynny alone.

'Come lad,' said old Jane, for today she looked more than her years; 'she'd want us to wear a brave face.' She put her hand through Richard's arm and somehow he forced himself to put his bowler hat on (his best bowler usually kept for Sundays) and turn away.

A flicker of sunshine again, as if Cynny were giving

96

Frances's memory a prod. Amongst them all as they made their miserable way out of the churchyard Frances alone knew a peace she couldn't explain, a secret that she shared with Cynny – and not the first secret they'd shared by a long way. She could have wept for Uncle Richard, for Dickie and Gina, for herself and the blank without the aunt who'd always been something special; but she couldn't weep for Cynny, it was as if she knew heaven had welcomed her. And something else she knew quite certainly yet she hadn't thought it out clearly – and perhaps never would, but with all the confidence of a fifteen-year-old she imagined she'd only have to give it some quiet thought and all the answers would be made known. It was all to do with something else the vicar had said: 'In the midst of life we are in death. . . .' That, then the sunshine, the message, as if to say 'In the midst of death we are in life'. Where was the barrier? They'd left Cynny buried deep in a hole in the ground, yet she was with them, she was with each one of them if only they'd stop weeping and let her in. She wished she could tell them, especially Dickie.

The solemn party walked back to Mallard Cottage where Betsy had put the leaf in the dining table and got a good hot meal ready. Nothing like a lining of food to put a bit of heart back, and from the look of them they could do with it.

'A good thing Gina's finished with school; old enough to look to things, Richard. You'll have to stop this rushing off each day, child, and try and keep the home right for your Ma.'

'But Grandma, I'm being trained. Ma knew. I can't –' there was a note of hysteria in her voice.

'Hush dear, we'll think about it all later,' Myrtle tried to soothe her.

'All very well, Myrtle. You've managed all these

97

weeks but you can't go on for ever running two homes. It's the girl's place, she has her Pa and Dickie to think of.'

'Indeed she has, Mama's right,' Ella decided. And at the turn of the century one wouldn't have expected anything different.

Silently the pretence of eating went on. Gina's vision misted, her throat was tight and her jaw ached as she tried to hold back her tears. No sound but for their knives and forks. She put food in her mouth and bit hard on it in her battle for control. When they saw her face crumple they all thought she cried for her mother, and she felt sick with shame that it wasn't so.

'It's not fair, Fran. Why did it have to be Ma? She'd never done any harm. And what about me?'

'Give him a bit longer, Gina, and Uncle Richard will buck up. It's not like him to be so – so sort of stiff –'

'I don't believe there's a God; it's all a lot of lies we're told to make us take what's coming and not grumble.'

'Oh Gina don't say that. It's like hitting at Aunt Cynny to talk like that. She always believed, she'll be so miserable to hear you talk like that.'

'She can't hear, can she? And she doesn't know what I feel. She's dead, as dead as these stones.'

They were at Tarnmouth, sitting on the shingle in the sudden early spring sunshine. A stolen five minutes while they waited until it was time to walk to King Street for their 'bus.

'Don't, Gina.' Frances's strong hand covered her cousin's and even in that brief contact she noticed how roughened her skin had become. 'There is a God, Gina. Look at the sky and the white gulls, feel the sunshine – and remember Aunt Cynny. How could she had been

98

like she was if there's no God? Why, you could feel the love she gave out.'

'Then what's he done it for?' Gina's voice broke. 'All she ever wanted was Pa and her home. If He's so kind and good what's He messed it all up for?'

'Don't know. She'd be so sad to have you miserable. It's hard to understand. And Uncle Richard, he must be so lonely.'

Gina didn't answer straight away. She'd bottled up her feelings over the months, frightened to show any emotion, even more frightened of recognising it in other people. Now she cried while Frances sat quietly by, not saying anything, not touching her. When at last Gina did speak what she said probably did her as much good as opening the floodgates of her tears.

'Pa's had a life, at least he's got something to remember. What about me? You don't know, Fran, how can you know? All I do is cook and wash and clean. I don't want to do it, I hate it, hate it. Looking after Pa and Dickie, that's all I'll ever do. One of these days Dickie'll grow up and get married and then I'll just be left with Pa. No chance of escape. It's not fair, it's just not fair. "A mercy you've got young Gina" Isn't that what Grandma said? They don't need a cleaner, they've got me. And Fran,' she gulped, 'half the time they don't even eat the things I cook. I do try, but it's not easy. Ma had had years of practice, cooking and spreading the housekeeping money round. . . .'

'Look, Gina, I'll get mother to have a talk to him. We'll sort something out. I bet you if you went to see Madame Zeigler she'd take you back even now. She seemed to have a fancy for you.'

'No. No, please Fran, you're to promise me,' Gina sat up straight, 'you're not to say a word to anyone, not even to Auntie. Promise me. Don't you see I can't let Ma

99

down like that? Promise me, God's honour. . . .'

'God's honour, if that's what you want.'

Perhaps Gina hadn't lost faith as much as she imagined, but neither of them noticed.

She blew her nose and straightened her hat. 'I just needed to let off steam. I feel much better now, truly.' She turned to collect up her shopping basket and get to her feet. Frances marvelled at her, her tears over and immediately she could look so pretty; in that as in so many ways she was like Myrtle. It was a rare thing for Frances to cry but when she did her face bore the traces for hours.

That afternoon was only one occasion. There were plenty more and, although Gina always insisted nothing should be said, bitterness smouldered.

There was the day Frances went to the shop and found her making a cake, Cynny's fat volume of *Mrs Beeton's Household Management* open on the wooden kitchen table.

'Don't know why I try; they won't eat it, I don't expect, or if they do they won't notice what they're eating. For all the interest they take in what I do I might as well be a machine.'

'It's rotten of them, Gina; they ought to think. Aunt Cynny must be jolly glad you look after them though,' she added timidly, watching for Gina's reaction.

It seemed acceptance was winning. She no longer doubted her Deity.

'She can't be glad to see the way they are though, the way we all are together,' she tried to keep her voice steady. Then: 'Fran – he even cries – last night I heard him. Didn't know what to do. I thought he wouldn't want me to see him and anyway – what could I say? It was awful, a grown man crying – Pa of all people –'

She'd kept her head bent while she blurted out this

100

latest trouble but now she looked up, straight at Frances. She was lost and frightened it was plain to see.

'The kettle's singing. While you get your cake in the oven I'll make a pot of tea, and let's call him up shall we.' Frances wanted to do something to help Richard, she wanted Gina to see she wasn't on her own.

But: 'I'm a bit busy just now; you get on without me', in answer to her call down the stairs gave her some idea of what Gina was up against.

So the months went by. Dickie left school at Easter and started an apprenticeship at the printers in Tarnmouth. Each morning by 6.30, a packet of sandwiches in his pocket, he'd be on the road pedalling the five miles. And Gina would have been up before him to cook his breakfast and pack his sandwiches.

Clement's allowance had always been sufficent to take care of fees so Myrtle shelved the problem of Frances's future by sending her back to school until the end of the summer and Frances shelved the battle she knew must lie ahead believing that in the course of those aded months she'd see a way. She wanted to stand on her own two feet but couldn't tell yet where those feet should be planted. Not so different from her classmates, she'd learnt her lessons, showed average ability, enjoyed the tennis court that was marked out on the lawn at Warwick House better than the sums that were chalked on the blackboard or the French verbs that seemed to have no relationship with any conversation she'd be likely to have. Her main interest was music and, late to start learning, her hours of practice had brought her to a standard that more than made up for wasted years. When for the remainder of her time at school she suggested she should take two afternoons off each week for fiddle lessons Myrtle agreed. What more pleasant that two trips to Tarnmouth, two tea-time treats at the Metropole.

When Frances spoke to her mother of girls who had left school and gone to work she only met with: 'I've so looked forward to the day when you're grown up and at home with me, Franny. We may not have riches but I'm thankful to say we can manage without your working.'

'Times are changing, Mama.'

'Well no need to bother our heads yet awhile. But Franny we could have such a happy time together. You're all I've got, remember.'

So for a start the battle went in Myrtle's favour, but it wasn't won yet. Once school was behind her Frances looked for a loophole and found it in the Tarnmouth Symphony Orchestra where she was welcomed into the first fiddles. Once a week they met for rehearsal and twice a year gave a concert at the Town Hall. It may not have been much but it was a start and that led her, after only a few months, into being invited to join the group of players with the Operatic Society – another evening a week for rehearsal. Because she'd found that much freedom she was prepared not to push her mother.

'Times are changing' she'd said often enouch to Myrtle, and indeed they were. Never had there been such an age of promise, such strides into a brave new world. No wonder at seventeen they wanted to spread their wings and fly, Frances and Gina too. No longer was the omnibus to Tarnmouth pulled by four grey horses. Now an autobus trundled over the bumpy road leaving a trail of dust in its wake. Men were striving to become masters of their destiny, conquering the air as their bi-planes travelled ever more miles, conquering time as their recordings took today's sounds into tomorrow and today's sights too as the moving pictures flickered on the screens. It was all new, all exciting and challenging.

A way to the future would present itself, Frances still trusted. The Symphony Orchestra, the Operatic

102

Society, and before long a suggestion from Dr Russell that she should join a quintet he was forming; Gina scowled petulantly, little did she suspect how her own life would be coloured by the effects of what she looked on as 'Franny's freedom'.

Chapter Five

Twice a year the Tarnmouth Symphony Orchestra gave a concert in the Town Hall, one in April, the second in October. The seats had to be filled to pay for the solo performer. Of course families and friends of the players could be relied on but they accounted for no more than a quarter. So the programme had to be chosen with a view to attracting the rest. For the last four months the musicians had practised. Now on the Wednesday of the great day they came together in the afternoon for a final rehearsal.

The overture from Mozart's *Magic Flute* was played from start to finish without a noticeable hitch. Beethoven always drew the crowd, and add to his First Piano Concerto Augustus Markhova (at considerable expense) and no wonder the hall was to be full this evening. For the rehearsal of course the great man wasn't there. He was to be met at the railway station at a quarter to six. In the meantime a student from the college was playing the solo piano, a young man with a talent that should take him far, and blond good looks to match. Dickie's fair curls were the colour of bleached straw, Leighton Tyrell's sleek waves shone like burnished gold. From her position in the second row of the first fiddles Frances could see no more, just his head and the set of his straight shoulders. Whatever Frances did she did wholeheartedly so on that Wednesday afternoon her attention was firmly on her music. At the end of the concerto she joined with the rest of the players in applauding him and as he bowed his head in acknowledgement she had her first real glimpse of this handsome young god.

'We're most grateful, Mr Tyrell,' Frank Baylis the conductor shook his hand. 'I speak for us all. A magnificent rendering, I hope we may ask you back one of these days in the near future for our evening performance.'

'I've enjoyed myself,' his smile enveloped them all, then he followed Frank from the platform.

Who would have expected him to be waiting when they broke for tea at the end of rehearsal, Chopin's First Symphony safely negotiated? It was patently clear who he was waiting for too. He'd obviously noticed her even if she'd not been watching him. Of course she was flattered and excited, and eighteen-year-old who'd met no one, especially an eighteen-year-old so eager for life. In the evening he stayed to listen – and to watch the striking girl who handled her instrument with such grace and ease. At the end of the concert he was at the door of the back stage room when she came out with her fiddle-case under her arm and standing next to him was Myrtle. So of course they were introduced and to be fair to him and charm he showed was his natural way and he viewed Myrtle with interest. Somewhere he'd heard that one should always look at a girl's mother – she would act as a warning – so no wonder he was impressed.

Yet as Frances came to the end of the day, one so much more exciting than usual, it wasn't he who carried her down memory lane. The day had been full of music (oh, he'd been part of it, his contribution an important part), all the effort of months culminating in moving along as part of that glorious sound, then the burst of applause lifting her right out of herself, or so she'd felt.

The next day Gina wanted to hear all about it and it was then that her meeting with Leighton took pride of place. The batter for a pudding was beaten for five whole minutes without Gina realising it as she listened. Afterwards Frances often spoke about him, to start with to Gina and then to her mother too. They knew he often came to rehearsals, not to play but to listen and wait to escort her to the omnibus. Gina knew too how often when Frances went off alone on her bicycle it wasn't for the solitary ride it appeared.

It seemed she wasn't to have a full-time career but up to a point fate had played into her hands. At Warwick House one or two girls wanted to learn the violin and still Highworth had no teacher. So Frances was asked to come each Wednesday afternoon, first for two pupils, then more. Certainly not full time but it wasn't long before she had two more on Monday morning. Add to that Tuesday and Thursday in Tarnmouth for her own lessons and a compromise between her own ambition and the wishes behind Myrtle's often spoken words – 'I've looked forward so long to having you at home' – seemed to have worked out naturally.

Gina's mouth took on a perpetual pout. Life wasn't fair. All very well for Fran to drop in at the shop – and she did most days – to help with the chores sometimes or go with Gina to market, easy enough to do that and then go off on her own affairs. She didn't know what it was like to be cooped up here all day. 'The family drudge, that's all I am, all I'll ever be', and she frowned at her reflection imagining she saw youth slipping away.

Richard would hear her banging the pots and pans, slamming the cupboards, and he'd scowl in puzzlement.

The girl was getting worse. Missed her Ma he supposed, but God knows so did they all. No use taking it out on each other. That he was anything but easy he didn't consider, that she was taking it out on the others she didn't know. As for Dickie, he was glad to pedal away in the morning; his working day was long and any evening he had left was spent more often than not playing darts in the winter or cricket in the summer. Home was no place to be. Such a cheery, sunny lad he'd always been, perhaps with his friends he still was, but the family saw little evidence of it. Unhappiness is like a cancer in a home, it spreads and deepens, seeming to feed on itself.

Myrtle was worried. In the first months after Cynny's death she'd accepted that things must be different and like everyone else (except Gina and Frances) had taken it for granted that the girl would stay at home and look after things. Cynny and Richard had been so close there was nothing she could do to lessen his grief and she'd known better than to try.

Cynny had been gone a long time now though, and gradually new habits form. So when Myrtle went past the shop she invariably called in, a few words for Richard and then upstairs to see Gina. From being 'Cynny's Richard' she came simply to think of him as Richard, a friend in his own right.

'Gina's gone off shopping,' he told her when she called one afternoon; 'won't be above half an hour. Come and keep me company till she gets home.'

She followed him into his workroom where he was busy repairing a tackle box that had seen better days. The glue pot was heating on a single gas burner at the back of the table.

'This is a cosy room, Richard. I like to see all your bits and bobs about.' She sniffed. 'It always has a peculiar sort of smell, all its own. Nice.'

'That's the old glue pot,' he chuckled; 'not what Cynny used to say about it. You wait a bit until it heats up!'

He'd never spoken of Cynny so naturally before. His first tortured grief he'd kept to himself and as time went on he only talked of her when he was especially low. This was different, easy, almost as if she were still with them.

Myrtle's voice was loving. 'Dear Cynny,' she mused. Then: 'If she's watching and can read our hearts she can't be happy to see Gina. She worries me, Richard; she's so on her own and nowadays Frances's head seems full of her teaching and one thing and another. This young pianist she's always talking about, he has something to do with it too. You'd think she'd have more thought for her cousin.'

'Naught wrong with Franny.'

'She always wants to be off on her own affairs. I never expected to be so much on my own once she'd finished with school.'

'Young Gina would like the chance to be off too. She thinks I don't know how she feels. Sometimes I think she looks on me as her gaoler you know Myrtle.'

'Don't say that,' her hand rested on his bare arm, for there in the shop he'd taken off his jacket on this October day of unusually warm Indian summer and rolled up the sleeves of his shirt as he worked. 'Dear knows, we don't want to be a burden to our children.'

'That's about it, that's about what we are, or I am at any rate. Here, take this chair, Myrtle. Slip off your jacket and hat and be comfortable. She'll be glad to find you here when she gets back. Tell the truth it's about the only time we get a smile out of her, when you come.'

'Poor Gina – and poor Richard too.'

'Ah, and young Dick. He gets his share of her black looks.'

He stirred the evil-smelling glue in its metal pot, then smeared some on to two edges of the wood. 'This poor old box has had its day. Hope I can make something of it. Belongs to Sam Childs. You've seen Sam, Myrtle, the old fellow who takes the milk round in a couple of pails?'

'Oh, I know, I've seen him. He hangs his pails on a yoke and bails the milk out with a battered-looking jug. Mr Parker's cart is so bright and modern and his churns so shiny.'

'Old Sam charges a farthing a quart less than Mr Parker. I doubt he scrapes much of a living.'

She watched how carefully he worked, trying to restore the fishing box. Her mind was on what he had said a few minutes ago: a burden on the children, and he'd meant it; his hadn't been empty words. How unjust. She looked round the room; it never changed she thought, the bare wooden table, a kitchen chair in front of it and the wooden armchair where she now sat by the empty fireplace, shelves stacked with stock and over near the window a large metal tank, empty nowadays but where the tiddlers had been housed, the net still resting across the top as if waiting for the next customer. Cosy had she called it? Certainly not its furnishings but, as she unpinned her hat and reached out to put it on the table, she felt happy to be there.

A burden indeed! 'I tell you what Richard, I'll cook up a special little something for supper. Leave the children to fend for themselves and come to the cottage. I'll see to it myself. What fun! Say you'll come, Richard; it's time we thought of ourselves for once.' Her eyes were bright, she looked as excited as a sixteen-year-old.

'That I will, Myrtle,' and seeing how eager she was for her evening entertaining he didn't even suspect she might be suggesting it out of kindness.

The afternoon was changed. Only an hour ago he'd rolled up his sleeves, thinking: 'Sticky day, unseasonal for October'. Now when he glanced out of the window to the long garden, he saw the gold of the leaves against the blue sky – strange, the last time he'd looked, all he'd noticed had been the decayed broad bean plants still waiting to be pulled up, and the runner beans soon to follow suit. 'October, Myrtle, and still like summer,' he said.

If Myrtle could have seen where Frances's own affairs had taken her on that afternoon she might have felt less contented there in Richard's workroom.

A bicycle ride, well nothing unusual about that. The girl didn't seem to know what to do to use her energy.

She was just nineteen, too young to know, some people might say, yet what can be more positive than the experience of first love? Even to a girl less decisive than Frances there's no room for doubts when mind and body awake to something they'd only dreamed of before. Hadn't she always know her body had been too eager, pushing ahead before its time? That was something outside her control, but what had happened to the lessons poor Myrtle had tried to teach her of decorum? 'It's not seemly to. . . .' this or that; how often her mother had said it.

The October sun beat down, there seemed to be no one within miles. Behind them from the wood came the song of the birds, the chuckle of a woodpecker; under them the grass stirred with insects, all part of nature's pageant. She felt him unbutton the high neck of her blouse, one button, two, three four; then starting from the waist she unfastened the remainder and pulled it loose from her skirt. She surprised herself, it was as if some force outside herself made her do it. Behind her closed eyelids her world was full of a blazing golden light as she raised her face to the sun. She felt his hand warm on her breast, she ached with a strange wild longing.

110

'Darling Frances, you know I'm in love with you.'

'Oh yes, Leighton, and me, I love you too.'

The golden light was blocked out as he came between her and the sun, then she felt his mouth on hers, his tongue teasing hers. Whatever Frances did had to be wholehearted, done with everything that she was. Now, even while she didn't wholly understand, she longed to be his, unfettered by the clothes that restricted them. If she'd stopped to analyse her thoughts – which she didn't for always instinct was her guide – she would have known that the abandon she craved would have been marred by the scratchy, insect-ridden ground, and in any case she wasn't completely sure what was involved. All she did know with certainty was that her body seemed to have taken control, her back arched, her legs ached with longing. She called it love; she was so sure.

The bright golden light was back in her head, he'd moved away. But still her eyes were shut.

'One day we'll be married. When we're ready, say you'll marry me?'

'Yes, of course I'll marry you, of course I want to be yours.'

He pushed her under-bodice up and she could feel the sun, unfamiliar, on her naked breasts. She moved her left hand to pull his head towards her, instinct still prompting her. She wanted to bring his mouth to her tingling skin.

That he took her hand and guided it elsewhere surprised her. She wondered what he was doing. The next second pulled her up short. The touch of his flesh as he pressed her hand to grip him brought her eyes open with a start. She'd had a vague idea of something of the sort happening. She and Gina, like growing girls of any generation, had whispered and wondered. Their actual experience had shown them no more than little Dickie on bath night, a far cry from what she saw now. Her racing senses were brought to a halt. The sight of his trouser buttons undone and the great angry column reaching skywards was so unexpected that her own tingling nerves turned back on her. Unbidden came the memory of a trip to the pantomine years ago, the magician who'd brought a gasp from the audience when he'd produced a white rabbit from his tall hat. A wild giggle rose in her but she repressed it – fortunately for the sake of Leighton's ego. He sensed the change in her, felt her draw away and feared the moment was lost.

'No, Leighton. Don't you see, it spoils everything.'

'How can it. Please, please Frances, you want to too, you know you do.'

'Of course I do.' Yes, of couse she did; why only a minute ago she'd been almost begging. 'But not like this. Don't you see, it spoils it? Soon we'll belong, properly, all of me, all of you.' All, not 'the thing' that had so unexpectedly come between them.

Now it was he who lay still, eyes closed against the golden glow, the column listing. She knelt up, fastening her buttons and tucking her blouse into her waistband.

'Frances come back. Touch me. Just touch me, kiss me just once.'

She leant forward. He felt the movement and as the column twitched expectantly to attention her lips fleetingly touched his. A moment later she was firmly anchoring her hat with its long pin and his collapse was absolute.

The afternoon couldn't be put out of their minds. Leighton knew they couldn't recapture the mood, at any rate not now, and when she suggested they should cycle back to Highworth to the cottage for tea he agreed. He'd been there once or twice, he was sure Myrtle approved of him and just at the moment his flagging spirit could do with her kindly attention.

112

'Drat the bell! How's a body supposed to get on?' Betsy wiped her fingers on a damp cloth. She'd not bargained for interruptions this afternoon. With the missus and Frances both out she'd promised herself she'd 'have a good go at getting the fruit stoned for m'puddings'. It was halfway through October already – not that you'd think so with this weather. She reckoned to have them boiled and put away ready for Christmas by the third week of the month, enough for themselves and 'that poor little Gina too'.

The bell pealed again. 'Hold on, hold on,' she muttered under her breath, 'got to get this sticky off just you be patient.'

Through the coloured glass in the front door she could see the caller was a man, tall, unfamiliar. Now what could a stranger want here? Only last week she'd heard that some beggarman had called at a house in Vatern Road. He'd been given food, and how had the rascal shown his gratitude? By slipping a silver vase in his pocket, that's how. She'd see no one got the better of her. Forewarned was forearmed, as they say; she'd just open the door a wee crack and size her caller up.

And a wee crack was all it needed. The tall man smiled and the years melted away.

'Well, bless my soul, Master Greg, come away in. The missus isn't home. Well fancy, you're a grown man. Well of course you are; we all move the same way.'

'It's you I've come to see, Betsy, not Mrs Ratcliffe. Is that how you call her?'

'Ah, Mrs Ratcliffe. Won't be home till tea-time I doubt. Come to my kitchen; real cosy I am in there.'

And so she was. A dish of stoned raisins on the table, the sultanas she'd been working on in a bowl and a plate covered with sticky pips at its side.

'I can see you are, and you look fine Betsy. The best day's work you did, coming here.'

'Things sort out. A bad business it all was. Can't pretend it sorted out for your poor father, but for me, yes, I'm well enough. And you, lad? How's this doctoring going? Fancy you a grown man and a doctor at that!'

'I'm not quite that yet, Betsy; next year before I'm on my own. I'm here for two months or so, helping Dr Saunders.'

'Time he put his bag away, if you ask me. Been muddly this many years. Still brings the babies into the world well enough but give him something a bit out of the usual run of things and – ah, muddle minded, like I say. All those years back with your mother, I could ha' done for her as much as ever he did for all his doctoring.'

'I've just come from seeing Grandpa, Betsy,' Greg changed the subject.

'How is the old gent?'

'Very frail, poor old boy.' The way Greg spoke showed clearly his affection for his grandfather. 'He said I was to come and see you – but that's not the reason I came; I would have in any case.'

'And so I should think. My! But you don't know how pleased I am. Such a good boy you've allus been to write to me like you have. Not one Christmas have you missed. I was thinking as I did m'tanas; soon be Christmas again, I thought, soon be looking out for my letter.'

He was ashamed. One letter a year, probably the only one she ever had and supposing one Christmas he'd forgotten!

'This year we'll do better than that, Betsy. I shall be in Highworth pretty well until the end of the year.'

While they'd talked she'd been making a pot of tea and now she took the cosy off and lifted the lid. 'Give it a stir I will. I mind you always liked it strong. Strong and no sugar, that was the way you took your tea even as a boy.'

'And still do. Betsy, I've something for you from

114

Grandpa. He said you'd remember it better than anyone else would.' He took a small jewellery box from his pocket and passed it to her. 'He's very poorly, an effort for him to talk much.'

'Must be past ninety. Wasn't a young man even all those years ago when first I went to work for him.'

'He said – oh, I knew what he meant although I didn't let him think I did, and you'll feel happier to know that he said it – there were things I ought to know. To give you this,' he handed her the box, 'and to say that he wants you to tell me. So I didn't give any hint that I'd known for so long what was wrong with mother.'

'He wants me to be the one to tell you?' She opened the little box. 'Well, well, fancy the old gent, keeping this all these years and then sending it to me. Here, put your hat off the table, there's a hook behind the door, and come and sit down for your tea. Good thing the missus is out; it'll take a while for me to find the words for this one, for I can see clear enough what he wants of me.' She took a locket from the case. 'This speaks his message. Dear me, what a muddly old business life is for some. Often I say to myself, Betsy my girl, think yourself lucky. Never did fall in love, you know. Used to wish I had someone to care for when I was young, but the more you see the more you wonder. Well now, where shall I start?'

'But you told me and heaven knows we saw the outcome. You remember, that very day you told me. Perhaps I take after Father, but I tell you one thing, Betsy, I'll never risk marrying and having children. I'm not going to be responsible for that.'

Betsy looked puzzled, she'd not followed his reasoning it seemed.

'I'll start before your Pa wed. I'd been in your grandfather's house since Mr Roderick was about the age you are now, and I was about the same. Oh, he had many a

115

girlfriend; bit of a lad for the ladies, always was; never seemed of a serious mind about any, mark you. Then he brought Judith Whitfield, as she was in them days, home. No beauty, he didn't pay court to her like he did to some of the young butterflies he'd had, but this was different. And my word how that girl adored him. Would have done murder for him if he'd asked. I'm not up in these things and, any road, who can say what one body sees in another? Like I say she was a plain enough sort of girl and he could have had his pick. I reckon there was something lacking in the sort of fondness he had for her. But make no mistake he did have a real fondness. Well time was to be the test of that. They were wed and took a house out towards Lewis. Whether he knew then what had ailed her father I couldn't say. Certainly I didn't know at that time, but mayhap he did and that was why they had no family. I stayed on in Hastings with the old gentleman so I don't know the rights of what sort of a home they had, but I always felt there was something he hadn't found in her. Your grandmother was alive in them days, no older than I am now but poor soul crippled up with arthritis she was. So they engaged a companion for her – a kindly way of putting it for the girl had to be more of a nurse, to tell the truth. Ah, I can see her now;' she drifted off into her thoughts; 'such eyes, the blue of steel. Never seen such eyes. . . .'

Greg frowned, waiting. 'Go on Betsy – about my parents.'

Betsy took no notice of his interruption. 'Sarah Dearlove was her name. Appropriate enough too. Right from the moment Mr Roderick clapped eyes on her I reckon it happened. Was when she'd been with us no more than a week he called; didn't often come as a rule. But after that he did, always about the place. Then on her afternoons off she'd go off, never saying where. It was,

116

oh, best part of a year before the day she told me she was going to leave. Asked her where her next post was – well, keeping to the point, hadn't a place to go, just running off she was, poor child, and by then you were already on the way.'

'Me! So she was never my mother – father's wife, mother as I thought her – she wasn't really my mother?'

'Now just you sit quiet and hear the rest. If the old gent, says to tell you I'll do the job properly and tell all I know. No dodging from pillar to post, just hear me on.' She picked up the locket again. 'Did you look at this?'

'No. Well, I saw it was a locket, I didn't examine it.'

'Then look at it now.'

He took it and opened the clasp. Two tiny miniatures in the oval frames, one undoubtedly his father, the other a young woman. Unsmiling yet gentle, he felt there was something familiar about her.

'Where did she go, Betsy? Where is she now?'

'Well, as I was saying, no place in mind to go to, but I had my suspicions what she meant to do. Terrible hard thing for a woman to bear a child out of wedlock twenty years back, bad enough today, but a cruel thing then. I may have been wrong but I think she saw only one place she could go – and poor soul that's where the Lord took her, but in His own good time.' Another pause, no doubt more memories. 'Such a to-do there was but Mr Roderick must have known about the way she was. Then it all came out, well in the house it did. Outside we kept it hushed up. What he would have liked was to marry her, no doubt about that, but what about his poor wife? Idolised him she did, wasn't natural the way she idolised him. I told you just now, anything she'd have done for him and what he asked was a deal to expect of any woman. Sarah stayed on in the house keeping herself out of the way if a caller should come. When the baby came it was to stay in the

117

family. I've seen since, but of course hadn't thought then, Mr Roderick must have know there'd be no other children. If poor Sarah had lived who knows what would have been the outcome. I think the two of them sharing a child would have been a bigger pull than keeping faith with his wife for all the fondness he had of her. To keep him she'd do anything, even take his bastard child as if she'd borne him herself.'

'And Sarah, my mother?'

'About twelve hours after you put in an appearance, no more than that, she lasted, and a mercy poor girl. He was there with her,' she sniffed, 'bad time that was. And downstairs Mrs Smart, young Mrs Smart I mean, she waited. First time it struck me there was something strange about her. My word but she was keyed up and no mistake. This little locket, 'twas all Sarah ever had of him, well, that and you. Often I wondered about it, what had happened to it. Fancy the old gentleman keeping it all these years and trusting me to tell the tale.'

'Who else Betsy?'

'Ah, who else? From the day you came into the world I had the care of you, and when you were no more than a month old Mr Roderick took the place in Matley Heights and I always suspected (not my place and I might be misjudging, mind) but I allus thought it was old Mr Smart put the cash into the timber business, set him up in a new start. Till that time, to be honest, he'd not buckled down, not like Mr James who'd already turned his bit of land up Oxford way into a good farm, or so I've allus heard. Well, you'd know the rights of that, you were packed off there often enough as she grew worse, poor soul.'

'It's funny, Betsy, once one knows, it all seems so obvious. Even the business. When I was a child I always imagined father such a successful businessman, but I've come to know since that the place ran on a knife edge.

118

Nothing got salvaged out of it once the debts were cleared. Poor Grandpa, from what you say he must have put a lot into it at the start too. Never criticises though, he never has.'

'A wise man your grandfather, Master Greg, allus has been. I dare say he'd look at his own happy home and know something of what Mr Roderick was lacking – and Mrs Roderick too. If she'd had from him the sort of love she gave, mayhap her poor mind wouldn't have had the strain.'

'Is there another cup of tea, Betsy?'

'Bless the boy, yes, pot's half full.'

As he drank he absorbed what he'd heard. A great weight was lifted. Later he'd think deeper, remember the poor creature who'd pretended he was her own, perhaps understand so much better now that he knew the truth. He'd wonder about the girl who'd died giving him life. How deeply had she cared for his father or he for her? The greatest love had probably come from Judith and what had his father felt for her? For her or for anyone? As a young child, even before he'd been sent away to school, he'd sensed that he was an inconvenience in the house, he'd supposed it was because he was young and dependent, if indeed he'd thought about it at all. More likely he'd assumed that it was the same for all children.

Another memory stirred, a home so different from his own that the impression had stayed with him all through the years. Only vaguely could he picture the room, the large table laden with fare, a decoration of neatly ironed washing overhead on wooden beams the whole length of the room. The scene was just a backdrop to an atmosphere he'd never forget.

'Do you remember the shop where I was sent to stay, Betsy?'

119

'Can't say I do Master Greg. You weren't often home, poor mite, off to school at seven.'

'Just before that. It was a shop in the High Street, fishing things, tennis racquets. . . . I can't remember their name even. Is it still there?'

'Sellwoods? You went to stay there? Well fancy that, I never knew, or if I did I never connected it.'

'Are they still there?'

'Oh ah, shop's there. Mrs Sellwood, good woman she was, she was taken three years back now. Sad to see how the place has changed. The missus she goes round two or three times a week and young Franny pops in most days to keep Gina company. Not the same there now, not without poor Mrs Sellwood.'

'You mean Mrs Ratcliffe from here? And did you say Franny?'

'That's it. She and Gina are cousins, the missus and Mrs Sellwood were –'

'But Betsy, I knew them. Why didn't you ever tell me who you were with? Frances – I didn't know her name was Ratcliffe – I call her Fran.'

'That's it, Fran or Franny, we mostly call her Franny.'

'What time do they get home, Betsy? Can I wait?'

So it was that when Frances and Leighton wheeled their cycles along the side path to the back of the cottage and then came in through the kitchen door they found him standing at the table with Betsy, both of them busily taking pips from the sultanas.

He turned as the door opened, wiping his fingers on the damp muslin cloth. The memory of Fran had stayed with him as a leggy child with tawny eyes like clear pools, earnest and trusting. He was unprepared for the tall woman who threw open the door. She was beautiful. Perhaps she always had been but he'd simply remembered that she'd been his friend when he'd been utterly miserable and frightened.

120

Before he could introduce himself or explain his presence she stopped still in her tracks. 'Greg! Why it's Gregory.' She held out both hands and he put his into them.

'My friend Fran.'

She'd not consciously thought of him for ages, years, yet now seeing him again pushed everything, even her afternoon on the edge of the wood, into insignificance.

'Oh Greg, I'm so glad to see you.' Then she remembered Leighton following her, she became aware of the familiar kitchen, of Betsy, and of a sense of surprise at the enthusiasm of her greeting. A hot colour suffused her face and neck, she felt he could read her mind. She hated the tell-tale flush but the more she tried to overcome it the hotter she became. All this time, and he'd not so much as sent a message by Betsy, and here she was making a complete exhibition of herself!

'I couldn't write to you, all I knew about you was that you didn't live at the shop. Remember?' She'd been right, it seemed he could read her thoughts. 'If I'd known your name I might have connected your mother with the Mrs Ratcliffe Betsy had come to – but you were just Fran.'

'Oh Greg, it is good to see you again.' So it hadn't been that he'd not cared that she was his friend. 'I didn't realise, I should have thought. I could have sent you a message by Betsy, or asked her for your address – but I thought you'd forgotten.'

'Fancy, well isn't that nice, you two being friends – and old Betsy never knew, well I never,' she stood watching them, a sultana split open in her fingers.

'Can I join in?' Leighton prompted. 'Aren't I to be introduced?'

'I'm Gregory Smart, a friend from the past,' Greg held out a hand.

121

'Leighton Tyrell, a friend – I trust – for the future.'
They shook hands and Greg read the message.

'Just let me finish these last few tanies and I'll get you some tea.' Betsy turned back to her job.

Greg declined the invitation to stay. Mrs Saunders would be expecting him his first day at the doctor's house. It seemed they all attended St Stephen's so he'd be sure to meet Myrtle after the service tomorrow.

'I'll see you at the church,' was all he said as he took Fran's hand in farewell, but something in the twinkle of those light blue eyes was disturbing. Minutes later Myrtle hurried in carrying a basket containing the makings of something special for supper.

'Bang goes m'puddings, never get the mixing done today now,' but being the treasure she was all Betsy said was: 'You do the frippery bits, I'll clean the veg.'

The 'Closed' sign was put on the shop before 7 o'clock, unusually early for Richard to draw the bolt across. Gina saw his preparations for the evening and her own mood took an upward turn, for her frequent depression came not only from being a prisoner at home but from the atmosphere there. Tonight she heard him opening and closing his wardrobe, she boiled a kettle so that he could shave for the second time in a day, she watched him polish his best boots and noticed that his collar was new and stiff from its packet. Later she'd make a macaroni cheese just for herself and Dickie; no need to rush. The kitchen took on a friendly air. Richard had become more of a gaoler than he realised. If he'd been less wrapped up in his own evening it might have occured to him that for once Dickie was apparently staying at home.

He'd already set out for Mallard Cottage when a

knock on the side door brought Dickie down the straight flight of stairs.

'This is Leighton. You all know all about each other,' was Frances's greeting. 'We've brought faggots from Mr Pringle's. Have you got lots of bread and butter, enough for all of us?'

'Oh, I say, that's splendid! Come on up both of you. Hey, Gina, it's Fran, she's brought a friend to meet us. Put your pans away, faggots for supper.'

It was so unexpected. The smile Gina turned on her visitors said it all. Faggots may not be everyone's idea of a treat, not even theirs for that matter, but the atmosphere more than made up for that. Could it be because Richard had been cheerful this evening? Was it the rare sight of a visitor, and such a handsome one too? Or simply because Richard wasn't there to watch them?

They soon got over the introductions and short-circuited the preliminaries in their hurry to get the faggots to the table while they were warm. Dickie took a tall jug to the Barley Mow for ale.

Gina's lovely face was flushed with pleasure; tonight everything was different, tonight there was magic abroad. Frances felt it too, it put her mind back thirteen years to the months she'd been part of her aunt's home.

'I always loved this kitchen.' She cut the steaming and highly seasoned faggot. 'My! but this smells good! Do you remember Tuesdays, having tea under the awning of ironing? One felt so safe, everything was sure and right.'

'That was Ma,' Dickie remembered.

'We still have an awning of ironing,' Gina defended.

'It's different.' For Dickie nothing would be the same without the Ma he'd held on a pedestal even while she lived. One of these days some poor woman would have a hard time living up to such a model.

Gina's mouth had the hint of a pout all too familiar.

123

'Isn't this fun,' Frances beamed across the table at her; 'we'll have to see if we can't get Mother and Uncle Richard together more often.'

Gina's good humour was restored. This evening she didn't want to think of parents, day-to-day monotony; this evening they were suspended above it all, or so she wanted to believe. Couldn't the others feel it too?

Perhaps they could. The meal over, they stacked the dishes and put them on the wooden draining board then took the playing cards from the dresser drawer. The room was soon full of young voices.

It had been Frances's idea to come. Leighton, his mind on the afternoon and his unfulfilled hopes, had thought of more promising ways of spending the evening. His only chance of getting her to himself seemed to be to walk down the dark lanes, perhaps to the river meadow, but the idea held little appeal even to him for the warmth of the day had gone as it usually does so late in the season. A still mist told them that winter was close. As for Frances, she'd suggested the visit to Gina as something of a refuge. Yet why? Only a few hours ago it was she who'd encouraged Leighton to their grassy shelter on the hillside, she'd wanted to hear the words he'd said, she'd wanted – no, she hadn't. She wouldn't let herself think about it. She felt somehow soiled; it had put a shadow across the romance she'd been building. Yet right up to the last she'd egged him on.

'Wake up, partner, your turn. Hearts are trumps remember,' Dickie kicked her ankle under the table as he brought her back to earth.

'I'm awake, I was just thinking what to play.'

The game went on. 'Our trick Gina.' Leighton gathered up the cards.

How funny, after all this time – why it must be eight years or more – but it wasn't like meeting a stranger. They

124

seemed to slot straight back into place. 'See you at the church,' he'd said. Well of course they would meet there, but she wanted to see him properly, to talk, 'mattering talk' as she thought of it. Perhaps she'd –

'Fran . . .,' three voices prodded.

'There's a ball at the college just before Christmas,' Leighton said as he shuffled the pack. 'How would it be if I get tickets for the four of us?' Plainly he was enjoying himself.

The stars stayed in Gina's eyes. To her a ball was as far removed as a trip to the moon. That she had no gown was a hurdle not to be reckoned with tonight. At the back of her mind unprobed was the certainty that Myrtle would support her and be sure that she was every bit as prettily dressed as Frances. She could almost hear the orchestra, feel the polished floor beneath her feet as she glided, gossamer light. . . .

The evening went so quickly, it seemed no time before Frances and Leighton left, he with a long bicycle ride to Tarnmouth ahead of him. The other two had only just come back upstairs from seeing them off when Richard's step was heard. Instinctively Gina and Dickie stood still and listened. A heavy tread, not a good omen! A glance passed between them, Dickie raised his eyebrows, Gina shrugged her shoulders. 'What's up with Pa?' and 'Don't know,' the silent question and answer.

'Enjoy yourself, Pa?' Gina made sure her voice was bright.

'Humph.' His look took in the untidy kitchen, dirty dishes and ale glasses, their playing cards on the table. 'A change to be somewhere comfortable I must say.'

'There's a drop of ale left. Shall I pour it for you, Pa?'

'No, not for me. I'm having a tot of something.'

He'd heard them laughing as he'd opened the side door, then the silence as they'd realised he was home. The

125

brandy was hot in his throat, fire water folk called it. God knows he could do with it, something to thaw the ice round his heart these days. This evening sitting across the hearth from Myrtle, the backgammon table between them, he'd come dangerously close to it melting. He'd been running away, hiding from the emptiness of his life. This was where he belonged, here with the children who watched his every move to see he showed no hint of the loneliness that squeezed the life half out of him. Another gulp of fire water.

'Did you have a nice supper? What did Auntie cook for you?' For Gina knew that Myrtle loved to prepare a special meal. Tonight's offering would have been her own not Betsy's.

'Ah, very nice. Some sort of beef thing with wine in it, all properly served on fine china, silver gravy boat. A creamy thing to follow, decorated fit for a banquet. Umph, what a meal!'

'We've been having a party too. Frances and Leighton – her friend from the college – brought faggots for supper.'

'Filthy things! Your mother would never have had ready-made rubbish in the house.'

'Oh well, Pa, we can't all dine off meat in wine and have our gravy in silver servers,' Dickie teased, trying to restore the atmosphere. Then more seriously: 'Ma would have been jolly pleased to see us enjoying ourselves at any rate.'

Richard gulped the last of his brandy and rinsed the glass under the dingy brass tap. Glad to see them enjoying themselves, yes, and so she would. And could she see? Could she hear them? For so long after she'd died he'd not even been able to think of the real Cynny, the woman she'd been before all the humour had been drained out of her, her spirit seeming to wither with her changing body.

Now, in that second, without warning she was with him, her kind face plump and smiling, her figure rounded, her voice soft. Earlier that same evening Frances too had know she was near, the secure loved feeling of Tuesday tea-time had reached out to her. . . .

'. . . to bed.' He didn't look at either of them, nor answer as they chorused 'Goodnight Pa' to his retreating figure.

Ice was easier to bear. Was it the evening with Myrtle that had done it or coming home from the atmosphere of her drawing-room to this? A home without a heart. Two brandies by the warmth of her fireside, the cold night air, another in his own unwelcoming kitchen, the lingering smell of faggots and ale. Then for a brief second Cynny lifting him from it to hold him in the love they'd shared.

Best suit, best tie, new collar, all forgotten. Sitting on the edge of the bed he buried his quivering face in his hands and felt the hot tears on his fingers. He wanted to cry aloud for the emptiness of his life. But the children mustn't hear him. If they realised the depth of his misery they'd watch him even more closely. 'Is Pa all right?', 'Keep an eye on Pa' and they thought he didn't notice!

He sank to his knees at the side of the bed, his nightly prayers no more than a wordless plea for some glimmer of light.

His tears were over. Perhaps the unusually rich food and drink had been too much on an empty stomach. To be honest his inside wasn't comfortable and as he bent to unlace his boots the floor moved before his eyes. Nonsense! He'd never had a better meal. It was coming home to the smell of those filthy faggots, enough to upset anyone.

He opened the bedroom door and shouted down the passage: 'Before you kids go to bed pull down the window and get rid of that damned stink.'

Dickie had already gone to bed and with the opening of the window the last of Gina's magic evening escaped.

'Mama, I'm not off on a trip to the moon. I'm only going for half an hour's walk. I need some exercise. I'll be back in good time to get tidy for church.'

'Funny child you are, always rushing somewhere. Mind you put stout boots on then, don't dirty your church ones.'

Silly to think he might come. He'd probably even forgotten where it was, and in any case since he was a visitor in someone's house, he might not be able to get away. She strode down the lane and climbed the stile, followed the path through the meadow to the stream and turned left along the footpath. The willow was shedding its leaves, not the green shelter it had been that other time, and as she came closer she could see he was there before her. With the honesty that was so much part of her she waved and quickened her pace.

'I hoped you'd come,' she said as she came near.

'I've been listening, like you told me – remember? – standing very still and listening to the stream.'

She nodded.

'Are things good for you, Greg? It was all so dreadful when it happened. I came here everyday and waited, I thought you'd come. Then I heard you'd gone away.'

'I wanted to come but in those few days while we were still in Highworth I was moved about, someone always seemed to be with me. First I was taken to that nurse, then uncle came, then Grandpa, they seemed to watch me every second as if I was a baby. And to tell you the truth I was frightened in case I got here and it wasn't what I'd remembered. I'd sort of hooked on to our talk here, it was a kind of anchor.'

128

'It must have been so dreadful for you. It's always the same here though, you should have come. I do when I'm bothered about anything.'

'Look Fran, look at the moorhen, it's after something.'

'Some poor little fish has had a short day.'

'It's nature's way. Fran, Betsy told me about your aunt. I can't picture it there without her.'

'No. And was that nature's way? She wasn't clever, some people mightn't have seen her as beautiful, but she was like – oh, like the spokes of a wheel, holding it in shape.'

'Yes, you could feel it.'

They watched the moorhen for a while in silence.

'Seeing you again after so long makes it seem like yesterday. Since she died they don't seem to move forward, just stand still and poor Gina has a wretched time.' Another silence. 'Greg,' she said after a minute, 'do you believe in heaven, in something after we die?' In hours she hardly knew him yet neither of them thought what she asked him strange.

'Yes I do Fran. I'm not at all sure what I expect but I have no doubts. This is only the beginning.' He sat down and held a hand to pull her to his side. 'A theologian might frown on my sort of faith but I believe that the Hand that made all this,' his glance encompassed the meadow, the trees, the stream, even the moorhen with its breakfast of fish inside it, 'understands how I feel. All that time I spent on the farm you know, one can't doubt when one watches the changing seasons, the animals bearing their young, the way nature provides.' He looked at her enquiringly, wondering if he'd said enough, too much perhaps.

'Go on.'

'Well, what we find when we leave this life must be a mystery until we get there. But, Fran, whatever God is must be in all that's good. In each of us there's some good

129

surely – and bad too – but it's the good that is given by Him. A baby new to the world knows nothing else. Remember Pandora's box? The rest is like that, we let it in when we lift the lid.'

'And heaven?'

'When we get to the next world I believe we shall understand so much that we can't know here: the good in everyone – something eyes can't see yet just occasionally one can feel the warmth that radiates from it.'

'Like Aunt Cynny.'

'Yes. I was only a kid, but I'll never forget.'

'But is she really gone, Greg? Sometimes I'm sure she isn't.' She almost told him about the day of her funeral.

'Fran,' he hesitated, 'you'll think me some sort of a crank, pi – I'm not – half the time I don't even go to church.'

'No, no I won't. I want us to talk; it's easy to with you.'

'Well, how can she be gone from you as long as you remember her and love her? The love that is part of you is close to her; that's the God given part, the part that one day will take over and then you'll be in what people call heaven.'

'How easy you make it sound. And what about her? We may hold her with us by still loving her, but what about her? Can she see us? My reason doesn't understand, yet my heart says she can.'

'Then listen to your heart, Fran.' He took his watch out of his pocket. 'I say, it's gone 10 o'clock already. Half an hour and we're supposed to be ready for church.'

'Oh, brother! I wish we didn't have to go. Old Reverend Carter is the dreariest of men.'

Steely blue eyes looked into tawny brown eyes, her words danced between them. They both started to laugh. 'There I go, lifting the lid of Pandora's box again,' she giggled. But there was nothing wounding in her words;

130

they helped the return to the easy companionship they suddenly both needed.

Instead of going home the way she'd come she walked with him along the footpath to the bridge, parting company at the corner of Bridge Road and High Street. Both of them tall, they walked easily together. He talked of his medical training at a teaching hospital in London, she of her fiddle, her few hours at her old school each week giving lessons. And music, of course, led to Leighton.

'He's a really splendid pianist; already he's played at one or two concerts and he's not out of college yet. He works so hard, quite five hours a day he practises.'

'Is he your beau? I mean, do you expect to marry him?'

'He's not given me a ring yet.'

'Are you in love with him?'

She hesitated, surprised that she should. 'Well, yes, yes, I'm sure I am. One day we'll be married.'

Greg didn't answer.

'And what about you? Have you a sweetheart?'

'No.' If forty-eight hours ago she'd asked him that question he would have felt trapped by fear. His grandfather, his mother, and what of him? He'd always thought himself sane, but so perhaps had they; even so a wife and children had been out of the question. Now he was conscious of a lightness of spirit. 'No, I haven't. One of these days when we have another of our deep down talks we seem given to that's something else I'll tell you.'

Monday morning found Gregory sitting by the elderly doctor's side in his surgery, for him a new view of his profession. The people he'd talked to in hospital had been the chronically sick, some who'd faced the dreaded ordeal of surgery, some who'd even lost limbs. Today he found sufferers of a different kind. There was old Jo Eggleton who humped the barrels at the Barley Mow, his task becoming increasingly heavy as bronchitis tightened its grip on his lungs, urged on by the evil smellings whiffs he smoked.

'Been sent to ask for a bit of help, Doctor, sir. The guv'nor, he said I've to come.' (So, no doubt the guv'nor intended to pay the bill. Who would have expected such generosity from the burly inn-keeper who nightly pitched his customers on to the pavement when they overstayed their welcome?)

Then a loud hammering at the front door and Mrs Saunders ushered in Mr Pengelley, the grocer, ahead of his turn and with blood seeping through the handkerchief he'd wrapped round his hand. His usually ruddy complexion was pale and he kept his gaze averted from the stained makeshift bandage.

''Twas the ham knife, took a bit near out of it. Dear oh dear me, feel quite queer . . .' whether from the sight or the loss of blood who could say?

A boy of perhaps six or seven, dressed in his Sunday suit and Eton collar for the visit, complained of sore eyes and a rash that Dr Saunders unhesitatingly pronounced as measles. Next a young woman with a black eye (that she could have tended with a piece of raw meat) and a swollen ankle, the result of tumbling down the stairs, she said. But her tears and sudden outburst of: 'I do my best, never sees the things what's right, only notices if I burn 'is dinner or lets me iron get too 'ot for 'is shirt. That's all 'e sees . . .' filled in the background.

So went the morning and for the rest of the day Greg accompanied Dr Saunders on his round of visits. His mind was taken up with what he saw; there was still so much he had to learn. Straight from the hospital and with his final examinations still ahead of him, there were some fields where he would outstrip the elderly practitioner, but what he did in Highworth was new to him. After only his first day there the direction he would take was clear. It was the cry of the ordinary people, their first fears of illness, even their need to talk to someone who would listen, this was what called to him.

But at the back of his mind through it all was the figure of a tall girl, her eyes clear and honest, her friendship sure. He hardly knew her, he told himself; why, they'd been children when they'd talked. Yet they'd not been children at play; even then they'd uncovered the secrets of their hearts, then and now too. That sort of friendship couldn't be counted in hours.

'Are you in love with him?' he'd asked.

'Why, yes, yes, I'm sure I am. . . .' Was she really so sure?

To be in Highworth gave Greg a built-in advantage, for as October gave way to November each evening the countryside was shrouded in fog. To travel from Tarnmouth and back in an evening was out of the question; the times of the omnibus would only allow Leighton half an hour or so with Frances. And to cycle the five miles over bumpy roads in that weather and then spend the evening chaperoned by Myrtle needed a stronger fervour than his! Once or twice he came when the breeze off the sea cleared the mist, but the elements seemed against him in that autumn otherwise he saw them in Tarnmouth.

We can plan our lives as we will but the pattern isn't of our own making. We are no more than the threads that are weaved. We may know what we expect but, like all patterns, one slight slip, too much of one colour, too little of another, and the balance is altered.

133

Chapter Six

Frances and Myrtle still went to Tarnmouth on Tuesdays and Thursdays and often Leighton joined them for tea at the Metropole. ('Such a dear boy,' Myrtle would say of him, adding silently 'A promising career ahead of him too, and such an exciting one.' Lovely to have Franny at home with her but one day she woud be sure to marry and really the idea of a concert painist for a son did have an appeal.) After its October concert the symphony orchestra didn't meet until February – many people found travelling to town difficult through the worst months of winter – so Leighton and Frances's chances of meeting were fewer.

While the fog kept Leighton in Tarnmouth, his loss was Gregory's gain.

'Poor boy, no parents to turn to,' Myrtle would say and at Betsy's: 'Never did have, never did know what it was to be cared for like a child should,' she was ready to show him what he had missed.

His welcome was warm and not for a moment did Myrtle look on him as a rival to 'dear Leighton' for there was nothing in his manner or Franny's either to hint at it. Often too Gina would be there. It took no more than 'I want to pin your dress sometime,' or 'You could stitch some of the seams if you'd like to help' and she was glad to spend her evenings at the cottage. No one at home wanted her company, or so she thought. As long as she kept them fed and cleaned the house that was as far as their interest went. Certainly Myrtle liked nothing more than to have the young people about her; often during that winter Dickie would join them. If only Richard would come too. She'd imagine him at home alone and tell herself it was for his sake she wanted him to share the warmth of her drawing-room. But was it? Whatever her reason, it made no difference; he didn't come. It was only on the occasions that she called at the shop and increasingly often sat with him, rather than going straight up to Gina, that she saw him.

The ball at the college was to be on the 16th of December. Gregory was due to leave Dr Saunders the day before. He watched the preparation of the dresses, for Myrtle's evenings were taken with them, and when he arrived to find Frances showing her mother how she looked in the finished result he was shaken by a sudden rush of jealousy of Leighton. Strangely in all these weeks he'd hardly thought of him.

'Well?' Frances turned to show him first the front and then the back. 'Shall I do him credit?'

With sudden clarity Greg acknowledged what he must surely have known deep in his heart.

'Beautiful,' he said. And Myrtle, engrossed on smoothing the back of the shoulders and flouncing out the skirt of the apricot coloured creation, took his words as a compliment to her work.

Only four days until the ball, only three until he'd be gone.

We've said, though, how one altered stitch, one pulled thread and the pattern can be changed. Early the next morning came just such an unexpected twist. It came in

135

the form of an urgent knocking on the front door of the doctor's house even before the first light.

Greg was the first downstairs, for the rest of the household wasn't yet dressed.

'I know it's early. Couldn't wait no longer though. It's the wife. Right since dinner yesterday Nurse Cox's been with her. Last year she had young Dan with no trouble, well nowt out of the usual. Can the doctor come? Oh there you are Dr Saunders sir, it's the wife, fighting for all she's worth, she is, but don't seem able to bring the babe. Never one for tears, but screaming out she is, orful to hear. You'll come, won't you, doctor, sir, you won't make her wait? Number 28 we are, you remember, top of Bridge Street.'

'Get along home, my boy. We'll be there as soon as you are.'

But he'd not taken into account the ice on the step. His feet shot out from under him and he fell with all his weight, putting out a hand to save himelf.

Gregory by then had brought the trap to the front door and was waiting ready to set out on their mission.

'You go on. You'll have to go without me. It's nothing, just a wrench, but I'll be no use without two hands.' Gregory had no idea what an effort it cost the old man to speak calmly; the pain of his wrist almost took his breath away. 'You can deliver a baby as well as I can, you've got all the instruments. Better on your own. If I'm there they may think I should be attending to it. Off you go now. . . .'

'Are you sure it's not serious?'

'Yes, yes, yes. Off you go.'

The great hall at the college was full of movement and colour. How pretty everyone looked; Gina let her eyes feast on the moving mass as the dancers waltzed by.

The dancing was in full swing when they arrived. The

136

trap that Richard had been offered by the owner of the ironmonger's had arrived late and Dickie was far from experienced. He'd driven a wagonette before, but always one belonging to friends, with someone at his side. This evening, as they all squeezed on to the bench, he was on his own. Getting the girls and all their finery to Tarnmouth was his responsibility. Fortunately the night was clear and dry and even more fortunately the pony wasn't of an excitable nature; it plodded peaceably along, not fast but showing no sign of temperament and Dickie knew when to be grateful. He was feeling every bit as conscious of his apparel as were the girls of theirs, for most of his savings had gone on the tailed suit and frilled shirt he wore and he wouldn't have been human if he hadn't hopes that the evening would prove the outlay worth while.

The pony was taken to the stable block and they followed the lights and music to the great hall.

'I thought you were never coming,' Leighton greeted them. 'I say. . . .' but he didn't continue as he looked at Frances, tall, almost stately, her apricot gown hugging her full breast and long slim waist, the matching flower in her coiled hair. Then he turned to Gina and she felt her cheeks grow hot. A new gown was so much rarer to her than to Frances and despite Leighton being no more to her than her cousin's young man his reaction was suddenly the most important thing in her world.

'You both look very grand,' he said, but she knew he'd not really noticed her, he'd glanced but not looked.

As the evening wore on he was to see her anew. So many people remarked on her.

'Who's the beauty, Tyrell?'

'You've met Frances before.'

'Indeed, she looks lovely. No, I meant the little dark fairy. Some people have all the luck. What about introducing me.'

137

If it had been said once he might not have noticed, even two or three times, but if anyone had been asked who amongst all the ladies caused the greatest stir there's no doubt the answer must have been Gina. Before she had been in the hall a quarter of an hour her programme was full, every dance taken. Frances was no wallflower but then she was looked on as Leighton's property so not open to offers.

The more Gina danced the more she glowed. Cinderella herself might have cast a jealous glance her way.

The next day saw her back at the stone sink, her dress shrouded in a sheet and hung away. For all the interest of last night's admirers today the college broke up for Christmas, they would all go their separate ways and by next term who would think of the magic evening – who except her?

In fact there was someone else who thought of it and remembered the stir she had created. Her loveliness was to be balm to his sore pride, but not for a moment was he to believe his hurt went no deeper than that.

The threads were tangling, the pattern must surely show a change.

Dr Saunders's wrist was broken in two places and proved to be slow to mend. Of course, seeing his plight, Gregory agreed to stay until he was fit to carry on alone again. For some time people had whispered that he wasn't the man he used to be. Many had turned to young Dr Hewitt who had opened a practice on Matley Heights, impressed by his up-to-date ways and perhaps especially by the fact that he travelled his rounds in an automobile instead of with a pony and trap.

Now the difficulty of using only one hand, his

dependence on his wife and on Gregory, the pain that gave him so many bad nights, all these things made it clear to him that he was no longer a young man. He wasn't able to bury his head in the sand any longer; it was time he made way for someone else.

'How long do you feel you can stay, Gregory? You've your examinations to consider. I ought to find someone else. To be honest I ought to let a younger man take over.' Was he watching the effect of his words especially closely or did Greg imagine it?

'If I'm useful to you I'd like to stay. General practice is where I belong, and you know I've a fondness for Highworth.' For more than just the place if truth were told. 'I could go back just to sit my examinations, stay with you until you're fit again.'

'It's been a great weight lifted to have you, my dear boy, indeed without you my practice would have gone. There's young Hewitt ready to take my patients. Yes, it would have been lost.'

Greg was as proud of himself as one would expect a young man to be at such praise.

Dr Saunders warned him: 'It'll be some weeks yet before this splint comes off. You'll get all the seasonal ailments to deal with. I'll be on hand of course.'

'It's what I want. General practice is for me, not hospital doctoring.'

'Ah,' the old doctor seemed to be considering him. 'Then, if you have a fondness for Highworth why not stay here? You have to qualify, of course, go and take your examinations, but there's no doubt you're ready, you're as good a medic as I've had the fortune to come against. What do you say? What about, when the time comes, putting your plate next to mine, eh? What about it then? Don't like to think of my patients going to that Hewitt fellow, even when I get beyond it, no, indeed, don't take

139

to the man at all. Time I stood to one side, made way for someone younger – not give up, mark you, dear me no, just step to one side. Well, and what have you to say?'

Greg's smile said it all. What a pleasant-looking young fellow he was, the old man thought, good white teeth, clear eyes, a strong grip to his hand. As if to prove it Greg took his good hand and shook it firmly.

'I'll do my best to see you don't regret it, sir.'

It was evening before he was free to tell his news, and where else should he go but Mallard Cottage?

When the bell pealed Betsy came from her kitchen to open the door and Myrtle from the drawing-room, curious to see who the visitor could be at this time of the evening. Not Leighton, for with a new term started at the college, Franny had gone off with her violin to play in a quintet he was arranging. Richard or the family would surely come straight in through the back door. She peeked at her reflection in the mirror of the hall stand, patted her hair, then ran her hand round her waistband. Just so would Gina have reacted without so much as realising she was doing it – but no bell pealed for Gina, playing patience on the end of the kitchen table as she waited for Dickie to get home from work.

'Why Master Greg,' Betsy visibly puffed up with pride as she listened to what he told them, 'if that's not the best bit of news I've heard since – well, since I don't know when. Doing your doctoring here in Highworth! There, Mrs Ratcliffe, what about that then eh? How's that for news?' She beamed as if the credit were her own.

'It's splendid. Your name on the brass plate, Gregory; just fancy. I believe we've a little Madeira in the decanter. Run and bring three glasses and come into the drawing-room, Betsy. We'll all drink to Gregory's future.'

'Isn't Fran in?' He tried to sound casual. He wanted to

140

tell her, he'd come straight here especially so that she'd be the first to know. Of course Betsy had been important too, but as Myrtle answered him he realised just how much it had been Fran he'd wanted to tell.

'She went off at tea-time to Tarnmouth. The college is back this week and Leighton is organising some sort of musical gathering, a quintet I believe. He asked her to take her fiddle along.'

And so he had, but when Frances arrived at his room she found she was the first one there.

'Am I early?' She looked at the fob watch that hung on the lapel of her coat.

'No, you're not early. Give me your fiddle-case and you can put your hat and coat in my bedroom.'

How strange it was, being here in the room where he slept. His hair brushes on the dressing table, a book by the bedside with a leather marker keeping the place. She would like to have known what he was reading but the influence of her upbringing was strong. The room was too personal; to pry would overstep the conventions. Indeed if Myrtle could see her here alone in his apartment, in his bedroom of all places, she would have been horrified. Trustingly she'd supposed the five players were meeting at the college and going together to the house where Leighton occupied the basement rooms.

He must have sensed her unease, for when she came back into the living-room he hardly glanced up. Time enough, the evening was long.

'Let's play something, Frances, just the two of us. Here,' he was turning over his music, 'what about this? I've borrowed the fiddle part for you.'

She smiled. Perhaps the others would be late. Just to be here alone with Leighton, making music together, the very thought was wonderful. It was something they'd not had the chance to do before. So they played, both of them

141

finding the experience strangely exciting, almost it was a form of love-making, the call of one instrument, the answer of the other. First the piano would lead, the fiddle follow; then the fiddle move on, seeming to beckon. He watched her, letting his glance follow her at every chance. How beautiful she was, her fiddle held so competently by her chin, her bow arm with its elbow high. He wanted to touch her, to feel the movement of her breast as she drew the bow across her strings; he could imagine the smooth silk under his hands.

'They're late, Leighton, surely?' They had come to the end of Schubert's *Valse Triste* and Leighton was again sorting through the pile of music.

'Frances – don't be cross. I didn't tell you when you arrived, I was afraid you'd not come in. They aren't coming this week; Hawkins hasn't got back yet and it's no use without a 'cello. Next week we'll start the quintet.'

She shouldn't be there, alone in his rooms. He ought to have told her!

'Please stay. Don't run away. What harm can it possibly do anyone if two of us make music instead of five?'

There was a difference though. With five of them playing the music would have been everything, with two it seemed to speak for them, say what otherwise wouldn't be said.

'Cézar Franck – I've always wanted to play this with you, Frances. It's only here that we can; you can't run away.'

'No, I'll stay, it can't hurt. But Leighton – Mama thinks it's a quintet. Don't say anything about the others not coming, not to her or to Gina or anyone.'

Why at that moment should she remember two steely blue eyes and imagine Pandora lifting the lid and peeping into the box?

The first chords of the sonata put everything else out of her mind. The minutes went by, the music took all her concentration. Only at the back of her mind did she think of the question and answer of sound, like the courting call of the male bird while the female comes tantalisingly close, only to retreat.

Leighton felt it too. The gas fire the only other sound, its continuous hiss in contrast to their give and take only adding to the sensuous pleasure. The last passage built to its tumultuous climax. He knew Frances was excited by it (of course she was, she'd played the fiddle part alone in the attic at home but never had she shared the experience). Then it was over. Silence, save for the hissing gas burner.

They avoided each other's eyes and he came to stand behind her, she supposed so that they could choose together what next to play. The room was warm, he'd had the stove burning for hours to be sure she'd not be cold. She was slightly breathless from her playing and quite unprepared for his hands holding her breasts and drawing her back to press close against him.

She remembered that other afternoon at the edge of the wood; for a moment she even wanted to remember it, she leant against him, excited by – by what? Him? The music? The unfamiliar experience of being here alone with him, the world shut out? So when he steered her towards the sofa she went, when he kissed her she pulled his head nearer; only when she felt his hand on her leg pushing her skirt above her knees did her feet metaphorically touch the ground.

'No, Leighton, you shouldn't. . . .'

'I should, I should.'

Above her stocking tops, pulling the leg elastic of her bloomers aside, then his fingers found their goal.

'Don't. Please Leighton, don't spoil everything.'

143

'How can it? Frances, I think of you all the time, I want you so, you're so beautiful.'

'Not now, not like this. One day it'll be right for us, don't spoil it.'

His hand was still now, hardly beyond her knee.

'One day we'll be married,' he spoke softly, 'when I can give you all I want to, but now is right. Didn't you feel it as we played? You know you did. You spoke your heart to me then, Frances; you want us to love, don't you, don't you?' Again his hand was moving upwards and his words were whispered, his face only inches form hers. His fingers touched her and he knew the answer without her speaking.

'I won't hurt you. It's your first time, I'll be gentle. Let me. Frances I can't sleep, I can't work. I've never felt like this for any girl before.'

Who knows what might have happened to the tangled threads if his next move had been different. Her eyes were closed, she was breathing deeply, frightened of where she was heading yet powerless to stop herself.

Her expression must have made him over-confident, for she felt him move away and busy himself with something as he spoke. 'I'll see we don't slip up; you'll be all right I promise.'

That gave her a moment to retrieve lost ground. She opened her eyes. His braces were unbuttoned his trousers too and she came face to face with the unfamiliar sight of a man's underpants and Leighton struggling to find release from the constraining garment. Her feet were more than metaphorically on the ground as she pulled away from him and stood up.

In a second the fiery column was freed.

'Don't be frightened,' he pulled her towards him and this time the hands that went under her skirt moved to her waist. She was a strong girl but she was caught off her

144

guard. She hadn't known what she expected but it certainly wasn't to find herself gripped between the knees with her underwear suddenly half way down her legs.

'I know what I'm doing, I shan't let it hurt, I promise. . . .'

Couldn't he sense the change in her?

'Leave go of me Leighton – you meant this to happen – that's why you brought me here.'

'Haven't I said I love you? You know I want us to marry when I can give –'

'Give! Take, more like it! Leighton, I'm going home.' She stood very erect, her five foot nine seeming to tower over him as he let go of her and lay back on the sofa. If Frances had come down from the heights it was obvious her words had done nothing to deflate him. He had a hand towards her, speaking gently as if he were soothing a frightened animal.

'I know how both of us feel so how can it be wrong? My thoughts are –'

'I don't want to hear your thoughts.' It's difficult to sound dignified with one's bloomers round one's knees. If she were to walk to the bedroom for her coat they'd be round her ankles. 'I'm going home. While I pack my fiddle away will you fetch my things from your room.'

He stood up.

'It shouldn't be like this, Frances. It could have been so different.'

'Indeed it could.'

One more attempt. 'Don't go. Darling, Frances, forgive me. Stay and make music with me. You loved me then.'

She didn't want to remember. But it was true, as they'd moved together following where the music had beckoned she'd known her body was alive with longing. She'd believed she'd loved him. Until he touched her? She

145

wanted to get away; to think or to forget, she didn't know which.

'Don't come with me to the bus stop. Just get my coat. Please Leighton.'

He turned away, but not before she saw that at last the mighty had fallen, and while he was in the next room she quickly bobbed up her skirt and adjusted her underwear. By the time he brought her coat and hat he'd buttoned away his hopes.

'You shouldn't go on this bus. You said you didn't want Mrs Ratcliffe to know there hadn't been a quintet – she'll know if you get home too early, and then you'll have to explain why you stayed at all.'

She wanted to be gone and even though she didn't answer him her expression left him in no doubt.

She believed it was he who'd spoilt the evening, enticed her there dishonestly (and that she would have accepted, after all it had given them an opportunity to play together) and all the time he'd had but one end in view. He said he loved her, but that wasn't love, or it wasn't what she wanted of love. Now she hurried to get away, pulling on her hat and jamming the long pin to anchor it to her hair. She wanted to be alone to lick her wounds for the hurt and disappointment she felt.

So she wasn't prepared for his sudden outburst.

'Dammit, looking at me like that! You led me on. All the time you played you knew where we were going. Pretty well begged for more when I touched you. Well, I've had plenty of girls, you're not the only one. But let me tell you something,' his face was only inches from hers, surely he must hate her to look at her like that, 'to do what you did is the lowest thing any woman can do. I don't think you've the slightest idea how near you came to – to – oh, never mind. Twice you've done it, well you won't again.'

'Leighton, I don't understand –'

146

'And I'll tell you why. You've got no warmth in you, that's why. Oh, you're keen enough, go through all the motions but when it comes to the point you're ice cold.'

'That's not true!'

'Oh? And how would you know it's not true? You're the sort who'd not touch a man without your gloves on. Well, if ever you do bring yourself to bed with a man – safely married of course – good luck to him!'

'How dare you talk to me like that. You don't know anything about me.' Her calm had gone by now, driven away by fear that what he said of her was true. 'If all you want is some whore, well, go and find one.' Her voice rose, for a moment he thought the couple in the rooms above must hear the disturbance.

She picked up her violin-case and turned towards the door. He'd had to hit out at her, to say what he had. But the thought of her walking out on his life was impossible. Anything but that, he'd accept anything so long as he didn't lose her.

'Frances, not like this. Don't go like this. Forgive me. Let's forget it all, pretend the evening didn't happen. Look, I won't come near you, just stay, don't go yet. We've said too much, beastly things we've said, just to hurt. Please, please,' his voice cracked, his mouth was working, almost he was crying.

If only she could have gone to him, held him in her arms, but she couldn't. Ice cold he'd said, and he must be right, didn't this prove it? Looking at him she felt nothing, no love, no pity, only humiliation on his account that he could behave like it. She wanted just to be gone.

'I'll be different. I won't touch you – not until we're married. You promised one day you'd marry me. Frances don't look like that.' He blew his nose, sniffed, made an attempt at control. 'I'm no different from any other man. It was being near you, here on our own. Tell me it's all

147

right. You'll forget it and we'll go on like we were. We'll get engaged if you like, I'll buy the ring –' he clung to her sleeve.

'Leighton, stop it, pull yourself together. We both know it wouldn't work. It would be wrong to try and forget this evening; we must always remember it. It's only music that holds us together; that's not enough for marriage. I'm sorry, Leighton; I wanted it to be different too.'

'Don't say anything now, think about it. If I haven't got you I don't care about anything. . . .' His voice rose hysterically, his bottom lip seemed to be jelly.

'I'm going. I must hurry for that omnibus.' And without a backward glance she went.

All the way home his words echoed in her memory. Twice she'd done it to him, led him on, he'd said, and he was right. How could she have let it be any other way though? Not purposely had she aroused him. It had been something outside herself, something that had drawn them both. And then? The omnibus rocked and swayed over the pitted road. The 7 o'clock from Tarnmouth was always full taking people home from work. She moved along the bench to make room for one more, but tonight she didn't listen to the snatches of chatter from her fellow travellers. Ice cold he'd said and perhaps she was. Certainly a dreadful revulsion had gripped her. She'd been on a downhill slope not wanting to stop herself and then, in a flash, it had changed. 'As if I'd hit a brick wall at the bottom of the hill. I couldn't have been different. Suddenly what we were doing was furtive, sneaky, I nearly said dirty but that's dreadful. It must be true, I'm the one who's not normal. Perhaps I'm like mother. Was that why her marriage went wrong?' She remembered Leighton's hands delving into her underwear, and her feeling of being imprisoned. The evening had put a barrier between them that couldn't be removed.

Most of the passengers were standing up ready to get off; she realised they were almost in Highworth. She followed, the last to climb down the two steps to the pavement. How could they meet again and pretend it hadn't happened? She'd walked away and left him, his face distorted by tears –

'Fran!'

So busy with her thoughts had she been that she'd not looked where she was going and had collided with someone at the corner of Duck Island Lane, walked right into him with no warning. That that someone was Greg was another twist of the threads.

'Your mother said you'd be on the 9 o'clock from Tarnmouth. I've just come from your house.'

'The quintet was cancelled.'

Why did he peer at her like that in the dim light of the gas lamp?

He could think of nowhere to take her so they could talk; here they were, only yards from Mallard Cottage, in a minute she'd be gone.

'Greg, is it too dark just to walk? I don't really want to go home yet.'

'Let me take your fiddle,' was his answer and they fell into step in an easy silence. If the pavement had been smooth she wouldn't have tripped, and if she hadn't tripped it's unlikely that he would have suggested: 'Take hold of my arm.'

On the bridge over the river they stopped. Leaning on the stone parapet they watched the golden light cast on the water from the single lamp.

Her evening had upset her, thrown her right off balance. Standing there with Greg, watching the dark water, she was surprised how far removed from it she suddenly seemed. Now she could stand away and view it. Greg was telling her of Dr Saunders's suggestion and she put her hand on his, a natural movement.

'I'm glad, Greg, ever so glad.'

'That I'm staying do you mean? Or that he's offered me a partnership?'

'That too, it's splendid. But I meant I'm glad you're going to be here.'

'So am I.'

A conversation that couldn't be said to be charged with romance. Between them there was a companionable silence and yet he was worried about her; from the moment she'd bumped into him he'd felt there was something wrong. Whatever it was must be to do with, Leighton.

'Fran, I'm not asking – but if you want to talk . . .?'

'How did you know there was something? I've not said anything. Oh heavens, am I so transparent? Will Mama bombard me with questions?'

'No. We've learnt to see beneath the surface, you and me.'

'Greg, I'm so mixed up. But the one thing I do know is that Leighton and I were wrong. And it's sad. I want us to share our music but we can't even do that anymore, everything's been spoilt.'

'Tell me, Fran.'

'You're a doctor, but I don't know if people talk about these things even to their doctor. Honestly Greg I was sure I was in love with him – you asked me once, remember? – I truly thought I was. Then this evening . . .,' and so the story came out, not all the details perhaps but enough for him to piece together the hour she'd spent in Leighton's basement rooms.

'You see, Greg, all the things he said to me, they're true. That's twice it's happened and something inside me suddenly turns; I can't help it. It's like milk, lovely creamy milk, then it curdles, goes sour, the richer the milk the sooner it goes off and there's no way of turning it back.

Supposing one day I think I'm in love again, actually get married? I'd have to do – well – be married properly, have children and all that, but it seemed, oh, furtive, revolting. . . .'

'That's because you weren't really in love with him.' He kept his voice low, matter-of-fact, only silently did his heart rejoice. 'Don't rush, Fran; one day it'll work out naturally for you.'

'But don't you see it mightn't. I thought it was real this time, – that's probably all I'll ever be capable of.'

'Nonsense. You're a warm, normal, healthy girl. It takes two. He's not the right one.' He musn't frighten her. If she suspected how he felt she'd rush from him just as she had from Leighton. His tone had to be positive, professional.

As they turned away from the river and back towards High Street he felt her arm slip through his.

'I'm glad you were here. We seem destined to hear each other's problems, don't we?'

His arm increased its pressure on hers; it seemed to accentuate what he'd said to her. Warm, normal, healthy. She found she could think of the evening now with no more than regret that she'd let any of it happen. As for Leighton, she felt nothing. Was that normal, healthy?

He left her at the gate of the cottage and she found it surprisingly easy to tell Myrtle the truth, not the whole truth but at least no lies. The quintet had been cancelled so she'd come home on an early omnibus and had been talking to Greg. Myrtle hardly listened, so often lately her mind was on thoughts of her own.

Leighton must have had more faith in Frances's love than one would have believed from the way he'd pleaded with

151

her not to leave him. As the hours wore on and he turned to the piano for comfort he remembered the first part of their evening. He knew how close they'd been then; the music had meant as much to her as it did to him. Once she realised what a void was left she'd welcome him again, she must. So, difficult though it may be, he'd give her a few days to miss him, time to forget what was better forgotten and to realise what she'd lost.

It wasn't until the Tuesday two weeks later that he sought her out and then with her mother present. There was nothing new in his coming to join them at the Metropole; he'd often done it before, knowing that's where they met after Frances's lesson. And what better time could there be to find Frances with her defences down than after an hour of music?

Myrtle saw him first. 'Look, Franny, here's Leighton. How nice.'

'Mrs Ratcliffe,' he bowed his head; 'Frances. I've been working my fingers to the bone, but I thought "Tuesday, I'll give myself an hour off". May I join you?'

'But of course, we'd love you to, wouldn't we, Franny.' It was a statement, not a question.

You'd think he would have been glad to see Frances's smile, but her welcome hit him harder than any look of displeasure. So might she have turned to Dickie or any family friend; to have him appear so unexpectedly seemed to upset her not at all.

'You didn't come last week, Frances, to the quintet?'

'But, Franny, you told me there wasn't to be a quintet. You must have been mistaken dear,' Myrtle was puzzled. 'You must have misunderstood.'

'I meant as far as I was concerned, Mama. No,

152

Leighton, I told you. You'll find another fiddler easily enough at the college.'

'But you were so keen,' Myrtle looked from one to the other.

'Mama,' Frances laughed, 'to hear you I might think you want to be rid of me. I'm already out one evening for the orchestra and soon the operatic society will start rehearsing again. Much better to find a fiddler who doesn't have a journey, especially in the winter.'

Later, as they came down the steps of the hotel he took her arm to hold her back out of earshot.

'Frances, when can I see you?'

'You're seeing me now, Leighton. It's no use. I expect you were right about me and it was all my fault, if so –'

'Franny, I see the autobus, we must hurry,' Myrtle called. Then to Leighton: 'Don't work too hard, dear; give yourself time to play too,' which surely was an invitation to Mallard Cottage.

He had to find another way of getting through to Frances. So it wasn't to the cottage he went.

'That young man of Franny's is upstairs. I suppose he must have thought to find her here,' Richard said on one of Myrtle's 'just passing' visits a few days later.

'He knows she's at the school this afternoon giving her lessons. It's early yet; I expect he's come to keep Gina company while he waits.' She was glad he'd come to Highworth. She'd not liked to ask (no use asking Franny in any case, she'd only tell what she wanted to) but it had puzzled her why recently there'd been no mention of him. For months, quite apart from his being a welcome visitor, it had been 'Leighton came to rehearsal', 'I'm going for a bicycle ride with Leighton', 'Leighton says' or 'Leighton does', then suddenly silence, his name never mentioned. She wasn't going to ask, she knew Frances well enough to be sure that way she'd learn nothing. But now he'd come

153

back and whatever little difference they might have had would be straightened; and how thoughtful of him to come to keep Gina company while he waited.

'Leave them to chatter, Richard, I'll not go up. He's sure to come to tea at the cottage, and it's nice for Gina to have someone to talk to.'

'If you're not in a rush, stay a while with me.'

They'd known each other since she'd been hardly more than a child in the days he'd come courting her sister. Yet lately they were seeing each other anew. Now as he pulled the wooden armchair nearer the fire in his workroom she noticed he'd brought a cushion from the parlour to put on it. Yet she'd never once seen him sit there himself; he always worked at the table and sat on an old kitchen chair.

'Thought you'd be more comfortable on that. It never gets used in the parlour.'

She knew the moment was important. He hadn't said it casually, rather she sensed uncertainty in his manner as he waited for her reply. He was watching her closely. The moment mattered.

'I'm always comfy here, Richard,' she met his look squarely. He deserved honesty.

Upstairs Gina had taken Leighton briefly into the parlour. Not for long though, for Cynny's practice of lighting a fire there on Sundays and special occasions was a thing of the past. These days there never were any special occasions and what was the point of lighting a fire on Sundays? The family no longer gathered there, parlour games and hymn singing by the piano (Cynny's ability had stretched as far as simple hymn tunes, preferably with no more than two sharps and always just so long as everyone sang loudly enough to cover the flaws) were no more than ghosts. Nowadays Richard invariably broke the Sabbath and carried on with his

154

repairs downstairs, Dickie found an excuse to go out and more often than not Gina went to Mallard Cottage.

'Can't we stay in the kitchen?' he said as she knelt in front of the fireplace ready to light the paper and sticks in the grate. 'Don't bother with that, Gina – it's warm out there.'

'If I'd known you were going to call I'd have made the room warm.'

'I just wanted to see you. Since the ball I've thought of you so often.'

True, so he had. He'd remembered her as the loveliest girl in the hall, 'the little dark fairy'. That she was Frances's cousin made her even more desirable. Just wait until word got round the family that he was giving her his attention, that would show Frances he didn't care.

'I've thought about it too, Leighton.' She said 'it' but surely she meant 'you'; wasn't that why she avoided meeting his eyes and why she flushed so prettily at his words? 'What a wonderful evening it was! Do you know, sometimes I can't believe it wasn't all a dream; I have to go and peep at my dress just to prove it really happened.'

'There'll be others, other balls, other concerts. On this Friday there's a recital at the Town Hall. Come with me Gina. It would be over in time for you to get home afterwards. It starts at 6 pm. Come in the afternoon and let me take you to tea first.'

How could he realise what it meant to her? Never in her life had she been invited out with a young man, and this wasn't just any young man, this was Leighton. Or did he mean that he and Frances were going to the recital and out of pity at seeing how pleased she was he'd come to see her, he was asking her to join them?

'Franny might not want a third.'

'Frances? But Gina, it's you I'm inviting. I'm not going with Frances.'

155

'I thought. . . .'

'That's nonsense. If you don't believe me, ask Frances. Please Gina come with me.'

She dug no deeper.

He wanted her for herself! Her eyes no longer avoided his, her pleasure was clear for him to read.

She wanted to shout aloud with excitement; it took all her self control to speak calmly – so calmly that her reply sounded stilted even to her own ears.

'Thank you very much. I'd be pleased to come.'

To set them on an easier footing she turned to lead the way back to the kitchen. 'The kettle's singing, I'll make us some tea.'

He followed her, the blow Frances had dealt his self-esteem already starting to heal. On Friday he'd take her to the Metropole to tea; that would please her. What's more, she'd be sure to come back to Highworth full of details of her outing.

He was prepared to enjoy the next weeks, confident that while he cheered Gina's dull existence Frances would realise what a fool she'd been. That anyone would get hurt didn't enter his head and certainly he didn't imagine his own feelings would be involved.

Friday was all she dreamed. Her foot tapped in time to the rhythm of the Viennese waltz as they sat at tea, she could hardly believe this was actually happening, any more than she could half an hour later when Leighton took her elbow in his hand as they walked along the Esplanade towards Broad Street and the Town Hall. In truth the recital itself wouldn't have been her personal choice, but she didn't consider that, much less acknowledge it, for this was Leighton's world and all she asked was to be part of it.

As they came down the wide stairway from the Town Hall balcony she tried to look knowledgeable as he talked

156

of the programme they'd heard. She nodded, managed 'Yes, I thought that too', and 'Well, of course I'm not a musician but I do agree', pleased with herself that at least she wasn't advertising her ignorance. It was a relief when in the foyer they bumped into a party of his fellow students, one of whom she'd met at the ball. She was sure Leighton was proud to introduce her, not suspecting why. The meeting came just at the right moment too, saving her from the more dangerous ground of music. If he invited her to hear anything else (oh, surely he must, he seemed to be enjoying her company) she'd find out first what they were to hear and learn something about it. Fran would help her.

He did invite her again, not just to concerts, but to tea, to the roller-skating rink where she acquitted herself with skill and grace, to the Music Hall where she laughed delightedly at the rough-and-tumble of the comic and joined in with the chorus singing, looking so pretty that he trod down the suspicion that she preferred the entertainment here to that at the concert hall. Then on the Tuesday before Easter when the term at college had come to an end he suggested she come to his basement room. She had been to all kinds of places with him unchaperoned, but this was something different.

'But Leighton, there's no one else there – I shouldn't. . . .' And perhaps she shouldn't but did he imagine just how much she wanted to?

'Dear Gina, how sweet you are.' He took her hand in his as they walked along Broad Street, her basket on her arm (she'd made shopping her excuse for an afternoon in Tarnmouth). 'You'll be quite safe, I promise you. I'll treat you as if you were my maiden aunt.' His blue eyes teased her as she knew she blushed and was ashamed. To her, Leighton and Leighton's world held all of sophistication; if he said it was right for her to go to his rooms, well then so it must be; right in his eyes and nothing more than that mattered.

'I know that, Leighton. Truly I spoke without thinking. Of course I'd love to come home with you. So much nicer than having our tea out.'

And a maiden aunt would have found his behaviour impeccable.

Each hour she spent with him she fell further under his spell and each hour she pushed thoughts of Frances further away. Not that Frances showed any sign of minding his apparent change of heart, Gina told herself, at the same time turning a deaf ear to an inner voice that reminded her: 'You hardly ever see her – you know you've been trying to avoid her these last weeks'.

No longer did she face each day with miserable resignation. Now she'd open her eyes aware that something good was just around the corner – and then she'd remember Leighton. The stone kitchen sink had lost its power to depress her. Perhaps her more cheerful state of mind transmitted itself to her cooking, adding a touch of lightness to her pastry or flavour to her stews, or perhaps she was just less interested in how her offerings were received. Either way she did what she had to do in the house – then at every opportunity she escaped. Just as Frances had thought a few months ago so Gina thought now: 'This is love'.

One might expect that Frances would have been less aware of the promise in each new day. If Leighton could have read her mind things might have worked out differently, but he couldn't; he could only imagine the gap his going must have left. In fact she missed him not at all. Even music had been no more than a common interest, a common love, for until that evening in his rooms they'd never played together. She'd not realised the extent she'd let herself be dominated by his personality. Now he was gone and she was free to be herself.

So each day was welcomed as something to enjoy and she hardly gave a thought to the fact that most of the good times were shared with Greg. Always it was fun to be with him, there was nothing they couldn't discuss, no secret compartments in their minds. Sometimes they'd go walking; sometimes she'd sit by his side in the trap as he made his round of visits; on Sundays he'd share a pew with the three from Mallard Cottage; and for months he'd been a frequent visitor to Betsy's kitchen and Myrtle's sitting-room alike.

It was a bright, wild day early in April. She'd been to Warwick House to give her Monday morning lessons and was walking home, fiddle case under her arm, head down against the buffeting wind, when she met him. Nothing unusual in that, Highworth was a small place and not many days went by when they didn't see each other. Why then was this one so special?

'I'm so sorry,' she said automatically as she bumped against someone; then: 'Greg! I'm sorry, did I hit you with my case? My head was down against this wind.' She held her wide-brimmed hat firmly on, it's ribbon streamer fluttering behind, while a flurry of last year's leaves and this year's dust scudded along the pavement.

'It's an ill wind . . . ,' he laughed; 'I was coming to see you. Fran, Dr Saunders doesn't need me anymore until this evening. When you've eaten your dinner, let's catch the autobus to Tarnmouth, have a stride along the cliffs. It's a day made for it. Or betters still, take your fiddle indoors now and tell your mother we're going. If we hurry we can catch the 1 o'clock; we can have something to eat later.'

'Yes, let's do that. Bother dinner. Do us more good to walk in the wind.'

159

Together they fell into step and hurried to Duck Island Lane. No time for more than a quick word with Betsy, for Myrtle was out, then they almost ran to the corner and reached the stop just as the 'bus chugged into view.

About half a mile before Tarnmouth they climbed down the three steps to the grassy verge by the roadside, where the path led to the cliff top. On an afternoon like this words would have been lost; battling against the wind they needed all their breath. An occasional glance of undisguised pleasure, her shout of 'Isn't this splendid' and his nod for reply. No more than that.

Even when they reached the foot of the cliff path and stopped in the newly erected shelter at the beginning of the Esplanade the magic of the wild afternoon still held them. Here the wind roared all around them, the waves crashed on the shore and they could taste the salt of the spray, yet they were enclosed in the pocket of stillness provided by the metal hut, Tarnmouth's latest pride built as a miniature of the bandstand farther along the sea front.

Her eyes shone with excitement as she watched the tremendous sea. She sat forward on the iron bench seat as if to be part of the storm. He let his gaze rest on her, loving her; she was his first love, she'd be his only love, he was so sure. And that was the moment that made this Monday afternoon something set apart from all the other hours they'd spent together, for at just that moment she turned to him. He knew her so well: she musn't be pushed, she must have freedom to find what she wanted So even before she was sure she hadn't imagined what she'd read in his eyes he looked away.

'Fran – Gina and Leighton – they see a lot of each other these days. Tell me, it's not my business if you like, but do you care?'

A moment ago she'd seemed to be caught up in the

160

tumult around her; now at his question her expression changed. He would have given much to recall his words; between them he seemed to see Leighton, handsome, talented, sharing her interests. What a fool he was, hadn't he known he must let her take her time?

If he could have read her mind he might have been cheered but her expression told him nothing as she answered.

'I want Gina to be happy, but Greg I wish she cared for someone different. Don't ever tell anyone I said that, will you?'

He shook his head.

'You mean you wish you and he –'

'Glory be, no, I told you all about that!' Her face flushed, she could feel even her neck was uncomfortably hot. 'I wish none of it had ever happened, even the good parts. It wasn't until afterwards I realised, all the time I was with Leighton, even when I imagined I was in love with him, it wasn't me at all, not the real me. It was what I thought he wanted me to be. I don't really blame him. Looking back I can see it was so much my own fault, being so stupid, not being natural. Perhaps Gina's not so silly and in any case she's such a dear, so gentle and sweet, he must surely love her.'

'That's what you hope?'

'If it's what she hopes. But really and truly I just wish she could fall in love with someone less clever, less ambitious, someone who'd care about her more than he would.'

'Perhaps he does,' and still he watched closely for her reaction.

'Well, let's hope so. Look Greg, just look at the sea! What are we doing sitting in here like a pair of poor old souls. Let's go and battle with the wind.'

That was in April, the daffodils in Myrtle's garden with

161

their trumpets beaten to the ground. By May they'd been tied in neat bundles and by the side of the short brick path leading to the front door hyacinths were a riot of colour, filling the air with fragrance. And still Frances hadn't stumbled on the truth.

Greg was a part of her daily life, she accepted him without question, almost without thought.

It was early one evening towards the end of May that in a blinding flash she knew. They'd been walking by the river (a favourite spot still, just as it always had been) and they'd stopped on the footbridge that led to the 'cowslip field' as everyone called the riverside meadow on the farther bank.

'Look, Greg, there's a kingfisher – don't move or we'll frighten him off.'

Greg was very still.

'Oh, now he's gone. But did you see?' she turned to him.

And what was there in that split second that told her? What was different from those other hundreds of times?

For so long he'd waited, never pushing her, never angling for the right moment. Without her he could never be complete. Surely she must one day see, one day realise that it was the same for her? Whether he moved to her now or she to him they didn't know, but as his mouth covered hers her eyes were wide open. She was like a wanderer who'd come home.

Their feet came back to the ground. They made their plans, they thought themselves masters of their destiny. But it's not so. The pattern is woven by a force stronger than our own.

Chapter Seven

The next day Gina heard the news of their engagement, her first reaction one of relief. Her pleasure was genuine for Frances but, more than that, for herself too. This must lift the shadow that threatened always on the horizon.

The previous evening Leighton had been in London taking part in a music competition. Today he'd be back and Gina had promised to meet him in Tarnmouth that afternoon. She could hardly wait. To close the door on Frances must open it for her. Surely, surely, he'd feel that too.

There was more of Myrtle in her than her inherited small, chiselled features and pretty face. Today she dressed with special care for her trip. Her wardrobe was small and what clothes she had were not new but she wore them with style; she pinned an early rosebud on her lapel, tilted her hat becomingly forward, put rouge on her lips and rosewater on her handkerchief. Always it gave her pleasure to make the most of her dress, yet today was something different. Only now did she acknowledge to herself just how much the shadow of Frances had clouded her confidence.

'Gregory Smart! She can't be!' was Leighton's

reaction. He looked strange; she couldn't say what there was about him – a tightness around his mouth a hardness in the expression in his eyes. She wished she had chosen her moment better, not blurted it at him almost the moment she'd arrived.

'But Leighton, Auntie came to tell us this morning, and I've seen Franny too. They're buying the ring in Tarnmouth this very afternoon.'

The silence seemed interminable.

'She's a fool,' he said at last. 'Why's she doing it? Why do you think she's doing it?'

'Well, because she loves him, I suppose.' She wasn't going to listen to doubts. 'What's wrong, Leighton? You said there was nothing between you and Franny, remember? That's what you told me.'

'Of course there isn't. But just the same she's a fool, she's buying trouble. What have they in common, tell me that?'

'I think there are other things more important than sharing the same interests.' Her big blue eyes were so earnest. If he read her heart, well, let him. Somehow she had to make herself enough for him.

What was going on in his mind she had no idea but with relief she heard him change the subject and suggest: 'Let's eat here, Gina. I want you to myself. Can you make us something?'

'Oh yes, I'd much rather. I like it lots more when we stay on our own.'

The stove at home represented hard labour; here in his basement rooms it was only one stage removed from heaven. All she asked was to make herself so necessary that he couldn't think of being without her; to serve him was her way to happiness. As she cooked their tea she heard the sound of his piano. Music was something outside her part in his life; she wasn't jealous of it so long

164

as it was a job of work shared with no one else. She even tried to show an intelligent interest and was sufficiently ignorant that she imagined any superficial knowledge she might glean to please him must draw them together, rather than put a wedge between them. Now she heard him playing the piano part of that Cézar Franck sonata but she 'didn't know the tune', as she would put it, and in any case she was far more interested in making sure she beat the egg whites just as much as she should and heated the oven to the right temperature so that the soufflé should come to the table at a dizzy height.

If she could have read his thoughts she mightn't have been as cheerful or as confident either.

The soufflé did all she hoped – and she hoped for more than she expected.

How lovely she was, he thought watching her, gentle and eager. Why, Frances wasn't to be compared, all hands and feet, he added spitefully. Not true though, his inner mind nudged him; you're only pretending. Remember her voice, her laugh, those wonderful eyes that so exactly match the colour of her tawny hair, remember the touch of her hands so strong and capable, the feel of her. . . . Damn it all, what had he to remember? Most of it had been in his own mind; all he'd had of her had been a tantalising moment.

'What's the matter, Leighton? You're not eating. Don't you like soufflè?'

'Yes, sweet Gina, I like it.' His hand reached towards her across the table, 'I like it and I like you sharing it with me.'

'Oh Leighton, really? I mean – you're not just being kind because you know how much I want you to say it?'

'Do you? Do you?'

She knew her cheeks were pink with excitement. The late afternoon sun was streaming through the basement window, shadows of people passing on the pavement above seeming only to isolate them from the outside world.

'I want you to need me more than I would ever want anything.' There, she'd said it! The words seemed suspended between them, waiting for him to take them up.

'Yes, I need you. You've no idea how lonely I am when you're not here.'

Across the table two blue eyes shone at him with open adoration.

'Come here,' he pushed his chair back and held a hand towards her.

She came. Such a slip of a girl, warm and eager as she let him pull her on to his knee. Near to each of them was a ghost of Frances. Leighton held Gina close, certain of her love, and he tried not to think of that other figure, the broad shoulders and full breast, the low tone of her voice or her deep laugh that was never a giggle, those clear eyes and vivid colouring . . . he'd not let himself think. Don't they say a drowning man sees his life flash before him? In that moment something of the same thing must have happened to Gina. There she was as a child with Franny; she saw every game they'd played, every secret they'd shared. She remembered the times she'd tried to talk of Gregory, and Franny's disinterest. 'You don't seem to care about him,' hadn't she said? She heard the two of them whispering their discoveries of adolescence, the echo of a more recent Franny with 'Leighton does this', 'Leighton says that . . .' In a split second of honesty she knew that she was only where she was because something had gone awry between the two of them; he'd only turned to her out of hurt. Even now, despite all he said, she knew, just in that 'drowning' moment, that she was but a salve to some wound Frances had caused. The joy of the moment was stronger than memories or conscience either. Franny could never have loved him as she did; he'd forget, she'd make him forget. She could make him happy, if only he'd give her a chance to prove it. She asked for nothing except to be able to make herself all that he wanted.

He was human; she was loving. For both of them that ghost faded.

The 6 o'clock 'bus rumbled towards Highworth without her and she gave not a thought to two hungry men waiting for their meal. Time had lost all meaning.

'My sweet Gina' he'd called her, and she heard it as 'I love you'. Well, perhaps he did, in that hour their world went no farther than each other.

Later as the 7 o'clock 'bus bumped and jolted on its way she sat on a bench by the window, very still and erect, her hands folded on the handle of her basket and her eyes straight ahead.

'Ticket, missie,' she heard the conductor say.

'Penny ha'penny please.' She passed two pennies and took her ticket and ha'penny change but didn't look directly at him. She felt there must be something about her, some sign that she was different from the girl who'd left home that afternoon. Her reflection in the none-too-clean glass window told her nothing, but she remembered peering closely into the looking glass on the chest in Leighton's bedroom as she'd tidied her hair and put on her hat, seeing the red patch on her chin. His face had been quite rough; she'd not noticed when he'd first kissed her, but later, his cheek moving against hers. . . . She glanced slyly at the two women sitting across the aisle from her, then lowered her gaze. No one appeared to be taking any notice of her; they were behaving as if it were any ordinary day. . . . She longed to share her secret, to talk about him. Imagine what Franny would say! Always things had happened first to Franny – well, not this time. Yet she musn't tell her; instinct warned her this was something that could never be shared.

'She wouldn't understand, how could she? Especially with Leighton – but in any case she couldn't know, she just wouldn't understand.' Gina had come a long way since she'd climbed the three steps on to the 'bus to take her to Tarnmouth. Frances may have been out buying an engagement ring, but it was she who'd learnt the secret of loving. Leighton loved her, her heart sang. 'My sweet Gina,' came the echo of his soft voice.

'Thank you, thank you.' Silently she gave credit wherever it was due. For a few moments he'd been hers, utterly hers. And the power she had would be hers again, and again. She'd bring him joy, she'd –

'Three 'apence, that's what you give me. This is as far as you go miss; 'nother 'a'penny to go on to the Market.'

'Oh, sorry, I was thinking about something else.' She jumped up, feeling every eye on her, every woman recognising her secret and reading where her thoughts had been.

Down the steps on to the pavement without a backward glance, then she looked up towards the kitchen window of the shop to find her father watching for her. She waved, only now realising that some excuse would be expected for her lateness.

'Why should I have to tell lies? I'm not their servant! I've been with my lover, how about if I say that? Lover, Leighton is my lover. Oh heavens, it's a different world there with him. Thank you, thank you. . . .'

'Hello Pa,' she called up the stairs. 'I met Leighton and he took me to tea. I just missed the 6 o'clock and had to wait, but I'll not be long with your food.'

'We're all having our supper with your Aunt Myrtle. Didn't you notice I'd shut up early? Better get a Sunday

168

dress on. I was just saying to Dickie we must put our best foot forward, eh, not let the family down. She's got the doctor and Mrs Saunders coming it seems.'

Dickie frowned. 'Don't see what's so special about him, not from what we've seen of him. Hope Greg turns out to be more of a doctor.' Then: 'Still, fancy Fran and Greg going to get spliced. Doctor's wife,' he chuckled, 'would you believe it?' He grinned, thinking of the tomboy she'd always been. 'Thought she'd get stuck with Leighton. He's all right mind you, but –'

'Leighton's going to be more important than any doctor one of these days,' Gina championed him, but the others hardly listened.

'Can I have that kettle of hot? I'd better have a shave when you've done, Pa.' Dickie had other things to think of than Leighton's rosy future, real or imagined.

Richard, cut-throat razor in his hand, was standing in front of the kitchen sink peering into the speckled mirror that hung from a string on the wall. Father and son bore so little resemblance to each other. Richard tall and straight, still a good-looking man, blue eyes that looked directly at one, no sign of grey in his light brown hair that receded now into a widow's peak he'd not had in younger days, an expression that told of patience and kindness. It was probably kindness that prompted him to swallow his words as Dickie took off his collar and tie and prepared to scrape off his imaginery bristles. 'Nothing to shave, lad, no more than a bit of bum fluff'. Tact kept him silent as he wiped the open blade and put the razor on the wooden draining board ready for his son.

In the meantime Gina took the second kettle and went to her room. Everything around her was familiar; the afternoon seemed almost like a dream. She slipped off her dress, her petticoat and bodice, then rubbed the soap between her hands. Stripped to the waist she smoothed

169

the lather over her shoulders, round her small breasts. It was real, it had truly happened, her body tingled with a strange new excitement; she closed her eyes, remembering.

'Going to be long, Gina?' she heard Richard call. 'Young Dickie and I are pretty well ready. Your aunt said about 8 and it's that now.'

'I'm hurrying, Pa. Won't be two minutes.'

He was relieved at her cheerfulness. To be honest he'd wondered how she'd take Franny's news but, bless her, he didn't know when he'd seen her so bright. What a good kid she was! She may think he didn't appreciate her but . . . 'And very pretty you look,' he said as she hurried along the passage from her room.

And so thought the rest of the party.

This evening Myrtle used her best dinner service, salvaged from her days in Belmont Road. Most of her afternoon had gone into the preparation of the festive supper (although it was Betsy who had cleaned the vegetables and battled with steaming pans) and the meal proved all she'd hoped. The mood of the evening was just as gay as she'd intended, the rise and fall of voices, the laughter, evidence of the party's success. Across the table her glance met Gina's. Dear Gina, really the child seemed to glow this evening. For a moment the disloyal thought came to Myrtle that to look at the two girls one might believe the evening were hers.

'Here's that piano-playing friend of yours, Franny,' Betsy called up the stairs, 'just coming up the path now.' She moved across the little hall to open the front door as Leighton raised his hand to knock. 'Saw you coming I did. No need to knock. I called up to Miss Franny that you were here. Scraping away up in the attic; doubt she heard me. I'll go and get her.'

'Don't you worry, Betsy, I'll get her. Is Mrs Ratcliffe not at home?' he remembered to add.

'No, just Miss Franny. Wonder she wants to spend all the hours she does with that fiddle now she's got so much to look forward to. You've heard, I suppose,' she puffed up her chest in pride, 'she's to wed Master Greg.' There, that should put this young man in his place. Never could understand what young Franny saw in him when Master Greg was there with his eye on her. She sniffed. 'Tell Miss Franny to stop her practising and come down. I'll make you a pot of tea and put it in the sitting-room.'

Frances couldn't have heard him come; she continued to play. Betsy went back to the kitchen as he climbed the narrow stairs, but she left the door wide open and strained her ears.

Then the music stopped. Voices. Were they coming down? No, it seemed not. She couldn't hear what they said but she knew it mattered, it wasn't simple words of well wishing; both of them were talking, a steady tone. Ah! Now the door was opening, they must be coming. She moved to the range and held the pot so that the steam from the kettle filled it, warming it. She'd better get their tea made. Wasn't that the fiddle again though? She put the empty pot on the table and went to the passage just as Leighton reached the bottom of the stairs.

'Don't worry about the tea, Betsy.'

Must say he sounds cool enough. But you can't fool Betsy, my lad, something's upset your applecart. 'Isn't Franny coming down?'

'No, she's practising and I mustn't stay. I'm on my way to High Street. Had to stop and give Frances my good wishes, that's all.'

She saw him out and closed the front door. From upstairs the fiddle played on.

Later when Myrtle came home she brought the

171

shopping into the kitchen and she made the tea while Betsy put cups and saucers on a tray.

'Put three, Betsy; we'll all have it out here. I dare say Franny will be down in a jiff.'

'Had that Leighton Tyrell to see her – to give her his good wishes, or so he said.'

'He didn't mention he'd been. I was with Gina when he arrived. No reason why he should say of course. . . . I was always very fond of Leighton, a charming boy.'

Betsy's sniff was her only reply.

'Time was when I thought he and Franny were heading for the aisle,' Myrtle mused.

'Never could understand it myself. She was such good friends with Master Greg. I could have told her he was sweet on her, plain as a pikestaff it was, yet she didn't seem to notice.'

'No more did I, Betsy,' Myrtle chuckled; 'it's all your doing, if you ask me; you willed them into it.'

'Was no need for it – but I would have done if I could. Fancy Mrs Ratcliffe, m'am, never cared for anyone like I have those two chillun, him from the day he was born and her from – what was she, nine? ten? – ah, tennish it must have been. And one of these days there'll be babies there, now we've both got things to look forward to.'

So Leighton's visit was forgotten, at least by Myrtle and Betsy. As for Frances, she wasn't likely to tell anyone what had been said up there in the attic.

'I didn't ask Mr Cowdery to tell him; I wrote the letter myself. But Greg, it makes me realise what a stranger I am to him. I'm taking it to Mr Cowdery and asking him to forward it. All I've said is the bare fact, that I want him to know that I'm to be married – to you, your name and so forth, that I've known you since we were children (I thought that sounded safe, sure somehow), and that if ever he'd like to write to me this will be my address after next week.'

All these years her father hadn't bothered, why should he care now? He had somehow to prepare her. 'One day I'll find him, show him how I am'; he remembered the little girl she'd been, so sure even then. Now, years later, she'd still been determined to do it. She turned to him, waiting for his answer, her eyes clear and confident. He couldn't bear the thought of her being hurt. He felt a wave of tenderness for her, a physical ache in the pit of his stomach.

'Fran, he may not reply. He may think it better not. He's never contacted you, birthdays, Christmasses –'.

'I've never forgotten him, I've always known that I'd write to him one day, but I couldn't do it until now. I used to tell him all my secrets, in my mind I mean. It's funny but you know I'd almost forgotten how much I used to confide in him; every night I'd unburden myself as regularly as saying my prayers. Even when I grew up. . . .' Not now though, she suddenly realised, not since she'd shared her thoughts with Greg.

In his mind that voice from the past echoed: '. . . one day when Mama won't cry.'

'How did your mother take it?'

'I've not told her.'

She knew a sense of shame as she said it; her conscience had been prodding at her already and she waited for him to say what she'd not let herself acknowledge. Her shame wasn't for deceiving Myrtle though, that's what surprised her; it was for disappointing Greg.

She felt his arms go around her. He was strong, he was her support.

'But you know you will tell her. We'll tell her together if you like, would that help?'

173

She could imagine Myrtle's tears, her trembling lip, the puzzled hurt that all these years she'd not been enough.

'No, I must talk to her by myself. You see that don't you – and Greg you understand why I had to write? When we have children, why, they'll be his grandchildren, whatever went wrong between them we can't keep that from him, or from them.'

He rubbed his chin against her forehead. 'Our children won't have much family. I've none to speak of.' His grandfather had slipped out of life without knowing he'd still possessed it, gradually drifting into unconsciousness that carried him over the threshold. A fair-minded man he'd always been as his Will had shown. 'Bearing in mind the monies previously made over to my late son Roderick Percival, I bequeath to his heir Gregory the sum of one hundred pounds and the ruby ring given me by my dear late wife.' The remainder of his estate, which amounted to no more than had cushioned Roderick, had gone to James, the diligent farmer from Oxfordshire.

Thoughts of the future pushed out her fears of telling Myrtle about the letter to her father. A life they'd build together, everything shared, a home, children, these were the things that mattered. They clung to each other and the letter was forgotten. In seven days they would be married. The house Gregory had rented in Matlock Avenue had been furnished with everything essential to set up home, and her wedding dress, sewn with such care by Myrtle, was hanging in readiness in her wardrobe.

As she pulled away from Greg she glanced at her fob watch and he could tell she was 'squaring her shoulders' for the job ahead.

'I'll do it now, as soon as I get home. I'll tell her and make her understand, and tomorrow morning I'll see Mr Cowdery.'

He didn't try to hold her back. If Frances had

something unpleasant to do he knew it had to be tackled straight away. Just for a second he gripped her hand and then silently he mouthed the words 'I love you'.

He'd said it before but never had they been so aware. The room was charged with emotion.

'And I love you, Greg,' her voice was low and steady; 'you're everything in my whole world.'

His Adam's apple felt twice its size, her tummy tied itself in knots.

She hurried home, determined to be loving and resolute, her size sevens planting themselves firmly as she went. The letter was in her purse. At last the time had come to turn the fantasy she'd created into reality. Or so she thought. But the evening was to change all that and by the end of the day the single sheet was no more than charred paper in her bedroom fireplace.

This last week or two it was no rare thing for the postman to lean his bicycle against the railings of Mallard Cottage. With the wedding so soon there was plenty the family found to write about. The time he was due along the lane usually found Myrtle near the window. Sometimes it wasn't just young Bill Stokes on his cycle, sometimes Mr Higgins came himself from the post office carrying a parcel. Today though she'd already had a letter from Ella this morning so she wasn't hopeful of anything else. When the rap came on the front door she was in the kitchen with Betsy. Without that knock they wouldn't have looked in the letter box until the next morning, and Frances might even have already left home to see Mr Cowdery. Without that knock things might have worked out quite differently.

Betsy was busy at the table ironing the chair covers she'd laundered ready for 'these folk we shall get coming

175

in, along with the wedding next week.' so Myrtle was first into the passage but Betsy was near enough after her to recognise the long parchment envelope.

Why should Betsy have had such a feeling of foreboding as Myrtle went into the sitting-room and slit open the envelope with the little silver paper knife she kept on her writing desk?

'Everything all right is it, m'um?'

'Why yes,' Myrtle marvelled at her steady voice, 'Yes, of course. Seems all the family are to be here for Franny's big day.' She folded the letter and put it away and Betsy turned back to her job. Now why should the missus have said a thing like that, tried to make her think the letter had come from one of the family? Something wasn't right.

Safely on her own Myrtle read the solicitor's missive again. 'But he can't do that, he can't. How am I to live? Oh, heavens above, how can he do it to me?'

'Did you call, m'um?'

'No, Betsy. Don't bother with any tea for me today, not yet at any rate. I want just to slip round to the shop for a minute. I've just remembered something I had to remind Richard.'

Now, why couldn't she have been honest? Betsy heard her run up the stairs to get her hat and coat and she felt helpless. Not for her to say: 'Just you tell, Betsy. Aren't I near enough family to share your troubles?' She put all her force into the frills of the chair covers, serving where she could.

It was second nature to Myrtle to care about her dress. Even today when the ground had been kicked from under her she automatically took a handkerchief from her sachet that toned with the flowers on her hat, shook rosewater on it and added a touch of colour to her lips. Then, the letter tucked inside her moleskin muff, she took her problem to Richard.

176

'I don't understand it, Richard. He says I shall no longer have to support Franny, but what about me? What about Betsy? Does he think we can do without a roof? My dear little home,' tears brimmed again; 'it's been such a happy place.'

'There now, we'll think of something.'

'But can he do it, cut me right down like that?'

'The letter came from the solicitor. If he couldn't Mr Cowdery would have told him so. It's not so little, Myrtle. Come now, cheer up, we'll work it out together.'

'There's nothing to work out. My rent and the grocer's bill comes to almost as much as that – and what about Betsy? What about coals for the fire and clothes for my back? He doesn't care. Perhaps he thinks I should find work, go as a housekeeper somewhere for my keep! And how does he know Franny's to be married? Not from me I swear. Gossiping busybodies; why can't they keep their meddling tongues quiet?'

'Perhaps he'll make a marriage settlement on the girl.'

'At my expense, yes, perhaps he might. He'd enjoy that, thinking of me going without to pay for it. I'll have to find a room somewhere, do my own cleaning, no more little treats, no more trips to the Baths for my back. . . .' By now the tears flowed unchecked.

'Come, come,' he put his arm around her shoulder, 'wipe your tears.' He wanted to hold her, to comfort her, yet just to have an arm around her aroused a tenderness that had subtly altered over the years. When first she'd been left on her own she'd turned to him, to him and to Cynny; she'd clung to him then and he'd given her reassurance. Now he was frightened to take her in his arms and surprised at his own feelings.

'You can't, you mustn't, think of going to rooms. Now listen my dear, there are two choices and I know which I hope you'll make. The first is that you live with Franny and Gregory; they'll have plenty of room and you know that's what they'll want. The second is this. Live here, Myrtle. Gina needs a woman, God knows I seem to have no influence on her. If I try and check what she does she thinks I'm chaining her to the job she hates. I don't know what to do with the girl and that's the truth. She needs a woman and you know how fond she is of you. Even young Dickie might spend less of his evenings in the alehouse with his friends if the house had a bit of comfort.'

'You're offering me a home?'

'No, not offering. I'm begging you. Until this moment I don't think I've ever faced up to how empty the place is, I've been frightened to I dare say. With you here . . . say you will Myrtle. You'd not have to clean, I'd get a woman for that. Make it a home again, bring some sort of love back into it again.'

'You really want me? Or are you just being kind?'

Her eyes would have melted any heart and the ice around Richard's had turned to a burning longing. He told himself it was because Myrtle had been a sister to him for so long; that must be why so much depended on her agreeing.

'I want you to come, I'm begging you to come. . . .'

'Then I will. That's what I'll do, I'll give notice at the cottage and once the wedding's over I'll sort things out and think to the future.' Suddenly she was excited.

'Yours – and mine too. Already there's something to look forward to.' His smile left her in no doubt.

'We'll make it a happy home again, Richard. Poor little Gina, it's been a lot for her to cope with.'

'Ah, she's done as well as she could. Just wait until she hears you're to be here! We'll see a smile the like we've not been favoured with for many a year.'

And so they did. Glad to have Myrtle, yes, but more than that. Surely this was her chance of escape.

An hour or so later Richard stood in the shop doorway seeing Myrtle off. In the early evening dusk the lamp lighter was on his nightly round and from the chimney of the ironmonger's opposite came the dark smoke of a newly lit fire. Winter would soon be here.

'I'll have to tell Betsy she must look for somewhere else.' Myrtle turned to him in sudden thought, 'Oh dear, fancy me forgetting poor Betsy. Says she's never been so happy as these years at the cottage. How I'll hate to do it. She'll not want for a reference but she's been like family, she's not young either –'

'Myrtle, Myrtle,' his eyes were teasing, he spoke softly, affectionately, 'you don't think young Gregory and Fran will let her go! And between ourselves I think there's nowhere she'd rather be than helping them set up home.'

'But of course. I didn't think. You know Richard I sometimes believe we don't always see the way we should be going. When I had that beastly letter – why hardly more than two hours ago, I can't believe it – I felt fate had struck such an unkind blow. But now I'm like someone who's found the missing piece of a jigsaw. In a flash it's all clear, almost ordained.'

'Bless you, Myrtle.' Then, squeezing her elbow in what he hoped was a brotherly way, 'I feel I should be grateful to whoever told Clement about Fanny, and I swear I'll try to see you never have cause to regret what you're doing. The home will have a heart again.'

She turned to him, all trace of her earlier sadness gone, her eyes clear and shining. What a difference it made to be needed. 'We'll make it a happy home, for the children and for ourselves – and for dear Cynny too, I like to think.'

If he'd felt uneasy about his strange excitement at the sudden turn of events, her remark quietened it. For a second Cynny seemed close, their own memories of her separate and private.

'Ah, nought but happiness where Cynny was. Her heart'll be lighter to know we're helping each other.'

When Frances read the letter from Cowdery & Elphinstone all her loyalty to her mother was aroused. That he could do such a cruel thing, he who she'd put on a pedestal all these years! Myrtle was hurt, bewildered; Frances, furiously angry and part of her anger was with herself. We know of the fire she made in her grate that night. It destroyed more than her message of friendship; it was a symbolic gesture.

'The 'ceremony' over she made ready for bed, washing in cold water from the china jug of her marble-topped stand, brushing and plaiting her long straight hair, barely thinking what she was doing, her mind busy with what her mother had told her.

'But, Mama, of course if you give up the house you'll live with us. There's lots of room, of course you will. And Betsy too,' she said when she'd heard the plans; 'Greg wouldn't hear of anything else.'

'No dear, you and Gregory should start on your own. If you'll find a place for dear Betsy it would be wonderful, but as for me, my mind's quite made up. Richard really does need me, Franny; he says they're all disorganised and it's no life for Gina. I dare say Leighton will whisk her away once she's free to go.' For a minute she'd been quiet as if weighing up how much she should say; then shyly, almost coyly, she'd looked up from where she sat at Frances standing in front of her. 'I'm really quite excited,' she'd confessed. 'A new start, to really be needed. You know, Franny, Richard says the house has lost its heart. I'll make them glad I'm there.'

180

'You've never been used to rough work, Mother.'

'He's going to get help; he said that too.'

'Pity he didn't do it for Gina if he can afford it now.'

'Poor Gina.' Her smile had shown her well pleased with the arrangements. Tonight she had no room for misgivings on her niece's account. 'Put another knob or two of coal on, dear, and run and tell Betsy we'll have our cocoa in here all together. Then we'll tell her.'

'No no, not tonight. It's for Greg to ask her to come. He will I know, but it's for him, not me to suggest it.' Her reply had surprised her mother. Frances usually made her own decisions. 'And there's no point in worrying her tonight for nothing.'

'No, you're right. Then run and make the cocoa. Bring it in for all of us just the same, but we won't say a word. I wish I hadn't to lose my pretty little home, but oh, Franny, I feel quiet delightfully excited.'

'Funny Mama.' Frances had laughed and in a rare moment of affection, or at least a rare demonstration of it, stooped and dropped a kiss on Myrtle's curly hair.

Of course Gregory made the same suggestion the next day but Myrtle wasn't to be moved; and of course he needed no prompting that Betsy's place was with him. It goes without saying that she needed no persuading.

All seemed set fair.

It was at 11 o'clock on the morning of the wedding that Myrtle heard the tolling of a single bell at St Stephen's. She was almost ready; any second Ella's carriage would be arriving, and in Frances's room she could hear bride and bridesmaid talking as they helped each other with their finery.

'Betsy, listen!' She hurried down the stairs and into the dining-room where Betsy was putting the finishing touches to the table. ('Fancy Master Greg's wedding and all of us having to stand up to eat. No room round the table

181

to sit, but it doesn't seem the thing at all to stand and hold a plate. Don't know what the old gentleman would have made of things today.') Betsy's thoughts were pulled up short as Myrtle came in. 'Betsy, it's a funeral bell. Fancy Franny having to follow a coffin up the aisle. It must be old Mister Duke from the farm; he passed away at the weekend. But to be buried today of all days. Why they'll hardly have him under the ground when we get to the church. Is it an omen do you suppose?' She held up crossed fingers of both hands. 'Wicked to be superstitious I know, but today should be full of joy. A funeral casts a shadow.'

'What rubbish the girl does talk.' Not like Betsy to be so familiar, something in the sight of Myrtle ('Bride's mother indeed! She looks no more than a child herself with her fingers crossed and those great eyes looking at me') made her forget herself. 'Omen indeed! Only thing that bell prophesises is that I'm going to be late for the church if I don't get a move on. Now then, everything's set out and ready except for the food and Mrs Ghrimes will be here in half an hour to see to all that while we're away. My, but you look nice, Mrs Ratcliffe, m'um; that hat fair sets you off a treat.'

So the omen was forgotten, Myrtle uncrossed her fingers and old Mr Duke, who'd farmed some sixty acres including cowslip meadow on the far bank of the river, was laid to rest. The tolling of the bell may not have been a sign of bad tidings for the happy pair but his death did indeed pull another thread into the pattern.

'Pa and Dickie are going to put all the furniture in the attic so that Auntie can have her own things in her bedroom, and we're having a shift round in the parlour too.' Gina chattered as she buttered the crumpets for their tea, assuming Leighton would be interested and not noticing his lack of response. 'Dickie's very put out about it all, Ma's things to be stored out of the way like that, but of course Auntie wants to bring all she can of her home. She has some lovely pieces. It's going to be far cosier; the sofa is in the kitchen now and one of the easy chairs. The only thing left in the parlour is the piano, even the rugs have been put in bedrooms. Do you want jam with your crumpets or cheese?' No answer. 'Leighton, jam or cheese?'

'Oh sorry. Anything you like. Listen Gina, I must talk to you.'

'Well? Here I am.' She laughed, so sure of herself, so certain of what he was going to say. She was free. No longer was she to be tied to caring for the family. All the months she'd watched Frances's preparations she'd been coming so often to see Leighton. The hours she's spent here had been the only hours that counted, and all the while she'd been frightened to look to the future. A vague 'one day' was at the back of her mind but what hope had she had of seeing a sight of it becoming reality? She'd tried to be patient, taken what happiness she could. Coming here to his rooms, she'd cooked for him, ironed his shirts, willingly let him make love to her when he'd wanted. Even to herself she'd not openly admitted her afternoons had fallen short of perfect, never for a moment had she hinted that anything was spoilt by the way he turned the key in the lock first or that to lie on top of his bed with her skirt and petticoat around her waist while he clambered on to her clothed except for his trousers wasn't what she'd expected of love. Even today, now that she was free and all their future was before them, he'd steered her to the bedroom just as if nothing had changed. When they were married things would be different; she'd thought it this afternoon just as she had so often lying passively as he

183

moved to a quick climax. Had she been able to read his mind as he'd rolled off her and lay panting by her side she might have lost some of her confidence. A few months ago when he'd first taken her to his bed he must have found her exciting, but 'about as thrilling as posting a letter' was the thought that had come unprompted today.

Still, she knew none of that and she turned to hear what he wanted to say, her huge blue eyes wide with anticipation, her answer ready.

'Gina, I've taken a post. I'm giving up these rooms when I leave college at Christmas and in the New Year I'm starting teaching.'

He was to have a salary, a teacher's wage would be enough to marry on. She waited, not interrupting him.

'It's in London. Someone at the college put me on to it, a friend who'd been studying the 'cello and who's father has a school.'

'London. . . .'

'Yes. I've been to see him, twice actually. You remember, I told you I was going to London.

'Playing, you said.'

'Well yes, I did. Didn't know if it would come off, you see, wanted to be sure before I told anyone. Well, I heard a few days ago. I've been putting off telling you all the week. Silly really . . .,' he hesitated, 'I mean, we both knew I'd soon be gone.'

She groped in her mind for something to say.

'. . . thought you were going to be a concert pianist.'

'Damn it all, I have to live, I have to eat. Dreams won't keep me. Mr Brindley has given me a bedsitting room with a piano, so I've every opportunity for practising. Decent sort of chap he seems.'

'You'll live in?' Of course, not for long, in her mind she heard his answer; only for as long as it takes me to find somewhere for us.

184

'Yes, no problem there. Really I've been extremely lucky.'

The butter on the crumpets had melted and cooled in a greasy yellow pool on the dish, no steam rose invitingly from the long poured tea. She couldn't look at him, she was frightened to trust her voice and the happy familiarity of the room was more than she could bear.

'What is it, Gina? Aren't you pleased for me? Tell the truth – and I wouldn't say this to everyone – as my last months at the college went by I was frightened to look to the future. Easy to talk grandly about being a concert pianist in the early days, but doing's not the same as talking. A piano isn't an easy instrument to earn a living with; no falling back on a place in an orchestra and until one's made one's mark concert engagements are hard to come by.'

'Yes of course I'm pleased for you.' Her voice surprised her; so calm, no sign that her breath felt trapped at the base of her tight throat. 'Leighton, I'm going to leave you to eat your tea; we've been talking and its got late. I promised Auntie I'd come home on the 5 o'clock 'bus so that I could help her sort her things,' she lied.

He looked at the small table, their meal set prettily, intimately, just as she always did it. Had he been rough with her, blurting it out like that?

'I'll come with you to the Square.'

'Of course you won't. You eat your tea.' She was already in his bedroom putting on her hat and coat, the atmosphere there stamping itself on her mind as if it would be there for ever. His brushes on the top of the chest, a tie hanging over the iron rail of the bedstead, a jacket on the back of his bedside chair. She didn't want to look; she was frightened to see the small intimate trappings of his life that had become part of what suddenly seemed no more than a glimpse into a promised

185

land. Can't live on dreams, he'd said. But that's what she'd been doing. She turned full circle, whether she wanted to or not her eyes devoured every detail. Then, shoulders straight (no doubt they were straight, consciously she held herself erect) she went back to the living-room.

'Gina,' he was watching her closely, 'you never expected things would be different, did you? We've had good times, but we knew I'd nearly finished at the college. . . .'

'I was just surprised you'd taken a teaching post. Look Leighton, I must hurry. Do eat your tea before it spoils.' And without another glance she was gone, to her credit her head high. He didn't need to be told what he'd done to her though; yet there was no anger in her, no ugliness. That may even be why he'd lost interest so soon; he'd found no light and shade, no heights and depths. The shame he felt as he heard her steps taking her up the short flight to the pavement outside was a rare thing.

She'd never felt so utterly alone. She travelled home, passed up her fare and took the halfpenny change, got off opposite the shop in the High Street, but she couldn't remember a thing of the journey. Then reality struck her. She couldn't go home, walk through the shop, up the stairs to the kitchen. Back to prison. She could see the upstairs rooms were in darkness but standing out there in the shadows she could picture it all, knew just where to put her hand on the matches to light the gas. The fire would need raking, supper had to be cooked. No, she couldn't, not yet. 'Please help me. I thought – you know what I thought. . . .'

Escape had seemed so near. She didn't want to think, she didn't want to look back, or forward either. The gears of the 'bus grated noisily and with a jolt it started on its way up the High Street to the Market Place; in the light of the gas lamp she saw the few remaining passengers rock in their seats. Then it was gone and she was alone in the street she'd known all her life, familiarity the reason she seldom really saw it at all. Tonight she did though. Her senses were sharpened, the early evening air carried a faint smell of smoke from the chimneys, each shop cast its separate pool of light across the pavement, some no more than a narrow shaft through the glass of the door, some with gas burners lit in their windows. She moved back from the street lamp into the shadows and looked along the High Street. Hopkins the outfitters with its windows crowded from top to bottom with hats, gloves, blouses, even underwear and elastic stockings; Booths the butcher next door with a row of legs of mutton and three whole pigs outside. Further down was Watson's grindery, with its sythes, riphooks, knives of all sizes packed in such tight rows one could hardly see into the dimly lit shop behind. Her father was standing on a chair now reaching into his window to light the gas; instinctively she pulled back further from the lamp.

'You never expected things would be different?' the question echoed. 'Of course I did, of course I did,' silently she screamed at him now. 'Did you think I'd do all that if I didn't love you, if you didn't love me? But you didn't. It was just a game – game? Dream? Now there's nothing, just nothing. Auntie's coming.' A sob caught in her throat as blindly she turned and, head down, hurried along the street. 'I was so pleased, so excited. You didn't seem to listen when I told you – and why should you? I thought it mattered that we were turning the furniture around, I thought you'd be interested. No wonder you weren't! London, a new life. As if it matters that we put the sofa in the kitchen!' A sob rose in her throat.

By this time she'd turned into Bridge Street away from the shops. There was no one about, the single lamp on the centre of the bridge parapet casting a stream of golden light on the water. Strange that she too should come here, just as Frances had after she'd left Leighton. There was no Gregory for Gina though.

She knew the path so well that even in the dark she could find her way to the towpath and there only yards from the bridge put out her hand to feel for the iron bench. The night wrapped itself around her, seeming to hold her suspended between a past she didn't want to think of and a future she couldn't face. The only sound was the gentle lapping of the water, hardly a sound at all.

Then something else! Everything, even Leighton was pushed out of her mind. There was a movement, someone walking uncertainly towards her. She sat rooted to her seat, so near the road yet the friendly lights of town seemed a million miles away.

Chapter Eight

'Sophie? Is that you, Sophie?'

The voice did something to allay Gina's fears, enough that she got up and moved as fast as she could towards the bridge.

'Sophie?'

'No. No, it's not.'

'Sorry, Miss, I just saw a movement. I didn't mean to frighten anyone. I'm looking for my sister.'

'I've not seen anyone,' she was still backing away towards the road; 'there's been no one here by the river.'

'She'll have gone to town, to market I dare say. Not so much as a wrap around her shoulders on an evening like this!'

By this time Gina had reached the safety of Bridge Street and the stranger was coming up the slope from the towpath.

'We've not been here many days you see. We're at Littlemore Farm. I took the cut across the footbridge yonder but I didn't expect Sophie would be in the dark. Perhaps you knew my uncle did you, old Mr Duke?'

'No, that is, I knew him by sight. I live in the High Street.'

189

'Then, if you're going home would you do me a kindness? Would you keep your eyes open for Sophie? If you find her could you bring her back along the road to the corner here. She's no place to be abroad at night on her own. I'll go t'otherway, up to market. Likely that's where she is. It's the lights, all the noise and bustle. . . .'

She peered closely at him as they came towards the end of Bridge Street and the lights of High Street gave them their first view of each other. At least thirty-five she guessed, one would hardly expect him to have an infant sister. Not a tall man, but there was a strength about him. His clothes were rough, the dark suit probably grey, she imagined, old and out of shape, but no doubt he'd come from working on the farm. The striped flannel shirt had no collar to grace it, not so much as a handkerchief tied around his neck and, like his cap, had long since known better days.

'I'll look for her but tell me what she's like. How big is she? How old?'

' 'bout my height, bit taller'n you I'd say, well built. Got her hair in a plait, you wont miss her. Not really a child, poor lass, not in years. You see, Miss,' she found herself avoiding his eyes as he spoke, recognising his concern and knowing how he hated to have to say what he did, 'she needs to have an eye to her. She's a touch fey if you understand me. Cares for me, looks after the home, but, well, she's not quite like the rest of us. . . .'

'I'll help you find her. I'll go to the left, you try the right and we'll come back to this corner. One of us will find her, you'll see. Oh, what's your name? If I'm to get her to come with me I must say who sent me.'

'Beg pardon. I should ha' said. My name's George Sullivan, but Sophie allus calls me Gee. Just say Gee asked you to look, she'll come with you right enough.'

As they looked both ways along the High Street and

could see no sign of Sophie she said: 'You keep her wrap with you. I only live at Number 18; if I find her I'll take her indoors and get something of mine to keep her warm.' So they parted.

It wouldn't be true to say her spirits had revived. Later the truth would hit her, later the utter emptiness of her outlook would fill her mind. She knew it, even now looking searchingly at each person she passed she knew it was like a dark chasm waiting to engulf her. Sophie was taking her through these minutes, minutes that would add to an hour. Then would come the next hour. She must concentrate all her attention on something else. That was the way to build a life again, one hour at a time. No memories; she couldn't bear to remember. Little by little she'd show them all she hadn't cared, she'd let him see – but she wouldn't. He wouldn't be here to see. Sophie, poor fey Sophie, she must have come along the dark lane to town drawn by the lights. 'And I think I've got miseries! What about her? What about him?'

There was no doubt it was Sophie. Not only was she the only person on the streets without a coat and the only adult with he hair in a long pigtail (a loose and untidy one at that), there was something about her that set her apart. She might have been any age, a sixteen-year-old over-developed with what was called puppy fat or a thirty-year-old with the innocence of childhood still with her. When Gina noticed her she was standing on the opposite side of the road in the shadows between two lamps, gazing across at the window of the pawnbroker's shop. Such an array of bric-a-brac was on display and behind it a large gilt framed mirror catching the reflection of the gaslight that hung from the ceiling. It seemed to hypnotise her.

'Sophie?' Gina crossed the road to her.

191

The unblinking stare didn't alter; it was evident she'd not heard her name.

'Sophie.' This time a light touch on her arm.

Far from being disturbed that a complete stranger should know her, Sophie looked for a second at Gina then beamed with pleasure.

'I met Gee. He's looking for you with a coat. You must be so cold.'

'Cold.' The woman, for looking closer Gina could see she was no child, rubber her arms, 'Ah, 'tis cold. Pretty, the shops, they're pretty. See the lights.'

'Yes, very pretty.' Slipping her hand through the older girl's arm Gina steered her towards Number 18. 'Is that why you came, to see the shops.?'

'Dark at home. We got no proper lights. Used to have lights where we were afore. Gee says it'll soon be all bright, Gee's going to see to it. Dark though. Don't like the dark.'

'Gee is meeting us at the corner but first come to where I live and I'll lend you a wrap.'

To Sophie it appeared to be the most usual thing in the world for a stranger to accost her and take her home.

Word travels fast in small places, so when they went in to the shop and Richard came from his back room he showed no surprise that the girl recently come to the farm should need befriending.

'Come and warm yourself by my fire while Gina gets you a coat.' He led her to his workroom. 'No panic for tea, Gina; best you see her right home.' Then to Sophie: 'You're new to these parts yet; we don't want you to miss your path in the dark. Young Gina knows the way well enough.'

Sophie beamed again, from one to the other and Gina left them to go and fetch the wrap.

'Nice. She's nice. Pretty,' Sophie pronounced.

Whether she spoke to herself or expected an answer wasn't clear, but thinking it might be her idea of conversation he replied: 'Ah, she's that. A good girl is Gina.'

At the sound of his voice she looked at him in surprise. Apparently an answer hadn't been expected. She must have approved of what she saw for again she smiled.

A minute later he stood in the porch and watched them disappear towards Bridge Street. Side by side they walked, then Sophie took hold of Gina's hand; not as a child might, but positively, holding it firmly and turning her head so that she watched her new friend as they went.

The next afternoon Gina told her story to Frances. By then her story was Leighton, he was all that mattered, and with his going her life would be even emptier than it had been before he'd played such a part in it.

Frances should have thought. She ought to have realised the hurt that Gina's matter-of-fact tone disguised. But Frances was no angel: only weeks into marriage she was remote from everything but the mysterious beauty of this new existence shared with Greg.

'I shall miss him, Franny,' Gina heard the words, almost as if someone else spoke them. The voice sounded small.

'You'll have to spend more time with me, Gina, and of course you've got mother coming so soon now.'

Gina nodded. What voice she'd had had disappeared.

Frances had been putting some letters and papers away in the bureau when Gina had arrived and now she picked up a concert programme and looked at it.

'The Albert Hall! Did I tell you we went to a concert there, Gina? It was all so grand. London is so bustling; that's the difference – and the underground trains, you should see them, even the way they rock you about is exciting. Here we always know what we shall see around each corner, but in London there are so many people, such a clatter. It was wonderful – and Greg knows his way about, knows just where to go –'

'He'll find it exciting – Leighton I mean – he'll soon get to know it all just like Greg does. He'll find it different from dull old Tarnmouth, make lots of friends. . . .'

'And so must you, Gina. You wont miss him nearly as much as you think.' She laughed as she went on: 'It seems a lifetime ago when I used to see him so much. I imagined I was in love with him at one time you know. When – well, never mind what happened – but after I broke away from him I was amazed. I didn't miss him one scrap. I missed going out, I suppose, but not him, not as a person. Yet I'd been sure I was in love. Greg knew; he said I wasn't. Greg said –'

'I've been to bed with him,' Gina's chin was high, 'not once, lots of times. I didn't just think I was in love with him. He's all there is, Fran. . . .' She clenched her teeth hard together.

'No, he's not, Gina.' How narrow Gina's shoulders were, Fran thought as she put her arm around her. 'One day there'll be someone worth your loving. If he were that do you think he'd take everything and walk away. He ought to be whipped – I'd do it!'

'He didn't take anything, nothing that wasn't his to take.' Her voice might still be small but Gina had found her dignity. Between the two girls the shadow of Leighton was driving a wedge.

They could hear Betsy coming up the stairs from the kitchen and Frances moved to open the door for her. It must be tea-time.

'There's a good girl; my hands are full with the tray. Now Miss Gina, you're ready for a nice cup of tea I

194

know, and I brought some cherry cake. Feels like old times making Master Greg his cherry cake again.'

'It looks lovely, Betsy. You've settled in, have you?'

'My word yes. Such a room I've got and a sitting-room of my own downstairs too. 'fore you take your leave just you pop down and see me; let me show you how well set up I am.'

'I will; I'd love to see,' and despite her own problems she meant it.

As the girls drank their tea and each ate a slice of Betsy's cherry cake (no bread and butter first, for tea was no more than a 'bite to keep you going' as Betsy called it, busying herself with something substantial for the evening when Greg came home) she found herself telling Frances about the Sullivans.

What Gina had said about Leighton and Frances's criticism of him spoiled their old easy relationship. Neither wanted to pick up the conversation where they'd left it. Gratefully they bridged the divide with Gee and Sophie.

Dusk fell early and by the time Gina went down to see Betsy on her way out it was nearly dark.

'I'll not come,' Frances had said; 'let her show you on her own.' Whether she stayed upstairs entirely for Betsy's sake Gina wasn't sure. She wished she could live the afternoon again and play it differently.

No doubt of the pride Betsy had in her sitting-room and it wasn't to be wondered at. Greg and Frances had helped her furnish it every bit as carefully as their own. The mahogany sideboard and chairs were a gleaming proof of her pleasure in her new state, the surround of the overmantle mirror with its side shelves bearing the small treasures she'd accumulated over the years; no less than three rugs were spread on the linoleum, the whatnot in the corner had belonged to Myrtle, the brass fender too had come from her parlour at Mallard Cottage, adding a sparkle of elegance. Only the horsehair sofa had been her own in the kitchen in Duck Island Lane and, somehow, it made the room more homely.

'Betsy, now it's all arranged how snug you are!'

'Ah, that I am, I wanted you to see it. But 'tis more than the trappings, it's that they've bothered to make it for me. I'd be happy enough to be with them if we had to make do with old orange boxes and that's the truth, but all they've done for me – well, I tell you, Miss Gina, I thank my Maker each day, that I do.'

'It's no more than you deserve, Betsy – you've been like family almost as long as I can remember.'

'Even so, I'm mindful it could have been a different story. It's being wanted, having people you love to care for, that's the hub it all turns on.'

Gina's voice had dried again, so in answer she dropped a kiss on Betsy's rounded cheek.

'Careful how you go now. It's a dark night for a girl out alone,' was Betsy's parting remark and the echo of it went with Gina as she made her solitary way home.

'Gina,' Richard called up the stairs a couple of days later, 'here's Miss Sullivan from the farm called to see you.'

Childish Sophie may have been but she'd remembered well enough the shop on the High Street and the gentle girl who'd led her back to Gee.

Then the next time the clanging shop bell announced her arrival there were customers and Richard told her: 'You nip straight up, you'll find Gina there.'

What they could have in common he couldn't imagine, but perhaps the truth was that her open adulation was balm to Gina's hurt in much the way that her own had been for Leighton when he'd lost Frances. Then too

Frances seemed remote these days. Was it marriage, was it Leighton or was it only fancy that she'd grown away? Sophie was filling a niche where under other circumstances there would have been none to fill.

'I like ironing, let me do it for you,' she'd say, or 'Let me shine those windows, I enjoy doing that.' Always she was ready with a smile, grateful for any kindness shown her.

When Gina would say: 'Time for you to go,' she never argued but just for a second fear would cast a shadow.

'Walk the lane with me, Gina; you'll walk the lane, won't you?'

So Gina would go with her, see her safely along the dark lane and into the farm kitchen with the lamp lit. But there was never any sign of Gee.

Then came the day that Myrtle's furniture was brought from Mallard Cottage and for the last time she closed the door on the home she'd loved. It was something she had to do alone. Even though Betsy had already moved to Matlock Avenue each day she came back to spend an hour or two helping Myrtle prepare for her move.

'I'll come for you, Myrtle, help you lock up. Escort you here in style, eh?' Richard had said.

'No, you be here waiting. I'd rather take my last walk round my little home by myself. Franny said she'd come, but no, I want to say my goodbye on my own.'

So many memories and, looking back, she remembered what was good, imagined that was how it had always been. She wiped her tears as she looked her last at each room, but it was the drawing-room that hurt most. How she'd loved it, the first room she'd ever truly been able to make her own. Now it was gone and what had she? A refuge given her in her brother-in-law's house, she who been looked on as the 'comfortable' one of the family. Often she'd pitied Cynny the drudgery of those rooms above the shop, but now she was glad enough to find

197

shelter there. The tears spilled as she considered her miserable plight. There was Frances so besotted with Gregory and her grand new life, what did she care for her poor mother? At least Gina would be glad to have her, no doubt of that. (She turned her thoughts away from Dickie, less certain there.) And Richard, she was sure of his welcome. She dabbed at her wet cheeks, then with one last look round the little hallway she went out into the winter afternoon. The cobbled pavement of Duck Island Lane had already taken on a different feeling; no longer did it mean home.

As she rounded the bend into High Street she saw he was waiting on the step, watching for her, eager to hurry to meet her. Dear Richard. Her pace quickened, almost she ran. Then he was by her side, her elbow firmly in his hand. It was early-closing day in Highworth so, free from the shop, he'd busied himself arranging her pieces of furniture that had come on the carter's truck, putting them in position as she'd decided.

Myrtle had never made enemies yet when on that first day she found Sophie in the kitchen with Gina she sensed the hostility. She couldn't have said how she knew for Sophie hardly said a word but occasionally Myrtle would glance at her catching her off her guard and read the expression.

When dusk fell as always Sophie asked that Gina would walk the lane with her and it wasn't until they reached the farmyard and could see the lamp had been lit in the kitchen ready for her that she said: 'She's there now; she won't want me. You come here and see me. Please Gina. Can we go to market like we did last week? Gee don't let me go on my own. You'd look to the shopping with me, wouldn't you? Please Gina.'

Gee had learnt from bitter experience what happened when Sophie shopped alone, filling her basket with fruit and sweetmeats, coloured ribbons and baubles, forgetting that meat and fish made up the most essential part of their daily diet. Until last week, when Gina had taken her, it had been his job. Sophie had accepted his ruling; in her mind all he did was right so she'd sat patiently in the cart and watched as he'd bought each week's food. Now she tightened her grip on Gina's arm and pleaded: 'Gee'll let me do it if you help me.'

'Yes, I'll go with you. I'll call for you just after dinner tomorrow. You tell him.'

So she went home and she didn't see Gee. But he saw her. From the shadow of the barn he watched her silhouetted in the kitchen doorway. He noticed how Sophie put out a hand to touch her as she said goodbye, touch her as a dog might pat one with a paw trying to hold one's attention. He understood. He thrust his own hands deep into the pockets of his old trousers, letting his eyes take in every line of her, every movement. Poor Sophie was less worldly than most, everyone who knew her recognised it, but she and Gee had much in common.

In the new gown she'd made especially to wear at Christmas Myrtle was as lovely as any girl. Not a line spoiled her soft skin, not a single thread of blood marred the whites of her eyes nor grey a hair on her head.

The family all went to St Stephen's on Christmas morning, Myrtle with Richard, Gina and Dickie, while Frances now sat further forward with Greg, sharing their pew with Dr and Mrs Saunders. Together they raised their voices to Salute the happy morn and after the service made a slow progress down the crowded aisle to the south door. Only with an effort did Frances hold her face into the subdued expression she thought was expected, for inside her she was beaming with happiness and pride.

From the well-to-do of Matley Heights to the humblest inhabitant of Roebury Buildings, the tenement block no more than a slum, Greg acknowledged greetings from them all. As they jostled their way towards the overcast winter morning she couldn't see him for he walked to her left and just behind, but she was aware of him in every nerve in her body. The sermon had been long, commanding them to love God with humility. Far from humble was Frances; but her pride wasn't for herself. Or was it? Because he wanted her? She loved him so much. As they were squashed closer into the throng that pushed towards the grey daylight she turned to look at him. If the vicar's words were to be believed what love and humility were in her may have been misdirected, but if God is Love then what she felt must surely have held something of Him. From a pew where Greg's one-time neighbours from Matley Heights were easing their way into the crowded aisle came a 'Merry Christmas, Smart,' but this time Greg didn't notice. Frances felt the pressure of his hand on her shoulder. She read a message in his light blue eyes; her tummy played tricks with her, tying itself into a knot just as it always had when something was almost more than she could bear. She turned her head away from him, the moment was too precious. His hold on her shoulder tightened and her humility was real as, silently, she said: 'Thank you'. Just a brief incident but etched on her mind for ever. Long ago there had been another, standing at the graveside where Cynny had been lowered. It was the same now, as if the clouds had parted and she'd glimpsed something beyond. This time though it wasn't just she who felt it, his hold on her told her.

Outside the family greeted each other with such gusto one might find it hard to believe they saw each other most days. But then, this was Christmas, the occasion merited special salutations before they moved towards the gate.

On a grave in the shadow of the far wall was a wreath of holly and ivy. Myrtle had made it, Richard had laid it there when they'd come to church last Sunday. Today as they moved off towards the street, the peel of Christmas bells ringing them on their way, was there one of them whose thoughts were with the woman who'd been the hub of so many of their Christmasses? Yes, just one; but his thoughts were tinged with resentment. Not against her, against his father.

'Look at him, arming her along as if she were made of Dresden china. Never fawned over Ma like it. Bet he never gives her a thought, poor old Ma. And look at her, what does she think she is, looking up at him like some silly doe-eyed kid. No fool like an old fool they say. Just wait till I tell 'em!'

The pavement was narrow, they walked in pairs. Richard and Myrtle led the way, he in his best overcoat with its velvet lapels, bowler hat, a new stiff wing collar and thin black tie; she in a dull pink coat with a fur cape around her shoulders and a fur hat the crowning glory to her lovely tawny hair. Following them were Frances and Gregory, the memory of that moment of nearness still with them. Not that they gave any sign of it, not for a second did she 'look up at him like some silly doe-eyed kid'. She held his arm lightly, looking back over her shoulder to talk to Gina, giving no hint of the bubbling joy that filled her. Greg glanced sideways at her, his beautiful Fran. Always to him she was that, but today she was beautiful by any standard. Her glossy straight hair was worn high on her head and this morning covered by a creation of Madame Zeigler's. Seldom had Frances gone to such lengths over a mere hat but she'd done it as a recognition of this, her first Christmas with Greg. Strange when one considers that he of all people would have found her perfect even in rags! The occasion had to be marked with something special and her rust-brown velvet coat had been left with the milliner so that the wide brimmed cream velour hat could be decorated with the exact colour. A trick of the light or were her eyes really the same shade?

Greg wasn't wearing anything new but then he was always so handsome, she thought, his shoes gleamed, the cape sleeves of his coat swung as he walked, the modern flat crown of his bowler was the very latest thing in fashion and yet he wore it with such ease. Indeed, he looked the perfect picture of a successful young man. He was watching her, she could feel it, and for a second her gaze met his. It really was an effort to concentrate on what Gina was saying.

'. . . used to come with you. It seemed strange without Betsy.'

Fran tightened her hold on Greg's arm, just to let him know she'd read and answered his silent message, as she replied: 'She wouldn't listen to us; we tried to persuade her to come. She wanted the morning to see to dinner, she said; everything has to be perfect. You know Betsy!'

'We suggested getting up early to help her but she wouldn't hear of it, would she Fran? "What?" Greg mimicked, "have you cluttering up my kitchen. No thank you"'.

'She went at 7 o'clock. She assured us that the Good Lord could be served better by her seeing his flock were fed than sitting for forty minutes or more listening to Reverend Carter,' Frances laughed, then in a voice unmistakably Betsy's went on: '"Enjoys his own voice, that one. Give me the 7 o'clock, something 'twixt me and my Maker, that's what I go for"'.

'Tut, tut,' Myrtle turned her head now and joined in the conversation, 'naughty of her to speak so of poor Reverend Carter. I'm sure he means well. It's just that he doesn't understand the jobs there are to do on Christmas morning.'

Certainly it seemed Betsy's time had been well spent. The goose was the work of a master, tender and succulent, the vegetables and sauce perfect. The pudding crumbled under Frances's spoon in a way that woud have rejoiced Mrs Beeton's heart.

They sat together around the large dining table, seven of them in all, for Betsy was there too.

'Oh no, Mrs Greg,' she'd argued, 'and this your first family Christmas in your own home. I'm very comfy downstairs, you know I am.'

'What rubbish you do talk.' As long as she'd known Betsy it had been 'Franny' but now it was 'Mrs Greg' and nothing would change it. 'You've always come with us for Christmas dinner to the shop.'

' 'tis different now. Whatever would old Mr Smart say if he could see me at table with the family?'

'He'd say "and quite right too",' Greg had come in as they were talking. 'Of course you'll eat with us. Why Betsy, it's Christmas, it's a party.'

'Oh, bless the boy! If you say so then I will.'

The gentle clatter of cutlery and china, the hum of voices; goodwill spread itself among them as the meal was despatched. It wasn't until Greg got up to fetch a bottle of port from the sideboard and Frances said: 'My, but aren't we doing things well! This is where I should suggest the ladies retire to the drawing-room. But I won't, I'll say, come on Gina, let's you and me give Betsy a hand,' that Dickie's voice cut in. At his tone they all turned to him, realising that what he said needed their attention.

'Before you go I want to tell you something. This is a good chance, everyone here together.' They waited. 'I'm leaving Parnell's, leaving Highworth. A mate of mine,

203

Eric Viner, and me, we're going to set up on our own. He comes from near Dover and we've got a place to rent over his way.'

'Set up on your own! What do you mean, set up on your own?' Richard looked at his son as if he'd suddenly grown two heads.

'Printing. We've taken an empty shop with rooms over. And why not? We know our trade. We've both got what we've saved, not that that's enough, but we're borrowing the cash for the press from Eric's father. He's in business, not just in a small way' (was that meant to cut?) 'he's done well, has four or five shops in the area and he's willing to invest in us.'

'Did it not occur to you to discuss your plans with your family?'

Betsy began to stack the plates, she wanted to escape downstairs. Not like Dickie to look so defiant, to speak meaning to hurt; not like his Pa to sound like some dictatorial parent of an earlier age.

'But, Dickie . . . ,' Myrtle started, her words dying on her lips at the look he turned in her direction.

No, Mrs Ratcliffe, m'am; can't you see what's amiss? Keep out of it, do. Out of it! You're in it up to your neck. But Betsy knew when to keep her thoughts to herself.

'I'm not a kid, Pa,' Dickie took a gulp of port, then went on: 'You didn't discuss your arrangements when you turned the home upside down – and you can't pretend it'll make any difference if I go, save to Gina maybe. You'll not be sorry not to have to get me my breakfast early of a morning eh, sis? Won't break your heart I bet on cold mornings.'

'You were doing so well at Parnell's, Dickie,' Myrtle tried again. 'A nice young lady, that's what you ought to have. . . .'

His expression spoke more clearly than any words.

'Get glasses for us as well, Greg. Let's all drink a toast to Dickie's venture.' Frances felt the tension, she knew they were on the edge of a precipice and so easily things might be said that coud never be wiped out. In a flash of insight she understood just how Dickie resented that his home – Cynny's home – had been altered to suit Myrtle. She was young, of course she could feel with him the urge to stand on his own feet, but it shouldn't have to be like this, not with spite.

If Frances saw his reasons it was obvious Myrtle didn't. She honestly had no idea that she was the cause of the rift between Dickie and his father. The home over the shop was more comfortable than it had been for years – 'ever' prodded a voice at the back of her mind only to be firmly disregarded, for whatever it had lacked in trappings in dear Cynny's time had been more than made up for by the spirit she brought to it. Really this was too bad of Dickie. Poor Richard looked quite unlike himself. If the silly boy wanted to throw up his job he should have talked about it to his father first, not treated him like this in front of all of them.

'Thank you, dear,' to Greg as he poured her port, and when Frances raised a glass to Dickie, Myrtle joined in the good wishes, her gentle smile no mirror to her thoughts.

The spirit of goodwill had spent itself. Despite the dull day the four young people went for a walk in the afternoon, Betsy stayed downstairs in her own room and Richard and Myrtle sat alone in front of the drawing-room fire.

'Try not to worry,' she laid her head on his arm. 'Likely enough he was showing off a scrap in front of the others, telling you like that. When he talks things over properly you may find his plans are well laid.'

'It's not just that. . . .'

'Then what? His home is comfortable. I suppose he wants to feel he's his own man, one forgets they grow up. And they forget parents have feelings. Naughty boy, to treat you like it.'

'Bless you, Myrtle. I don't know what I'd do without you.'

They'd been friends for more than half her life, yet suddenly she felt she saw him anew. But was it so new? Hadn't she known for a long time something was slumbering at the back of her mind only waiting for the right moment to wake? How silly to feel like this. Shy? Frightened? A little of both, but most of all wildly excited.

If Dickie had thought the look she gave his father after church was 'like some silly kid' it's as well he couldn't see her now, her eyes clear and shining, her lips parted.

'Myrtle.' He took her hand in both of his and felt her fingers clinging to him. 'My darling girl.' The soft hand was raised to his lips. Then she was only inches from him, his grip hard on her shoulders.

'Richard.'

He could feel the warmth of her breath, she was only inches from him as she whispered his name.

'Darling girl, my precious flower.' His arms were strong, the moment was theirs and neither of them fought what was happening to them.

Then just as suddenly she pulled away, not able to look at him.

'No, Richard. No. We musn't. How can I live in your home – ? Don't you see?'

He was breathing heavily but not touching her now, leaning back against the arm of the sofa.

'Richard . . .?'

He nodded. 'You're right, I know you're right. Just once I must say it. Myrtle, I love you.' As he said the

206

words he looked directly at her, raising her chin and willing her to meet his gaze.

'Darling Richard.' Gently her fingers caressed his cheek. 'Just once I'll be honest too. I love you, Richard. Until now I don't think I knew what love meant. When I married I was hardly more than a child, I knew nothing, there was so much I hated. . . .' Then she went on: 'Now here I am not even young anymore. How people would laugh to see a woman of my years feeling like this. But now I know what love means, now I'm ready.'

Her great eyes looked trustingly into his, her hands were on his shoulders, and once again she was close in his arms. As a young man he'd fallen in love with Cynny, he'd loved her truly and devotedly. If she'd still been here Myrtle would have been no more than a sister who looked to him for help. But Cynny wasn't here and at twenty he'd never loved with the intensity that he did at fifty. The scent of Myrtle's lovely hair, her small soft body clinging to him, the echo of her words 'I love you . . . now I'm ready' put everything but her from his mind.

The walk did much to restore Dickie's good humour. He talked about his plans and, after all, they were all young, all in sympathy with his need to spread his wings.

When they came home they didn't go up the steps to the front door, but through the gate at the end of the back garden and to the back door leading down the passage to Betsy's room and the kitchen quarters. The walk made him feel better and leaving the others with Betsy he went up the basement stairs determined to be pleasant. He crossed the hall and opened the drawing-room door. The back of the sofa was towards him, neither Richard nor Myrtle heard him come. They hadn't yet lit the gas although daylight was fast fading and in the glow of the firelight they were aware only of each other.

As quietly as he'd come so Dickie went.

The next day he took the train to Dover. No one was at home to see him go and in his present mood he felt that was another proof of how little they cared. Boxing Day and the shop still closed, Richard and Myrtle had gone for a stroll saying they'd not be above an hour and Gina had been asked for tea at the farm. 'Always with that simple woman these days,' he thought; 'even Franny seems full of her own affairs and I suppose Gina's just glad to be out of this place. Wish she'd stayed home to see me off though.' He almost talked himself into believing they'd gone out purposely but the truth was he'd not said he was going so soon. 'Wouldn't have gone, not yet anyway, but I'm not staying here to watch Pa mooning over her. Silly damned old fool, here in Ma's home too. It isn't her home now; she'd not recognise it. Stuffed all her things in the attic, he has. Well, I'm beggared if I'll stay here and watch them canoodling. Her and her pretty ways. Serve her right if the old man put her in the club, damned if it wouldn't.' All this time he'd been stowing his few possessions into an old wicker grip of his mother's he'd found in the attic. That it was hers somehow helped him; he didn't want to take anything of Richard's. He supposed the photograph of Cynny packed carefully between his shirts was really his father's but he overlooked that. It was all he'd have of home.

The note he left was short, telling them that he'd gone, saying he would write when he was settled. With a grim pleasure he addressed the envelope to 'Pa and Gina' then left it on the kitchen table. Even that was different; the same old wooden table that Ma had kept scrubbed each day, but covered these days with Myrtle's deep pink chenille cloth, and the old kitchen curtains had been replaced by those from the cottage. The sofa brought out from the parlour (now known as the drawing-room!) had been transformed with cushions. Couldn't Pa see what she was doing? He'd taken her in out of charity and she behaved as though she did them a favour to alter everything; and the old man lapped it up. Well, let him!

He bit his lip as he clattered down the steep straight flight of stairs to the side door, his ungainly basket strapped and carried under his arm. The few pounds he'd saved were safely packed, his train fare and a shilling or two to spare in his pocket. Just for a moment he was frightened, didn't feel half the man he had with that glass of port in his hand yesterday. No turning back now – 'not that I would' – the sooner he left Highworth the better.

'I'll write,' he'd said in his note. Three times a day the postman cycled down the High Street with his bag of letters. Richard watched at first expectantly, but as the weeks went on with less hope. It was March before the promised letter came and for all it told them Dickie might not have waited so long. In truth he'd started to write more than once, then pictured his letter's arrival at the love nest his father must be making by this time and the words wouldn't flow.

So when finally he put pen to paper the missive was brief. It gave them his address, told 'Dear Pa and Gina' that trade had started to come in, but there was nothing of his life, no reference to the past and no mention of the future. Richard read it alone in the shop, puzzled and hurt.

When he handed it to Gina she gave it less than her full attention. Partly that was the fault of the few stark sentences but the truth was the suggestion that Gee Sullivan had made to her that morning pushed everything else into insignificance. When she'd finished reading it she held it out to Myrtle.

'Have you seen it yet?'

The first thing Myrtle noticed was that short though it was she'd been excluded. 'May I?' she asked Richard.

'Of course you're to read it, as if you need to ask.'

Her expression gave nothing away. Neither of them had any idea how furiously angry she was that Dickie could behave like it. She wasn't blind, she'd seen how often Richard had casually looked out of the kitchen window and up the High Street around half past seven each morning when Bill Stokes the postman made his first round, how he managed to be in the front shop when the 10 o'clock delivery was due and the same at 3 in the afternoon. Every envelope brought to him the look of hope she could hardly bare to see, for it was always followed by disappointment.

'Sounds to be settled,' he said now; 'trade come in, he says. Can drop him a line now, eh? Why don't you write Gina, he'd like that.'

'Would he? He didn't seem in any hurry for letters, nearly three months before he let us have an address. Still perhaps I will. I've news of my own to tell him. Pa, I've been offered a job – well not really a job – at the farm. Gee has asked me to go there as a sort of companion housekeeper, to run the house. Poor Sophie, she does her best but she does need help. And she likes me to be there.'

'And what sort of a life is that for you? Poor girl, try she may, but she's no companion for you. To go there each day – why you'd have no freedom, you'd not even be able to go to Franny's. Don't you rush into something you'll regret.'

'I'd be free to go where I like, he's made that very plain. And Pa, I wouldn't go each day; I'm to live there, take over running the house. He's out from morning until night, except for dinner of course. Sophie would like it. She shouldn't be on her own so much, she gets so nervous when the daylight goes, she –'

'Live there!' Myrtle interrupted. 'But Gina how can you think of living there? That would leave you father and me on our own. Whatever would peopole say? It's quite different all of us sharing a home together.'

'People say? Of you and Pa? Oh, Auntie that's ridiculous. As if anyone would give it a thought. You're our aunt. Whatever could anyone say?'

Myrtle felt the hot colour in her cheeks; she avoided Richard's eye. Ridiculous! So that's what Gina thought. Middle aged, beyond the interest of gossiping tongues.

It wasn't until later in the day when Gina had gone to tell Frances what she intended that Richard said: 'If she thinks no one will raise an eyebrow so much the better. And Myrtle, flower, whether Gina's in the house with us or not will make no difference. You know that, don't you? I'll not use you wrong; you'll always be safe here with me.'

'Dear Richard. Yes, I do know. If my conscience would let me do it I'd give him his freedom even after all these years. Dear knows I wish I had my own. But I can't. Marriage is until death and to have it dragged through the courts – it's too dreadful to imagine, all the beastliness resurrected. He's not kept faith, but I can't break vows because I want something else. Is that selfish of me? Ought I to put you – us – first?'

'I would we could, but my Myrtle is what she is and that's how I love her.' Gently he held her hand to his lips.

'We'll be very happy here, the two of us. Things we can't share, but plenty we can.' There had been much in marriage she'd hated, things she didn't want to remember even from this distance of time. It was as if her spirit was pulled in two directions, one wanting to be one with Richard while the other loved the intimacy of their days yet clung to the privacy and freedom she'd grown used to.

She was safe with Richard. It never occurred to her to doubt his word.

'But why do you have to live there? I would have thought you would have liked it now with Mama at the shop. You're pretty free these days. You can go there when you want without moving in surely?' Frances couldn't understand why Gina, who'd so hated her years of housekeeping at the shop, should want to tie herself to being a paid domestic.

'You're as bad as Pa! Don't you see, I'm to do just what I like there. Anyone would think I was going to be a scivvy. Not that that would be anything fresh, it's all I've been at home. Franny, I'm to turn the farmhouse into a home, arrange things how I want. There's no comfort there. Old Mr Duke was a queer old man, the house is full of heavy Victorian furniture, all good things mind you but quite out of place with those low ceilings and beams. All he ever lived in was the kitchen and it's the same now. He was very well off, you know, and he left everything to Gee.'

It was still the same, only the kitchen and their bedrooms used, and although poor Sophie did her best her skills went no further than seeing them fed – and that not appetisingly – scrubbing their clothes and cobbling the mending. As for Gee, he seemed not to notice; dingy or bright, dirty or clean, the house didn't bother him.

Why then had he begged her to come?

'You can have a free hand, get rid of anything you want to, replace it if you think it needs. I don't know anything about these things – but I'm not short of a pound, and I tell you it's up to you. Do anything you like if you'll say you'll come.'

Yes, she believed she could. It wasn't simply what he'd said. Yet he'd given no hint beyond those words. Could it be just for Sophie's sake he wanted her there? Her family may not have said so but she knew well enough that they considered him rough and uncouth.

Well, what if they did? They and their working-class respectability!

Now here was Frances, so pleased with herself in this ugly house, frowning in judgment over whether or not she ought to take up Gee's offer. Did she suppose that being married and having a home of her own gave her the right to give advice? Why, the farm could be a hundred times more attractive than this tall grey building with its basement and three stories above, half of it not even used. In her mind's eye Gina could see the old open hearths with log fires warming the rooms into life, herself the pivot on which everything turned. If somewhere in the picture was a Gee who bore little resemblance to the one she knew, one who was cared for and groomed, it was no more than a shadow and she hardly realised its existence.

So despite Fran's: 'Don't rush into it, you'll regret it. Heavens, you'll work harder there than at the shop and it's not even your own home', she smiled a secret smile and went her own way.

If sometimes during those months Leighton had thought of her and the hours he and Gina had spent together, it was to imagine her settled back into the life he'd temporarily helped her to escape. Things might have worked out very differently for her, the threads twisted to alter the pattern, if just once he'd written to her, but he didn't. Certainly he may have thought of her from time to time, but his new post and even more important to him his first public engagement early that year set his sight on the future. She was no more than a comfortable memory.

Frances could have changed Gina's fate too, if only she'd taken the trouble to see a little deeper, or even Myrtle. Couldn't any of them recognise her need? Love should breed love, yet the dazzle of it seemed to have blinded them both.

Chapter Nine

'I hear a motor stopping now; that must be Mr Greg home.'

As Betsy spoke Frances looked at the clock on the mantlepiece. Already it was half an hour after their usual dinner time and even if the children hadn't learnt to tell the time she knew from the petulant and argumentative tones from the playroom overhead that they were both hungry.

No rare thing in a doctor's life that he should be delayed, but Frances liked them to sit down to the table together. It was a rule that occasionally had to be broken for there are limits to how long children's hunger can be held at bay. On the days when they had to feed without him she'd say to Betsy: 'You three have yours, just keep mine back until Greg gets here.' But this wasn't to be one of those days. Today the five of them would eat in the breakfast-room together.

The household had grown in the five years since Greg and Frances had married, grown to the extent of Alexandra, by this time just four, and Matthew, nearly three. Then there was Daisy the living-in maid who worked under Betsy's rule. 'Like family' they'd always said of Betsy and now, with two children and another on the way, she held a unique position somewhere between housekeeper and nanny, with a hint of honorary grandparent thrown in. As we've seen at mid-day she ate with the family, just as she did at breakfast; then unless Frances had any special plans the rest of the day was her own to go out if she wanted but more likely to stay in her own room or 'see over Daisy', as she called it. In fact young Daisy had been taken under her wing, and altogether the house ran very smoothly.

Tea was Frances's special time. She didn't eat with the children at 5 o'clock but she always tried to be there, looking forward to it as much as they did. And how the old customs held! One plain slice first, then at least one with jam or potted meat before any cake or tinned fruit. It was unheard of for Greg to share these tea-time hours. Only on Sundays could he hope to be at home and Sundays had a flavour of their own.

Now Frances went to the window and watched as he climbed off his motor cycle then reached into the sidecar for his bag.

'Good, now we can eat. Will you tell Daisy we're ready, Betsy, while I get Alex and Matt.'

'They sound to be hungry.'

Frances laughed. 'They'll be better humoured when they've been stoked up.' Then, calling up the stairs: 'Come along, Daddy's home. Are your hands still clean?'

The answer was lost in the clatter as they hurtled out of the playroom racing each other to be first down.

In the five years Frances had subtly altered, not aged so much as developed. She'd had her two children with as little effort as she'd expected and four months into the next pregnancy anticipated nothing different this time. Energy and well being (oh, occasional bachache but she wasn't prepared to count that) culminating in two hours of the sort of agony that made her bite her lip until it bled

215

(she'd not have it said that she screamed!), then it was all over. Tall and long backed she carried her babies easily and regained her figure quickly. Two down, two to go, was the way she thought of it; one this year and fourth in about eighteen months or two years, say in the winter of 1914. Life hadn't been all domesticity and childbearing. Fit though she'd been, the idea hadn't occurred even to her that she might continue teaching at the school once she was pregnant. Reluctantly she'd asked them to find a replacement but Highworth still didn't aspire to a fiddle teacher apart from her. To appear in front of children in her condition would certainly not have been acceptable so sadly she'd given up the lessons even though a day never went by without her playing and she'd taken part in the quintet in Dr Russell's music room in Tarnmouth each Wednesday evening until a week before Alexandra's arrival, missing only four weeks before she and her fiddle were back amongst her friends. As one might expect Myrtle hadn't approved ('Oh dear, Richard, what's the world coming to with the young people? Flaunting herself in her state. It's not seemly, it's time she learnt to keep herself to herself.')

She hadn't agreed to go back to Warwick House again, for what would have been the point when she intended a family of four? One of her pupils, Dolly Drake, was the eldest of six children, herself nearly fifteen. When her mother called to ask Frances if she could continue with her lessons she was delighted and from that small beginning came other pupils. Now, while one stone gatepost of number 46 Matlock Avenue bore a brass plate announcing it was the residence of Doctor G. Smart MB the other carried another, this time wooden and painted with the words 'Frances Smart, Teacher of Violin'.

And Greg, what had the years done for him? These days he ran the practice alone, for after a bout of influenza

216

the winter before last Dr Saunders had given up. Life was certainly busy, no one to share the night calls, the epidemics or the weekend emergencies, but as he'd always said general practice was where he belonged. People were important to Greg; those who sent for him readily enough with no concern for his halfcrown fee, and those who more often than not put off asking for help long after it was needed for fear of the bill. He'd learnt to recognise where he was most needed and if he'd had all the halfcrowns he'd earned on his 'dropped in for a minute as I was passing' calls he would have been a richer man.

Frances knew he'd been on one of those visits this morning when during dinner he told her: 'I was passing Molly's this morning so I dropped in.'

'How was she? Did she tell you anything?'

'Putting two and two together I imagine the main problem is the usual domestic one. She said she'd be bringing some things she's mending back on Thursday, so see I remember to put up a bottle of tonic for her.'

Molly Durham stretched her meagre housekeeping money by taking in darning. Betsy was clever with her needle but, knowing Molly, even she didn't argue when Frances found work to send out to her, sheets to be turned sides to middle, socks re-heeled or shirt cuffs turned. She and her drunken husband had five children living and three more in the churchyard. Now she was well on the way to producing yet another. Of what he earned as a humper in the market all too much was handed over the counter of the Barley Mow and she'd had to learn in her twelve years of marriage how to stretch what he gave her so that each hungry mouth was given something each day; the more mouths to share, the less each had and the something was never enough. To see her one might have imagined her nearer fifty than the thirty-three that was

217

the truth. Like so many around her with families to care for, when things were short it was the mother's ration that was first to be cut. When Molly came to fetch her bundle of mending Frances always had the same old feeling of shame at her own good health.

'More cabbage? What about you, Mrs Greg dear? And there's still some meat too. Come on now, and you Mr Greg, with an afternoon in the cold ahead of you.'

'Betsy,' Fran laughed, 'you'd have us like barrels.'

'I hate to see waste. A mite more for you chillun, eh?'

'If I had anymore I'd have no room for the plum duff, Betsy.' Alexandra was old enough to have learnt the lesson of tact. 'And I don't want to miss that.'

There was a solemn dignity about her that never ceased to surprise Frances. Her pale fair hair hung straight in a silvery cloud to her shoulders, her huge eyes the same colour as her mother's but with a seriousness that seldom sparkled with fun. She seemed to radiate a gravity unknown to Frances.

Young Matt was far more transparent. He pushed his small knife and fork together, his freckled face assuming an expression of unconcern as he peeped first at his father and then his mother. She knew she ought to see the offending pile of cabbage under the blade, but it was impossible to resist him.

'It looks as though you'll have to eat it yourself Betsy or let Daisy have bubble and squeak for her supper.'

Matt leant back in his chair perched on a bound volume of the *Ladies Home Journal* topped by a cushion. His expression relaxed, the camouflage must have been successful! Betsy was beginning to stack his plates.

'Too full to eat it all are you, Matt?' His father sounded pleasant enough.

Matt fell into the trap. 'Yes, Daddy. That's it, I was full.'

218

'Just four plates then, Betsy, Matt won't want any duff.'

'Yes I will. S'my favourite, Betsy made it 'cos it's my favourite. I do want duff.' There was nothing uncertain about Matt's expressions, they changed in a second from one mood to the next. Now his face was pink, his bottom lip stuck out defiantly but he fooled no one, they heard the tears in his voice. 'I've got room for the duff, I helped Betsy do the stones. Dad, I –'

'One big forkful then, that's all it'll take; there's a man.' Betsy heard his voice break too and wanted to save him. 'There's a man, then I'll be able to get a plate for you too.'

He heard the kindness in her tone and felt her support. 'It's cold. Hate cabbage.' He was pleading now.

'Then eat it up quickly. Bite and swallow before it gets colder,' Fran encouraged.

Greg said nothing as Matt forced the mushy green mass into his mouth and with his eyes closed and his small face contorted with revulsion forced it down. Then: 'Good fellow. Now he deserves a slice with plenty of fruit, eh, Betsy?'

Alexandra watched in silence. It was impossible to guess what went on in her head.

Betsy fetched the plum duff and a jug of steaming custard. First she served Frances, then Greg.

'There now, isn't that a lovely piece. See all those raisins,' she said as slice number three came under her knife and was put on a plate and smothered with custard. 'Best give that to Matt, hadn't we?'

Little Alexandra's voice gave nothing away. Always she was served after her father.

'I'm older than Matt, I come next. And I ate my cabbage.' She didn't quite look at anyone in particular, simply stated a fact.

'Oh Alex,' Fran started, 'as if –'

'She's quite right. Alex next Betsy; it's her turn,' Greg decreed.

'Thank you.' Alex took the plate that was passed to her.

'S'not fair,' Matt glowered at the pudding that was finally put before him; 'you said I could have lots of raisins. Alex had that good piece.'

'I'll change with you if you like.' Alexandra pushed her plate across the table.

'Well, I declare! Such a fuss and then you don't want it.' So often Frances was at a loss to understand the little girl's reasoning, but it seemed that where she got left behind Greg managed to keep up. Now, she noticed a look pass between them. It seemed they were both satisfied that justice had been done.

'My first call after dinner is to the farm. Someone brought a note round from Gee. He wants me to call and see old Sam, the drover; his chest's bad again.'

'Can we come?' Matt spluttered through a mouthful of pudding. 'Please Dad, can we come?'

'Why don't you? You could walk back.' Greg looked down the table to Fran.

'I've got a lesson at four we couldn't stay long. I haven't seen Gina for weeks though, I've a mind I will.'

'Yes, Mum, go on Mum, say we can.'

'Don't talk with your mouth full, Matt. If we do go you'll have to come back in the pushcart, I shan't have time for you to dawdle.'

'I'll run. I can run as fast as she can,' he nodded his head indignantly in Alex's direction.

'Pusher or not at all. And what about you, Alex? Will you walk it?'

'Do I need to come, Mummy? Can't I stay with Betsy?'

'Bless the child, 'course she can stay with me, Mrs Greg, if you're not needing her.'

'Well, I don't know. You deserve a break, Betsy.'

'I won't be a nuisance, I won't spoil Betsy's break, honestly.'

'You could do with some fresh air, I should hae thought.' Greg looked at Alexandra, her face always so pale, her thin little frame so different from Matt's. Despite her being sixteen months older and four inches taller there was no doubt who was the more robust.

'Tell you what,' Betsy suggested in her honorary grandparent voice, 'Alex and me'll take a walk round to the shop for half an hour, see Mrs Ratcliffe and your uncle.'

'Oh yes, let's Betsy. Please Mummy, I won't be any trouble?'

So it was agreed and while Alexandra was still independently struggling with the buttons of her gaiters Frances and Matt were on their way to the farm. Travelling was so easy, Fran thought. Even on a day as windy and cold as this it was lovely to snuggle into the sidecar with Matt on her knee and the chair roped between it and the pillion seat of the motor cycle. In the summer they took the hood off and felt the wind on their faces but today she was glad to be inside. No wonder Greg wore his leather helmet and goggles and a big scarf pulled up over his chin.

In the farmyard he off-loaded his passengers and the pushcart and drove straight on to the cottage to start his afternoon round.

'See Unc'e Gee, come on Mum, Unc'e Gee, see Unc'e Gee,' Matt tugged her in the direction of the barn.

'What's this then?' Gee appeared. 'Gina's already gone, said you were expecting her round your place.'

'We came the long way round,' Fran heard herself lie, 'or we'd have met her. I thought we'd said here; how silly of me.'

'Ah well, your Betsy'll see she waits for you. One of you must have got the arrangement muddled – her, like as not.' Gee threw the stub end of his hand-rolled cigarette into a puddle and turned back to the shed.

'Unc'e Gee,' Matt grabbed his jacket, 'show me the a'mils. Please. Let's see the pigs and things, c'mon, please pigsandsings.'

'Along you come then. Best to carry you; it's a real mud bath in that yard. Won't keep him above a minute or two, Fran, but we can't send him home without when he's come special. If you want to go in the warm I'll bring him over to the house.'

From where they stood near the barn Frances could see the window of the farmhouse kitchen and she knew Sophie was watching.

'All right, I'll go and see Sophie.'

'Bit down she is today, with Gina going off again. Don't take it amiss if she's none too friendly. Just that she's jealous on account of Ginny spending all the time with you she has this last week or two. Get's low when she's alone too much, poor lass.'

Frances waved towards the still figure watching them and picking her way between the puddles went towards the house. Now what was all that about? What was Gina doing? She'd not seen a sign of her for three, perhaps four, weeks. Spent so much time together lately? Arranged to meet today?

She seldom came to the farm. As a rule Gina would cycle over to her instead for here Sophie made their old natural chatter impossible. It was like having a censor vetting their conversation, a silent censor at that, for she'd sit close to Gina saying nothing, just watching and listening.

There had been great changes in the farm in the five years. 'Do anything you like,' Gee had told her and Gina

222

had taken him at his word. No oil lamps these days. Even Gee hadn't intended the money to fly as it had in the early months of her residence, but he would refuse her nothing and it seemed electricity was to bring light to their life. New rugs, new curtains, a carpet on the stairs and comfortable chairs in the sitting-room where a fire was lit each day. He'd agreed to it all and in return, feeling herself to be appreciated at last, Gina had accepted him for what he was, given friendship to them both and found life surprisingly pleasant. When he'd suggested she might marry him she hadn't hesitated; she'd changed the house into what she wanted, so she'd change him too. He was generous, Sophie was doggedly devoted to her, the future held security. ('No penny pinching. Why, even Fran and her doctor husband have to watch their money in a way I've never had to since I've been at the farm.') She was too close to realise that was no recipe for marriage. She'd loved once, she knew all about heartache and disappointment. With Gee she'd be safe from all that, no one could hurt her.

Frances stood further away. She'd seen the picture more clearly. As she tapped on the back door she was conscious of a feeling of fear for what Gina was doing. It was as if all this time lying dormant in her had been a premonition of trouble. She'd not let herself acknowledge it, yet in the last five minutes she'd seen it all. How long was it since she and Gina had talked honestly with each other? And whose fault was that? Hers, for being too smugly pleased with life? Gina's for withdrawing behind a veneer she used not to possess?

No answer to the tap, yet she knew Sophie had seen her coming. She wouldn't try again, she'd escape while she could, before she said the wrong thing. Seen so much of each other these last weeks had they? She had no idea what Gina could have told them.

223

When Gee found her waiting for them by the barn all he said was: 'Poor Sophie, takes it hard she does when Ginny pushes her off for someone else. I'll go up to the house in a while, see she's all right. Don't you worry 'bout her.'

It wasn't Sophie she worried about. Gina was on her mind as, when they got home, she and Matt set out his farmyard in the playroom, as she gave her 4 o'clock lesson and later played a game of snakes and ladders with Alex before her bedtime.

That evening it was nearly 9 o'clock by the time the door was closed on the last of Greg's patients and they were able to put more coal on the fire and settle down to enjoy what was left of the day. These hours were always precious, all the more precious because they could never be certain of them; at any time they could be cut short by an urgent call. Tonight they were left in peace.

Sitting on the little stool before the blaze Fran leaned back against the arm of his chair. With darkness the wind had dropped and in its wake had come a steady heavy rain.

'This is nice.' She would have purred if she'd been a cat. 'Just listen to it on the window.' The sound made the fireside an even better place to be.

'Umph.' He took a cigarette from his case, lit it from a taper standing in a box on the hearth, then passed it to her.

'Thanks.'

His own pipe burned steadily, he stretched out his long legs. 'Tonight may there be no new babies, no sudden colics. . . .'

'Amen to that.' She leant forward, hugging her knees, her cigarette sending up a thin blue coil of smoke. (This new habit of hers of smoking was yet another Myrtle found impossible to accept.)

'Something up, Fran?'

'With me? No, I'm fine, we all are. We're so lucky, Greg. Is it having so much that makes me blind?'

'What's worrying you then? Something is.'

'It's Gina. She wasn't there; she'd told them she was coming here . . .,' and so she told him. 'It was as if I'd always known something would happen, had been waiting for it. Yet I hadn't suspected anything.'

'It may be nothing. They may be an ill-assorted couple but then to outsiders so are a good many. She's never appeared to be miserable, has she? He's sure to mention your going there even if it's just to ask her who mixed the arrangement up, then she'll come and see you. She'll talk to you.'

'I hope so. Gina's never been strong like me; she's soft, gentle – like mother.'

He laughed. 'Come on, my Fran, you and your strength. Time you were in bed.'

'Is that an invitation?'

Gina was forgotten. They heard Betsy shooting the bolt on the front door, then Daisy's tread on the wooden back stairs as she went up to her attic room. The busy day was over, night closing in.

She did think of Gina again though as she looked in to see Alex and Matt were covered ('if only she had children, but she had nothing – a pretty house is cold comfort') and as she undressed and finally climbed into the double bed with its hot water bottle.

Feeling Greg's arm about her she forgot. She rubbed her cheek against his face sniffing the faint lingering smell of his shaving soap, she felt the warmth of his body close to hers. If she had room for anything in her mind except themselves it was an echo of his words: 'Please not tonight, don't let him be called out tonight. No babies, no emergencies. . . .'

'Fran, Fran.' He hardly knew he said her name. To Greg 'Fran' and 'love' were synonymous.

225

Later she lay still by his side, wide awake now and listening to his deep, even breathing. She wished he'd wake, she wanted to tell him. Five years, how many times must they have made love, yet each time it burst on her like a miracle. She kissed his shoulder. 'Greg, Greg, wake up, Greg.' But he didn't hear.

Only minutes ago every nerve in her had urged her on to the tumultuous climax they'd shared. Now, lying in the darkness with her eyes wide open she was filled with a great peace, her hands resting as if to protect that new life in her. So still, no sound but the steady patter of the rain. Then the first flutter of movement from the child, so slight she might even have imagined it. It was enough to prod her memory, to make her think of Gina, to wonder at the rainbow she was chasing.

'I'm so grateful for all I have; thank you for my blessed Greg and for the children, this new one too. I do thank you for being so good to me. Please help Gina to find happiness. I don't know what's wrong but I just feel something is. Surely if you could let her have a baby things would be better for them. She loves babies and you know how good Gee is with Matt; he'd love to have a son of his own. Well, you don't need me to tell you that, you must know much more about it all than ever I could. But if it helps for me to pray for them, please hear me. . . .'

In his sleep Greg turned to face her and she took his hand drawing his arm around her.

Faintly she heard the clock on St Stephen's tower strike the hour, 11 o'clock.

'They asked me to stay to supper, that's why I'm late. I knew you wouldn't mind,' Gina called as she took off her hat and coat and hung them in the hall.

'Here, let me take your gamp. I'll stand it in the sink,

226

it's too wet for the hall stand.' Sophie put her hand out for the dripping umbrella. 'I put some food by for you but I suppose you'll not be wanting it if that Franny's been feeding you.' She was so transparent.

Seeing her expression Gina felt a pang of remorse. In fact she was ravenously hungry and that, too, made it easy for her to smile and say: 'It looks too good to waste. I can find a corner for it. We didn't have anything much.'

'You'll like this. I made it special 'cos I thought you'd both be ready for it, out in this weather. Not fit for a dog, and you know how easy you catch cold. Wonder that Greg didn't bring you home in the sidecar, letting you walk on a night like this!'

'Greg wasn't home, he'd been called out.'

Gee sat by the kitchen range, his boots off and his feet on a stool in front of the blaze. The paper was unopened on his knee. He wasn't reading, he gazed vacantly into the burning coals, his shoulders hunched. Gina had long since given up all hope of the moulding she'd intended. She accepted because she had no choice and she tried not to see. Now she found herself looking at him afresh. His work-roughened hands rested on the wooden arms of the chair, their nails none too clean; his face was lined and the dark shadow on his chin showed her he'd not shaved today. His mornings started too early for such refinements, but usually he was to be found in front of the kitchen sink when she or Sophie wanted to be there dishing up the supper. This evening, with her out, his old habits had come to the fore. With only Sophie there either he'd not bothered or not remembered.

'Your feet dry yet Gee? Ought to have changed those socks, you did, get your death.' Sophie gazed at him with loving concern.

'Ah, pretty well dry now. You got us a good blaze going Sophie lass.'

His praise was all the reward she asked. She beamed with pleasure. Despite the attention Gina always gave to her she'd changed very little. No longer was her hair left to hang in an untidy pigtail, for each morning it was plaited and pinned into a bun, her clothes were becoming to her age; she could go about without attracting attention. But under all that she was the same, asking nothing but kindness and affection, ready to serve those she loved and bestow that beam of gratitude if they praised her.

'Why aren't you in the sitting-room? It's much more comfortable,' Gina asked.

'This does us, don't it, Gee. I didn't light the fire in there this afternoon with you being out. Gee likes the old kitchen well enough and 'tis a dirty day to carry mud through on to those nice rugs.'

'Oh well, I'm going to have a bath then go to bed.'

Gee stirred himself to look at her. 'Best thing. Don't want you catching another cold. I'll go and light the geyser. When you've got that supper down you you just come by the fire while the water hots up.'

She wished he wouldn't be kind, not tonight. A minute ago she'd seen him as a stranger, a middle-aged man, workworn and dirty. Now, as he padded out to the room she'd persuaded him to have built behind the kitchen to house the new enamel bath, she couldn't bring herself to look at him. She was ashamed.

Half an hour later lying in the bath her shame turned to anger. It was his own fault. In the beginning she'd tried, first with gentle hints and then outspoken criticism. Why did he have to come to the table without a collar and necktie, dry his steaming wet feet in front of the fire, wear the same shirt for a week if she didn't hide it from him? And as for his underwear, she closed her eyes as if to try to escape the memory of those woollen combinations. Once a week he took a bath and if she didn't seize her

228

opportunity then and exchange them for fresh ones he might well wear the same pair all through the winter! Day or night he was never parted from them.

'Don't you stay in there and get cold, Ginny. Come and rub dry afore the fire. There's only me here. Gee's gone to make sure ol'Sam's settled for the night.'

Draped in a large towel Gina came to the kitchen range where Sophie took her nightdress and held it to warm. 'Is Sam still poorly then?'

'Ah, had your Fran's Greg to see him. Wonder she didn't tell you. That's how it was she came, in that side-care of his. Silly girl getting her arrangements wrong; still, she'll have told you. Fancy not saying doctor had to come to poor Sam.' Sophie sniffed. 'Still, that's folk for you. Don't give a worry for anyone outside theirselves.'

'A good thing old Sam's warm and indoors this weather anyway. Oh Sophie, my nightie feels lovely and toasty.'

Sophie passed over her slippers and held her dressing-gown. The bad moment was over but Gina wasn't risking any more pitfalls. She'd said she was going to bed after her bath and that's what she did.

Two warm bickers wrapped in towels made the deep feather mattress inviting; she snuggled down. Now at last she was by herself, she could think, re-live the hours of these weeks, remember every wonderful second.

He must be coming back; she heard his step in the yard, then the back door being opened, his feet stamping as he kicked the mud off his boots, voices, his and Sophie's, the rattle of cups as one of them made cocoa. All the familiar sounds, no more than a background but enough to intrude on her secret world, to jar on her thoughts. Even with the covers pulled over her head she couldn't shut out the reality.

Surprisingly when there was so much to fill her mind she was lulled by the warmth almost straight to sleep.

229

'Ginny,' she heard his voice in the dark, 'I came up early too.'

She remained turned away pretending she hadn't woken.

'Didn't put the light on, but Ginny, don't go off to sleep yet.'

His hand was rough and cold but she musn't flinch or he'd know she was awake. To breathe as if she were asleep was almost impossible as she felt her nightgown being pushed up but it was the movement of him unbuttoning those combinations that defeated her.

'No, please, Gee, no, not tonight. I'd just got off to sleep and I've got such a tummy ache.'

'You seemed all right downstairs.'

'It just hurt a bit. I thought a hot bath would help but I think that's going to start me off. I can't help it Gee; you know how I get.' He heard her voice crack, tears were near.

'Come on now, Ginny, don't cry lass. Cuddle up against me.' He eased her towards him, gently, accepting her excuses. She knew she ought to be grateful but the arm that came around her, clad in the long sleeve of his woollen combinations, was about as comforting as a prisoner's shackles. Was it that stale sweat on his underwear that hung on the air, or the farmyard mud or worse on his books by the chair?

A sob rose in her throat and she gave up fighting it. Just to think of the wild joy of those few precious hours, she couldn't bear it. And now it was all over; tomorrow he'd be gone. It wasn't fair. What had she now to hope for? All these years she'd accepted. If she hadn't been actually happy at least she'd not been miserable either. Life had seemed to have compensations. Now though she saw them for what they were. The house she'd transformed, the garden she'd made, she'd believed it had mattered.

230

She'd delighted in pretty clothes and enjoyed Madame Zeigler's salon every bit as much as did Myrtle. Gee's working days were long, he got up so early each morning that often he'd go to bed before her and be asleep when she came. His demands were few and she accepted with a good grace if no enthusiasm. These three weeks had turned her world upside down; how could she ever slip back into the groove her life had run in before? The tears were hot on her cheek, loudly she cried, hearing herself with surprise and finding some sort of bitter relief in the depths of her misery.

'Hey, hey, Ginny, don't you cry like that. Here, you take hold of this brick, the extra warmth will help you back to sleep.' He eased his wrapped brick across her so that she could hold it against her.

If he'd been demanding, angry, if he'd shown anything but this constant regard for her she would have found it easier. It was like kicking a faithful dog to be unkind to Gee, or Sophie either. She gulped.

Help me, dear God, I'm so alone. I try to be what they expect, well I have tried until now, but surely I deserved something. Isn't that why you gave me this chance, let me have these few weeks? Now he's going, I'll never see him again, and how can I go back to living like I did? It's like letting a prisoner free for a day then putting him back behind bars. Please, please, help me. I've got no one. Are you punishing me for marrying Gee without loving him? But don't you see that's not fair. There's Franny so full of herself, one baby after another and you'd think Greg was head and shoulders better than other men the way she dotes on him. Can't you see it's not fair? She'll never pretend to have tummy aches, for her it must be like. . . . Still she snorted. All the years ahead and I have nothing. Please, please won't you help, I don't know how, but. . . .'

231

Another gulp, but she didn't know. Sleep had overtaken her.

'Ginny,' his rough hand was gentle as he rubbed her back, 'there, Gin, there. . . .' There was little that Gee wouldn't have done to ease any pain of Gina's, but he was helpless. Not for a moment did he imagine the ache was in her heart, which must surely tell something of their four years together.

Now she was still, only an occasional convulsive sob catching in her throat as she slept. He kept his hand on her as if he believed he could transmit some of his own well-being to her. Soon the only sound was the rain beating against the window.

The farm was too far out of town for Gee to hear the chimes of St Stephen's, but from downstairs in the hall came the strokes of the hour. The old grandfather clock that had belonged to his uncle and come to him, like so much else with the farm, wheezed itself into readiness, chimed, then struck eleven.

If Gregory and Gee had had more in common the girls would never have had any barrier, veneer, call it what we will, between them. As it was the four seldom met socially, unless it was at the shop for some special occasion. Myrtle's birthday perhaps, or, very rarely these days, a visit from Jane Pilbeam. Since Ernest's death Jane had lost much of her spirit, she was aged; to make the journey by train to Tarnmouth and then autobus on to Highworth was almost beyond her. The last time she'd come she'd made it plain: 'If I'm to see my family they must make the effort. Fairly shook the life out of me coming all this way. Yes, next time you will have to come to Ella's place, isn't that so, Ella?'

So that was the end of that excuse for a family party.

232

There was the annual fête in the Recreation Grounds and surely there wasn't a person in Highworth who stayed away from that. Wednesday was early-closing day and for more years than anyone could remember the last Wednesday in July Highworthians had donned their best attire and gone to the Recreation Ground bent on pleasure. Even then though, while the family sought each other out. Gee had other things to do. All the farmers from round about vied for the rosette for the best-decorated wagon, the best-groomed horse, good-humoured rivalry which drew them instinctively after the parade to the far side of the field where they were content to 'leave the lassies to the fun' and make the day little more than an extension of the Friday Cattle Market.

It was the same when there were concerts in St Stephen's Hall, usually three or four in a year. Frances was always asked to play the fiddle, accompanied by the church organist, and all the family would go, all that is except Gee. 'You take Sophie along. She'll enjoy it, she always does, but I've things to get done,' was his unfailing excuse, and taking Sophie along meant she clung closely to Gina's side.

It wasn't that he and Greg didn't get on; like most men they were prepared to accept each other, finding nothing to dislike; nothing to draw them together either, they seemed poles apart, which was surprising considering the long holidays Greg had spent on his uncle's farm in Oxfordshire. As an idealistic boy he'd seen farming as man's perfect work, toiling to help reap the harvest of nature's cycle. Gee appeared a far cry from James Smart—not because of his suit that might have been borrowed from his scarecrow or the mud that permanently caked his boots. James had somehow instilled in his nephew the glory of creation while Gee had grown up to see the land as a tough master.

Gina had wept 'I have no one' and mixed with her very real loneliness was that old tinge of jealousy. Frances had Greg and the children too, but more even than that, she had friends, she had a life full of interest. There was her music, the people she shared it with; one or two evenings each week she'd go out – the quartet, some practice or other; then there were the Grantleys and the Deans. That was what hurt most. Douglas Grantley taught at a boys' school near Tarnmouth. A friend of Greg's, he had a wife, Celia, and a young son. The men were friends, the women were friends and so too were the children. Recently Dr Hewitt had taken a partner, David Dean; again he and Greg were friends, so were Louise, his wife, and Frances. Louise must have been some years older than her husband and singularly plain, or so Gina considered, with her hair pulled into a mean-looking and unbecoming tight knot, her steel-framed spectacles permanently slipping down her short nose. A sallow-looking woman, yet despite appearances being against her, she'd produced three noisy and high-spirited children and Frances seemed to have already made a close friend of her. As with the Grantleys it was a family friendship. Gina was outside it all. She'd called once or twice and found either Celia or Louise with Frances, she'd heard the romping from overhead in the playroom and felt like an interloper. Yet Frances hadn't noticed, she loved having visitors, the house came alive when it was full of young voices and skirmishing. She should have understood, if anyone knew how Gina's mind worked it should have been her, but in her own pleasure she looked no further.

Greg had said he was sure Gina would call and explain why she'd covered her tracks yesterday and Frances waited, hopefully. Sure enough about 10 o'clock she heard her voice, still talking to Betsy as she came up the stairs from the basement.

'I'm in here Gina,' she called; 'I hoped you'd come.'
Immediately Gina was on her guard.

'About yesterday you mean?'

'Greg said you were sure to come and tell me. I hoped you would.'

Greg said! Couldn't Gina just imagine them, cosily discussing her from the security of their snug, smug fireside!

This morning she'd watched for Sophie to go out to collect the eggs, then she'd taken her bicycle from the shed, left a note saying she'd gone to the drapers to buy ribbon and pedalled to Frances. She'd wanted to talk to her, needed to confide, as at one time they would have; in Frances's understanding she'd recall what these last weeks had meant. Suddenly she knew she couldn't, to find words was beyond her, it would be belittled in the telling. Of course Fran would listen, then later probably she and Greg would discuss it, pity her for her empty marriage. Pity? Memories crowded in. Let them keep their sympathy, she needed none of it.

'It was a bit naughty of me to fib,' she laughed, surprised at how well she lied, 'but usually if I go out Sophie's with me. She doesn't expect to come here, you see, she never has. Once in a way I do like to go to Tarnmouth on my own. Is it very selfish? She'd be hurt if she thought I fibbed to escape – don't say anything will you.'

She'd tipped the scales. The sympathy would be directed towards poor simple Sophie, it was she who'd been tricked, it was her life that held so little colour.

Human nature is complex. Gina had wanted to share her secret with Fran because in talking about it she thought to establish it as a lasting recognised part of the fabric of her life. Yet now she said 'poor Sophie' but her pity went much further, it even took in Fran and her

235

humdrum respectability. How many of these comfortably married women – Fran or her friends – had been blessed as she had? 'Blessed amongst women'; the biblical term came to her as for the first time she looked down on Fran from her own superior position.

'You know I won't say anything,' Fran promised.

'I don't usually cheat her. It was just bad luck that the one time I do it you should call.'

'But Gee said –'

She got no further. The door opened and there was Greg, still wearing his leather coat and helmet and cupped between his hands a floppy-eared, bright-eyed puppy of indeterminate breed.

'Oh you sweet thing.' Fran reached to take it. 'Whose is it Greg?'

The little dog was passed to her, small, trembling and none too clean although it hadn't inhabited the world more than five weeks.

'Yours I thought. We can't let it go, Fran, can we? I had a visit in Silver Street, they'd three puppies. Two had been found homes but I got there just as this fellow was being put in a cloth bag with a brick tied to it. His brothers were rather more handsome –'

'Hush, he'll hear you. . . .'

'You like him, don't you Fran? He's a good little chap.'

In gratitude for his reception the puppy licked her face. 'Look Gina, isn't he gorgeous. What is he Greg?'

'Just a dog, eh? A bit of this and a bit of that. His mother wasn't too certain as to her own origins so heaven knows what our young friend will be, or how big he'll grow.' He fondled the puppy under its chin as he spoke.

'He's a mixture, aren't you, pet?' Fran rubbed her cheek against his rough black-and-white (or would-be white) coat. 'We'll call you Mixie.'

'He can stay then?'

'Of course he's staying.' She stood him on the ground where he stood shivering and looking from one to the other, then, fear getting the better of him, whimpered and left his first puddle. 'Oh, glory be, it's easier with babies. You've got a lot to learn, my little lad. Watch him while I get a cloth.'

The children were called down. Mixie was made part of the family.

Alexandra hung back. She wasn't nervous but she always needed to take her time. While Matt went straight to Mixie she stood close to Greg and watching for her reaction he put his hand on her sleek silky head.

'What about him then, Alex? Do you think we'll be able to make him happy? He looks a bit frightened.'

'Oh yes, Daddy, we'll take care of him,' and as if to prove her good intentions she moved closer and stroked the pup. Matt was already full length on the ground, eyes level and on equal terms with his new friend. Mixie's tail thumped, Matt's eyes sparkled; Matt beat a tattoo with his fingers, Mixie sprang at them delightedly.

Greg had more calls to make, he'd not come to stay. Gina had only stolen a few minutes and had to stop to buy ribbon on her way home.

'Oh, I meant to tell you,' Fran said as she went with her to the gate, 'when I was at Dr Russell's a couple of weeks ago I heard, and then I didn't see you or I'd have said before, Leighton has been back at the college. He may still be there for all I know. Percy Scott was called away and Leighton was free. Apparently they've always kept in touch.'

'You meant to tell me! As if I need you to tell me that Leighton has been back!'

She didn't give Frances time to reply, the last world had to be hers. No queen of drama would have made a better exit. Sitting erect – even if she did wobble as she pedalled

237

hard to put space between herself and Frances – and
without a backward glance she conveyed the impression
that Leighton's visit had indeed been on her account. The
wobble was overcome; as she gained speed so she gained
dignity.

That was at the beginning of December and with each
passing day Gina hugged her secret more tightly to
herself, glad now that she hadn't told her story to Fran. At
first there was no more than a golden memory, then it was
tinged with hope, hope that grew into confidence and
finally certainty. She knew then what she must do.

At the start of the New Year Leighton was to sail for
America. 'A concert in New York,' he'd told her with
pride, 'and who knows where it may lead? I shall come
back; we'll be together again, Gina,' he'd added seeing
her expression. If the Gina of old had had half the warmth
and abandon of the woman she'd become now things
might have been very different for them.

So Gina set out on the next step. A solitary ride to
Tarnmouth; the Post Office there was safer from prying
eyes. He'd told her where he'd been living, a lodging
house in Bayswater. Timidly – for telephones were an
unfamiliar experience to her – she asked the operator for
the number.

What had she expected to come from that call, what
had she hoped? The future had been an unknown blank.
This was the dividing line between what had gone and
what was ahead.

When the next autobus left Tarnmouth she was on it.
Like a spider trapping a fly Highworth was waiting for
her, her father's shop, the housewives hurrying along the
High Street their baskets on their arms, an errand boy
whistling as he pushed his bicycle from Mr Pengelley's
yard. The trap closed. It wasn't the first time. Leighton
had gone away, he'd given up his room and gone to spend

238

Christmas with friends. No he wouldn't be returning and no they didn't know where she could find him. Not the first time, and yet it wasn't the same. There was something about her now that nothing could cast down. He may have gone but he'd come back and nothing could take from her what she had.

That night when Gee went early to bed as he usually did, she followed him almost immediately; as a rule she left time enough for him to be asleep before she stole in by his side.

She'd seldom refused his love-making – the odd headache or pain perhaps – but at least in the first years she looked on it as right to keep her side of the bargain and she'd submitted passively enough. But for months now she'd avoided his advances. There was something akin to Sophie in Gee. He held his beautiful Gina on such a pinnacle; that she had married him never ceased to fill him with humble gratitude.

Tonight she climbed into their bed, moving close to him with a shiver.

'Cold, Ginny?'

'Umph. Make me warm, Gee.'

He didn't need twice asking; his warm hand rubbed her back as he held her to him. No man could have had more, his lovely dear Ginny turning to him for warmth and comfort. He wouldn't have been human if he'd not felt a stirring in his blood.

She'd said she was cold but her hand was warm enough. Never before had she unbuttoned his combinations. His breath quickened with excitement; her fingers touched him; from the opening in that despised garment she eased his eager flesh.

'Ginny lass.' He may have been humble in his adoration but he was no lover; her touch was his invitation and in seconds she felt his full weight crushing her, 'Ginny lass . . . it's always just me . . . I wish you . . .'

'Hush, hush;' she held him tenderly, or so he believed, wanting it to be finished but this time thrilled by the secret she cherished. What she did was part of it, she went through it almost willingly. So soon it was over, the seal on her secret secure.

The next afternoon the glow of well-being was still with her. She saw that Greg's motorcycle was in the yard and knew he'd come to see Sam. The old man still lingered but none of them expected he'd last. He was sinking, they knew it; even his wife, a tough dark-eyed woman of Romany stock, was recognising the truth although she'd not admit it. Perhaps it was partly fear that made her stubornly insist: 'He do seem a bit brighter'n yes'erday,' each morning when Gee went to the cottage, for what would become of her when a new drover had to be housed?

Gina pulled the kettle to the front of the range and stood the metal pot to warm. As soon as she saw him come out she'd make the tea.

'You're a friend,' Greg smiled as she called to him. 'That cycle is no way to get around in this lot,' 'this lot' being yet another day of wind and rain.

'According to all the rules it should be you who needs doctoring, you must be soaked through. It's all ready to pour. Come in the warm.'

'I never seem to come to any harm no matter what it chucks at me, but I promise one thing, Gina, soon now, as soon as we can rise to it, we're going to have a motorcar. Fran's going to drive too.'

'Fran! Oh, what an idea! Anyway it'll be months before she can think of such a thing.' To say it without that old jealousy! She felt like the Cheshire cat, nothing had the power to get rid of her smile.

240

'Better an motorcar than that bicycle she tears about on still.'

As if answering its cue they saw a bicycle, unmistakably Fran's, being ridden into the yard. But it was Daisy who slipped from side to side on the saddle in her effort to reach the pedals, her relief at finding Greg still there plain to see.

'Dr Smart,' she shouted as she hopped off and ran towards the already opened kitchen door. 'Dr Smart, sir, you better come quick. I been chasing round after you. Betsy says come quick. It's the missus. Betsy said –'

But he'd gone.

Chapter Ten

Afterwards she couldn't remember how she'd come to trip at the head of the stairs, for that's what had happened. A long straight flight with nothing to break her fall until, outside the surgery door, she'd hit her head on the corner of the marble-topped table. Betsy and Daisy from downstairs heard the crash and between them managed to shift her into the empty surgery and lay her on the couch.

'Oh, mercy me! Oh, lawks Betsy, whatever are we to do? Bleeding everywhere, did ever you see such a gash! Fit to kill her. Oh lawks . . .'

'Now then my gal, just you pull yourself together. You and me, we've got to find the master and get him home, that's the first thing. And no frightening the chillun either, mind you think of them. Downstairs with you and get me a bowl of warm water with a lump of salt in it. If those chillum come down I don't want them to clap eyes on this mess. Don't gawp girl, water, quick as you can and quietly mind.'

'They won't hear, up to their tricks again sliding down those attic stairs, that's what they're up to, and just listen to that Mixie, barking fit to raise the dead. Oh dear oh lawks –'

'Hurry up girl do.'

She hurried, unnecessarily tiptoeing across the hall and down the basement stairs. From the top of the house came whoops of glee and Alex and Matt bumped their way down the lino-covered top flight, then ran up again accompanied by a pup even more excited than they were themselves.

'Come on now, luvey.' Once she was on her own with Fran, Betsy gave vent to her feelings. 'Come on now. Open your eyes, there, there, come on luvey. . . .' She'd never felt so helpless as she chaffed the lifeless hands.

Greg's list was checked to find out where he was and Daisy sent off to search for him on a bicycle sizes too big for her. And of course when she heard what had happened Gina took her own cycle and went with her to Matlock Avenue. By tea time she'd fetched Myrtle and cycled back to the farm to ask Sophie to warm the spare bed.

To pack their night clothes and be taken to the farm was a rare treat for the children, but that night they felt uncomfortably guilty to be enjoying any of it. Betsy had told them: 'Mummy's had a tumble but she'll rest better if she knows you're having a happy time with your Aunt Gina', but Greg hadn't even seemed to notice that they were going. That was what was wrong; a treat like this was special, yet no one seemed interested.

Once they got to the farm they cheered up. Sophie fussed around them, Gee let them put on their coats and come with him to check that the cowsheds were shut for the night. That nasty empty feeling they'd had was fading and really it was fun to make toast in front of the kitchen fire and spread it with honey made by Aunt Sophie's own bees.

At 8 o'clock Gina took them upstairs and what excitement that was! No candles and hissing gas at the farm, but a switch that flooded their room with light and a double bed that promised scope for endless fun, used as they were to separate rooms.

'Bad thing, a tumble like that,' Gee said to Gina later as they sat at the supper table. 'Well on the way with the child from the look of her too.'

'She'll be all right,' Gina was sure. 'A nasty cut on her head. Leave it's mark, I wouldn't wonder, but Franny's ever so strong.'

'Likely. Well, let's hope you're right, poor lass.'

Of course I'm right. Gina was ashamed at the unbidden thought that came uninvited and unchecked. She's never had a day feeling poorly. About time things went right for me and wrong for her. Ashamed, and frightened too. I didn't mean that, forgive me. You know I didn't mean it.

But didn't she? Could it have been no more than fear of tempting providence that made her beg forgiveness? Surely not, with so much shared and for so long.

'I'll go round first thing in the morning. You'll keep an eye on the children, won't you; let them help you? She'll be better by tomorrow, I'm sure she will.'

But by the morning the baby was lost and one look at Greg told her the night they'd had. Myrtle had proved herself strong in an emergency before and so she had this time. All night she'd been by Greg's side ready to fetch and carry; not once had she flinched. They'd gone through a night that neither of them would ever forget and although, as the next morning Fran was carried off to Tarnmouth Hospital, she didn't realise it then, there had been brief moments during those hours when she too had seen and comprehended their and her own plight; never for long and only as something looked at through the wrong end of a telescope, watched as if she had no part in it.

The days that followed built their own routine. Once

the shock passes a routine is a great strengthener. Afterwards they would look back at 'that bad time when Franny was so long in hospital' as a period totally devoid of bright patches, but of course it wasn't so. Each day had its moments of hope, of relief, even of laughter. When the ambulance carried her away there had to be hope, for to lose that would have been to lose faith and that was all they had. As the surgeon worked they could do no more than pray and trust, whether from faith or a superstitious fear that to doubt was to tempt fate. After the operation was over any superstition was forgotten; they knew where to send their silent thanks. By then relief and hope grew and strengthened together. That Fran could have no more children meant nothing. She had two already and plenty of women who, year after year were brought to bed in labour, would have been grateful to change places with her.

And laughter? That followed readily enough. As their spirits bounced back from the depths there was an extraordinary need in them to see the lighter side of life. Them? Greg certainly, Myrtle too and the faithful Betsy. As for the children, they watched the adults and took their lead from them. The mood of the house lifted; with relief Alex and Matt felt it and their own took colour from it. They became more boisterous than they'd ever been, they played harder, giggled more readily and cried when normally they wouldn't. And Gina? For her there was reason for joy indeed.

Alex and Matt were no longer at the farm. For the few days they stayed there, it was a relief to Greg to have them away from the tragedy that loomed. For a few days too it was the same with the practice: Dr Saunders took Greg's surgery for him and even made his calls while Fran was hovering on the brink of two worlds. Then the cloud lifted, Greg's mind began to function. Fran would be well. His first need was the children, to bring them home, to keep the house alive; rather like keeping a hot brick in the bed to make sure it would be ready when a loved one returned. So in Fran's house everything had to run as it always had.

By the end of January although no date was fixed for her to come home at least a pattern for living had emerged. Myrtle took the 'bus almost each day to Tarnmouth, Greg went on his motorcycle, Gina visited her less often but then it was Gina who collected the children and took them to play at the farm. Out of necessity a routine grew and it strengthened with confidence for the future.

When word reached Dickie he wrote to Fran and Greg, but then he always had. His periodic letters to his father said little and he had no intention of going home as long as Myrtle lived there 'queening it with the old man' as he believed (whether she was housekeeper, companion or mistress he didn't want to know). As he'd settled in Kent it had always been Frances who'd been sent a true and often vivid picture of his life. He'd described the rooms above the little printing shop, the mixture of discomfort and fun that made up his bachelor days, even the occasional and never serious sweethearts. Even more important, with Frances he'd reminisced: 'Easy to tell old Fran things. It's a bit like talking to Ma – a lot of Ma in her, always was.' And if Frances had known that's what he'd thought she would have been flattered indeed. So his concern was evident in the letter he sent to Matlock Avenue, his answer to his father stiff and formal. The longer time went on the harder it was to write.

Richard was in the shop on his own sorting and grading a supply of fishing floats the postman had brought that day and, at the same time, watching for the 4 o'clock 'bus from Tarnmouth to stop across the road. He'd been upstairs to stoke up the fire in the parlour and draw the damper back on the kitchen range; no need to let the coals roar away in there, they'd eat on the little table by the fireside this evening. The prospect was pleasant, he whistled quietly to himself, things were very comfortable. Young Fran was getting well again, Myrtle had started to look more like her normal self. For the first few days he'd been worried. His dear Myrtle – the hours she'd spent nursing, lifting and carrying too he didn't doubt. She'd looked quite worn out. The first evening she'd been home he remembered how she'd fallen asleep by the fire. Thinking of it he stopped whistling and a tender look softened his features. Fancy crying like that when she woke, crying because she'd slept. 'As if I wasn't caring. You know I care, Richard; I'm just so tired. Oh dear, I ache like an old lady of a hundred.' Her hair had fallen in whisps out of its pins, her lovely eyes were smudged with sleeplessness; nothing of the girl in his Flower that day. He'd never loved her more.

The bell of the shop door broke into his thoughts.

'Hello Pa. I've just taken the children home so I thought I'd pop in. All alone? Is Auntie upstairs or isn't she back from the hospital yet?'

'She'll be along as soon as the 'bus gets here. Run up and pull the kettle forward so that we can make her a cup of tea when she comes, there's a good girl.'

'Yes, all right. I'll wait and see her. I wanted to see you both especially.'

'Oh?'

She heard the question in his voice but didn't rise to it. Her news was too important to be handed out piecemeal. She'd wait until they were both listening and then make her announcement.

The autobus drew to a stop and Myrtle climbed down the steps. From upstairs Gina watched her; she heard the

247

shop bell and waited. They'd come up now for their tea. She made it ready. After a minute she went to the head of the stairs and listened. Could something be wrong? It seemed not; she could hear them talking, their voices sounded normal enough. They seemed to find plenty to say. Myrtle was laughing as she talked.

Gina looked back at the empty kitchen, the ghost of her old life here touched her shoulder. Ghost? Almost she could hear her mother's voice, here in the kitchen that had been hers for so long. 'What's that pout doing on your face? Put your lip in before you step on it! I declare you've got that black dog on your back again.'

Despite the memory she couldn't help it; the pout set firm. She'd hurried here so excited. He must have forgotten to tell Myrtle she was upstairs. Either that or it wasn't important enough to make them hurry.

'Hello Gina.' Ah, they were coming. Myrtle was calling up the stairs as she led the way through the door from the shop. 'I've just been telling Richard the news. Franny's going to be allowed home. It's only four weeks but they say she's done splendidly. She'll have to rest, of course; no lifting or stretching – have to give that fiddle a miss for a few months I expect. But isn't it wonderful? She looked so bonny this afternoon, sitting out of bed too. Oh, good girl, you've made some tea, I'm wilting for a nice cup of tea. Yes, she looked almost herself. Thin, dear me but she has got thin – and between ourselves that's such an ugly mark on her brow, always will be I dare say.' As she spoke she took off her hat, a velvet creation of russet brown decorated with autumn berries, and put it with her muff on the dresser.

Fran! Fran! Even today when she had so much to tell Fran had to come first.

'We'll have our tea out here in the kitchen then Richard can hear the shop better. You pour dear, you made it.'

'Pa, Auntie,' Gina passed them their cups, 'I came especially to tell you something. I've got news too, wonderful, marvellous news. Pa, you're going to be a grandfather, what do you say to that?'

'Why Gina, that's splendid. And I'll wager Gee's pleased with himself, isn't he?' Richard kissed her brow. 'And you're feeling well?'

'I'm ever so well. I never expected to be; one hears such stories. Perhaps I'm to be like Franny, she sailed through.'

'Poor Franny,' Myrtle frowned, 'she didn't sail so well this time.' Then she opened her arms wide to Gina. 'Bless you, I've never been more pleased. Franny didn't give us time to be kept waiting, hardly beyond her honeymoon. I was so afraid there was some reason when you went so long.'

Gina hoped her face didn't look as warm as it felt. Between them all she seemed to see Gee. She could imagine just what they had wondered, probably even talked it over together.

The bell rang and with a quick pressure of his hand on hers Richard went back to the shop.

'Well it happened at last. I did wonder too, Auntie, if anything was wrong with me. You know all the problems I always have, not like Franny.'

'Dear me, yes, so you do. But it was Gee I wondered about. Ever since Sophie said once how ill he'd been with mumps the year before they came here. I've heard say that mumps can do that you know, stop a man siring babies. Still you'd have known if he weren't – if he didn't – no need to fear though; now we have the proof of it. When is it to be?'

Apparently it was to be about the middle of September.

When Gina was ready to leave Myrtle asked her: 'Are you on your cycle dear? It's quite dark out there now.'

'No, Auntie. My cycle's in the shed and that's where it's

249

staying. After waiting all this time I'm not running risks. Greg said only the day of Fran's accident that he wished she'd not ride hers. I'm not courting trouble.'

'Very wise too.' It seemed they'd forgotten that Fran's fall had been in the house not on the road. 'Never could tell Franny anything; not that I'm criticising, don't think that.'

'Of course not.'

'But you know Gina, even today sitting by her bed would you believe she was puffing away at a nasty cigarette? It's one thing for the menfolk to have a smoke but I do so dislike it in a woman. Can't understand Greg encouraging it.'

'Perhaps it helps her, Auntie; she must feel so down. Poor Fran coming home with everything so different. Don't like a woman to smoke you say, but think how she must feel, hardly a woman at all now.'

'Nonsense dear. She has two lovely children. What does it matter if she's done with all that business? Plenty for her to do with the family she has already.'

And so there may have been but that didn't make it any easier for Fran to accept. She was twenty-seven years old. It wasn't the baby that she'd lost that wounded her (saddened her, yes, but that she could accept); she didn't even mind that her family was restricted to two. What she did mind was that she was to have no say in it. Her body had functioned so effortlessly yet here she was barren, sexless, or so she thought on her worst days.

Mustn't do this, can't do that, no lifting, no shopping, no playing the fiddle! To start with she didn't argue but her strength soon returned, it always had.

'Picking up nicely, don't you think?' Betsy said.

'Too thin, but the roses are back in her cheeks,' Myrtle agreed. 'Over-rides anything, you know Betsy. She seems not to brood about the babe.'

It was early spring, Frances had been home about two months and was back into her old routine none the worse for all that had happened or so she was determined to appear.

Betsy often called at the shop if she was in the town; when she'd worked for Myrtle they had got on well, but these days, probably because of her unique position in Fran's house, they were friends. Now she put her cup and saucer on the tray and stood up.

'I must get along. First I'll just rinse these cups.' Habit died hard.

'As if you come here to do the washing up. Hark, here's Richard on his way up the stairs,' Myrtle turned with a smile as the door opened. 'There's still a cup in the pot, I expect you've come for a re-fill.'

'No, no more. I've brought the post up. This just came for you.'

'For me? Who's it from?' She was always pleased to get a letter.

'From Cowdery & Elphinstone from the look of the envelope. They're early this month, it's not the twentieth yet.' He passed her the letter.

'Well I'm off. I'll leave you to read your post.' Betsy picked up her bag and gloves. 'Don't bother to come down with me, I'll see myself off the premises through the shop. When you hear the bell it'll just be me going.'

Myrtle slit her envelope carefully with a paper knife. ('Don't haggle it,' she'd said so often watching Frances tear the flap with her fingers.)

Downstairs the bell jangled; Betsy had gone.

The letter was short. The now very elderly Mr Cowdery regretted to inform her of the death of her husband on the tenth day of April. She would appreciate that the allowance paid to her would cease with effect from that date and the enclosed was therefore the last payment to be made.

'But I can't believe it! He wasn't ill!'

251

Richard came behind her and read over her shoulder. 'How would we know?' He waited a few seconds, then, quietly: 'You know what this means. . . .'

What a moment for a customer to choose!

'I'll have to go down and see what they want. I'll get rid of them as soon as I can,' he said, then hurried down the stairs leaving her still gazing at the sheet of paper.

In the parlour she sat on the edge of her favourite chair which, like most of the furniture in that room, had come from the cottage. There was to be no more money – fancy, Clement died! – nothing coming in each month, nothing for her 'little treats' and pretty clothes. Clement, so tall and forceful. In truth she'd always been in awe of him even in those early days. Who would have believed then that it would all have ended like this? Dead! And after all these years if they'd passed in the street would they have known each other? 'Dear knows, we scarcely did even in the days we were wed!' But that was it. They always had been wed, she'd been a married woman and as such hadn't broken the rules to live here in Richard's home. Things would be different now. And wasn't that what they wanted? Richard had recognised it as soon as he'd read the letter. 'You know what this means. . . .' Yes, she knew. She bit her lip, excited, nervous, eager, relieved, shy; such a mixture of emotions fought in her.

The years had been happy; probably living here had been the happiest time in her life even though it had meant giving up the cottage. She and Richard were very comfortable. Right at the start he'd told her he'd never expect her to do the rough work and he'd kept his word. Two mornings each week Mrs Tulley came and while she scrubbed and polished Myrtle took the opportunity to give herself an outing, a trip to Tarnmouth or a call on Franny or Gina. Then with her own money in her purse she'd been free to buy a hat if it should beckon to her from

Madame Zeigler's window, to take a Turkish bath and even, on her own these days, to have her tea afterwards and listen to the music at the Metropole.

There'd be nothing of her own in her purse now though. All she'd have would be the little bit she'd managed to put by. Her vision misted, a tear spilled. Life really had been so pleasant. That Clement should cease to provide had never entered her mind. How unkind fate could be, how unjust.

'You know what this means. . . .' Oh yes, she knew. Dear Richard, truly she loved him. Hadn't she said so all that long time ago? 'Now I know what love is, now I'm ready,' she'd told him. So why was she hesitating?

He was coming back.

'Tears?' How dear she was, how tender hearted, to be touched by Clement's death after all he'd done to her.

'No, well, only that it's a shock. He wasn't old.'

'About my age I'd say,' Richard remembered.

It was that that sorted out her jumbled thoughts and showed her which were the things that counted. She stood up and put her hands on his shoulders, gripping him hard.

'Oh don't, don't say that!' Supposing it had been Richard!

When he kissed her she clung to him. She was free, she was in love with her dear Richard, the doubts had vanished, taking her fears with them. They were to nudge their way back again later on when he'd gone down to close the shop and she was alone cooking the supper, only to vanish as they sat together planning the future as if it were to differ from the present. But then in one respect it would. As she pulled the covers over her shoulders that night and burrowed down between her familiar sheets she thought about it, imagined the room down the corridor that had been Richard's as long as he'd lived there, his and Cynny's too. For a long time sleep eluded her. First she lay on her left side, then on her right, sure that he must hear her every movement. All the time she'd lived here her bedroom had been her own private place, she'd shut her door never questioning. Because Clement had stood between them that corridor might have been a thousand miles long. Now there was no Clement, nothing but two walls and a few feet of passageway. Tonight she knew he'd be awake just as she was. She wished she could sleep. Let the future take care of itself. It wasn't that she didn't love him, of course she did. She'd hated it so much though. There now, she'd admitted it. It had been a duty, never any more than that. And what about him? Her mouth felt dry with fright. No virgin bride could have been more apprehensive than Myrtle.

'Heavens above, I'm not a girl. I'm forty-six and he's ten years and more older. We're beyond all that, he won't expect it.' But as she thought it and imagined starting life with a Richard who didn't desire her she felt a strange and sickening disappointment.

What prompted her she hardly knew except a new sense of freedom and a need of reassurance, his reassurance. The night was far from warm but she didn't stop to put on a dressing-gown.

He heard the door open. The shaft of moonlight fell across the centre of the room the white-clad figure moved silently into it.

'Richard.'

'Flower.'

She came to the side of the bed and found he'd thrown back the covers and was sitting on the edge. Her doubts and misgivings were melting, her arms came around him and she felt his head against her breast. Surely he must hear her heart, it seemed to echo through her body.

'There's only you and me Richard. We can do as we want.'

'Sweetheart, I want just you. If only you knew. . . .'
'I do know. Hold me Richard, please, hold me close.'

'I thought you'd be so happy for me,' Myrtle's hurt surprise was real. 'All these years I've struggled on my own, all these years I've been tied to a mistake I made when I was hardly more than a child. Surely you can't grudge me affection and companionship for my declining years?'

To look at her, declining years were not even on the horizon!

'Oh mother, how you do exaggerate. Struggling and alone indeed! When were you either? And of course I'm happy for you. It's just that for Papa to die and all it means is your freedom seems – oh, surely you can see?'

'Do you expect me to wear widow's weeds for a man who ruined my life with his infidelity?'

'More likely by marrying you in the first place.'

'Oh no, never that. Why, Franny if I hadn't wed him I'd have been without you. How can you ever think my marriage was a mistake?'

Her eyes still had the look of a wounded terrier and now they brimmed with unshed tears at the thought that Franny could imagine she'd ever regretted rushing into wedlock at an inexperienced eighteen.

'But are you sure this time, Mama?' The old name escaped Frances. 'After all you've shared a home with Uncle Richard for years enough. It will hardly cause gossip now. And anyway who's to know you're free as you call it?'

'You don't understand. Franny, never once has my dear Richard taken advantage of my homelessness. I couldn't have stayed there if he'd acted differently. All the time I had a husband he never once made a wrong

255

move. Now there's nothing to hold us back, we shall make arrangements just as soon as I can get a copy of the death certificate. I'm going to Tarnmouth this very afternoon to ask Mr Cowdery to arrange it for me. And Franny', her mood brightened, 'while I'm in town I thought I'd just pop in to see Madame Zeigler. I want something really special for my wedding day. That's not too naughty is it? No more money coming in now. All that has to stop. For my wedding day though I surely deserve something pretty? It does seem unjust to think how comfortably off that harlot must be. None of it was of my doing; you'd think he –'

'Mother, don't talk such rubbish. Papa had every right to leave anything he had to whom he liked – or loved.'

A tear spilled. Myrtle wasn't used to being spoken to sharply.

'It's all very well for you with a husband who must be making a good living. Not that I'm criticising my Richard. I wouldn't change him a jot. . . .' She forgot her woes and turned to Frances with something like girlish enthusiasm. 'Be happy for me, Franny. I want you all to share what I feel. We won't have riches, Richard and me, but oh such a weight has been lifted to know that I'm free. If only we could put the clock back a few years, have more time to look forward to. When you're young you take it all for granted. But Franny, we have a right to something surely? Fate won't rob us too soon.'

'For you of course I'm happy and for Uncle Richard.'

'Bless you.' Then, timidly: 'I believe Cynny would be happy too. I'm not stealing anything that was hers you know. I wonder if you are old enough to understand.'

Frances remembered Cynny, the home she and Richard had made where as a child she'd loved being above anywhere, a place that had echoed the harmony in their lives.

'Yes Mama, I understand. Auntie Cynny understands too, I'm sure she does. I wish Dickie would too.'

'Silly boy behaving as he does. You surely don't blame me for his cruel treatment of my Richard?'

Overnight he'd apparently become 'her' Richard. Frances turned away. Suddenly and without reason she'd had enough; she wanted her mother gone. It took all her self-control to stand erect and expressionless. It was a physical effort and one that frightened her. It happened so often, this desolate emptiness. She clenched her fists as if that way to dispell the fluttering that seemed to fill her whole being.

'I know we're very different, you and me, Franny, but I didn't expect you'd want hypocrisy from me over your father.'

'And I don't.'

'You looked at me as though I were a naughty child. I don't understand you. If you could so much as remember him or if he'd wanted you when you held out a hand of friendship then I could –'

'Of course I remember him!'

'Remember what you've liked to imagine more likely.'

Frances's jaw ached with the effort of holding it firm; she had to breathe slowly, consciously. But why? Suddenly without cause and from nowhere this dreadful enveloping fear.

'Do look at them.' Myrtle spoke from just behind her. 'How they love young Mixie.'

Outside on the grass Alexandra and Matt were playing wheelbarrows, with Mixie leaping excitedly in front as they plodded forward.

Frances looked but she hardly saw. Her throat was tight, her palms wet, her heart beat as if it would choke her. Outside herself nothing had any reality.

'Dear me, what time-wasters little people can be! I

257

could watch them all day. But if I'm to get the 2 o'clock omnibus to Tarnmouth I must go home and give Richard his dinner.'

'Give him my love,' Frances heard her own voice, 'and Greg's too.'

'Yes dear, of course I will. I thought something a soft shade of violet would be a change. It's a long time since I've worn violet. Am I too old?'

'Mama, you'll never be old.' And she meant it.

The sudden wave of affection she felt was her undoing. The door had hardly closed on Myrtle before she flopped into an armchair. Old? Age came when hope vanished. She felt as old as time, as empty as the shell of a withered nut. Her eyes closed but the hot tears escaped to roll down her cheeks; she could taste the salt of them. Outside one of the children must have fallen; it sounded like Alexandra crying. Fran heard but it was as if all her power had gone, and her interest too. Usually she would have hurried down ready to pick up the pieces, bathe and bandage or simply kiss better. If she were to stand now she felt that her legs woud give way under her; they were empty, like her mind and her heart.

Betsy's voice was added to Alexandra's wails and Matt's protests that: 'I didn't, you're a fibber, I didn't. Wasn't my fault.' Then as the victim was taken off to have her knee washed and covered his short-lived flare-up was forgotten and he shouted after them: 'Me and Mixie'll wait here. Tell you what Alex, you can have an extra go 'cos you fell over. Mixie! Come on boy, here, Mixie, fetch!' She knew he was throwing stones for the puppy to chase. Often enough she'd told him not to do it but today she didn't care.

The clock on the mantlepiece ticked loudly, Mixie barked, Matt laughed, the clock ticked on, then Alex was back outside, peace restored and the game re-started, the

258

clock struck, Fran's eyes were still closed but now the tears were dry on her face. To weep needed energy and feeling; she had neither.

'Fran,' Greg spoke from the doorway, 'Fran.'

Was she asleep? It was as if he'd been waiting for this. Ever since she'd come home from the hospital she'd worn an armour that even he hadn't been able to penetrate. They'd all said how bright she was, how quickly she'd returned to normal and like a fool he'd wanted to believe.

With foreboding he came near her. 'Fran, you're awake. Don't pretend, not with me.'

She opened her eyes and looked straight at him but her expression said nothing.

He sat on the arm of her chair, his arm around her.

'I just met your mother, she told me. I'm sorry Fran; now it's too late to hope.'

She nodded, gripping his hand.

'It's not just that.' Her jaw was stiff with unshed tears and at the sound of her voice her misery and fear welled up. Myrtle could weep quietly, sadly; not so Fran. She sobbed loudly, uncontrolled and uncaring, she held herself away from him, there was no reason in her. Wildly she beat her clenched fists on the arms of the chair and what words she managed to throw out were barely intelligible. She felt herself sinking; she wanted to sink.

It had to happen. For weeks he'd been frightened the bubble must burst. He should be thankful he was here with her. The minutes seemed endless, her crying was demented. She didn't notice when the door opened a few inches or hear Betsy's: 'Oh lawks, whatever's amiss?' When Greg replied by shaking his head and whispering: 'Keep the children downstairs', it was outside the orbit of her misery. Her hysteria gradually spent itself and Greg slipped to his knees in front of her holding her shoulders but she seemed unaware of him. Slumped in her chair her now swollen eyelides closed again.

Her face was a mirror to her soul, the ugly scar on her forehead emphasised by her pallor, lips slightly parted and even now her breath occasionally catching in her throat.

'Tell me, Fran. Let me share. Is it your father? Is it the baby?' He gathered her in his arms; she didn't struggle but neither did she respond. She leant against him, a dead weight.

Drawing back he took her by the shoulders and this time shook her.

'Tell me, I say. Whatever it is it's my concern too. Do you think I felt no grief for the baby? I wanted him too. Let me in, Fran.'

She shook her head. At least she must have heard him.

'It's nothing. There's nothing – I'm empty – inside I'm dead.' Again the tears but this time she didn't fight when he held her, but how much comfort he gave her he couldn't tell. 'It's all such a waste. Papa – I never knew him, Greg, now I never can.'

He knew his Fran so well. Even now she wasn't telling him the whole truth; he recognised better than she did herself how she clutched at her father as an excuse for what she couldn't face. At least though she'd drawn him into her unhappiness, she'd called him by name.

The tears must have helped her, for she pulled back from him and sat up.

'Can I have your hanky,' she sniffed; 'I must look a sketch. Don't let Alex and Matt see me.'

'Betsy's giving them their dinner. Here.' As she wiped her face and blew her nose he lit one cigarette and passed it to her, then another for himself.

'Thanks.' She puffed it gratefully and again lay back with her eyes closed.

She had to ask him. All these weeks when sudden moods of depression had frightened her she'd been too much of a coward to put her fears into words. This had to be the moment. Why else had fate sent him home early, put him there with her when nothing else mattered but this one burning question?

'Greg, I have to know –' she started, but he hadn't heard.

'Call myself a doctor! They all said how well you seemed, bright and over it all. Any doctor worth his salt would have seen!'

'So I'm right. Greg, I want the truth. Please, please, I can accept anything that's honest. I'd rather know, truly I would. Like this don't you see I can't trust anyone, all of you treating me like a child – or a fool. It was the fall, wasn't it, the knock on my head? I understand. You don't have to protect me. All I want to know is, will I always get these fits, or less often, or more, is this only the beginning? Sometimes I feel like I always did, then suddenly – I can't keep hold, there's nothing but emptiness, no hope, no sunshine. . . .'

'Fran, sweetheart, why couldn't you have let me see? Oh damn it all, I shouldn't have needed telling.'

'What will it be, Greg?'

He tilted her chin forcing her to meet his gaze.

'The knock on your head was superficial, a surface cut. A nasty gash but just a flesh wound, nothing more, I promise you. That you get fits of depression has nothing to do with it. I should have warned you that you would. Precious few people go through the surgery you had without after-effects like it. It's just that you seemed so on top of it all.'

'You mean there's nothing wrong with me? Swear to

261

me Greg; put your hand on your heart. I didn't damage my brain? I want the truth, don't try to be kind, please swear it's the truth.'

'I swear to you Fran there's nothing wrong with your brain. You're miserable, although you may not realise it, because you can't have children. But sweetheart, does that really matter so much? It doesn't to me.' He threw his half smoked cigarette into the fire. 'Fran, when you were taken into hospital, when we thought – thought . . .,' he didn't go on, but held both her hands tightly in his. 'We've both had our own private hells Fran, but they're behind us.'

She laid her hand on his head, then, her cigarette following his, put her arms around him and held him. Somehow their roles had reversed, she'd become the comforter. The road ahead that half an hour before had been empty now beckoned to her. She'd touched her lowest ebb. It was as if some evil spirit had been exorcized, her soul had found itself again. If moods of depression hit her again she could understand and so they would never take control.

To remember her father – or the father she'd created in her mind – was to remember the horror of those stormy tears, the sick dread that her reason was going. The two were confused in her memory. Whatever happiness she'd derived from her childhood dreams was lost. Later she might be able to look back on the day, but not now, not yet. She wanted only to forget.

It was the last Wednesday in May when Richard and Myrtle were married. Only the family came to St Stephen's and of them one was missing for Dickie didn't want to be part of it. He wrote explaining how busy he was and sending a wedding gift, an easy way out but the bridge between them was too formal, charged with memories better not resurrected on that special occasion.

After the ceremony the family gathered at Matlock Avenue and as far as he could Greg left the day free of visits. Betsy rose to the occasion with a saddle of lamb fit to grace any table and a wedding cake that made Myrtle blush with pleasure as prettily as any girl-bride. This was one of the rare occasions when work on the farm hadn't been allowed to come first; Gee and Sophie were both there, she as excited as a child at her first party – indeed, it very likely was. Gina carried her lost waistline with a pride that on anyone but her Myrtle would have considered unseemly. At home she'd taken over the spare bedroom to be made into a nursery and had already moved into it.

'I sleep so badly Gee if we're together, I can't seem to relax. I'm frightened of disturbing you.' She'd made it plain right from the first week that any idea he'd had of making love must be forgotten: 'After all the trouble Fran had I'll do nothing that might hurt this baby,' and so he'd agreed. He was as overjoyed as she was with her news. At last there was to be a child and for that he was prepared to accept anything.

Today he hoped the happy pair would get on their way soon after the meal; he had a lot he'd rather be doing at home. By the time he could get back and out of his best clothes the day would be all but wasted. Sophie looked to be enjoying herself; couldn't say he was but Ginny had wanted them to be there and he'd not disappoint her, especially now. He wondered what she and Fran were talking about so seriously; Ginny looked puzzled, she was frowning, biting her lip. He went to join them.

'. . . had had a letter, he actually showed it to me thinking I'd be interested. Oh, here's Gee,' Frances turned to smile at him, 'I was saying to Gina how splendid she looks.'

263

'Ah, that she does, pretty as a picture,' he agreed. It hadn't sounded as though that had been what she'd been telling Ginny, but there was no doubt of the truth of it.

The hum of conversation went on, the family was revelling in a party.

It wasn't until evening, home again and alone, with Gee outside in the sheds and Sophie shutting the hen houses, that Gina let herself face what Frances had told her. She seemed to hear the echo of Leighton's voice – 'A recital in New York and who knows where that may lead?'

Chapter Eleven

'The old year's going out on us all in a happier state than it found us, that I will say. Couldn't let the day pass without slipping in to wish you both joy in the next one. 1914. How it does go on, seems no time since we moved into the new century.'

'Indeed it does. And you, Betsy my dear, may 1914 be good for you too,' Myrtle answered. 'This one's certainly been a year of change, but Franny's well and now there's Gina with that darling little Nicholas. As for Richard and me, we're quite the Derby and Joan,' not a description she would have welcomed from anyone else!

'Ah, all set fair now it seems. We can do without any upheavals in this twelve month. Let things rest as they are, that'll do me nicely.'

It was as well none of them could see ahead.

While Betsy visited the shop with her message of goodwill, so Frances and the children took theirs to the farm. Matt was outside with Gee but the others were in the sitting-room where the fire burned all day now for Gina didn't intend that Nicholas should breathe the air of the kitchen, neither the smells of cooking nor the cold gusts from the back door. As a child her favourite game had been with her dolls and pram; now she doted on her son, seeming to care for nothing else.

Alex leaned over the Moses basket where he lay, a basket that had taken Gina weeks to prepare, lining it finally with white silk and only after he'd been born adding the finishing touches of blue satin ribbon.

'Not too close, Alex; don't breathe on him, dear,' she admonished the little girl.

'Aren't you going to pick him up, Auntie? His eyes are wide open.'

'Put him by the fire, Gina. Take his nappy off and let him kick.' Fran too bent over him. 'Nasty old napkin; you want it off don't you?'

Gina picked him up but had no intention of exposing his baby manhood and certainly not on the draughty floor. Really Fran did have the strangest ideas.

'What a year it's been, Fran.' She ignored the suggestion, rocking the baby gently as she talked, 'and I wonder what the next will bring. You'll be walking won't you my little man – look Fran at his hands, aren't they perfect! What will he do with them I wonder?'

'Expect he'll help Uncle Gee milk the cows, Auntie,' Alex suggested in what she considered a suitable adult tone to be included in the conversation.

'Nonsense, indeed he won't! Fingers like that weren't made for labours of that sort.'

Alex turned pink and moved back to shelter behind her mother.

'A pianist?' Frances couldn't help it. She excused herself even if it were hitting below the belt. Gina asked for it, looking down her nose when she talked about Gee, and taking that tone to Alex too.

Gina didn't answer, just fondled the tiny fingers. Then: 'Do you suppose he'll come back soon, Fran, Leighton I mean?' It was the nearest she'd ever come to confiding her secret.

'The last I heard he was still in America. He's travelled and been well received I told you; then he's going to Austria. He expects to come back in the summer, he said. Gina, I doubt if we shall see him; he'll have got too grand for Tarnmouth.'

'I'm not Tarnmouth. I tell you it was different last time, perhaps we'd both of us grown up.'

'You want to look at what you've got and be thankful. Not many people have the adulation that's given to you, and he just about worships the boy.'

'Of course he does. You're beautiful, aren't you my pretty? Come on, smile,' she tickled the pink cheek, 'smile at Mummy.'

It seemed she wasn't to be drawn.

So started 1914, a year that was to make an indelible mark on the page of history, but no one thought so in those winter days.

Of the successes chalked up to the year past, one Betsy had overlooked in her recital to Myrtle was Greg's Renault. He'd purchased it in the summer and learnt to master it quickly enough on the empty roads of the day. Then it had been Fran's turn to take the wheel, and during the weeks of autumn whenever he'd had the chance he'd called for her to come for a spin and, more exciting, to be the one to drive even if it were only on his round of visits. Myrtle tut-tutted at an act so unladylike, Gina watched with secret envy, the children with open admiration and pride. Certainly through that winter the motorcar proved its worth. When Greg made his daily round the weather ceased to be the hazard he'd come to take for granted on the motorcycle.

It was in March, at the end of a morning surgery, that he came upstairs to find Frances. He needed to go to Tarnmouth to the hospital; if she'd like to come too he'd take her to lunch in town.

'I've spoken to Betsy. She'll fetch the children from Miss Blake's,' for now they both went to a kindergarten school on Matley Heights.

Frances needed no persuading. Five minutes later she sat at the wheel while he cranked the starting handle. Life was so good. Again she was bursting with health and energy.

'Drop me at the hospital if you like, I can walk along to the Metropole to meet you,' he suggested.

'No, it would be wasted on me to have a vehicle. I'm going to have a good windy walk.'

'Then I'll take the wheel when we get to the beginning of the cliff path. You're driving jolly well, Fran.'

She coloured with pleasure.

'It's such fun bumping along all on our own.'

The engine was noisy, journeying was no time to talk. When she chugged to a halt at the end of the cliff walk she reached to the back seat to collect her muff and purse, then dropped a kiss on Greg's cheek.

'Life's so good, isn't it?.' She was poised to go yet not quite going. 'Are you ever frightened Greg that we're too lucky?'

He took her hand, caressing it with his thumb.

'As long as we never take it for granted Fran, never forget to be grateful.'

The road on the outskirts of town was empty, the day of the mortorcar was young yet. She moved towards him on the benchlike front seat, putting one leg over his and wriggling between him and the dashboard.

'What's this? My lucky day?' He was laughing now, that serious moment gone as he hugged her close to him.

'Move across, you chump. Greg, not here, Gr –' his mouth closed hers.

To laugh and kiss at the same time was no new thing to them.

'Unhand me, woman, I have work to do.'

'Move along then, ass. You're driving now, remember? I'm going to get out your side; it's easier than climbing over the brakes.'

He slid along the seat but didn't leave go of her even after they'd changed places. The laughter was still there but there was an overtone of tenderness.

'If I had you at home you wouldn't get away so easily. Look at the state you're sending me away in!'

'If we were at home I'd not let you go.'

The laughter died; tenderness was uppermost as he kissed her and watched her climb the stile to the cliff walk.

The wind was from the west, strong but not cold. Once on the cliff top she strode briskly towards town and the harbour enjoying the wildness, the flying clouds. Too early yet to go to the Metropole and the town with its busy shops held little appeal for her, so when she'd made her way down the slope to the beginning of the Esplanade she went to the shelter by the beach. She hadn't planned to go there. Fate must have led her.

One person was there already, a thin whispy-looking woman, perhaps forty, perhaps nearer fifty, not poor to judge from her dress, but colourless.

'What a morning!' she greeted Frances; 'it almost takes the breath out of one.'

'It's glorious though, isn't it?' It made Frances want to run and leap but she felt she could hardly say so, so she finished lamely: 'Not nearly so cold.'

The stranger turned to give her her full attention and Frances was puzzled by the sudden twinkle in her expression. In truth Ada Stokes, as she was to learn was her name, had understood the unspoken answer.

'It's lovely to see somone young and full of life.' She said it without envy. 'I've been ill, I'm not usually as limp and frightened of a puff of wind.'

269

'Oh, I'm sorry. Then it's probably no morning for you to be out.'

'My husband has brought me down for a holiday, away from the smoke and fog of the Midlands. I mustn't waste the fresh air just because of a blow of wind.'

'It'll do you good, I expect, as long as you don't get cold.'

'The South always does me good. I was reared in the South, in Dorset. Went North when Jack and I were married. He'd just gone into practice in those days in Lancashire, amongst the mills, and what with the rain and fog, to say nothing of the smoke that hangs so low, it's no wonder one feels out of sorts. This winter has been a bad one. I try not to make a fuss, but bronchitis pulls one down so.'

'A practice you say? Your husband – what does he practise?'

'Medicine. That's what made him insist I must get away for a while. He's come down with me but won't be able to stay. He'll leave me here for a month and by that time even up there it should be spring and I'll be able to cope again.'

Of course that gave them a common talking point, both married to doctors. Twenty years may divide them in age but they spoke the same language.

When finally Frances said she ought to go, she was meeting Greg for a meal, Ada stood up too.

'So am I meeting Eddy. Just for a treat we're eating at the Metropole today. I'm not staying there, I'm farther along at a place called Victoria House, but today he went to the hospital and left me on my own this morning so he said he'd take me somewhere nice to make up for it.'

'Then we'll walk together. Greg and I are having a treat today too,' a remark which lost it's ring of truth when they entered the diningroom and she was greeted by name.

They reserved their tables, two separate ones, then went on to the enclosed sun terrace to wait. Eddy Stokes had been to the hospital to look up an old colleague of his, Greg had gone to see a patient and talk to the surgeon who was now in charge of the case. Fate was having a busy time, it seemed, for Eddy's ex-colleague was that same surgeon, and so the two men met. Both were going on to the Metropole so what more natural than that they should drive in Greg's Renault and, finding their wives already together, what else but alter their reservations for two tables to a single one for four?

And briefly that's how Greg came to have a partner, and not before time for his list of patients had grown out of all recognition from that he'd taken over when first he'd worked on his own. So many of those who previously had called in Dr Hewitt had held much the same opinion of him as had Dr Saunders and once the senior partner they'd considered too old for the job had retired one after another they'd decided it was time for a change. Six years ago the smart end of town, those who could afford to call a doctor without fear of the bill, had gone to Malcolm Hewitt and the poor end to Greg. Now he had patients from the large residences on the Heights to the meanest dwellings in Roebury Buildings. Some paid their bills as soon as he sent them, some had their halfcrowns on the mantlepiece waiting, a few asked him to wait just a few days and still there were many who didn't send for him even when they should for half a crown in his pocket meant less in the children's stomachs and they had little enough already. He'd learnt a good deal as he made his visits and he still tried to keep an eye where he thought it was most needed. In a big town he couldn't have known.

It took some weeks before Ada and Eddy Stokes moved South. He had to sell his practice then find a house near enough to Matlock Avenue that he and Greg could both work from the same surgery, an arrangement that suited Ada admirably for after all these years at last she would be able to call her home her own.

They came at the end of June and already there were rumblings in Europe of the troubles ahead.

'There must be something absorbing in that newspaper,' Myrtle thought as she came through the doorway into the shop. No clanging bell today for in the heat the door was open. 'He doesn't even notice me.'

And she was right. With his daily paper open on the counter in front of him Richard frowned over what he read.

'A penny for them?'

'What? Ah, it's you, Flower. I didn't hear you. Penny for them indeed. Nothing but trouble wherever you look.'

'Oh dear, more bother with Ireland, is there?'

'Ireland could be pushed into the shade the way things are going. Read this will you,' he turned the newspaper towards her; 'where's it taking the world?'

The murder of Archduke Francis Ferdinand meant nothing to Myrtle beyond sympathy that the poor man could meet such a fate. It was obviously something worrying, a sign of underlying currents outside her understanding.

'Oh, dear, dear, dear.' Then resting her hand on his: 'But it's a long way away, Richard. Why? What has the Hapsburg throne to do with our dear land?' Almost she pleaded for his reassurance.

'Yes, a long way. Don't you worry your head with problems we can't solve. You've right my Flower.'

She smiled contentedly and folded the offending newspaper away. And she was but one of millions. The affairs of mid Europe were far away from their safe island. They had the sea and the most powerful navy in the world between them and all the unrest that had a quality of unreality about it.

'I wanted to tell you Richard, I've just been to Franny's and I met Greg's partner and his wife. Very nice people, they seemed, quite middle aged. I dare say Mrs Stokes is my age (she looks older, I thought, but it wouldn't be kindly so suggest it; poor woman she seems so frail and whispy), and I found her so pleasant. I'm to take tea with her tomorrow.'

The Archduke was forgotten, mentally she was deciding which dress she'd wear and whether she could find enough roses in the garden to take a bunch. Forgotten he may have been by Myrtle but even if it was all far away it was news, a talking point in the Barley Mow and every bar up and down the country, in every home too.'

Gina pushed her perambulator to Matlock Avenue that afternoon. Troubles on the Continent meant only one thing to her. She found her cousin on her knees weeding the flower border, her sleeves rolled up and her neck buttons undone in a way that would have earned her mother's disapproval. The heat that summer was intense; day after day the sun blazed down from a clear sky. Even the elderly said they'd never known a June like it. Matt and Alex were clad in nothing but their underwear as they splashed in a few inches of water in a zinc bath on the grass.

'Gina, what nice surprise. You look boiled. Don't you just wish we could be like these two and wear nothing but our boomers?'

'Don't splash towards Nicholas's perambulator, will you children. You do look lovely and cool.'

'Can we see Nicholas? Is he awake?' Alex ran forward

273

and after one more big jump into the water Matt climbed out of the tub and followed her.

'Careful, careful. Don't touch him, dear. Do mind you don't get his covers wet.'

'I should think he'd welcome it today,' Fran laughed, 'the grass is bone dry Gina. Aren't you going to let him have a crawl?'

'No, I'll keep him where he is. There are ants and insects in the ground. I don't like him down there. Mind, Alex, don't breathe over him, dear.'

'Glory be, an ant or two won't kill him! Still, as you like. Do you want to pull the seat into the shade?'

'No, it's lovely here. Fran I only popped in to ask you – this news today, this murder of some Archduke, I don't understand it but Gee says things are looking bad and I'm worried.'

'But Gina,' Frances fell into the same trap as so many, 'its miles away. I know it's awful if you're caught up in it but how can it affect us?'

'Well Leighton's out there, isn't he? You said he was coming home in the summer. That's why I came round, I wanted you to find out. That friend of his, I forget his name, someone you said he writes to, Franny ask him if he's had any news. I just hope if he's still there he sees it's no place to be and comes home.'

Frances frowned. 'Gina, he may even be home already. Don't you see, if he'd meant to come back here he would have written to you himself?'

'How could he write to me? I've got a husband to watch my every move!'

Frances picked up her small gardening fork and turned away, once more starting to pull out the weeds, and with a force that clearly showed her anger. That Gina could speak about Gee in that tone shocked her, Gina who'd always been gentle.

'Yes, you've got a husband and a good husband he is. It's a lucky thing for you and for Nicholas he's the man he is. He's so blindly besotted with you; you're not being fair, Gina.'

She spoke quietly but that didn't disguise her feelings. She could have let her tongue lash as it wanted and the children wouldn't have noticed. They were too busy having a noisy water fight while the baby shrieked with delight to have time for mothers.

'I think you're unkind, Franny.' Gina wasn't Myrtle's niece for nothing. 'Even the little pleasure I've had you grudge me. Three weeks, that's all I had him for. Gee hasn't been hurt by it, he didn't even know. But Leighton will come back, I know he will. You don't understand, it wasn't just something flighty, it was. . . . I remember thinking then,' her chin was high, she wanted to hit back at Frances and her criticism, 'how much I pitied you, so comfortable and unemotional with your dull home and family, you didn't know the miracle of those few short weeks. They had to hold so much they were worth all the misery. Of course he'll come back. And when he knows. . . .' her gaze rested on Nicholas and her words died away.

'Oh Gina, what a mess.' Fran knelt back on her heels completely untouched by the remarks that had been aimed to wound. 'And if you're right and he does, what of Gee? Doesn't he deserve better than that?'

Betsy was coming down the path armed with a tray; Gina was spared finding an answer.

'A nice cool drink of lemon, I thought you could all do with one.'

'Betsy, you must be a thought reader. Come and sit down. Up you get Gina; we'll move the seat across by the trees,' for Frances knew the portly and thickly dressed Betsy wouldn't welcome the sun beating on her.

275

So peace was restored before it had quite been lost.

Not so in Europe. The story has been recorded often enough of the trouble that was brewing across the water, how Austria declared war on Serbia accusing her of the Archduke's murder, how Russia backed the Serbians and Germany the Austrians. July saw diplomatic threats, by the end of the month those threats had turned to real war and the huge conscripted armies were mobilised. Fance was Russia's ally so Germany moved to attack France, planning a wheeling-army movement through neutral Belgium and so to strike at Paris.

How long could people continue saying: 'It's too far away to affect us' and 'Thank God we have the sea to cut us off from all the madness'?

The news grew graver with each day and yet while the sun blazed down on their parched and peaceful land it was impossible to suspect they hovered on the end of an era. Those who remembered war would think of 'our dear boys fighting the Boer', far away indeed, something that had made little difference to anyone at home.

The Germans moved through Belgium and Britain's blood was up. On the first Sunday in August an ultimatum was sent; 'withdraw your armies from Belgium or you'll have us to reckon with.' That should show the Bosche where he stood, that should call his bluff! England was prepared to wait until 11 o'clock on Tuesday night for an answer, midnight on the Continent. If no such undertaking came we should be at war.

The nation held its breath. Still the sun beat down from a cloudless sky.

The Monday was Bank Holiday. By tradition the family had looked on it as a picnic day, the meadows by the river had been the usual place when Frances, Gina and Dickie had been children. Things were different these days. For one thing that same meadow belonged to

276

Littlemore Farm, to Gee and so to Gina; for another, Richard wanted to spend the day gardening and Myrtle delighted in watching him as she sat and stitched a new blouse, such a pretty shade of blue and the length of material had been a bargain she couldn't refuse. With the Renault to take them further afield Greg and Frances decided to go to the far side of Tarnmouth away from the crowd that thronged the beaches near the Esplanade.

In the North the mills were closed; this was the week of the annual holiday. The railway had been crowded on the Saturday and in Tarnmouth, the same as in most holiday town along the coast, landladies were able to put signs in their front windows saying 'Boarding House Full'.

Alex, Matt and the hamper were installed on the back seat, he in his best sailor suit and Alex in a white sailor dress. Today Frances was wearing a candy-striped dress with a wide white belt and collar, and on her head a hat not unlike Alex's with its turned up brim and streamer of ribbon. Even Greg was clad for the holiday in his brown-and-white blazer and straw boater. Underneath the air of festivity was a feeling of disbelief; they couldn't even try to look ahead; of today they could be sure, of tomorrow too, but beyond that was a blank, something they didn't want to probe for hope hadn't yet died. So they looked no further than the moment and never had they appeard more gay than as they set out. The children clutched their pails and spades and between them on the seat was the hamper full of sandwiches, cake, lemonade, apples off the tree at the bottom of the garden and a bottle of water and a bowl for Mixie. They knew just what was there for half the fun had been helping with the preparations. As for Mixie, he stood on Frances's lap with his nose hanging over the top of the door and his tail

277

beating a tattoo on Greg's arm. The Smarts were in festive mood and if their gaiety covered a fear they wouldn't admit, it was lost on children and dog alike.

If they'd stayed near the Esplanade they would have been able to change into swimming costumes and go into the sea, for Tarnmouth prided itself on its bathing machines and golden sand. That would have meant sharing the beach with the crowds of visitors while just a mile or so farther along they were almost by themselves. The children were allowed to change on the beach and Greg took off his shoes and socks and rolled his trouser legs up to his knees to paddle with them. Fran had loved to swim even as a little girl. Sitting on the sand with the hamper went against the grain, but it was too small a thing to mar the fragile perfection of the afternoon. She watched them as they played on the water's edge, Matt with his boat attached to a long piece of string, Greg helping Alex with her castle, then, leaving their things safely out of the way of the tide, all of them climbing on to the rocks hunting for baby crabs. She wanted to impress the image indelibly on her memory, the sight, the sounds, the warmth.

And if war came, why had she this sick dread? She reasoned with herself, trying to tell herself that what they had was safe. Wars were for soldiers. 'Why, I don't even know any soldiers, or sailors either.' It was the newspapers that caused so much of the hysteria one felt all around; they tried to make everything larger than life. Anyway of course Germany would promise to withdraw its soldiers from poor little Belgium. She imagined, or tried to imagine, what it must be like to be there. What right had she to all this, here with her family, loving Greg so much that sometimes it frightened her, her darling Alex and Matt, Matt such a bundle of affection and joy, growing up so fast and always trying to ape his father. She had everything she could want – and Mixie too she added, watching as the little dog jumped from rock to rock, his tail wagging as if it had gone completely out of control.

What about those poor women in Belgium, women who'd been children when she was a child, probably played the same games and (except for the language) sung the same songs? What must they be feeling today? Supposing those dreadful German soldiers were here in Tarnmouth, in Highworth, marching down their streets, demanding shelter in their houses. . . .

'Don't look so worried, Fran.' Greg had left the children and come back to her. 'There may be good news by the morning.'

She nodded.

'Greg, we're so lucky. Just think, if you were a soldier, or in the Flying Corps, or –'

'The Flying Corps. That's what's so different this time, Fran. If it comes, and please God it won't there's the air bringing a new dimension. We've always sent our armies abroad and the navy's kept us safe. This time, if this time comes, things must be different. That's what makes it so difficult to see; different, but how?' He took her hand and for a second held it very tight. 'Just look at those children won't you.'

She nodded. They both knew the moment was precious.

By the next night no answer had come from Germany. 11 o'clock was the final hour. At town centres everywhere people were gathered. In London thousands thronged outside Buckingham Palace and in Parliament Square. If no announcement was made when the hour struck they would know that war had come.

Greg and Frances drove to Tarnmouth and joined the crowd outside the Town Hall at about 10 minutes to 11. The excitement was almost tangible; if that great bully

279

had to be taught a lesson these then were the folk to teach it. The minutes ticked on. From London word was to be sent by telephone to civic centres. The Town Clerk would come out on to the steps as soon as he had anything to tell them.

The hour struck, the tension grew. By then the crowd had swelled, filling the Square, holiday makers and locals alike. George Dudsbury the Town Clerk owned the brewery and was probably the largest employer in the district, a familiar figure. 'Come on George,' came murmurings, dividing visitors from Tarnmouthians, and 'Buck up, Georgie, surely you've heard summut by now.' It was nearly a quarter past 11 when the rotund and rosy brewer came to the head of the steps, his usually cheerful expression missing. Even those who weren't familiar with him recognised who he must be for as the hour had approached he'd donned his black robe, his wig and frilled jabot.

Silence.

'Please, please, don't let it happen. . . .' Frances took hold of Greg's hand and felt his fingers tighten on hers.

'It is my duty to tell you,' the Town Clerk spoke as loudly as he could and all over the Square people stood motionless, seeming to hold their breath as they waited, 'that by 11 o'clock no reply had been received from Germany. We are therefo . . .' The rest of his sentence was lost.

'War! This means war! We'll show the swine!' Wasn't there a note of hysteria in their cries? 'War! War!'

The moment would stay with her forever, even as she lived it she knew. The stillness and silence rent, the Town Clerk turning back, her throat tight with an emotion she didn't understand. Then someone not far in front of them took off his hat and shouted: 'Three cheers for the King, Hip, hip. . . .'

A roar, the second one even louder, her voice and Greg's as strong as any; by the third cheer she felt her lungs would burst. To shout was to show one's strength, strength that had conquered her earlier fear.

Outside the King's Arms on the other side of the Square, as the last cheer died down, a man started to sing.

'God Save Our Gracious King,' he sang. There wasn't a man in the crowd who didn't pull his hat from his head. As a prayer the National Anthem was sung. Hysterical excitement had given way to a new resolve.

How hard to sing when your throat is closed and you are blinded with tears. Greg's grip tightened.

As the last notes died they turned away, his arm around her shoulder to save them getting separated in the melée. They walked to King Street where they'd left the Renault and then started for home, a silent drive. They couldn't know how much their lives might be affected, no one could know for the world had never seen a war such as this one was to be.

The night had stirred all their love for their country, their way of life, even of each other and all that was worth fighting for. Amongst such feelings words had no place.

They called at the shop where Richard was still up waiting for them. Myrtle heard them and put her wrap on to come to the kitchen to listen to the news. Tonight all Frances's senses were sharpened; she felt she was seeing her mother with a new clarity and realising for the first time that she was changing with the years. Her lovely soft skin had lost the bloom of youth; perhaps it was seeing her with her hair hanging around her shoulders and no touch of colour on her lips.

'Oh dear, dear, dear,' Myrtle turned a puzzled look on them all, 'how can the governments be so silly? Now our poor soldiers will have to go and fight over there.'

'Bad news indeed. A forlorn hope that they'd have

281

pulled back, but God alone knows where this'll lead us all,' was Richard's comment.

'Now don't you worry, dear,' she said to Frances, for a single tear and her eyes were red and tonight had been full of emotion that had left its mark on her. 'Be thankful that dear Greg isn't a soldier, or Dickie either.'

'Amen to that,' Richard agreed, 'and Gee too. Farmers will be pushed to keep the nation fed, the German navy's a force to be reckoned with.'

'Dear, dear,' Myrtle hated to see Richard so glum, 'who would have thought at the beginning of summer we'd see things come to this. Shall I boil a kettle? Wouldn't you two like a cup of cocoa? You'll need something before going to bed.'

'No mother.' Greg was watching her fondly; a cup of cocoa her answer to war. 'We'll go straight home. At least we know where we stand now.' He kissed her. 'Get some sleep; we shouldn't have got you up.'

'Indeed you should, Richard has been watching for you. Yes, we'll put an end to this day; by the morning things always look better.'

A forlorn hope. They put an end to the day, an end to the life they'd taken for granted for nothing would be the same again.

Tarnmouth emptied of its visitors. A few stayed for their full week but most went home. The days were charged with emotion as soldiers took leave of their families and bands played them off to battle. 'Goodbye old chap, good luck' from fathers whose hearts were bursting. The English hate to show their feelings. Railway platform partings were little more than a quiet 'God bless you' as wives kissed their husbands, mothers their sons, 'Come home soon'.

Impossible though it seemed it was really happening. The British Expeditionary Force with its small Royal Flying Corps set out for France.

The printers must have been working overtime for wherever one looked yet another poster had appeared. The British lion bearing a Union Jack was poised to spring from the hoarding opposite Richard's shop, at its feet two bones, one Germany and the other Austria. The slogan, 'Any more to come?' showed the strength the people felt; they were ready to take on any who rose against all they held dear. 'Men of Britain – Enlist Now', 'Your Country's Call – Enlist Now'.

And enlist they did in the first red-hot keenness, queuing outside the recruiting offices. Patriotism, determination to revenge the ill done to a small country, a chance to escape from the narrow confines of their small-town lives; so many reasons, each man obeying his own particular call.

What was he thinking about standing gazing out on to the twilight of the Avenue? All day he'd been quiet. Was there a problem over a patient? Or was it what he'd read in the newspaper that morning of the fighting still going on at some place called Ypres?

She'd been upstairs putting on her hat and coat; this was her evening for the quintet.

'I'm in good time, Greg. I'll walk to the 'bus stop.' She never took the motorcar on these trips; he didn't want her out on the road alone in the evening in case she should have any trouble; she drove well enough but a breakdown would be beyond her.

'Greg, did you hear? I said I'm just off. Why ever don't you pull down the blind and light the gas, it's gloomy in here.'

283

'Fran, I must talk to you.'

'She glanced at her fob watch. A good thing she'd got ready early.

'Yes? What's up, Greg? You looked miles away, is something wrong?'

'That's just it, that's what's wrong. I'm not miles away, I'm here and I shouldn't be. You know, don't you – Fran, they need doctors, chaps out there are getting wounded to keep us safe at home. I can't skulk here looking after measles and pregnancies!'

She put her fiddle on the table, suddenly it weighed a ton.

'Enlist you mean?'

He put out his hand and she went to him, standing by the window in the fading light.

'If I were anything but a doctor I might find excuses, but Fran think of those poor devils and not enough medics to care for them. Tell me you understand. I have to go, please be with me not against me. Fran?'

She leant against him. Just for a moment she saw again a sunny beach and re-lived a sick dread of a future she couldn't imagine. This must have been the unknown shadow.

'Would you have me do anything else?' He lifted her chin and peered closely at her.

She shook her head. 'Greg, I wouldn't have anything about you different. I'm proud you are as you are – just ashamed of me – I don't know how I'll be brave enough.'

'Yes, you will. We have to, sweetheart. And don't imagine I feel too brave either, but we can't sit back and let other people fight for us. There's so much at stake Fran; we've got to win this war, and when it's over we shall have the right to the sort of life we've known.'

'I know what you say is true, but you – out there – I feel so helpless, useless.'

284

'I don't think it'll be any easier for you than for me; sometimes to wait and worry can be worse. I've seen that at the hospital. There's more than one kind of suffering.'

The light had almost faded but still they stood where they were silhouetted by the uncurtained window. For the past month there had been no street lights in the towns near the south and east coasts and before they lit the gas they woud have to be sure the blind was down and the curtains closed.

'Does Eddy know how you feel? He might not have come if he'd realised.'

'I've not told him I'm going but there's no doubt he knows. He can manage. I was on my own before he came. At my age he'd do the same.'

She'd been clutching at straws. Of course Eddy would manage and if he was overburdened he would be able to take heart from the fact it was his war effort.

'David has never suggested going. I suppose he'll stay on with Malcolm Hewitt.'

'David isn't as fit as I am. He told me once, there are things he can't do – a dicky heart.'

Another straw broken.

'Fran, you'll miss your 'bus. I'll run you to the stop.'

'I'm not going. You tell me you're joining the army and you expect I want to rush off and make music.'

'Yes darling, I do expect it. It's because that's how we behave that we shall win this war. Chin up, love, show the Bosche what you're made of.'

At that moment she felt she was made of cotton wool.

Even then they lingered. Once they lit the light and took a step forward they would have accepted the path they knew they had to tread. By the time they drove into the Market Place the ominbus was waiting at the terminus; she was only just in time.

Fran surprised herself that evening. If, a few hours

285

earlier anyone had told her that Greg was to enlist and she would spend her evening as if the day had been no different from any other, she wouldn't have believed them. Yet the young woman who sat with her fiddlecase on her knee as the 'bus carried her the five miles to town gave nothing away by her expression. In Dr Russell's drawing-room she set up the music stands, a job she'd fallen into and which had become a habit, remembered to enquire after Mrs Russell's toothache, appeared to give all her attention to the 'cellist as he told her of his daughter's prowess on roller skates and found herself carried along by Beethoven and thankful that he demanded all her concentration.

Only as she was putting her fiddle away and loosening her bow did the enormity of what Greg had told her cut her off from her surroundings. Ypres and the horrors the daily newspaper reported, Greg a part of all that, a home without him. . . .

'Mind how you go now, no moon tonight.' Mrs Russell was seeing the first departing player on his way. 'Carrots are what we need, they say carrots help you see in the dark.'

Carrots! Seeing in the dark! As if any of it mattered. He was going, that in itself took the meaning out of her days, but more than that he was going into a man-made hell. Later she would find the way to pray, beg that he'd be kept safe and brought back to her. Now it was too soon, even prayer was beyond her.

'Have you a minute, Frances?' she heard Dr Russell say.

'Yes,' an automatic check of the clock, 'ten minutes before my 'bus is due.' She was surprised to hear her cool reply and pleased with herself; this was what Greg wanted of her.

'I thought you'd be interested. There's news of young Leighton Tyrell.'

'Good news? Did he get out of Austria in time?' It was as if Gina stood at her elbow.

'No fear of him getting himself tied up where there's trouble! It seems as far back as April he thought it wiser to get out, "Europe", he said, "was no place to be". So he took himself off to the United States out of harm's way.'

'America? Not home?'

'A talented young man. Perhaps we should be glad he's not getting himself mixed up in the mess we're all in. Sticks in the throat though I must say.'

'That was in April. There was no thought of war in April. He'll come back, Dr Russell. I expect he hears what people say and thinks it won't last. Some say even now it'll be over in a few more months.'

Dr Russell was no longer young. At twenty, no matter how one fears the present, there is always a future, something to strive for. At seventy there is the past, the present and, in 1914, a mist of uncertainty.

'I don't know, my dear; I see no end to it. And young Tyrell, well let him stay away, I say. When this lot's over, if over it ever is, he can stay where he's run to as far as I'm concerned.'

Frances listened to what he had to tell her. For Leighton she cared nothing; he could stay away or return home, it mattered not at all. That he should have sought sanctuary in America disgusted her when all around her she saw young men flocking to the call of duty.

But that was only half the story, it was the other half that must surely make his departure final.

Chapter Twelve

The next day Greg went to offer his services to his country. Doctors were needed, there was no doubt of that. At Ypres where the first days of the battle had gone in favour of the Allies, the tide had turned. The Germans had battered the British line, breaking through, then being forced back; with attack and counter-attack the storm had raged for nearly a month. Newspapers were graphic in their descriptions and now that Greg would soon be part of the horror it took on a new meaning to Frances. 'A number of casualties', 'many of our soldiers lost'. 'German losses high'. 'field hospitals dealing with casualties under heavy bombardment'. The November fog hung heavy on the streets of Highworth muffling sound. Was it possible that so few miles away across the Channel this hell was a reality? It seemed as dream-like as memories of the relentless sun, the laughter, of the summer that had gone.

They knew that he would be called quickly but even so when Betsy came into the breakfast-room with the morning mail they were none of them prepared.

'One from Dickie. Fran, you open it,' he passed one of the two envelopes across the table.

'What's the other, the buff one?' She knew, even before he answered.

'It must be . . .,' he took a knife and neatly slit it open. 'Yes, it is; it's instructions for where I report.'

'When?' How could she sound so calm?

'Monday, next Monday.' Then he grinned at the children who'd been watching, looking from one to the other of their parents, puzzled and insecure. There was an atmosphere they didn't recognise, they were uncomfortable. Frances hadn't noticed, Greg was more sensitive. 'How about that, I'm to be a soldier! What do you say to that, eh?'

For a second they could find nothing to say to it. Matt was the first to speak. If Dad could smile like that then everything must be all right.

'I say, Dad, are you going to fight the war?' No doubt of his pride or his confidence. He knew very little about what war meant but lately everyone had been solemn and worried. Once Dad took a hand in it he'd sort it out. Here was something to tell the lads at school.

Alexandra smiled too. She felt it was expected of her but she wasn't as quick to adapt to the idea of a father in khaki; how could she be? She wasn't as young. Soldiers went away. In her mind she had pictures of men in uniform fighting each other with guns and swords. She'd seen pictures in the newspapers of men sprawled in the mud and she was old enough to read the words underneath, words like 'killed', 'bloody', 'missing men'. She smiled back as Greg wanted but it tore his heart to see her.

'Good girl.' He spoke just to her. They always understood each other.

He passed the letter to Frances. He was to go to a training base in Wiltshire. But he was a doctor and would serve as a doctor; what army training would he need for that? Wiltshire was safe, some sort of a reprieve, but it couldn't be for long.

It was such a short time since he'd enlisted, not much more than a week. Of course she'd told Myrtle and Richard, Myrtle had told Gina and Gina had come round as soon as she'd heard. But Celia Grantley had been there and they hadn't talked alone and even if they had it's more than likely Frances would have forgotten to pass on the news about Leighton; Greg had pushed it out of her mind.

The days that were left melted into just so many memories. Monday came, damp and unseasonably mild. Mixie with the uncanny instinct peculiar to dogs of his doubtful ancestry knew something was afoot. Wherever Greg went he padded after him and when the time came for him to go he picked the little creature up and was rewarded with a face-wash of enthusiasm.

'No, old chap, you can't come. You stay with Betsy,' then putting the wriggling dog into Betsy's restraining arms he stopped to kiss her. 'Take good care of yourself and of them for me.'

'Ay, that I will. And you, just you get back here quick as you can.'

He turned and left her; he knew her well enough to pretend he hadn't noticed the way her mouth trembled.

Fran drove him to Tarnmouth and like all the other thousands hid her heart as she kissed him goodbye.

'You'll be home soon; you'll get some leave and Wiltshire isn't far.'

'Yes, of course. Even a weekend I could manage from there. Chin up, Fran.'

'It is.'

'I know. Good girl.'

He squeezed her hand and picked up his grip from the platform. The guard was ready with his flag. She watched the train steam out, she walked out of the station and back to where they'd left the Renault, she cranked it into life ('whoever saw a woman swing a handle like that, it's not natural' Myrtle's voice echoed), she drove carefully down Station Road and into Duke Street, now busy with horse and motor vehicles alike. A fortnight ago if she'd been told that today she would have said goodbye to Greg and the old way of life she would have been filled with panic, yet here she was driving back to the home he'd left and the world looked no different. Women doing their shopping (more often than not buying more than they needed for fear of the shortages that might be ahead), an errand boy on a bicycle too large for him (she made sure she left plenty of space between him and the motorcar), a man up a ladder pasting yet another poster on a hoarding ('Women of Britain – say "Go"').

She was out of town by now, the road empty before her. Take each moment as it came, that's what she must do, each moment and each hour. Before today had come the thought of it had been some sort of impossible hell, yet here she was living it. It was no more than time to be endured; the seconds would tick away; good and bad alike it would all pass. Just be patient, face each day and look no further; time would bring him back again.

When she arrived home she found Gina waiting for her.

'I've asked Betsy if there's enough dinner for me to stay. Is that all right Franny?'

'As if you need to ask.'

'I thought if you were by yourself you'd be moping, not eating properly. I know what it's like to feel miserable and have no one to talk about it to.' A gentle reminder perhaps of the days of her captivity over the shop, but it was lost of Frances.

'Something smells good,' she changed the subject. As if she could even start to talk about it, and what was there to say? She was ashamed to hear her stomach rumble hungrily, the appetising promise of beef stew and

291

dumplings wafting up from the kitchen reminding her that neither she nor Greg had eaten their usual breakfast.

'I'll put the cloth on,' Gina offered. 'Just you and me?'

'No. Betsy always has dinner with us.'

Gina had imagined a cosy tête-à-tête (with Nicholas of course). Betsy was a dear but her presence would prevent the baring of souls she'd looked forward to. With Greg gone Franny would belong to her again, things could be as they had been years ago.

'Don't you tell me you're not hungry now.' Betsy spooned Frances's stew from the tureen. 'Just you eat it all up.'

'I will Betsy. To be truthful I'm ravenous.'

If she'd played with her food and made a pretence of forcing herself both Betsy and Gina could have accepted it. There was something almost indecent in her hunger. Greg would have been glad to see her attacking her meal with such fervour, Frances knew he would, but even so she was ashamed. Her mother wouldn't have approved behaviour like it!

The numbness was going, reality making her aware. The chairs had been moved into different positions (Betsy must have been at work while they were at the station), grouped around the oval table so that no one sat exactly in Greg's place yet neither was it empty. To think about it hurt too much. She knew herself to be a coward but ony by concentrating on the unexpectedness of Gina's visit, on the flavour of the stew and the suspicion of herbs in the dumplings could she get through. This was what Greg wanted. ('Oh Greg, where are you now now? Do you feel torn to pieces too, lost, frightened? Greg, Greg, Gr . . .') She pulled her thoughts back; Gina was talking.

'. . . I don't blame him either. He and Dickie have both worked so hard and now they're doing well. It's not fair to expect him to manage on his own. If Dickie goes he'll have to take in someone else.'

Frances's heart warmed to Dickie.

'Dickie is sure to feel the way he does.'

'It's one thing for Greg. After all Dr Stokes will keep the practice going; it'll be waiting for him to come back to. But what would Dickie have? I expect really I'm just frightened for him.'

'Ah,' hardly more than a sigh from Betsy. For Dickie or Greg?

'He wouldn't be an officer like Greg,' Gina went on, 'just an ordinary soldier, a Tommy Atkins. You don't have to actually worry about Greg even though you'll miss him Franny. It's a different way for the officers; he'll even have a batman to look after him. Pa was saying that doctors start off as captains. Not like Dickie, just a private. They're the ones we have to worry about.'

Betsy sniffed. 'Worry about them all, privates and generals alike. Please God you're right about our Mr Greg though. Mayhap they'll send him to one of those hospitals in England. The poor wounded soldiers that come home need doctors enough.'

'Well, wherever they send him, Betsy, he won't be anywhere where there's the real fighting. The poor wretched men get carried back from the line and taken off where it's safe to be cared for.' Gina wanted to reassure Frances.

Food was one thing, conversation another. Frances let them talk as she ate her way through her dinner, even silently passing her plate for a second helping of gooseberry tart. Not that she wanted it but it was easier to keep chewing than to chatter and she recognised that Betsy had opened one of the jars of fruit she'd bottled especially to tempt her, gooseberries had always been her favourite.

293

Daisy came up to collect the dishes. Betsy took herself off to her own room. Gina settled down by the fire, this was what she'd been looking forward to.

'We shall have to keep each other company Franny, both of us are so much on our own.'

'What rubbish! You're not on your own and I'm most certainly not.'

'Oh, we have the children I know.'

'We have Greg and Gee. And there's enough to be done without looking for ways to pass the time.'

Gina forgave the terse answer, after all poor Franny had good reason.

'As far as I'm concerned,' Frances went on, 'with Eddy having surgery here I shall still take the messages, carry on the same as always. I want to get some extra teaching too. There won't be much coming in now and anything I can earn will be useful. Then we must do what we can for the war, Gina.'

'I suppose you think I should be helping on the farm, but honestly Fran I'm just not made for that sort of work.'

'You could go to the Red Cross Centre. They want people to roll bandages and that sort of thing. I intend to go at least one afternoon a week.' Then she thought of what Gina had said and laughed. 'You, on a farm! No, Gina I can't see you behind the plough!'

'Anyway I have Nicholas to look after. Franny – what can have happened to Leighton, hasn't that friend of his ever heard?'

'Oh, heavens, I'm sorry Gina, I forgot all about it. It was just as Greg enlisted, I didn't think –'

'Well? He's home safely?'

'No Gina and he's not coming. He recognised there was trouble brewing and he went back to America last April. He'd made good friends in Germany; he didn't want to get involved if there was war. And Gina, he went back

294

there instead of coming home partly because of a girl, a German girl living in the United States. They were expecting to be married, oh it must have been last week.'

Gina picked Nicholas up from the rug where he'd been busy pounding a rag doll with a wooden hammer he'd found in a box of toys that had been fetched downstairs for him.

Frances went on: 'Apparently he knew this girl before he went to Austria, then he stayed with her relatives in Germany. She's a pianist too. . . .'

'I don't want to hear about her. He was in love with me, he was coming back to me, he promised.'

Frances was ashamed to see the hurt in Gina's eyes, ashamed for Gina and for herself that she cared so little. 3 o'clock. Where would he be now? When would he have a chance to write to her?

Whatever he's doing, please be with him and let him know I'm with him too. It must all be strange, a different sort of life for him. Please take care of him, help him to adjust, don't let him be miserable. She'd found her way to her first prayer and as she shut her mind to Gina and her memories of Leighton's promises she petitioned not for herself but for Greg. Let him know I'm with him, she begged. A silent plea and a silent answer, for as clearly as if she heard the spoken word she knew; she wasn't alone, she never could be alone. She didn't try to understand but it was as if her spirit and Greg's had come together. Let him know I'm with him, and she was sure he did, just as she knew he was with her. What was it he'd said so long ago, that there was a goodness that was God in each of us? Was that what it was, her thoughts and his reached out at the same time, that part that was in each of them come together? It was beyond her reasoning, beyond anyone's for there was little logic in her thinking, just faith and a sudden happiness. Nothing could ever keep them apart.

295

Thank you. It's just as if he'd put a hand on my shoulder. Let it be like that for him too.

'. . . day we'll neither of us forget. Greg gone and now you tell me this! Oh, Franny, there's nothing as pure and precious as a babe, is there? Come on my sweetie, we have to go home. Give Auntie Franny the hammer, hold your hand out Franny and see if he knows.'

The baby hung on to the hammer but he obligingly planted a wet and dribbly kiss on Gina's chin. Whatever she thought her life was lacking Nicholas was her consolation.

A day to remember indeed, the 9th of November. Just wait: let the seconds turn to minutes, to hours, to days then weeks, Fran had resolved. So time would see Greg through his training and she through the weeks of waiting.

A man got off the omnibus opposite and crossed the road towards the shop. In the gathering gloom of tea-time December he was hardly more than a shape, a shape and a walk that turned the clock back seven years almost to the day. By the time he reached the porch the jangling bell had told him his father had seen him.

'Dickie, Dickie my boy!' All the antagonism faded in the surprise of his sudden appearance and in Richard's welcome the bridge was built between them.

'Pa, bit of a shock, eh?'

Seldom was Richard lost for words; now all he could do was grasp his son's small frame in a bearlike hug. Unmanly behaviour, out of character for either of them, yet serving them as words couldn't.

'Come, come in, let's have a look at you. Pull down the blind on the door and I'll put a match to the gas.'

Seven years had turned the curly-haired cherub of a

youth into a curly-haired cherub of a man. Hard to say where the difference lay, in the fine network of lines around his eyes perhaps, but, more, in their expression. There was a confidence now that he'd lacked; his expression seemd to say 'Smal I may be, but I'm a man for all that!' And Richard? Dickie's memories of him had been as of two people, the father of his childhood, cheerful, dependable, then the man who'd dominated their lives after he'd lost Cynny, his moods setting the tone in the house until he'd lost faith with the past, or so it had seemed. He was older, no doubt of that, heavier in his build and these days he viewed the world over the top of a pair of half-moon spectacles. A gentleness about him recalled the man of the earlier age, almost Dickie expected to hear his mother's tread on the stair. It hadn't been easy to swallow his pride and come home but there could be no place for that sort of self-indulgent stubbornness in today's world.

'Pa, I had to come and see you first. Couldn't join up and feel that we – well – you know –'

'So you're going too. First Greg and now you.'

'Us and millions more. Sooner we settle the swine the sooner we can get on again.'

'Doesn't make it any easier even if you're right. Not half an hour ago Bill Pearce was in here, the postman you remember; tells me his lad's done the same thing. Signed up this morning.'

'Alf Pearce? I remember Alf, he kept rabbits. When I was a kid we had one from him. Ma got it and you made a hutch – for a surprise, d'you remember, Pa?'

'There's not much I don't remember, son.' He trod a tight-rope but had to do it; 'Are you man enough to understand that yet I wonder?'

Dickie had always looked one straight in the eye.

'I'm man enough to take it on trust. Will that do?'

297

'Your aunt will have the kettle hot. We'll lock the door and go up in a minute. Dickie – you'll treat her right, won't you, not just for my sake or hers, for your Ma's too? She'd undestand. I often think about her and – well, she'd get no pleasure out of knowing we were lonely and miserable, not Cynny.'

'Don't push me, Pa. I'll treat her right, as you put it. I'm glad you've found a way to be happy.'

'We'll not talk about it after this, son, but I must just say one bit more, then it's done.' and it shows what a jolt his emotions had had when Dickie walked in for him to be able to say it at all. 'I'll never love your Ma the less because I love Myrtle. Affection's not a thing we have just so much of to share around.' His tone made it clear, that was the end of the heart-searching. He took a breath, shut the drawer of the counter and locked it, then: 'Now if you'll push that bolt across we'll go up. Won't hurt to close up early for once.'

It had been Dickie's idea to enlist for some weeks. The headlines in this morning's newspaper had told him he could wait no longer. Yesterday the Germany navy had shelled the Yorkshire coast. Figures weren't known yet but many hundreds of civilians had been wounded, over a hundred killed. The reports told of buildings on the seafront, amusement palaces, boarding houses and homes, scarred and battered; he'd thought of Tarnmouth, of Dover, friends of the past and friends of the present. What was the Bosche planning: Belgium yesterday, England tomorrow? Dickie had packed his grip, his hour had come.

He was only in Highworth for two days, time enough to give his name to the Recruiting Officer, to see Gina, to spend a few hours helping Gee (strangers to each other yet in step from the first), to have a morning with Frances and an afternoon at the bottom of the garden with a fishing rod in his hands and ghosts for company. Then, with the latest contingent, Alf Pearce amongst them, he was bundled into an open lorry and driven to Tarnmouth Station. From the shop porch Richard watched him go. He raised his hand in farewell and was answered by a cherry grin and a two-handed thumbs-up sign. Upstairs Myrtle watched too and waved from the kitchen window trying not to mind that Dickie didn't raise his glance. As the crowded vehicle rounded the bend and disappeared from sight she went down to the shop.

That was on the 19th of December. For Frances the waiting was nearly over; one more day and Greg would be home.

That first Christmas of the war had a quality of unreality about it. Too soon for shortages to have bitten hard, the shops were piled with luxury foods for those who could afford them; war toys were every small boy's dream – canons, cavalrymen on horseback, boxes of metal soldiers, dolls like drummer boys ready to perform at the turn of a key; yet the preparations for the festival were made with a feverish excitement, an unnatural haste as if to pack a lifetime's jubilation into two short days. And for some it was already too late. The force which had set out for France in August was by now almost destroyed, experienced soldiers had been replaced by raw recruits, hospitals were full and the sight of men in the strange bright blue uniform of the wounded was a constant reminder as the shoppers filled their baskets.

Seven precious days of leave. When Greg first arrived it seemed so long, but seconds melt into minutes, then into hours, time takes everything away; wasn't that the thought that had bolstered Frances during the weeks of waiting? Nothing must mar the time they had, not even thoughts of how soon it would end. That he was home for Christmas had to be enough. She festooned the house with holly and ivy, the tree in the hall was the finest they'd ever had, Betsy cooked a whole gammon just as she did each year and Gee called at the house himself, a rare thing, to bring them the fattest goose from the farm.

'Why Gee, it looks as though it ought to be wearing the prize rosette. It's a splendid bird and it's been plucked!' Frances admired it. 'Who plucked it?

'Aw, that didn't take me but a few minutes. With Greg home you none of you want to be wasting your time on those sort of jobs.' He brushed it aside as nothing but she'd seen Betsy struggling most of an evening with the feathers of a goose and tearing her fingers into the bargain. Gee's workworn hands were so cut already that a tear or two more would go unnoticed.

'Gee,' spontaneously Frances leant forward and kissed him, 'you're one of nature's gentlemen.'

He coloured. 'Get along with you, Franny. There's me stuck here safe and doing the job I like – be a pretty poor thing if I couldn't give a few minutes of m'time. Best be getting back to it. I was thinking – don't expect Greg's got an hour to spare, but tell him I'm sorry he wasn't in. If he feels like looking in at the farm – but he'll be busy, don't push him.'

'He won't need any pushing, but he'll probably have the children in tow, at any rate Matt. He never misses a chance to come to the farm and so far neither of them have let Greg out of their sight.'

'The lad needs his father, boys do. Tell you, Franny, I'm looking forward to my young Nick tagging along. Later on, just till Greg gets home permanent you understand me, you ought to send Matt to me sometimes. He likes to help and, tell you the truth, it suits me to have a nipper along.'

300

Greg and Gee had known each other for years of course, accepted but never ventured below the surface. That same feeling that time was short must have nudged them towards each other; just as this year Christmas had to hold a concentration of rejoicing so one week of leave had to by-pass the superficial. Willingly Greg accepted the invitation to the farm.

'Gee, while I'm away keep an eye on Fran and the children for me. I just mean let them feel you're here if –'

'Depend on it and I'm real glad you ask me. Don't like pushing myself on them but you have a word with Franny. I did suggest that Matt might sometimes like to give me a lift with the work.'

The idea that five-year-old Matt might effectively give anyone a 'lift' was over optimistic.

'Have you lost any of your lads?' Greg asked.

'Ah, two gone. Certainly plenty to keep me busy here. Days are so short this end of the year. You just caught me fitting this new share, then I'm off back to the ploughing. The new lad I've taken on is good enough with the animals but can't make a straight furrow to save his life.'

Greg took his watch out of his waistcoat pocket and checked the time. A quarter to ten.

'Tell you what, let me go and put some old clothes on then I'll give you a hand. I used to fancy myself behind the plough when I was a kid.'

''Struth man, you're on leave, you can't waste your time here.'

'To be honest Gee I reckon walking your field might be just the therapy I need. Give me twenty minutes and I'll be back. Fran'll put me up a sandwich. Where am I ploughing?'

'Longacre, just beyond this grazing meadow. Are you sure you mean it? What'll Franny say? Time's something you haven't got much of.'

301

'Fran will know you'll be doing me a favour.'

So, of the seven days, that was one lost to the family, but he was right; Fran did understand. If he'd been a fisherman the river would have called him but he'd lost interest in his fishing rod almost as soon as he's started holidaying on his uncle's farm.

Strangely Frances was happy to stand back during the days, to watch him with the children playing games, listening to them reading, encouraging Alex as she practised carols on the piano, or sometimes to leave him alone with Betsy. Their nights were precious and their own.

By Christmas Day his leave was drawing towards the end but they wouldn't look ahead yet. After the morning service (and a forty-minute sermon that had needed a restraining hand on Matt's swinging legs) Myrtle and Richard came to Matlock Avenue and this year Ada and Eddy Stokes added to the number. How loudly they all sang the carols, Alex manfully working her way through her well-practised repertoire while they called on good Christian men to rejoice and all ye faithful to come. If her small fingers hit an occasional wrong note no one minded; Frances kept them on course with her fiddle.

So soon it was over and by Boxing Day they could no longer pretend. Tomorrow he'd be gone; already Frances felt hollow with dread. Consciously she watched each movement, listened to each word; none of it must ever be forgotten. How long would memories be all they had? She wouldn't think, she daren't. This time it wasn't six weeks in Wiltshire, this time it was France.

The children went to bed, Betsy had 'a few things to do' for Boxing Day or not she wasn't going to intrude on their evening. Yet once by themselves they had no need for words, didn't even want them. Side by side they sat on the chesterfield in the firelight, the branches of holly behind the pictures casting odd and unfamiliar shadows on the walls.

'I'll go down and get you some supper. We won't disturb Betsy,' Fran said as the clock struck 9.

'No, don't. I'm not hungry – are you?'

She shook her head.

'Would it be indecently early to go to bed?'

'There's nothing I can think of better than to go to bed with you indecently early,' her laugh was a brave attempt but it held no mirth.

'Tonight we won't sleep, Fran.' He turned towards her, his hand under her chin. 'I don't want to waste a second of our time with sleep.'

There was no hiding from it any longer, the night was all they had.

Their bed was warm; Betsy always put hot bottles in early in the evening.

'Fran, I want to love you, not once, but again and again, Fran, Fran. . . .'

'I want it too. The whole night's just ours.'

Their emotions were almost at bursting point, only in loving could they give expression to what they felt. They strained towards each other, their movements fierce, wild, their climax electric and over so soon. Not just once but again and again, he'd said. They hadn't intended to sleep, but nature got the better of them.

It was hours later when they woke, not knowing who stirred first.

'What's the time?' she whispered, afraid of the answer.

He sat up in bed and felt for the matches, then lit the candle on the table.

'Twenty to six. We've a long time yet.'

They lay very still, the candle flame flickering, not a sound anywhere. Then she heard her tummy rumble; it seemed to be turning somersaults.

'Help me to be brave, Greg,' her whisper was hardly audible.

They turned to look at each other, the tic in his cheek speaking for itself.

'Fran,' so quietly, 'it's really happening to us. Stay near me.'

She understood what he meant. 'You know I do, always Greg, wherever you go, however long, always I'm with you, part of you.'

'I know and I'm with you. My darling, my darling. . . .'

Silence, their hands clinging tightly to each other.

'Fran, whatever happens –'

'Don't Greg –'

'No, hear me – whatever happens nothing can alter that. I'm part of you, you're part of me.'

At a quarter to six in the morning the world is distant, it's a time for souls to meet.

She nodded. 'Always Greg, whatever I'm doing my heart's with you, Greg.'

'And you're to promise me one thing. You're not to be sad –'

'How can I promise that? Without you there's nothing.'

'Yes, sweetheart, there is, and you'll never be without me. Whatever the future holds for us I want you to be happy. . . .'

She moved closer to him. 'Hold me, Greg, hold me close; I want to keep this moment always.'

He held her. Their whispered words had held all the solemnity they'd brought to their marriage vows, they'd neither of them realised it was leading them into physical love-making and yet what other way was there for them? Their movements were slow, charged with tenderness, their eyes were open, it was a communion of body and soul alike. And afterwards they neither of them slept;

304

now their time must be counted in minutes, no longer in hours.

That morning Betsy called the children, gave them their breakfast and walked with them to school. Frances and Greg had already left. The roads in Highworth were empty except for a few cyclists and the milk cart. It was barely light, the noise of the motorcar seemed to broadcast to the world that he was going. At the far end of the High Street on the corner of River Way stood St Stephen's Church. Greg said something to her as they came towards it, she slowed down and the motor chugged to a stop. The door was never locked, they knew that, not that visitors were expected at that hour of a Wednesday morning.

They went up the gravel path, quietly lifting the latch and pushing the heavy oak door. Did they go to beg for his safe return, or to remember the vows they'd made there together, to plead that the world would find its way back to sanity, to promise in the sanctuary that had been part of their lives that however long they might be separated they'd never be divided, or was it to find courage, reassurance? Outside the grey light of early morning was dim; as they entered it the church appeared hardly out of darkness.

It was ten minutes later when they came out, both walking tall and straight. She got back into the driver's seat, he cranked the engine then climbed in beside her.

The postman's visit became the focal point of her days. Not that she had time on her hands; at home she had seven pupils by that spring and she'd agreed to go back to Warwick House on Monday mornings. Then there was what she called her war work; Wednesday afternoons at the Red Cross Centre where she rolled bandages or did

305

anything else that was asked of her. Messages had to be taken for Eddy and the surgery, occasionally a call would be urgent and, just as she had for Greg, she would get out her bicycle and go to find him on his round of visits. Her days were full; that was the way she wanted them; with time on her hands she couldn't disguise her torment of fears. At night, alone in the darkness, there was no escape. At times he seemed so near she could almost hear his step, his laugh, but at others she couldn't reach him through the wild and terrible imaginings of her mind. There were times when she could pray and that way she must have found comfort for usually she'd fall asleep even while she pleaded, but there were others when to pray was as impossible as to hope.

'Post's gone by, Mrs Greg dear. I just happened to notice him,' Betys greeted her. It was in August, a day of hazy blue sky and the promise of heat. This morning she'd been so sure there would be a letter, it was nearly a fortnight since the last. She'd woken early, keen to be up. Today she would hear. . . .

'The mail must be held up somewhere, Betsy.' It was up to her to keep the house cheerful, it took its colour from her – 'happened to notice him' indeed; she knew well enough how Betsy watched from the semi-basement kitchen window. 'When we hear we'll get two or three letters together again.'

'Ah, that'll be the way of it. Now then, look what Mr Gee just brought round for your breakfast!' On the table was a joint of smoked bacon and already she'd cut five good rashers from it for the pan.

'Gee, at this hour of the day?'

'Had to take his boxes of veggies to Mr Pengelley himself; said the lad hadn't turned in. Been hinting of signing up it seems. His brother's going, so Mr Gee says it looks like he's seen the last of him.'

306

'I read the other day that a lot of farmers are starting to take women.'

'Stuff and nonsense! A good help in the dairy or with the chickens, farmers' wives always have been – not that Gina ever took to it – but a good deal on the land is just plain hard graft, too much for a woman.'

The seed was sown. Frances was as strong as many a man or so she liked to think. And that's how it come about that she started to lend a hand on the farm. In the beginning that's all it was but two things she found. The first was that it wasn't possible to divide her life into segments and give of her best to any of them and the second that her faith in her own strength had been well merited.

''Tis a bit of extra I can do for this war;' Betsy suggested. 'You leave the surgery messages to me and the Red Cross too. Daisy'll run off to find the doctor if there's a need.'

'Betsy you work too hard already, you deserve what little time you have to yourself.'

'If there's a body who shirks an extra job at times like these then may he be ashamed. You know you feel the same way, dearie. It's all very well to do a comfortable day's work; what we need is to feel burdened. That's the only way to be part of the struggle. Mr Greg, Dickie, you – and there's Gina, she does her Red Cross now. You just let me do the doctor's messages and roll your bandages.'

So, except for Monday mornings when she still went to Warwick House, Frances worked on the farm as hard as any man and dug a straighter furrow than many. Her lessons had to be fitted in but what else had she to do with her evenings? The quintet and the orchestra had both been put in cotton wool for the duration.

Batches of mail, gaps in between, days of hope, days of gloom, but each that went was one more crossed off.

307

'Time like an ever rolling stream. . . .' they sang on many a Sunday morning in St Stephen's, indeed it was the only certainty. So the year went on, the seasons passed. With a sense of shock Frances would see patients of Greg's, wives and mothers of people who'd been part of the fabric of his work, wearing the black arm bands of mourning. The first brave confidence had gone, all that was left was dogged determination that however long it took the only end possible was victory.

On the mantlepiece in the drawing-room stood a framed photograph of Greg, he'd had it taken when four days leave had given him a chance to see Paris. It was the only picture they had of him in uniform, unsmiling; his eyes seeming to follow one, he looked as though he were listening. Frances thought of it as her's; that he was away was her loss, her tragedy. When she chanced on Alex alone in the room gazing at the framed face with a secret smile she drew back unnoticed. A hundred memories flooded her mind; the silent secrets she'd shared with her own father, the place she'd built for him in her childhood. Until that moment she'd imagined she was filling Greg's role a well as her own, not letting the children suffer the loneliness of not having him. As if it were possible, and how wrong of her to try! To unashamedly miss him was their right, to be needed was his. She saw now that her own cowardice had tried to push him out of their lives. It had been easier to assume a forced cheerfulness, keep everyone busy, to avoid acknowledging her own unhappiness and so smother their's. For that was what she'd done; she'd thought to prevent it but she'd smothered it.

That was the day she altered the position of the chairs around the oval table again.

'Why are we sitting differently?' Matt asked, 'I'm squashed up against the leg, Mum.'

308

'That's how we always used to have the chairs, don't you remember? That's Daddy's place at the end.'

'I remember,' Alex said. 'That's nice, Mum; it looks as though he'll be back soon.'

Frances nodded. Alex at nine was growing up.

The chairs were only a symbol. She resolved that from then on he would be talked about with honesty, never again would she pretend. This was his home, without him it was as empty as – as the Renault standing idly in the shed now that there was no petrol.

Hurrying to the farm on her bicycle a few days later she glanced across at the shop as she passed. Nearly 9 o'clock and the 'Closed' sign still on the door; she'd never known Richard to be as late. In normal circumstances she would have wondered about it and pedalled on. In 1916 a break from routine was all it took to arouse a sick dread they'd all come to know.

She propped her bicycle against the kerb and went down the path to the back steps that led from the garden to the kitchen. No need to bring anyone down to the side door, and the shop would still be locked.

'Coo-ee,' she called as she let herself in. 'May I come in?'

Myrtle heard her and came down the passage to the kitchen. She was still in her dressing-gown, her hair tumbling around her shoulders. It must have been years since Frances had seen her like that and even at a moment like this (for she recognised without being told that this was no ordinary morning) she knew a feeling of loss. Her pretty Mama, she was middle-aged, this morning she was almost old.

'Is something wrong? I saw the shop was –'

Myrtle didn't answer, there was no need. Her ready tears spilled as she passed the cablegram across the table. Even before she read it Frances knew what it would say, Dickie's war was over.

Something had woken her. She lay still and listened. What it was she couldn't be sure. Thunder perhaps, the air was heavy enough. There it was again, a distant sound, but no clap of thunder lasted as long as that. Gunfire? But guns didn't sound like a far-off earthquake. She'd heard them firing sometimes when the Zepplins had strayed off course and crossed the coast nearby, loud, separate bursts, each a positive sound that rattled the windows.

She threw off the single blanket and went to the window. Instinctively her hand felt for the envelope that was on her dressing table, it had come only this morning but already she'd read it until she must have known it by heart.

'Four o'clock in the morning,' he'd written; 'everywhere is uncannily quiet. We've moved forward; we're ready and waiting, that's how it seems here. No one knows when the push is coming, us least of all, but rumour is rife. They say when it come this will be "the big one".'

She remembered his words, 'the big one', and without a doubt she knew what she heard must be gunfire. A steady rumble as if far away the earth trembled. To hear it here, in England! How many miles away was she – forty?

'No, no,' she whispered, 'stop it, please; don't let it be happening.' Her hands were clammy and trembling, her mouth dry with fright. 'Let me wake and find it was a thunderstorm, let it be just a dream,' but the envelope she clutched was real enough. 'The big one' they were calling it, waiting for the casualties they knew would come.

His words came back to her. On the next page he'd written as only in the middle of a silent night he could. 'Do you remember the feeling of those days before it all happened? Memories are my constant companion. Walking on the cliff top together, bicycling along the lanes, the willow tree by the river, Sunday mornings in St Stephen's, watching you sitting up in bed, a baby at your

310

breast fixing you with a stare of unblinking concentration – Alex? Matt? Both, I suppose. A thousand things I remember, every inch of your precious body, the sound of your voice, your laugh. Fran, my love, my only love. I thank God for memory, it's the dearest of His gifts.'

His letters were usually much less sentimental but that one had been written in the small hours and now in the small hours she remembered.

At the breakfast table Betsy gave her a searching look but said nothing. Not like Franny to have red eyes in the morning. Good thing children didn't notice these things.

'Betsy I shall be late home today. I've no lessons and if the weather holds Gee wants to finish getting the hay in. You children can come to the farm after school if you like; Auntie Gina said she'd give you tea.'

The news was greeted with excitement. Alex always liked to go and see Gina. Sophie made her feel uncomfortable sometimes, she wasn't sure why, but it was worth that to be able to help put Nicholas to bed. As for Matt he liked nothing better than to help on the farm. A big boy for his years, at nearly eight his 'helping' was beginning to almost be worth having.

The day was the 2nd of July. They none of them knew as they started out that yesterday had seen the beginning of what history books would call the Battle of the Somme, a battle that was to rage for over four months. Before long news started to come through, and as a background to what they read time and again they were to hear the rumble of that distant hell.

The hay was in, the corn waiting to be cut. Frances had been working in the field all day, bent double picking up potatoes. By the time she got home all she longed for was a hot bath and bed.

'This came Mrs Greg, duckie.' Betsy came to the bicycle shed to meet her; 'not ten minutes ago the lad

311

brought it. Thought I'd best open it up.'

Frances took the cablegram. She'd never seen Betsy cry before.

'Oh, Madame, don't you just long for the pretty shades we used to wear! A soft pink, or bronze for these first autumn days.'

Myrtle took the hand mirror Madame Zeigler passed her and turned to view the effect of the back in the long looking-glass on the wall.

'To get the dyes is becoming impossible.' The milliner too yearned for the colours they'd taken for granted. 'Everywhere it's the same; clothes are so drab, and as for those ugly skirts cut high above the ankle – not many women improve their looks by showing their legs to my way of thinking – and so straight. Less material, less style. For my hats I do try to make up in elegance what we have to lose in colour. And, sadly, nowadays there's many a lady who dresses in shades of mourning.'

'Indeed, and I among them.' In a second her eyes filled; the dark grey hat became an acceptable symbol of her suffering. 'A step-son who's been as dear as a son since he was a babe, then a son-in-law. This dreadful war, there seems no end to it.'

Madam Zeigler had shared Myrtle's joy and sadnesses since as a girl bride she'd come to the salon on the very first day it had opened, over thirty years ago. With the coming of the war there had been whispers of internment; no one had ever doubted her origins or the trace of an accent there'd been no reason to suspect. Her papers had been checked and word had soon spread. Madame Marte Zeigler had been born Miss Mary Bugler. Her Viennese training had been behind the pseudonym; a clever idea it had proved too for no matter how chic her hats Miss

312

Bugler's charges would have been shillings less than Madame Zeigler's.

Now she asked: 'Is there no news of the doctor?'

'Nothing. Three weeks and still nothing. How can a man be lost? To say he's missing, as if he could disappear!'

'We cannot start to imagine. But it's almost harder for her than to be told he's been killed; just never to know what's become of him. . . . How is she?'

Myrtle's tears had overflowed to roll down her cheeks. She dabbed them with her handkerchief, comforted by the faint lavender smell as she shook it from its freshly ironed folds.

'She says so little. I can talk to you Madame, I know you understand. If I try to speak to her about it it's as if she's made of stone. I can't get near to her and – oh dear, forgive me,' the tears flowed faster, 'you wouldn't credit the way she is with the children. Yesterday at tea I had a premonition she needed me, I went to call and when I got there, what do you think I found? She'd pushed that motorcar out of the shed and she and the children were polishing it as if their lives depended on it; she was chivying them along, even making some sort of game of it.'

'Poor girl.'

'I don't understand her. Always she must push herself against every hurdle. If only she'd let go, cry, accept. But no, Franny has to battle no matter what the cost.'

'Poor girl.'

Betsy watched too and waited to pick up the pieces when Frances could battle no more. Gina watched, always hoping tht when Frances accepted what they all felt must be the truth, when Greg was finally gone, then she'd be the one she would need and the old love between them would mean what it had as they'd groped their way into adolescence.

313

And Frances herself took each day, worked until her body ached, lived in limbo, neither past nor future having any place. It sounds easy; she forced herself into believing it was what she had to do. To the children all she said was: 'Daddy isn't able to write to us for a little while,' and they'd become so used to accepting things they couldn't understand that they didn't question. Somewhere he lived; if he didn't surely she'd know.

Sometimes she'd dream he was slipping into a dark abyss as she reached out to him. That her arm could stretch to lengths that seemed limitless was reasonable, such is the way with dreams. More than once she woke crying; in sleep she had no power over her behaviour. Then she'd know herself lost, alone, nothing but misery and helplessness ahead. At other times her dreams would bring him so close he was a part of her. She'd wake with her faith restored, able to hope again and to pray. That was the only way; her trust must be strong, for herself and even more for him.

The days of September saw the harvest carried in. She left home early each morning and come back only when the daylight faded. Betsy shouldered all the burdens of the house. By the time she wheeled her bicycle up the side path the children would already be in bed and she would have been away for twelve hours or more.

On this particular evening Betsy heard the back door and knew she was home, then called her into her sitting-room. 'This came for you, Mrs Greg, duckie.' She took a letter from the mantlepiece. 'Came this afternoon. I all but walked it round to the farm but – well you'd best go and read it on your own. I've put a match to the fire upstairs for you.'

Frances took the letter. She and Betsy looked at one another, neither wanting to face what they feared. Someone else had written. Hadn't they heard of this sort

314

of thing, a senior officer saying how much he was missed, how proud she must be. . . .

She haggled the lip of the envelope open but she didn't go upstairs. This time she needed to share; her face was expressionless as she read.

'Well?' Betsy prompted softly.

A sob caught in Frances' throat, she tried to breath steadily but she felt she'd choke as she fought against her tears.

'Franny, lovey, there, there child. What is it they've told you?'

As if she were indeed a child again France flopped into a chair and clung to her old friend, her face buried in the soft bosom that over-topped her corsetted form.

'. . . prisoner . . . wounded. . . . Betsy, he's alive, Greg's alive . . . found him. . . .'

'Alive! Mr Greg alive! Thanks be. Didn't we know it duckie?' Words straight from her heart. 'He's out of it now child, he'll come home to us soon as it's all over. There, just you cry it out, poor little soul, bottling it up all this time. All over now dearie. Nothing's going to hurt him now; we'll have him home sound as a bell.'

That was in September, the war just two years old. Even more than before Frances had only one goal, victory. She worked with an energy that seemed endless. At the end of the day she only felt satisfied if her muscles ached; she needed to be physically exhausted in her effort to beat the Hun. When Daisy left to work in a munitions factory they didn't replace her, partly economy and partly patriotism. To employ a girl in the home was to help the enemy.

For weeks they waited to hear from him. How long Red Cross letters took they had no idea, or even how soon he'd be well enough to write. Wounded? How badly wounded?

When his letter did come it dropped through the letterbox just as Fran was crossing the hall on a morning when for a moment Betsy's back must have been turned to the kitchen window and she didn't 'happen to notice'. His own writing, not the same neat quick hand as she'd been used to, but his own. She flopped on the bottom stair and tore the envelope open.

'Mrs Greg,' Betsy shouted as she clumped up the basement stairs, 'are you coming for your breakfast? Chillun are on with theirs, the porridge is out. Did you hear me –? Why child, what is it?'

'A letter, Betsy it's from Greg, he's written himself.'

'Thank God for that. Then he's well again?'

'Getting well, Betsy. It was his shoulder and his arm. But he's getting better, he can write.' Only half a page and that with difficulty. Until Frances held his letter in her hand she'd never let herself admit how frightened she'd been. How silly to cry now, to feel the tears running silently down her cheeks.

'I'll tell the children tonight,' she gulped. 'I must go and wash my face. Silly isn't it . . . can't seem to talk about it . . . tonight I'll tell them.' She wasn't as strong as she'd tried to believe.

Another haymaking, another harvest. These days her hands were so chapped that even the strings of her fiddle cut them.

'Oh Franny, your poor hands.' She'd called at the shop on her way home, the bearer of a dozen large brown eggs from Gee. Myrtle took them gratefully enough but the gift was marred by the sight of the hands that passed them. 'They used to be so nice.'

Frances hid a smile. So nice? At the time it had been: 'Such a pity; a dainty hand is an asset to a woman.'

316

'As nutmeg graters they'd be useful.'

'Oh dear, Franny, what's it doing to us all?' Myrtle's eyes were as clear as ever they'd been, the whites as white, surrounding irises the same tawny brown that seemed now to mirror the anguish of a troubled world. Her complexion had lost its glow, the skin was just as soft but youth had gone. Indefinably Myrtle had aged; perhaps without realising it she'd given up the battle now that she was secure in Richard's devotion. To him she never altered, his lovely Flower. Life had been kinder to her than she realised for without Richard's unfailing love she would have been fighting a losing battle.

Now she looked at Frances, her brow furrowed. 'Even now Franny you don't see a grey hair on my head. At your age you shouldn't have that streak, the colour has almost gone. You always did take after Clement but I did think you'd inherited your colouring from me. You must try and take care of your appearance, dear. Remember it's easier to protect it than to win it back once it's lost. When dear Greg gets home he'll want to find you as he left you.'

'Oh mother,' she pretended to make a joke of the warning, 'you're not suggesting I change the habits of a lifetime now! Anyway my genes seem to have come from father's side so I'm a hopeless case.'

Myrtle would have been pleasantly surprised if she could have been a fly on the wall as her daughter made ready for bed that night; a hundred strokes with the hair brush, then vaseline on her hands so thick that she had to cover them with an old pair of cotton gloves. Ten minutes in bed and the gloves came off, there were limits to what she could endure but at least the warning had sown its seed.

The history of the war has been written times enough, its battles and losses recorded. In a backwater like Highworth how closely one was involved depended so

317

much on the people one loved, where they were, how often letters came, whether instead of a letter with a Field Post Office frank on it there came the buff envelope everyone dreaded. Food grew shorter, queues for what little there was outside the ration grew longer, but all that was superficial. The daily grind was broken by an occasional concert in St Stephen's Hall, a whist drive in the Institute, a singsong with a silver collection for the boys at the front and just before another Christmas came around a variety show to raise money for Red Cross parcels. Out of the usual path of the Zeppelins, that was the domestic scene in Highworth. Trade in the shop was as brisk as Richard had ever know, for there were a good many who had more to spend than they'd been used to; these days there was work for everyone. Extra to spend, extra trade, yet it brought little cheer for by then no one dared to look ahead and hope to see the light at the end of the tunnel. Places they'd never heard of became household names, Vimy, Passchendale, and others that already held memories, came into the news again, Ypres, the Somme.

The end was coming but no one suspected it anymore than they had seen what was ahead of them four years before in the last golden days of peace.

So at last it was over and the prisoners were the first to come home.

Frances and the children were on the platform ten minutes before the train was due. Four years since he'd seen her; would he find her terribly changed? Any amount of vaseline hadn't been able to work the miracle she'd hoped for. Nothing could take away the streak of grey in her hair above the scar on her temple crows feet were etched around her eyes. Before she'd left home she'd examined herself critically; four years had left their

318

mark. She'd bought a new suit for Greg's homecoming. No chance of anything colourful but the donkey brown, cut to the new shorter style and worn with a brown velvet wide-crowned tam-o-shanter, suited her in its simplicity.

And if she'd altered, what about the children? Alexandra's face was white, she chewed nervously at her lips, glanced at Frances with a quick smile that was no smile, then back down the track. Matt, standing by her side was already the taller of the two, larger boned, his face hadn't her fine cut features. Even topped with its grey cap his tawny brown hair grew with a mind of its own, springing into a wave that escaped and stuck out over his left ear. His freckled nose and ready smile never altered, the same at ten as it had been at two. Frances looked at them trying to see them with Greg's eyes; it was easier than to imagine his reaction to the changes he must find in her.

The signal dropped, the train was coming, her heart was beating into her throat. On the platform she could feel the surge of anticipation; they weren't the only family waiting. As the carriages snaked slowly in one could feel the tension, everyone posied ready to spring to life. This was it, the minute had come, the seconds all ticked away and time was bringing him back. Suddenly she didn't know how she could face it. Alex touched her hand, looking for reassurance or giving it? Doors were being thrown open, one or two people shouted as they recognised some uniformed figure.

No sign of him. He hadn't come! 'Please God don't let him not be here, please let me see him. . . .' Not known how to face it had she imagined? 'Where is he . . . please God, please. . . .'

'There he is! Dad! I see him. Dad!' It was Matt who spied him first and rushed through the throng to meet him. Frances and Alex saw him at the same second. The child stepped back, her face no longer ashen but now with

319

two unnaturally bright patches on her cheeks. As for Frances, she was rooted to the ground, her legs had lost all power of movement.

Then he was there, only inches from her. He put his grip on the ground, she felt his fingers under her chin holding her face towards his as he had a thousand times. From nowhere Myrtle's voice echoed telling her to take care of her looks, he wouldn't want to find her changed. In the first moment he saw the lines at the corner of her eyes, lines she'd not had four years ago, but above all he saw the expression in them just as he'd dreamed. Gently he kissed her.

Then he turned to Alexandra, stooping to hold her close and then feeling a sudden bearline hug as her reserve melted.

'We'll have to go on the 'bus Greg, there's no petrol.' Such banal words but they're easier than the profound and at least they showed her she hadn't lost her voice.

'The 'bus is fine.' Neither had he.

He was home, wild joy was coursing through her. Minutes ago she'd felt she'd lost the power in her legs, then her voice, now to think clearly was beyond her. Walking by her side his hand gripped hers; just in front of them Alex and Matt led the way to the 'bus stop each holding a handle of his grip. This was the moment she'd dreamed of, to touch him, to see him strong and well, such happiness was almost too much to bear, certainly too much to more than blindly live through until her reason returned!

Poor Betsy. She who'd been their prop and stay all the time he'd been away, she was ashamed that if tears had to be shed they should be hers.

So much had to be packed into the day; a visit to the shop where Myrtle shed tears that 'the poor dear boy had come home to them' and more for 'poor dear Dickie', a bottle of home-made wine (blackberries picked over two years ago) opened on Richard's insistence. All that within half an hour but then that's what war had done to them, they'd all learnt that, whether tragedy or joy, sometimes one must skim the surface, that was the only way to survive.

Then at last it was evening, the children in bed and asleep, the gas turned down and a fresh log thrown on the fire. In the shadows of the flickering flames they were alone again; so much to say with years to make up, but time enough later. His arm was around her, her head on his shoulder, the only sound the rhythmical ticking of the clock on the mantlepiece. Seconds, minutes. 'This too will pass, this precious evening.'

Later he lay in the luxury of the deep warm water, his own bath again. He could hardly believe it was happening to him. Surely he'd wake as he had so often and find himself in the narrow bunk that had been his quarters for two years?

Fran came in carrying two towels.

'These are lovely and warm.' She spoke. No dream did that and no dream wrapped the soft white towel around him as he stood up.

'Greg, Greg,' she laid her head against him caring nothing for the wet, 'you're here, you're strong and whole, it's not changed you. I thought. . . .'

He held her close. They were too full to speak but this wasn't like the first moments at the station, this was real, her feet were on the ground. She ached with love for him as he sat on the edge of the wooden casement of the bath and reached to take her on his knee. Somehow though she slipped out of his grasp and kneeling in front of him laid her cheek against his chest. She kissed his shoulder, his chest, gently laid her mouth against his stomach, his groin, she burned with a need to serve him. She knew

321

what she did and seemed driven by something outside herself. Later she would lie close to him, fulfilment would be for her as well as for him. But not yet.

'Fran, Fran, careful Fran, you shouldn't,' he whispered urgently. But she knew she should.

To kneel before him, to show her love in this special way was what she wanted above anything else. He felt the warmth of her mouth, his fingers moved on the back of her head and suddenly, holding her close, too late now to pull away. His blessed Fran, his blessed love. The agony of the years was wiped clean, he was home.

And in her folly she thought they could turn back the clock, pick up the threads of the past.

Chapter Thirteen

'So lovely to have things normal again, Franny. Dear Gregory back to his doctoring and you at home where you should be. I expected that by this time you would have stopped going to Warwick House; there can't be the need of it any longer.'

'Of course I shan't give up teaching, Mother, why should I? To be honest I miss the farm but that's all in the past. Gina says Gee can get all the labour he wants now that the men are coming home so fast. A lot of them have no job to come back to – their wives must have been better off with their few shillings a week army allowance.'

'Oh dear, poor souls. Still I'll be bound they're happier to have their menfolk home. No allowance can make up for their being away.' To Myrtle that was the end of the matter. It was bad enough that all these months after the end of the war they had less food in the shops than there had been before the armistice. At least with the soldiers getting back to their old lives there must be a move towards sanity.

So much worried Frances. At least men coming back to look for work gave her something she wasn't frightened to clutch at. Deep in her mind, constantly nagging at her, was Greg. Was she being as short-sighted as Myrtle? Four years of a life so alien to his nature must leave him changed, but it was over. What was the use of brooding? They had so much to be grateful for. As Myrtle said, daily life appeared to be normal again, at least for them. Sometimes everything was as it had been and she'd be filled with thankfulness and relief, only to find that suddenly something would trigger off his resentment and the anger she'd come to dread.

Men were coming home to unemployment, she'd said to Myrtle. That was something to do with it. She knew well enough the visits he made, often unasked and unpaid, on men who'd been promised a Country Fit for Heroes, only to come home to 19s a week dole and to feel themselves on the human scrapheap. Joining the army had been a release from unemployment for so many and now their hunt for work must start again.

Newspapers spoke of the new industrial boom; in many places there was evidence of it, but not in Highworth. There the owner of the timber yard that had once belonged to Greg's father was the largest employer, for the rest there were a few shops, glad to take back the men who'd been there before, and four years' accumulation of repairs and odd jobs.

Each day Greg went on his round of visits, sometimes to homes as comfortable as his own but often to homes that disgusted him. That things hadn't improved during the war he could understand but now the months went by and still nothing was done. As long as the shillings came in each week for rent the landlords and council alike looked no further. He was ashamed and filled with burning anger.

Frances's war had been one of shortages and anxiety, hard work and anxiety, loneliness and anxiety, of dreams of a future as golden as the past, and always anxiety. Now that golden future had become the present; only in Greg was the difference. It seemed to her that while to have him home was all she'd asked, it wasn't enough for him. She was hurt, angry and resentful and most of all she was at a loss to understand.

'Have to find you a soap box, my son,' Richard said tolerantly. He and Myrtle had been passing the house that afternoon on their customary Sunday stroll when Alex had seen them through the window. They'd needed no persuading to come in then, finding Greg had been called out, to wait to see him and finally to stay to tea.

Watching him Frances tried to hide how worried she'd become. That quick frown was so unlike him. 'You're strong, you're fit, you've not changed,' she'd said when he'd come home, her heart full of thankfulness. She'd been confident, not for a minute doubted he'd slip back just as she would into their old ways.

Letting her thoughts wander she'd missed what he was saying: '. . . conditions that breed disease. Have any of you seen inside Roebury Buildings? Of course you haven't. Mould on the walls, leaking roofs, one lavatory between four families –'

'Hush Gregory dear.' Myrtle didn't offend him as anyone else migh have; he knew there was no pretence in her embarrassment.

'Mother,' he'd been warming to his subject – even without Richard's soap box he'd held the stage – 'if you could just see it you'd understand. Hovels to live in and some of them with no more than 19s a week to pay the rent and keep their families. A boom is coming, they say. Precious little sign of it in Highworth.'

'Perhaps dear if they were to move to where the work is, even to Tarnmouth?' Myrtle hoped her suggestion might put an end to the conversation; these discussions with Gregory were all too frequent, and she found such talk uncomfortable.

325

'Move? What building is there? A few houses on the west side of Tarnmouth. And how can people uproot their families to go anywhere where the work is? Nearly three quarters of a million families are homeless, homeless and hopeless. And here we sit with the table piled with food, seeing no further than the end of our noses. Doesn't a man have the right to the dignity of providing for his own wife and children? When I think how they must have longed to come home – and for what?'

'But Gregory, what can we do for them? How does it help these poor miserable souls for us to get upset? Surely, dear, that you look after them is something; at least you've nothing to reproach yourself with.'

'And so we accept, God forgive us.'

The shrill bell of the telephone just outside the dining-room door put an end to the conversation. Young Mrs Carrington from Matley Heights had gone into labour; would the doctor come. A first baby, he knew he had no need to rush, but he knew too that Ella Carrington was highly strung and already terrified.

'Yes, I will, but tell her there's plenty of time, give her a cup of tea and try and get her to eat something . . . yes, that's right. . . . I'll not be more than ten minutes or so. I'll get the car out straight away.'

Frances listened to his reassuring voice; that was the Greg of old. A minute later hearing him crank the Renault to life she wouldn't have been human if she'd not thought: 'Well, at least that's one call he'll be paid for today.'

For a first baby Ella Carrington made short work of her confinement and he was home again before 11 o'clock.

Poverty was the enemy, the enemy of those who suffered it, of he who longed to fight for their sakes and saw no way and of Frances because all too often his battling soul was carried out of her reach. Not so tonight. To bring a new life into the world, healthy and perfect, was a fresh miracle each time. She could tell from the sound of his tread on the stairs that all had gone well. Tonight he wasn't a fighter, or if he was it was without bitterness.

'Your Sabbath hasn't been exactly a day or rest, has it? Eat these sandwiches Betsy left covered for you and then let's go to bed before anything else happens.'

'Share them with me. To be honest I'm not hungry, but we daren't leave Betsy's sandwiches.'

He must have been hungrier than he'd realised, the cold beef sandwiches soon disappeared between the two of them.

Upstairs he sat on the side of the bed watching her plait her long hair for the night. Did she will his mind to follow hers? Certainly she tried to. It was she who opened her arms to him, holding his head to her breast, she who slipped her nightgown from her shoulders and let it fall to the floor. Not a word was spoken or needed. The devils that so often plagued him were quiet, Fran was his refuge and strength. As her body thrilled to his love her heart was at peace and afterwards the miracle of what they'd shared still held them. So often she imagined his frustrations to come between them, but not tonight. The emotion of the moment, the intimacy of darkness, all played a part. In that moment she knew nothing had changed.

He'd been home for a year, he'd seen an epidemic of influenza that had waged through war-stricken Europe taking its toll of young and old alike. What he saw all added fuel to his fire; without proper housing and warmth, without enough food, what chane had they?

327

Moving among the sick it seemed he had a built-in immunisation; his own good health never let him down.

By then demobilisation had brought everyone home, some to work, many to none, but lack of creature comforts appeared only to make them take their pleasure where they could. There was no doubt of the bumper crop of babies.

It was early in 1920, 2 o'clock on a cold morning in February and for hours he'd been with Betty Hogg, one of the patients he'd dropped in on over the years, helping her bring her fourth child into the world. Now, the baby was safely delivered and the same neighbour who'd taken the three older children to 'turn in with my lot' had been left to do the honours in the one and only bedroom.

Gregory scrubbed his hands in the wooden-handled round bowl in the kitchen sink while Jo Hogg poured them both a cup of strong tea.

'Are you fixed all right to be home with her for a day or two, Jo?' for Jo was one of the lucky ones, out of work before he'd gone off to war he'd found a job now driving the brewer's dray.

'Effie Hume, that's Effie with her now, she'll keep an eye. And our young Cissy's rising ten now; she's a help about the place, she'll stay home from school for a bit. Was these walls what must've started her off; got up the steps this morning she did trying to scrub the mould off them. Felt so well she said, thought she could manage.'

'She's been very fit this time, Jo. And the baby's a fine lad, small but with a good pair of lungs.'

'Don't know how you do it, Doctor, straight I don't. Fair turns my stomach to hear a woman screaming out like that. She sets great store by you; "be all right when the doctor gets here", over and over she said it. Tell you one thing,' he took a gulp of the unpalatable brew, 'what a woman has to put up with ain't that much easier than what we saw on the Somme and that's the truth.'

Greg gave him a smile, thinking what a good lad he was. In years there was little between them, the expression was born of the Somme perhaps, shared memories that made an invisible bond between so many men.

If the 'good lad' had realised the results of his next remark he might have kept his thoughts to himself. 'Talking about you last night we were, Bet and me. Pity they haven't got one or two like you at the Town Hall, we were saying; might get something done about these old places. Never have sight nor sound of any of them; glad enough to get our votes then that's the last of it. Too far out of Tarnmouth for them to bother, I suppose. Never hear a squeak out of that Councillor Henderson. He's supposed to be our man in Highworth, isn't he?'

Out of acorns. . . .

'You don't think I'd stand a chance, is that it?' Greg said the next morning to Fran. He'd taken her support for granted. If even she doubted him then he must have a steep uphill battle ahead.

'It's not that. Greg, surely to goodness you've got more than enough to do. As it is you're here little enough.'

'What do you think though, Fran? Would people have enough trust to support me? There's so much needs doing. You've heard me talking about it often enough. Those poor devils feel they've been let down, they think Highworth's out on a limb and it's true. That's the way it always has been. We've been lucky; it's never mattered to us.'

'The more you do the more they'll expect of you. That's what I think, if you really want to know! You'll be rushing off to council meetings, always at their beck and call for something.'

'If I get elected. . . .'

'If! Of course you'll get elected. You're bound to be elected.'

He heard the impatience in her voice and frowned, puzzled.

'What's up, Fran?'

'Nothing. No, that's not true. I just think it's a pity you don't think more of your own family and less of every lame dog who hasn't the gumption to look after himself.'

'That's not fair! Fran, it's just not like you. Our children never lack for love nor yet for food and comforts.'

She swallowed, her throat was dry. At the other side of the breakfast table Greg sat very still, only the tic in his cheek betraying him. They both knew that whether or not he stood for the municipal election was no more than a part of it. This was something deeper than the few hours of each week he'd spend in the council chamber.

I should stop, she thought. I've said enough, too much. If all he wanted was his home, the children, me, if all that was enough and he didn't care then he'd not be Greg. He always has cared. Isn't that why he's a doctor, isn't that why the people love him? But it's not fair, we have so little of him and it'll be less . . . I shouldn't say anymore. . . .

But she did. 'You do have a family. They may not be neglected enough for you to find interesting –'

'Fran, we can't talk now. I've got surgery waiting.'

Late though it was they'd still been sitting at the breakfast table. It has been nearly 4 o'clock by the time he'd got to bed, Betty Hogg and baby comfortably settled. He hadn't intended to be slow, but despite getting up at the usual time, lack of sleep had probably made everything conspire against him. A cut on his chin while he was shaving, an broken shoe lace, a nagging headache even though he tried to ignore it, and then as if

330

she sided with the enemy Fran sounding unapproachable and critical. He wished he'd not told her yet about Jo's suggestion.

Now he stood up, carefully rolling his serviette and putting it back in its ring. The children had gone to school, Betsy was downstairs. Only Fran was left at the table. There was something in the droop of her shoulders that touched him, his rising anger evaporated and as he passed her he laid a hand on her head.

'Try and understand, Fran. We can't talk now, I must go, but try and understand. They need someone who can put their case, fight their battles. . . .'

She nodded. So silly to feel like this. Hadn't their fight always been his? There was nothing new in it. Yet it was as if she saw him being pulled two ways; she and the family on one side – and what on the other? Social injustice, poverty, broken promises made to men who'd fought believing in justice, bad housing, disease, ignorance, these were the things that tugged at his conscience. She heard the door close; he'd gone downstairs to morning surgery and she knew she had no choice but to accept. In all the years of separation she'd never felt more alone.

That was in February, three months before the election. Word soon spread that he was interested. That he'd be everyones' choice was a foregone conclusion to Betsy, who could see no other way and of course wanted to talk about it when she took her weekly order to Mr Pengelley. No better way than that of broadcasting news. The red-faced and talkative grocer enjoyed his piece of inside information.

Another local purveyor of news, written and verbal, was Bill Pearce, the postman. He heard the rumour first in the Barley Mow a week or so after Jo Hogg had sowed the seed.

'Just the one this morning,' Richard looked up as he

331

came in to the house with a letter in his hand, 'and that's for your wife.'

'Ah, thanks, I'll take it up to her. From her sister by the look of the hand.'

'That daughters of hers, I heard a whisper that her husband's to go on the council. That right is it?'

'Likely he will. Certainly he's going to stand and I'd say his chance is as good as any.'

'Ah, better, if you ask me. Real fine lad. Good many years it is since we've had need of a doctor but he came to my Liz, must be twelve years or more back, when she had a nasty fall. No airs and graces, not much than a lad those years ago but seemed to know what he was at. Well, he'll get my vote and I'll see to it Liz gives him her's too.'

'There were plenty more who shared his view. With patients in all quarters of Highworth he was a popular doctor, added to which good looks never did anyone any harm. Women had fought long and hard for their vote, at least some of them had. Now it was partially theirs; those over thirty could go to the polls – could, but not necessarily did. They'd vote for Gregory though, that was different, he was someone they knew. It would be good to have someone at the Town Hall at last who understood their problems and especially good to know they'd helped to put him there.

So Greg took his place on the Tarnmouth Borough Council representing the outermost ward of the district, Highworth, the one-time neighbouring village that was steadily becoming more closely linked with town. At last he had a platform, served on two committees, the Health and the Housing, and at that point he was confident his fight must be as good as won. In his ignorance he believed it would be so easy.

332

The meeting had all the signs of a long sitting. Elderly Donald Spiers, the Committee Clerk for many years, opened his notebook and laid out three sharpened pencils on the table in front of him, then turned to the agenda as if he hoped some of the items might have been miraculously erased.

He scribbled the names of those present at the top of his first clear page. 'Not much hope of getting home before 11 tonight. That Dr Smart'll have plenty to say on this lot. Shared sanitation; Beaconsfield Buildings; vermin in butcher's shop – wonder where that is, have to warn Maudie to keep clear of it when I hear; probably in Highworth though; doesn't miss a trick that one. My but it's hot in here tonight; cut the air with a knife before the evening's out, what with the heat and the smoke from their pipes. No way to spend a summer's evening. You'd think they'd got no homes to go to. Damn this collar, I told Maudie not to starch it so, cuts like a knife,' and he eased his boney fingers around the edge of the offending wing collar trying to keep it away from his scraggy chicken neck.

Even as he let his thoughts ramble his pencil was at work noting what was worth noting, leaving out what led nowhere. He'd done the job so many years it had become second nature and he knew too which members might drop their pearls of wisdom and which would seldom merit a mention in the minute book.

Item Three: Shared Sanitation. For nearly an hour the subject was bandied about the table, and on one side were aired expressions such as: 'a public duty it is amoral to ignore' and 'spread of disease in an area of society least able to fight it', even 'and did our sons and brothers give their lives for their families to be used like this? For many of those living in the squalid conditions I've described are indeed their orphans and windows.' Donald Spiers let his

333

pencil fly. He did wish they'd get a move on but he had to admit that young doctor m'lad from Highworth had a gift for words; even in these few weeks the minute book bore evidence of it. Spoke a deal of sense too. Fit for Heroes they'd said. He saw little sign of it.

The Borough Treasurer was on his feet now. That made easier recording, he could guess what he would say. No money to spare, it hadn't been allowed for this year.

By the time Greg reached Highworth it was nearly midnight, the hot evening had turned to a hot night and distant thunder rumbled.

Fran was waiting for him in the dining-room.

'Fran, it's always the same, can't afford this, can't afford that. . . .' As he spoke he flopped into a chair at the table, unsuspecting that her greeting might have held any resentment that having stayed out until this time he even now brought the arguments of the meeting home with him.

'That's an answer everyone can understand. And of course it's an infallible argument, Greg. Whether it's with the housekeeping or the nation's wealth, money isn't elastic.'

'But, dammit, where are their priorities? They aren't reasonable. Do you know they're putting a new hard surface on Gravel Hill. The old track isn't good enough now that there are so many motorcars it seems! Wouldn't a bit of plumbing in those dreadful tenements be a better way of using the rates? And the War Memorial – as if the poor devils wouldn't rather their families had a lavatory with a chain to pull than see their names on a slab of granite – of course they would.'

She didn't answer. She wanted to change the subject.

'I'll cut you some cold meat, you must be starved.'

'No, I don't want anything.' He felt her hands massaging the back of his neck; even against his will it was

334

relaxing him. 'I'm so damned ignorant, Fran. I only know what I want to know, there's so much more. Highworth is just a drop in the ocean.'

His voice was tired, he was coming back to her. As he relaxed so her own resentment faded.

'I suppose wherever you serve you have things you want to see done. If you were on the Highways Committee you'd want something for the roads. Then there are the schools –'

Not a clever move on her part; he jumped at the cue: 'That's another thing, we should do more for the children. If they don't think it necessary for any other reason they surely can see that a strong country has to be a healthy country. The council ought to send doctors to the schools, take up cases parents have neglected – ignorance, poverty, laziness, whatever the reason the children shouldn't have to suffer for it.'

The gentle massaging went on.

After a minute or two: 'Come on, Fran, cold meat sounds good after all. Let's go down to the kitchen, I'll eat down there.' He stood up and turning to her tilted her chin in the old way, then touched her mouth lightly with his. 'You're a good lady, my Fran, to come home and find you waiting, it's like – like –'

'I know what it's like,' she rubbed her cheek against his, the hours of waiting, her angry loneliness, forgotten; 'It's like I feel when I hear you coming. Closed in, warm, safe. . . .' She chuckled: 'Fifteen years Greg, I never thought people felt like this after fifteen years.'

His hug said it all.

'Come on, woman; the spirit may be willing but the flesh is hungry.'

'I know what I want to know,' he'd said, but one couldn't fight battles without knowledge of the enemy's defences. So he read, always realising that the problems he cared about went so much further than Highworth or Tarnmouth. The so-called boom couldn't last; in the first hungry market of peace the workers had wanted increased wages, and employers had paid, sure of the demand for their goods. War-torn Europe couldn't afford our exports; 1921 was only the beginning but already the warning signs were there. Beaconsfield Buildings had fallen into even worse decay and although one or two families had moved into new council houses in Tarnmouth there were more ready to replace them.

Greg's battle went on, his and those of others like him all over the country, but despite them the number of families needing houses rose, the number of babies born rose, only the number of jobs fell.

It was a glorious evening in June the following year. In the Recreation Ground the Highworth Boys' Eleven were playing the Tarnmouth Under Fourteens. The shadows were starting to lengthen but even so late the sun was still warm, its golden light shining on the cricket pitch and dazzling Matt who stood poised bat in hand before the wicket. Even with his face screwed up against the glare there was no doubting his enjoyment.

'He's growing up so fast.' Fran might have been talking to herself, for only she knew how much more her one short sentence meant. She wanted to hold this precious moment, impress it on her mind: the sight of the boys, the ripple of excitement as Matt hit the ball to the improvised boundary, the sound of the evening call of a blackbird, the clear blue sky, Mixie lying across her feet content to sleep with his eyes open and no more than an occasional twitch hinting that he was dreaming. This was no ordinary evening; it was a rare thing for Greg to be free to come out with her, taking time off to watch cricket, but it was rare for more reasons than that. She closed her eyes; she'd

336

captured the sight and now, as Greg clapped Matt's boundary, she wanted to absorb the sound.

Concentrating on the murmur of the summer evening Greg's voice broke the spell. Instantly her eyes were open, even as he started to speak she knew just why the evening had been special. Years ago there had been a dividing line in her life, her fifth birthday. Was this to be another, would she look back and think 'that was before the evening we watched the cricket match' or 'that was soon after that evening Greg told me'?

'Fran, I came specially this evening because I want to talk to you. I thought here no one would interrupt us.'

'Just talk? Or about something special?'

'About the future.'

Her tummy turned its first somersault. She didn't know it was no more than flexing itself for the antics it would perform later.

'Yes?' Did he know how frightened she was? Yet there was no logic in her fears; she had no idea why such a premonition of disaster should flood over her. Everything she'd been seeing and wanting to cling to nudged at her consciousness, mocking her. The evening had been precious because she'd believed they'd shared it and all the time he'd come with her to talk about a future that suddenly frightened her.

'At the next General Election, Fran, it's been suggested that I should stand for Parliament. I've not said I will. If I got in it would mean changes for all of us. What do you say?'

She didn't say anything.

'You're surprised. Well of course you are, so was I. But, Fran, the problems we have here are universal, don't you see –?'

'Surprised? No.' How flat her voice sounded, yet he didn't seem to notice. 'As you said it I had a strange

337

feeling, as if I knew, as if I'd heard it before. . . .' Mixie couldn't have been asleep. Greg may not have suspected how she felt but the little dog stood on his hind legs, his paws on her lap and his trusting eyes gazing unblinkingly at her. She picked him up, glad to have something to do with her hands and glad to rub her cheek against his furry face and be rewarded with a lick of pleasure.

'Here's Alex.' Greg changed the subject. 'We'll talk about it later. I don't want to tell the children yet, not until I decide – we decide.'

'Dad, there's a message for you. Mrs Higgins, number 4 Craven Road. Can you go straight away. She's tipped a pan of boiling water over her foot. Her daughter came. Betsy told her to bathe it in cold water.'

'I'll go home from there, Fran', he said as he stood up. 'I'll see you there.'

Alex stayed, the game went on, but the magic, like Greg, had gone.

The game finally ended, they walked home. Matt had to talk to Greg about how he'd bowled Sam Briers out and how his own innings had come to an end with the loss of the middle wicket. Then Alex sat down at the piano, as she often did in the evening, and even though Frances said tonight she didn't think she'd get her fiddle out the girl seemed content to play on her own. Since it was usually encouraged this evening could be no exception.

Then at last, the long hours of daylight fading, Fran and Greg were alone.

'Well?' It was obvious he was eager for her answer, sure she'd feel the honour of the suggestion just as he had.

'But Greg it's ridiculous. You're a doctor. If you did some worthless sort of job it would be a different thing.'

'I don't understand you. Fran if one wants to get anything done there's only one platform and that's in government, or at least in the House.'

Her gingery eyes flashed. 'There are plenty of places to get things done. Weren't you getting things done this evening when you rushed off to Mrs Higgins? It's people who count, you always said so. Is it still people, or is it power?'

'I don't understand you, you've never talked like this before.'

'Supposing, just supposing, you were elected to Parliament. Oh yes, you'd feel fine, no end of a big fellow! I doubt if you'd find the time to worry about Highworth except as the stepping stone to the platform you're so interested in. What about the people here at home, patients you've cared about for years? Away there in London, do you think you'd be a fraction of the help to them you can be here?'

He took her by the shoulders, turning her to face him.

'Is it because I'd be away so much, is that it, Fran?'

It was almost as if she stood outside herself, hearing it, watching, pulled along on a tide she couldn't stem. He'd stand for Parliament, he'd win the seat, he'd be swept away, his sights fixed on some Utopia he'd never achieve. They were puppets, somewhere outside themselves the strings were being pulled. Her tummy was the only reality, its rolling and fluttering of earlier had gone to the next stage; she could hardly stand straight for the knots that tightened inside her.

'Away so much?' She had to hurt him. 'As far as Alex and Matt are concerned when do they see you now? And as for me, I'll have the bed to myself, that's about the only difference it'll make.'

'Fran, Fran,' he pulled her into his arms, a chink in her armour had let him see what he'd never con-sidered. Fran was jealous!

Even her knotted insides took second place, wildly

339

she clung to him. 'There's work to do here, Greg, people who need you.'

'Sweetheart, the country's bigger than Highworth, problems don't stop at Highworth.'

'We could move somewhere else, get another practice.'

'Any doctor can do what I do here, or in any practice.'

She move away from him. What was she fighting? From the mantelpiece his framed picture seemed to watch her. How many times she'd looked at it during those years he'd been away, looked and taken comfort from it, so sure that once he was home they'd pick up the threads, re-weave the pattern. Never before had she been so aware of the march of time; the boyish face in the sepia photograph had come a long way to develop into the Greg of today. But what about her, had she grown too? Certainly she wasn't the girl who'd driven him to Tarnmouth and bravely seen him off to war. Of course she wasn't; the four years of struggle had seen to that. Then he'd come home. She'd wanted to stop the clock, even to turn it back, but one could never do that; time and experience twisted the threads. He'd moved forward, she'd stood still and, worse, she'd tried to pull him back.

'I'd be asking you to make sacrifices.' He moved to her and turned her again to face him. 'We'd not have the income, I'd be away more than home. Fran, I know all that. Darling how can I do anything different, be asked and not accept the challenge? I am as I am, I must at least try. I probably won't get in, a parliamentary constituency isn't Highworth you know.'

'Of course you'll get in.' She heard her reply as an echo from the past.

'It's me, Franny. Are you in?' Gina called up the basement stairs.

340

'Nice surprise. What are you doing here at this time of day?' For she sometimes saw Gina in the mornings but tea time revolved around Nicholas.

'I came to say don't worry about Matt. Nicholas met him coming home from school, he's at the farm.'

'He'll like that. I wondered where he'd got to; not that he hurries himself, the young rogue. Alex has been home for ages.'

'Is that her playing the piano? Well, of course it must be. Hasn't she come on well.' Gina glanced unconsciously in the mirror hanging over the fireplace, pulling the dusky pink toque more firmly on her head. Today's short hair styles with her natural waves suited her. Her even features needed no help from 'a woman's crowning glory' as Myrtle thought of hair, and at thirty-seven she was as pretty as she'd been at seventeen. At that moment she had something of the same petulant expression as she'd so often worn in those days too. 'It doesn't seem just, Alex able to play like that and enjoy it while there's Nicholas mucking out cowsheds. Your Matt loves the farm too but it doesn't alter him. I can't explain, Franny, but with Nicholas it's more than enjoying working on the farm; purposely he copies Gee in everything, takes a delight in it. And Sophie's so stupid, she glories in it and encourages him.'

'If you left them all busy, Gina, you don't need to hurry.' Frances knew when to steer the subject into happier channels. 'We'll forget them and have tea together. That's a smart hat, it suits you. Is it new?'

Gina smiled again. 'I went to Tarnmouth this morning. I know it's sad that Madame Zeigler has given up, but really, Franny, although Auntie Myrtle will miss her, and lots of older women too, for one age Suzette has much more flair. You ought to go and see her.'

'Perhaps I will. Take your coat off, Gina. I expect Greg

341

will be back soon; he's supposed to be at a Housing Committee meeting at 7.'

'Franny, you'll laugh when I tell you this; it just shows how muddled people can get. When I was in Tarnmouth I bumped into Madame Zeigler – fancy, there was I with Suzette's hatbox in my hand too! – but anyway what I was telling you was, she said she'd heard that Greg was going to stand for Parliament – Parliament mark you, not the Council!' She laughed, delighted at the joke.

Franny apparently didn't find it funny.

'You sound surprised, Gina. I wasn't. He's not given his answer yet.'

'Parliament! Greg! Well, of course I was surprised. I mean, I'd never thought of it. His interest have always been here – London is so remote.'

'He'd stand for Tarn Valley, that's not remote. And politics are all about people surely.' When she felt any criticism, it was surprising how strong her defence could be.

'Remote from us though, from you, from his home. I don't know anything about politics. I've only voted once and that was for Greg for the Council. Well, of course I voted then, he's family. Gee was saying though that Tarnmouth is staunch Liberal but Greg's views are more radical than he thinks people would swallow. I say, I don't understand these things, but he says that if Greg's too radical it might help whoever stands for the Tory Party. Do you understand it all, Franny? I never have worried my head with these things, but I don't want to see you left on your own again. Men just aren't fair, are they? It isn't as if Greg hasn't a good comfortable life here.'

Hearing her Frances felt a sense of shame, not for Gina so much as for herself. Had her own reaction been so different?

'If he stands he ought to be elected. Have you ever

known Greg to be mean or unkind? No, he's good, through and through. If he's prepared to do it then every single person should vote for him and be grateful.'

'My word! But what a champion.'

A champion? She should be, she ought to have nothing but pride that he was as he was. Hearing the way Gina spoke had filled her with shame that her own selfish feelings had been so much the same. 'I am as I am,' Greg had said; and weren't they all!

Greg didn't get away from his patient in time to go to the meeting. Usually Eddy took any calls on the evenings he had to be in Tarnmouth but not today. No woman in the middle of a miscarriage can be expected to change doctors, so by the time he got away it was already after 7 o'clock and having parked the motorcar and come into the house downstairs – and stopped for a minute or two with Betsy – he heard the sound of music from the drawing-room. Often Alex and Fran played together now, in music they found a companionship they'd lacked previously. Matt was busy with a keep net, trying to remember the way Richard had told him to mend it. On Saturday he'd arranged to go fishing and it was no use having nowhere to put his catch.

'Don't stop,' Greg said, taking in the sight of fourteen-year-old Alex at the keyboard and Fran standing close behind her, her fiddle tucked comfortably under her chin. Sitting cross-legged, Matt surveyed his handiwork then looked up with his usual grin.

'D'you reckon that'll hold, Dad?' He held out the net.

He believed it had his father's full attention as it was examined. 'Take a pretty strong fish to break it, I'd say.'

The music flowed on. It was a moment he'd remember. Had he the right to do it to them? If only Fran could understand, feel as he did about it.

'Well?' Fran's voice brought him out of his reverie. The

music was finished, Alex closing the lid of the piano. How long he'd stood gazing into space he didn't know. She only said the one word. He understood her question and knew the moment mattered.

'I have to do it, Fran. If I didn't I'd never live with myself.'

She stood her fiddle on its side on the piano, unscrewed her bow and laid it carefully in front, moving slowly, playing for time while she found the courage to meet his gaze. Six eyes watched her, even without looking at them she knew.

Then she turned, not to Greg but to the children: 'It's time you heard the news too. How would you feel about having a Member of Parliament for a father, eh?'

Whatever her reservations it seemed they had none. Suddenly the tension broke, forgotten in the excitement.

Never had Matt been out so late, nearly midnight and the crowd was still gathering. He wished everyone knew who he was, that he could stand at the top of the steps of the Town Hall and announce that he was a part of it all, his father one of those three candidates who watched and waited for the votes to be counted.

Gina hadn't let Nicholas come ('well, he's not important; Dad's only his sort of uncle'). She'd said it was too late for a nine-year-old to be out and Sophie had been glad to stay with him. The thought of a lot of people jostling together in the dark was quite dreadful; she'd much rather stay at home in the warm. Tonight there was a feeling of winter in the air for all that it was only October.

Betsy, Alex and Matt had gone to the farm for tea, then Matt had helped with the milking. Nowadays when Gee said to him: 'Coming to give me a lift. . . ?', whether with milking or haymaking 'a lift' from Matt was worth having. Nearly fourteen by that autumn of 1922 and as tall and well built as one would expect for a son of Frances and Greg.

It had been after 10 o'clock when they'd piled into Gee's motor car, Betsy sitting in the front next to him while Gina, Alex and Matt squashed into the back. By then Greg and Frances would already have been inside the Town Hall. Alex had imagined it: the long trestle tables where the counters sat, the policemen guarding the doors, the hiss of the gas and the rustle of the ballot slips the only sound. She knew because they'd told her about it after the Council election two years before. She wished she could have been there with them, and yet it would be almost too dreadful, waiting, not knowing. . . .

Inside the Town Hall Frances felt something the same, her tummy was rolling over and over alarmingly, her mouth so dry that to lick her lips didn't help. Only minutes now and they'd know. Perhaps the Tory, Henry Humphreys, would win; then Greg would put the whole idea behind him, see that his work was caring for the sick. And yet, and yet. . . .

Then it was over. The Returning Officer took the paper that was handed to him, not giving a sign of what it told him as he led the way to where they must line up at the head of the Town Hall steps.

The Square was crowded, a cheer of anticipation went up from somewhere over by the King's Arms, then silence as they waited. She tried to catch a glimpse of the family but couldn't see them.

'I now have the results of the voting to elect a Member of Parliament for the constituency of Tarn Valley.'

Ah, now she saw them, just to the left of the steps. Betsy was standing in the middle, one hand on Matt's shoulder and one on Alex's, both of them taller these days

345

than she was herself. Fran imagined how they'd come by their place in the front: 'Just move along a bit will you. Make a space for the chillun to get through.' Taller they may be but to her 'the chillun' they still were.

'I shall read the results in alphabetical order. Henry Humphreys, Conservative: 5,102.' (A cheer from the crowd.) 'Malcolm Richards, Labour: 1,259.' (And another, far louder than the first; perhaps all 1,259 of them had turned out to give him support!)

Then a pause. The cheer died away, the night seemed to hold its breath. Standing by Greg's side Fran gripped his hand and felt his fingers tighten their hold. It could only have been seconds that they waited, long enough for him to turn his face towards hers, to look deeply and questioningly at her, long enough for her to see the tell-tale tick in his cheek, and for her to tighten the stranglehold on his hand. '. . . Smart, Liberal:' the Recording Officer was already speaking, that sudden silent question and answer seemed to have destroyed her power of concentration. '12,105.' (This time it was a roar. She clenched her teeth hard together.) 'I therefore declare that Gregory Smart is duly elected Member of Parliament for Tarn Valley.

The cheering went on, grew louder, everyone seemed caught up in excitement. There had been 6,361 people who'd voted against him but one wouldn't have thought it to hear the uproar.

No doubt of the volume of Matt's contribution. Frances couldn't hear his voice but she knew from the vigour of his clapping and stamping of his feet. Alex stood on Betsy's other side, quite still, her face not clear in a night of shadows but it was easy to picture the luminous grey eyes and the two bright patches of colour on her pale face. His children, his family, it was his moment and so it was their's.

346

She felt his arms around her just for a moment, heard his whispered: 'Fran, we did it!' We? Their lives would be different, his and her's too, but together they must step into this new role. 'I'm part of you, you're part of me.'

It was a heady moment. Her quick hug had to speak for her. Later he would be just her's but now he belonged to these people who had put their faith in him. She watched as he stepped forward from the line, raised a hand to the crowd and started to speak.